Praise for the novels

"A fast-paced, lushly described historic... romantic and ultimately hopeful, *The C......... .... Secret* is a riveting story of intrigue and love in wartime." —*Shelf Awareness*

"Beautifully structured and well-told with authentic historical detail… another top historical novel by Ackerman." —*Booklist* (starred review) on *The Codebreaker's Secret*

"Once again Sara Ackerman delivers with a riveting novel of WWII-era Hawai'i. Her vivid storytelling makes the island come alive around you. A plucky heroine, a decades-old mystery, and a stirring romance make this book positively unputdownable!" —Amanda Skenandore, author of *The Second Life of Mirielle West,* on *The Codebreaker's Secret*

"This historical fiction novel is empowering… Deliciously visceral, readers will be transported into the dreamy Hawaiian backdrop." —*Bookriot* on *Radar Girls*

"I trust this author to bring me a great story: filled with excellent research, vivid descriptive details, characters to root for, and engaging from page one." —*Reading Ladies Book Club* on *Radar Girls*

"Ackerman's winning historical novel is fast-paced and rife with nonstop action, romance, and suspense." —*Publishers Weekly* on *The Lieutenant's Nurse*

"*The Lieutenant's Nurse* illuminates the attack on Pearl Harbor with a riveting drama told from a unique perspective. Sara Ackerman brings a time and place to vivid life, putting a human and heroic face on events that changed history. I savored every page!" —Susan Wiggs, #1 *New York Times* bestselling author

Also by Sara Ackerman

SARA ACKERMAN

THE UNCHARTED FLIGHT *of* OLIVIA WEST

mira

mira™

ISBN-13: 978-0-7783-6951-6

The Uncharted Flight of Olivia West

Recycling programs
for this product may
not exist in your area.

Mira
22 Adelaide St. West, 41st Floor
Toronto, Ontario M5H 4E3, Canada
BookClubbish.com

Printed in U.S.A.

For Lucy & Kitty,
my most faithful companions.

1

THIRTY-SEVEN MINUTES

Olivia
San Diego, 1920

Livy had been coming to the airfield for months now but still had yet to go up in an airplane. On weekends, when Pa was out fishing, she would offer to wash the planes or do whatever odd jobs she could for a penny, while watching planes go up. Always hoping to get a ride, but so far out of luck. Though not for a lack of trying. She had been pestering Mr. Ryan for months now. "Paying customers only," was his standard response. "Or students." But so far, all students were men. A sixteen-year-old girl had no business in a cockpit.

Ryan Flying Company and School of Aviation was on the edge of the Dutch Flats alongside the San Diego Bay and the Marine Corps Recruit Depot, a long Spanish-style building with a tall bell tower in the middle. Palm trees neatly lined up in front like green soldiers at attention. When the tide pulled out, you could smell salty brine and decaying sea life. The hangar was modern and clean, but it was plopped on a brown expanse of hard-packed mud that kicked up dust when dry. Of late, the place had become a magnet for all things aviation.

Mr. Ryan had begun letting other people park their planes here free of charge, and customers flocked for the sightseeing tours.

On a warm Sunday in March, after surviving a long sermon at church with her mother, Livy beelined it to the airfield. A new pilot had been hired for the tours and she was hoping he might be a softy, and maybe, just maybe, she could persuade him to take her up. Such a gloomy and gusty day, with dark clouds threatening rain, meant less people taking a tour. It also happened that Mr. Ryan was in Los Angeles for the week, and what he didn't know couldn't hurt him.

Livy was hunched over, wiping down the wheels of Mr. Hall's biplane, when she heard the incoming engine. She stood up to watch the wobbly machine approach. A storm was brewing to the south, you could taste it in the air, and that always made the pilots nervous. She watched the plane make a precarious drop before leveling off, and then come in for a hard landing. As soon as he came to a stop, the new pilot hopped out of the plane, waiting for his customer and holding a hand out when she finally disembarked. A red-haired woman in heels, face white as chalk.

Livy walked over, wiping her hands on her overalls. "How was it up there today?"

The woman staggered past Livy without even a glance. "Never again."

The pilot trailed behind his passenger and shrugged. "What can I say? Usually, they're begging for more."

Once the woman left, zooming off in a shiny Model T, Livy moseyed over to the hangar and stood in the doorway. The pilot was at the counter drinking a Coke and studying a clipboard. With his goggles pulled up on his head, his thick blond hair stood out in all directions, as though he'd stuck his hand in an electric socket.

Livy cleared her throat.

He looked up. "Can I help you?" he asked.

"I'm Olivia West. I work here."

More like volunteer and hope that people would pay her, but she could dream.

"Oh, right. Mr. Ryan said you might be here. I'm Heath Hazeltine, new pilot." He was staring oddly at her, and for a second she wondered if she might have grease on her face, like she often did while working here, but then he said with a shake of his head, "I was expecting something different."

"I come in on the weekends, wipe down planes and other odd jobs," she said, for some reason feeling like she had to explain, then added, "I'm learning to fly."

That was a stretch, too, but she did always listen to the pilots talk, watch how they got the propellers spinning and closely observe the takeoffs and landings. She knew which part of the runway was more rutted with potholes, and which angle was best for approach.

He cocked his head slightly. "That so?"

"It is."

One side of his mouth turned up, just a hint. "I didn't know women could fly airplanes, let alone teenage girls."

Livy felt her whole face go red. "I'll be seventeen in four months. And I'll bet I know more about airplanes and weather than you do, especially down here in San Diego."

All she really knew about him was that he'd come from Los Angeles and had flown in Hollywood some, doing stunts. No one had mentioned anything about him being so young. She had been picturing some old guy with a sun-beaten face and graying hair.

"Feisty. I like it," he said.

She stood on her tippy toes and straightened up, all five feet three inches. Though her thick curls tucked under the hat added some extra height. "Take me up, and I'll teach you a thing or two."

He laughed. "What can *you* teach me?"

When he smiled, his whole face changed, making him seem even younger and a little less arrogant—and painfully handsome. Livy felt a swoosh in her stomach and her cheeks tingled. He couldn't have been much older than twenty, and yet there was a certain worldliness about him. She found herself wanting to impress him.

"Like I said, I know everything there is to know about this area. What have you got to lose?" she said.

He looked at his watch. "My new job, for one. And I have another tour in twenty minutes, so even if I wanted to, I couldn't. Want to help me patch that big pothole in the runway?"

None of the other pilots ever offered to fill the potholes, they always figured someone else would do it. The mud stuck to everything and gave off a rank odor, and a lot of them saw it as beneath them.

"How about I go fill those holes for you, and you take me up after your tour," she said.

She thought he was going to refuse her, like Mr. Ryan always did, but instead he nodded and said, "You're on."

Disbelief flooded through her. "Really?"

"Really. Now get out there before my next customer arrives."

But the passengers never showed up, most likely on account of the weather, and the books were empty after that. Heath helped Livy up onto the wing with a big, rough hand and a rock-solid arm. He moved like a man who was extremely comfortable in his own skin, as though the world rotated on his time. Livy decided that he was the perfect man for the job. You wanted your first time up to be memorable, but also to be survivable. Confidence was an asset.

"Sure you want to do this? Those clouds look formidable," he said.

Livy had noticed the band of charcoal clouds at sea, heralding the foul weather moving up from Mexico. A sudden chill came over her, and she tried to blot out the memory that always accompanied storms blowing in. The dark thing that would always be with her, always haunt the recesses of her mind. Blinding salt spray, cold waves smashing over the bow and washing everything from the deck, the sound of her name being stolen by the whipping wind. *Olivia!* The last moments of his chafed hand holding on to hers. Her heart began to squeeze in on itself, but she willed the thoughts away.

This storm was likely to be a bad one, but hell if she was going to blow her only chance to fly. Timed right, they'd be able to outrun it.

"Positive. From the looks of it, we have about thirty-seven minutes before that front hits here. Just head north along the coast and we should be back in time."

She climbed into her seat, and he leaned in and tightened the belt on her waist. "Thirty-seven, huh? Not thirty-six?" he said, close enough that she caught a whiff of mint and salt water.

When he pulled away, their eyes met. Chocolate brown with flecks of fire. Her first instinct was to look away, but instead, she held his gaze.

"Nope, thirty-seven. Let's go, we're wasting time," she said. "Oh, and you'll probably want to come in from the east on your approach. The wind will swing around coming in off the ocean when it moves in."

When he stepped back, he almost fell off the wing, catching himself on the wire. They both laughed, breaking whatever strange thing it was that had just passed between them. Without another word, he hopped in and started up the engine. After a few sputters, it chugged to life. Livy slid her goggles on, and made sure her cap was strapped tight. The whole plane buzzed, sending vibrations from the tips of her toes to the crown of her head. As they bounced down the runway, gathering speed, she could hardly believe her luck.

One, two, three. Liftoff.

The shift from clunky and earthbound to weightlessness was unmistakable. Everything went light and buoyant and yet Livy was pinned to her seat as the plane went up. It was a steep climb and all she could see was sky in front of her. She let her head fall back and closed her eyes, imagining herself as an albatross soaring. The hum from the wires that held the wings together grew louder the faster they went. Heath let out a holler and Livy found herself half laughing, half crying. It was even more wonderful than she'd imagined.

When they banked to the right and leveled out some, she saw that she had a bird's eye view of San Diego Bay, Coronado Island and the city itself—white buildings, red roofs and palm trees. The wind from earlier had died down, leaving an eerie stillness in its wake. They flew toward the cliffs of Point Loma and beyond that, the blue Pacific. There were none of the usual bumps and drops that everyone talked about. It was smooth sailing and she was in awe.

About six minutes out, the nose of the plane suddenly pointed skyward and they began climbing sharply. Pretty soon, they were nearly vertical. Livy knew all her specs of the Curtiss JN 4 "Jenny"—top speed was about eighty miles an hour, she dove well, but when climbing fast, she had a tendency to stall. So, what the heck was Heath doing?

Just when Livy felt like she might slide out of her seat backward, he leveled out and plunged them into a nosedive. If she had any food in her stomach, it might have come out then. Even though she was strapped in, she braced herself with her arms as she watched the beach below come up fast. Heath let out a whoop, as if he was having the time of his life.

Next came a series of loop-de-loops and barrel rolls that had her head spinning. It was hard to know which way was up. And between the thrum of the engine and the roar of the wind, it was so darn loud. Every now and then, she checked the wooden struts on the wings to make sure they were holding. This was not your usual sightseeing tour, and Heath was pushing the plane to its limits, obviously trying to make some kind of impression. She knew she ought to be terrified, but she was loving every minute.

When he seemed to have run out of new acrobatic moves to perform, they turned around and headed back toward Dutch Flats, directly into a wall of slate-gray clouds. Livy was finally able to lift her arm to check her watch, and was surprised find that they'd already been up thirty-two minutes. She peered over the side. Beneath them, the water was sleek as oil, but up ahead, there was a line of chop. The wind was coming.

She pointed inland, and yelled, "Head in," though her voice was lost in the noise.

Heath stayed on his course. The men on the boat had been like this, too, discounting her words. Except for Pa, and Orlando, her uncle. But Orlando was gone now, forever a part of the sea. Pa blamed himself, but Livy knew in her heart the accident was entirely her fault. Which was why she refused to step foot on the boat again.

Flying south over the water, the plane suddenly dropped, launching her stomach into her throat. The feeling was completely different and far more unsettling than the orchestrated dives. They bumped around for a bit, and then lurched to the right. The plane felt as though it was about to flip, when it righted. Livy pointed inland again, this time more vigorously. They were almost to the line where the water went from smooth to frothy whitecaps. Even heading inland, they couldn't avoid the front, but at least they'd wouldn't be flying in a crosswind. They had stayed out too long and now they would pay.

Heath banked to the left, and flew toward the city. They were buffeted around like a lost seagull, though the wings on their plane were proportionately much smaller and less aerodynamic. With each hard bump, the wires made a strange plucking sound and the wings creaked and groaned. Thirty-seven minutes out, they flew straight into the edge of dark rain and screeching winds. Nothing could have prepared Livy for the way the plane slammed this way and that. Up and down and sideways. Dutch Flats was close, but in these conditions, they'd be lucky if they made it.

Heath yelled something, but she couldn't hear. And now, it was impossible to see anything through her goggles as the rain came in on them from all directions. She closed her eyes and pretended she was out on a boat in rough seas, being tossed around. The feeling was similar and she realized how much she missed it. Water currents, air currents. Same thing. Here there was just a longer way to fall.

A couple minutes later, they were miraculously still aloft, though descending quickly. Livy wiped her goggles and was able to make out the flats below them. Heath had listened to her after all—they were approaching from the east and coming in fast. No more than thirty feet off the ground, a strong gust pushed the nose of the plane down, so that Livy was face-to-face with the rutted runway. A strange sense of calm came over her.

So this was what it was like to die. She didn't fear death so much as leaving her parents behind. Images from her life played in her mind—Pa dunking her in the ice-cold ocean when she was just a wee thing, meeting her best friend, Aurora, on the beach in the driftwood hut all those years ago and the all-encompassing smell of her mother's rose perfume, sharp and beautiful, just like Ma. They were flashes and then they were gone.

A second later, Heath somehow leveled out the Jenny, and the wheels struck hard ground, tail skid digging in. One of the wings tipped to the side, dragged for a moment and then lifted. They came to a stop. The engine sputtered off. Livy said a silent thank-you to God, untangled the scarf around her neck, unbuckled the seatbelt with shaky hands and stood up. Not a peep out of Heath. She turned around and found him leaning over, his head against the control panels.

"Mr. Hazeltine? Are you okay?" she said, unsure whether he was Heath or Mr. Hazeltine to her.

He didn't move. Livy climbed out onto the wing and jumped to the ground. She was weak-kneed and perspiring despite the rain and cold, but otherwise felt okay. More than okay, actually—she felt invigorated, electric.

A second band of rain was moving in quickly and she wanted to get inside, but couldn't just leave him. At long last, he sat up, running his hands through his hair and mumbling something unintelligible to himself. In one fell swoop, he hopped out and dropped to his knees, kissing the smelly earth.

He stood and wiped his palms on his flight pants, making eye contact for the first time since they'd set out. "Thirty-seven minutes," was all he said.

She shrugged. "I told you."

He turned and walked to the hangar. Livy followed. The wind had begun to wail through the trees, bending them sideways and tugging at the metal eaves of the building. Once inside, they slid the door shut. Livy pulled off her goggles and cap, and shook out her damp hair. Heath stared at her for a moment with an unreadable expression.

"What?" she asked.

"You're not even scared a lick, are you?"

She was shaken, to be sure, but ever since the day on the boat with Orlando, she seemed to find herself tempting fate, as if daring God to take her, too.

"Oh, I was. But I've been through much worse. My pa is a fisherman."

And I've stared death in the face.

He tried to unbutton his jacket, and she saw that his hands were trembling so much that he couldn't get ahold of the buttons. When he finally did, he tore it off and threw it on the counter.

"I'm sorry. I should have listened to you," he said, looking her straight in the eye.

"We made it, that's the main thing."

He grinned. "I have a feeling you're going to make a damn fine pilot. I'll even teach you myself, if you like."

It took every ounce of energy to maintain her cool. "You would? For real?"

"If we can convince Mr. Ryan. I'm going to have to tell him how miserably his plan failed."

Her hair stood on end. "What plan?"

A guilty look came over his face. "Just between you and me, Mr. Ryan said that if I took you up, to make sure to scare the living daylights out of you. That way, you'd get off his back. Nothing personal, you know. He likes you—he just doesn't think girls should be flying airplanes."

The whole world narrowed down to a pinhead, the words thundering in her ears. If there was one thing Olivia West knew about herself, it was this: tell her she couldn't do something and she would prove you wrong, whatever the cost.

2

A CURIOUS APPOINTMENT

Wren
1987

Wren opened one eye, the familiar crack in the ceiling directly overhead as it always was. Good news, she was in her own bed. Bad news, her head felt as though someone had taken an axe to it in the night. She reached around, found her tie-dyed tank top and pulled it across her eyes to try to block out the annoying morning sunbeams. Her skin felt clammy, her mouth parched. In her mind, she flipped through the previous evening's events, trying to remember what exactly had brought her to this state.

The only problem was, it wasn't just the evening's bad decisions that had brought her to this particular moment, it was an accumulation of a rotten few months, and really a rotten year.

Someone started pounding on the door. She groaned. *Not now, Mr. Fukuda, please not now.*

"Miss Summers, you in there?"

She didn't answer.

"Miss Summers, I left you five messages. You pay rent today or you're out."

She held her breath, as if that might somehow help, only

to almost pass out. Wren normally only drank beer or wine, and not too much, and now she was paying for deviating from that norm.

Eventually, Mr. Fukuda gave up and she heard his rubber slippers slap their way down the lava rock path away from her tiny dungeon studio. Houses in this part of Kaimuki were a quarter the size of regular houses, and Wren lived underneath one with her windows just above ground level, facing east. Her only roommates were giant flying cockroaches, geckos and the occasional stray bufo toad. She had lived here for two months and twenty-two long days. It was a big departure from the two-story Manoa cottage she'd lived in for the past two years with Joe, but it was all she could afford on her own. Actually, she couldn't afford it. Hence, Mr. Fukuda at the door.

Wren was an artist. Or actually, a craftswoman to be precise. She made light fixtures from wood and glass and sold them to shops around the island. For whatever reason, her creations had yet to take off in the huge way she had imagined, which was why she was still waitressing on the side. Gina said it was because her prices were too high, but blown glass was expensive—what could she say?

As she lay staring up at her latest piece, a hanging row of blue orbs full of tiny bubbles, last night started to come into focus in flashes, and then all at once, she remembered what drove her to asking the waitress for tequila shots.

"You sure you want to do that?" Gina, her wing lady, had asked.

After helping Gina hunt for vintage fabric for the aloha print dresses and handbags she sewed, they'd stopped into the Harbor Pub for pizza and a sunset beer. Every time Wren went out these days, she avoided the usual places because she didn't want to run into Joe and *that girl*. Harbor Pub wasn't in their usual repertoire, so she felt safe being there.

They were one beer in, waiting on their Canadian-bacon-and-pineapple pizza, when Gina said, "Oh, fuck."

Wren followed her gaze to see Joe headed for a table in the back, pulling a dark-haired woman in a mini skirt and high heels by the hand. For a moment, Wren's vision went funky. She wiped her eyes to make sure she was seeing correctly, which she unfortunately was. A wave of disbelief, hurt and rage crashed through her, wiping out all common sense.

"You want to go?" Gina asked.

"Absolutely not. We were here first. I refuse to let him ruin my life."

Even though he already had. That was when she ordered the shots. Then another round. They ate dinner and Wren pretended she was okay, going through motions of chewing her food, even though she tasted nothing. Not once did Joe look their way, but she got a feeling he knew she was there. That weird way he bobbed his neck when he was nervous, and a woman's sixth sense.

When they left, instead of going home, which would have been the smart thing to do, she persuaded Gina to drive them to Mama Mia's Pizza, the outdoor restaurant she had been "let go" from the previous week for giving away too many of her waitressing shifts. There, they played INXS and Guns N' Roses on the jukebox, drank margaritas and flirted with college boys from UH. She hated every moment, but this was what single women did these days, wasn't it?

"How old are you?" the hot one who reminded her of George Michael kept asking.

"Too old for you."

"Come on. You're gorgeous."

Wren finally relented. "I'm twenty-six."

He leaned in and whispered in her ear. "I like older women."

From there, things went fuzzy again. Wren remembered being squished between two of the guys, each one with a hand on her thigh. Things went black and then she recalled all six of them skinny dipping at Kaimana, one of them losing his shorts afterward. It was a miracle she didn't drown. Did she kiss George Michael? She might have. Which was okay, as long as she hadn't done anything else, which she was pretty sure she hadn't.

Joe had been the only man she'd been with in almost three years. When she fell, she fell hard and fast and less than a year later, he'd put a ring on her finger on the beach at Waikiki. Finally, at long last, Wren would have her own family. But choosing a wedding date proved elusive, and there was always some reason to keep pushing it back. *Sorry babe, it's just not a good time, we have the hotel opening that month. I have to go to Cabo with the boys.* A little voice in the back of her head started whispering *run*, but Wren ignored it.

Five days a week, Joe put on one of his twenty-three Reyn's Spooner aloha shirts and drove his BMW 325i to Bishop Street, where he worked for Alexander & Baldwin doing vague business activities. His father bought him his own membership to the Pacific Club, where he played paddle tennis after work and drank *pau hana* drinks every Thursday with his downtown buddies. He was also handsome and intelligent, if not a little too buttoned up. She could overlook buttoned up, because she was the polar opposite and opposites definitely attracted.

Where Joe never had a hair out of place, Wren's lived in a low, loose ponytail at the base of her neck, with stray brown curls always escaping. Joe had a closet full of business suits, while the only suit Wren owned was for swimming. He was a social butterfly, but she loved being alone with a book or a stray cat. He loved money, she never thought too much about it. Joe Montague. Good family, good education, going places in downtown Honolulu, major asshole.

Their differences were so glaring, you'd need shades, and yet Wren had had herself convinced they complemented each other perfectly. Until the morning she found pink lipstick and perfume on his shirt. Eighty-four days ago. Turned out he had a thing for his coworker Julie. Wren had been blindsided. The most pathetic part of it all was that she would have stayed with him had he shown even one drop of remorse. It must have been some primitive part of her brain wanting to fight for the man even if the man was all wrong for her. Not only had Joe been unremorseful, but he'd wanted to keep seeing Julie. Wren cried for five days straight, until Gina came to her rescue with a few wise words.

"It's been scientifically proven that all you need is sixty days to kick a bad habit, cold turkey. That's really what Joe is anyway. A bad habit," she'd said.

Gina had never been too fond of Joe. She tolerated him because she knew Wren loved him. Looking back, Wren wished she had listened to her friend. Friends always knew best.

Now, she made up for it by following Gina's advice. Moving out and cutting off all communication, and almost convincing herself that she was over him. She'd survived every woman's worst nightmare! But the minute she'd seen him with Julie last night, she'd crumpled. Joe's hand belonged to her, it was not meant to be wrapped around someone else's hand in this lifetime.

Now, she lay in bed reliving last night's encounter. Could she have behaved differently? Gone up and said, *Hello, I'm the fiancé whose life you ruined!* Unfortunately, Julie was striking, with dark hair and pale eyes, even if she did have big hair and excess eyeliner. Wren had been replaced, just like that, and it made her want to crawl in a hole and die, just like her old cat Olivia had done.

The phone rang, causing a new throbbing behind her left ear. What time was it? And why did the ringer have to be so loud? She let the answering machine get it. Maybe it was Joe, calling to apologize and tell her how much he missed her and what a massive blunder he'd made.

But it wasn't.

"Hello, I'm calling for a Miss Wren Summers. My name is Bob Simms. I'm an attorney with Young Brothers. Please give me a call at 867-5308 at your earliest convenience, I have an important matter to discuss with you."

Wren wrinkled her nose, wondering what an attorney could possibly have to discuss with her, then turned to the clock and bolted upright when she saw that it was almost ten. Sleeping this late was completely out of character for her. She tore herself out of bed, went to the bathroom and turned on the cold water only, pulling off her underwear and stepping in. This was her tried and true remedy for most things. All the while, she tried to figure out what business Bob Simms had with her. Was she in trouble? Oh, shit. Maybe she'd done something nefarious last night. Perhaps acted out one of her fantasies about slashing Julie's tires or smashing in her car windows.

She called his office as soon as she got out. "This is Wren Summers, returning a call from Bob Simms."

"Miss Summers, may I set up an appointment for you to come into our office?" his secretary said.

"Would you mind telling me what this is about, first?"

"Mr. Simms would prefer to tell you himself."

"Am I in some kind of trouble?"

"No, Miss Summers, we're an estate firm."

Her brain wasn't firing on all cylinders, but she was quite sure she didn't own an estate.

"I don't have an estate."

The woman on the other end laughed, but let out no more information. "How about 4:00 p.m. today? We had a cancellation."

"Hang on, let me check my schedule."

She checked her planner, which had nothing written on it all week except for Sunday: *"Hike with Gina."*

"I suppose I can make it," she said.

She took down the details, ate two powdered-sugar donuts and a banana and went back to bed.

When Wren woke up the second time, she felt much better. Did this count as alcohol poisoning? How people drank like this on a regular basis was mystifying. It was unlikely she would ever drink tequila again. Her eyes were still bloodshot, and she kept catching whiffs of her own breath. Her olive skin looked washed out, but she managed to make herself presentable with heavy concealer and mauve lipstick.

The office of Young Bros. was across the street from Alexander & Baldwin, and she began to wonder if this had anything to do with Joe. It must—what else would it be? She drove around the building three times before she found the entrance, then backed out and parked three blocks over to avoid the hefty parking fees.

The nineteenth-floor office had smooth paneled wood and etched glass doors, and smelled of money. She sipped hot coffee and munched on shortbread cookies as she waited for Bob, growing more curious by the minute. A door opened, and out stepped a silver-haired man in a gray suit.

He gave her a practiced smile. "Miss Summers, I'm glad you could make it," he said, reaching out to shake her hand.

"My pleasure."

They went into his office and he shut the door, then pulled a chair out for her at a long koa wood conference table with one very lonely looking manila folder sitting atop it.

"Please, have a seat," he said.

Wren sat.

"No doubt you're wondering why you're here, so I'll get to the point. Your great-aunt Portia has passed on, and she's left her estate to you."

The news came out of left field. She had met Aunt Portia a couple times as a young girl, and Portia would call the house every so often to speak to Wren's mother. Wren always knew it was Portia because when she answered, there'd be silence in response to her *Hello.* The poor old woman could hardly hear. Wren would then pass the phone to her mother, who would yell into it. *We are doing well, thank you!* Portia was her father's aunt, but since her father hadn't been in the picture much, neither had Aunt Portia.

"I'm sorry to hear that she passed. How old was she?"

"Ninety-two. Emphysema got her in the end. Now, I understand this may come as a surprise to you, since you two haven't been in touch in some time, but she was clear that you were to inherit everything."

Wren felt a tingle of excitement. She recalled that Aunt Portia lived in an apartment in Waikiki and had once worked as a teller at First Hawaiian Bank, but not much else.

"What exactly is *everything*?"

He opened the manila folder and slid her a piece of crisp white paper and an envelope.

"No money, I'm afraid, but there is a property on the Big Island."

She frowned. "What about the apartment in Waikiki?"

"That, she was renting," he said, apology weighing down his eyes.

"The Big Island, you say?"

"Yes, have you been?"

"Never."

"The land is outside of Hāwī, across the channel from Maui, beautiful place. A hundred acres with an old barn and a grove of mac nut trees. Someone tried to farm it once, but now it's overgrown. The barn is a teardown from what I understand."

Wren was hit by another wave of hangover. Or was it something else? Tears pooled in her eyes and she began to hiccup.

Bob sat quietly, waiting for a response. She started crying in earnest then, and he went and got her a box of tissue.

"Sorry," she said, taking a handful.

"Think nothing of it. Comes with the territory."

The tears stopped but the hiccups continued.

"This is such a surprise, and I'm curious why she didn't leave it to my father, or anyone else. Do you know?"

"I think you'll find your answer in that envelope."

"Miss Wren Summers" was written in shaky cursive on the front. She opened it and pulled out a piece of folded lined paper. The writing inside was even shakier.

> *Dear Wren,*
> *My father left this land to my sisters and me, and now I pass it to you, the last woman in our line. This is a special place and it's been sitting idle too long. It is time to change that and make something of it. Best of luck.*
> *Portia*

Wren felt a strange current running through her hands as she held the paper. She didn't want to put it down. This deaf great-aunt of hers, who she barely knew, suddenly seemed so intriguing, so relevant. Wren's grandmother had been the youngest of three girls, but she died the year after Wren was born. Growing up, Wren's mom didn't speak of Wren's father or his family, so one whole side of her bloodline was a mostly blank slate. She wasn't just an only child, she was an only child of an only parent who was also an only child.

"The property has been put into a trust in your name, so as long as you are alive, it belongs to you," Bob said.

"And when I die?"

"It goes to your daughters."

"Presuming I have any," she was quick to say.

Kids were no longer on her radar. At all.

"If you weren't to have any daughters, then you would choose another female heir."

Who would have known that Aunt Portia was such a feminist?

"What if I decide to sell it? In all honesty, Mr. Simms, I have no idea what I would do with one hundred acres of land in a remote part of the Big Island."

"If you sell it, half the proceeds go to charities."

"Which charities?"

"Animal charities."

At least Aunt Portia had good taste in that department.

He added, "I just write up the papers. People come up with all kinds of stipulations, and this one is quite straightforward. Keep in mind, you can always turn it down."

Wren sighed. "I don't want to sound ungrateful. I guess I'm just overwhelmed and caught off guard. Can I take a few days and get back to you?"

"Better yet, why don't you fly over and see the property. Then you'll be in a better position to decide." He leaned back in his chair and crossed his legs.

She should. But airplane tickets weren't cheap. And how would she get around? But then something dawned on her: if she went, and decided to stay, she would be on the far end of the island chain from Joe, with no chance of running into him. It could be just what she needed, a forced exile. It would also be impossible to drive past his house at odd hours of the night, just to see if Julie's car was parked out front. It always was.

"Which airport would I fly into?"

"Waimea. They stopped service to 'Upolu last year. I could arrange a ride if you need one," he said, then added, "And if money is a concern, I can offer you a flight coupon. We fly to our office in Kamuela on the regular and I have a whole stack."

"That would be wonderful! I'll book a flight as soon as I can," she said, feeling cautiously optimistic and desperate to get out of town.

3

SHOW US THE MONEY

Olivia
1927

Everyone always said that landing was the hardest part, but Livy loved landings. There was a certain predictability about them. You were almost to your destination, and even though a handful of things could go dreadfully wrong, you knew what to expect. In her mind, navigation was the tricky part, especially in weather. Poor navigation skills would cost you dearly, sending you smack into the face of a mountain or off course and out of fuel, wondering where in God's name you were. Over land you had a chance, but over ocean, forget about it.

Today, none of that mattered. Conditions had been perfect. Clear blue skies, light winds, balmy temperatures. The wheels had touched down light as a hummingbird. After helping the Los Angeles passengers deplane, she unfastened her flying cap, shook out her hair and made her way toward the hangar. After close to four hours of flying round trip up and down the coast, her legs were stiff as planks, her lips chapped. But she wouldn't trade it for the world. Flying was her life.

Years of toil had brought her here. Not a journey of a thousand steps, but a thousand hours in the air. Or actually, more like four thousand seven hundred twenty-two. But who was counting? She was, actually, in her logbook. One of the diligent requirements of being a pilot.

On the approach, she'd noticed an overabundance of cars parked at the field, lined up all neat and orderly. The guys sometimes congregated here on Fridays, but this was much more than usual. A mass of men was spilling out the door, all crammed together. Livy could hear Mahoney's voice, but only picked up a word every so often over the chatter.

Eager to find out what was happening, she tippy toed to try to see over several wide sets of shoulders. Ernest Callahan and Bill Hoover were both regulars at the airfield, but the other guys she had never even seen before. When Bill caught sight of her, he gave her a nervous smile, but he did inch over so she could get her nose in. The buzz in the room was palpable, and mingled with cigarette smoke and all those male bodies, it felt more like a speakeasy than an airplane hangar.

Mahoney—who had just bought out Mr. Ryan and was the new owner at the ripe old age of twenty-six—was standing in the front of a packed room. "And fellas, this is going to make the world forget the name Charles Lindbergh. His flight was a cakewalk compared to this. The prize, well, it's the same as the Orteig Prize. A cool twenty-five grand."

The roar of voices erupted in the room.

"Sign me up!"

"You'd have to be insane."

"Show me the money."

A couple of guys stood up, clinked bottles and danced around. Others were shaking heads. Mahoney raised his deep voice. "Second place gets ten fat ones, too. And I'm willing to fast track and discount any of you a plane, should you decide to enter."

Livy whispered to Bill, "What the devil is he talking about?"

"A race to Hawai'i."

Her pulse kicked up a notch. This was news. Big news. All

anyone at the airfield had been able to talk about these last three days was Charles Lindbergh and his famous flight across the Atlantic. With good reason. The *Spirit of St. Louis* had been manufactured right here in San Diego at the Ryan Airlines factory. Mahoney's crew had put together the plane in record speed, calling it the Ryan NYP—for New York to Paris. And she along with the rest of the guys had actually met Charles Lindbergh on several occasions. Charming and humble. An overnight sensation.

But Hawai'i?

Mahoney put his fingers in his mouth and whistled at the unruly group, getting everyone's attention again. "I know this probably is not a reality for many of you, but give it some thought. Happy to help any of you get your application in, too."

Livy's exhaustion from the flight evaporated. Her mind began hatching a plan. With that kind of prize money, everything could be right in her world again. Two birds with one stone.

The next morning, she came in just after sunrise. Pink clouds rose above the inland hills like heaps of spun wool. Mahoney was an early bird, and a sucker for chocolate cream puffs, which she picked up on the way in. She wanted to catch him alone, and was thankful to find him out back, sweeping the sidewalk. A stickler for perfection, he kept the place shiny as a showroom.

"Morning, boss," she said, holding the pastry box out so he could see it.

The whine of a de Havilland engine started up behind them. He waited until the plane taxied down the runway before responding.

"Something tells me you didn't come here at the crack of dawn just to satisfy my sweet tooth," he said, broom moving across the freshly laid asphalt.

Mahoney knew her too well. Over the past few years, once

he'd taken over the business from Mr. Ryan, they had developed a nice rapport. After her first flight with Heath Hazeltine, a fiery crash the very next day had led her mother to forbid her from stepping foot near the airfield. Livy bided her time, focusing all her energy in schoolwork—namely mathematics, until her eighteenth birthday, when she announced her plans to take up flying and make something of herself. Ryan had been dead set against it, Mahoney had been all for it. He wasn't tied to convention like most of the guys and understood her predicament—of being a female in a male-centered world.

"The only catch is, Slim, you gotta fly better than anyone else here, and never give the boys a damn thing to complain about," he'd told her.

Six years later, here she was.

"I heard about the Race to Hawai'i and I want to enter," she said, getting straight to the point, which was how you had to operate with Mahoney.

Mahoney laughed. "You really are something, you know that, West?"

She made no mention of not being invited to the meeting, which she was sure was intentional.

"If you sponsor me, and loan me a plane, I will make you proud," she said.

He folded both hands on top of the broom and looked at her with something like pity. "Not a chance, Slim. And it's not that I don't believe in you, because I do, but those race officials will never go for it."

"Why don't we let them decide?"

"Look, you have a good gig here with the airlines. Don't waste your time on this. It's gonna come up a dead end," he said, eyeing the box of cream puffs. "And even if I wanted to help you, no financier is going to back a woman on this flight."

"Think what it would do for your business if I won."

"I'd be crucified for being an irresponsible schmuck if anything happened to you. You know that, Livy. And I have plenty of business after Charlie's flight."

A part of her knew he was right. But damn, she wanted this more than anything she'd ever wanted. Lindbergh was partly to blame. But even before him and his outlandish idea of making the crossing alone, Livy often daydreamed about what it would be like to fly out to the blue horizon and beyond. The freedom, the escape, the adventure.

"What if I find a backer? Will you help me with a plane, like you offered to help all the other guys?" she asked.

"Ah, hell, don't make this harder than it has to be."

She had seen what went on with Lindbergh. How Mahoney and all the guys on the project had lived and breathed *The Spirit of St. Louis* for months, skipping meals and even sleep, until the very afternoon they had all stood and watched him take off from Dutch Flats. Warm afternoon sun glinting on the wings. Even a few tears were shed, as if they were watching their very own child leave the roost.

"I'm not asking for something custom like Charlie's. Just something that can be fitted with enough fuel to get me to Hawai'i."

"You mean you and your navigator?"

"No, just me."

He frowned. "If I thought you were a little loose in the skull before, now I know you've lost your marbles," he said, tapping two fingers on the side of his head.

"Charlie knew he had a better chance going alone, and he did. He made it. So, why couldn't I? You and I both know he hardly knew a thing about navigation when he arrived here," she said.

"He remedied that pretty darn well, I'd say."

"I have a head start."

Mahoney had been her greatest ally in the flying department.

He'd stood up for her countless times in the past. Now, she'd thought she'd be able to wear him down, but he wasn't budging.

She opened the box and held it to him. "How about a cream puff?"

He took one and bit down, closing his eyes, chewing slowly, oblivious to the powdered sugar collecting on his upper lip. Livy waited as he finished it off in three bites.

"You know what happened to Rogers and your buddy Hazeltine. If they couldn't make it with all those navy ships to show them the way, what makes you think you can all by your lonesome?"

Hearing Heath's name caused an undesirable sensation below her rib cage.

"Lindberg makes me believe it. And Hazeltine is not my buddy, for the record. I haven't spoken to him in years."

Since he made off like a stinking coward, a coyote in the night. Heath had joined the navy, and two years ago, along with Commander John Rogers, had made a failed attempt at Honolulu. Livy had followed the story, purely out of aviation interest, she told herself. Two P-9 Seaplanes had taken off from San Pablo with a string of destroyers laid out across the Pacific to bounce radio bearings off. Somehow, they went off course and disappeared.

For a tense nine days, the world held its breath, Livy included. Then, as if in some strange mirage, they appeared off Nawiliwili Harbor on Kaua'i, having fashioned a sail out of fabric from the wings. A submarine towed them in. The plane had traveled four hundred fifty miles that way, unable to transmit on their radio and nearly missing O'ahu. A few big rain squalls had generously provided them water, and the crew had become unlikely heroes. Two years later, Lindberg made everyone forget.

"I heard from him last month. He's leaving the navy," Mahoney said.

"Good for him."

"Maybe one day you'll forgive him."

Maybe one day I won't.

"I'm not here to talk about Heath Hazeltine," she said, softening her approach. "Please, Mr. Mahoney, won't you help me?"

He looked away, studying the clouds, taking in the mud-packed runway and checking the windsock. Livy followed his gaze and thought perhaps he was actually daring to imagine her flight.

"Look, I would if I could, but it's not gonna happen this time. Sorry, kid."

4

THE TROUBLE WITH FOG

Olivia

Fog posed a problem for any aviator. And summer in California was a fog lovers delight. It crept in over the water, enveloping the coastline and sending smoky tendrils inland. On some mornings, the blankets of white were so thick, visibility went down to less than twenty feet. If you flew too low, treetops appeared suddenly, scratching for the sky. Fog was disorienting at best, deadly at worst. You could easily lose your bearings and fall out of the sky, as many pilots had done.

Livy drove home that afternoon through a white haze, both excited and nervous to break the news to her pa. She found him at the rough-hewn cedar table on the back patio, tinkering with the drowned radio, which he'd been trying to repair for months now. Ever since he'd lost his boat. He barely acknowledged her presence, mumbling a preoccupied hello as she stood there in silence, working up the nerve.

Livy threw down the newspaper, which had a big photograph of a man named James D. Dole on the cover.

"Have you seen this?" she asked.

San Francisco—In light of Lindberg's successful flight
across the Atlantic, James Dole, Hawai'i's Pineapple King,
is offering a prize of twenty-five thousand dollars for the
first flier and ten thousand for the second to make the
nonstop flight from the West Coast of North America to
Honolulu. Fans of aviation all the world over will not have
to wait long, as the prize is ready for the taking. Dole has
stated that he has high hopes for an abundance of qualified entrants, in the hope that this contest may be doubly
successful, first that it may cost no brave man either life
or limb and second that the continent and Hawai'i may
be linked by airplane.

He kept his nose buried in the radio. "Sounds like trouble,
you ask me."

"You don't even know what I'm talking about."

"I know the tone of your voice. Which means I know you've
got something up your sleeve. Something about an air race,
perchance?"

"So you've seen it, then. I'm going to enter," she said.

He sat upright, pulled his spectacles down and examined
her, a smile spreading slowly across his face. His smiles were
few and far between this days, so this was more than welcome.

"Shoulda known it. My little bird wanting to spread her
wings."

"Pa, I'm serious."

"I know you are. Do me a favor, though. Don't mention this
to your mother or you will make both our lives hell."

"Don't worry."

Livy had already thought of this. Always a worrier, her
mother, Bee, had developed a stubborn and mysterious rash
once the boat ran aground. She'd been to every doctor within
a twenty-mile radius, and no one had been able to help. The di-
agnosis: hysteria. Without even mentioning the race, she could

picture her mother's response. *We just can't take another loss, dear. No, this would certainly push me over the edge.*

"There's one more thing," Livy said.

"What's that?"

"I want to fly alone."

Pa's shoulders tensed for a moment, then he cleared a space on the table, went to a shelf and pulled down a dusty bottle of tequila. He had a stash of the stuff hidden in a hole in the ground out back. He poured shots in two mason jars.

"I know better than to try talk you out of it, so here's to showing the world how it's done," he said, raising his glass.

They downed their first shots, and she knew another one was coming.

"Where there's a will, there's a way."

They drank again, and the alcohol caused a lightening of her limbs. A weight lifted off of her, knowing she had his support. Not that she ever doubted.

"To strong wills," Livy said.

He downed the shot and slammed his glass on the wooden table. "Strong wills and a turn of the tides."

If anyone on this earth had a strong will, it was her pa. He was a self-made man, going from errand boy to deck hand to running his own boat in less than two years. Then later, when Livy was old enough, he took her with him and taught her the ways of the sea. Intuition and determination had served him well. He had weathered the loss of his first mate in a storm. But this latest tragedy, the loss of his boat and his livelihood, was proving harder to overcome.

He tried to pour them another round, but she put her hand over the glass. Pa looked her in the eye for a few moments, then said, "I don't want you to do this for me, Olivia. I'll find a way through this mess."

She wished she could be so sure. You could only borrow a boat so long—they cost an arm and a leg these days—and in recent months, his hair had gone from thick brown to thinning and gray streaked. The boat that he had borrowed from their old neighbor one week out of the month was barely seaworthy, so that added another element of concern. Not being in the sea as much, he seemed to be withering before her very eyes. But even before the loss of the *Lady Bee*, he'd had to go farther and farther offshore, or down the coast into Mexico to find enough tuna to keep them afloat, which was why they'd been where they'd been when they went aground. New territory and heavy fog made for poor bedfellows.

"It's my fault," she said, voicing the words she'd been keeping inside for months now.

She had known there would be a sudden upwelling of fog that day, and hadn't said anything. Granted, she was in Los Angeles on a flight, but she could have called him. Could have found a way.

He grabbed her wrist, hard. "This needs to end right here. You can't go on blaming yourself until the end of time, just like you do for Orlando. Misfortune is part of life, and it's not our job to stop it. Our job is to keep living with everything we have."

Livy pulled her arm away. "If I had called you—"

"Baloney. And don't tell me this is why you want to go it alone on the flight."

She shook her head. "Not at all."

Absolutely.

"I know that look, Olivia. And I suggest you get that notion out of your head. You're far more likely to get yourself in the race if you have a man along, as much as you hate to hear it."

A breeze came in the window, blowing his hair around and bringing with it the faint smell of fish. Fish and her pa were inseparable, and she realized then that she would fly around the whole globe if she had to for this man.

★ ★ ★

Getting in the race proved harder than Livy thought it would be. Ever since her conversation with Mahoney, she had been pursuing other options, but slamming up against wall after wall. She'd tracked down a banker in San Diego, a movie magnate in Los Angeles, an oil heiress with enough money to buy a hundred airplanes, and even Norman Goddard, a fellow pilot who ran another airfield in San Diego. All turned her down. Meanwhile, entrants were beginning to stack up. A Hollywood stunt pilot in Los Angeles named Art Goebel, newspaper magnate William Hunt's son Jack, and a crew from Michigan who planned on bringing a schoolteacher named Mildred along for the ride.

Then, word began circulating that a man named Ernie Smith was side skipping the Dole Air Race—as it was officially called—altogether and making his own bid for Hawai'i. For half a minute, Livy thought maybe she ought to just set out, too, since no one wanted a woman pilot in the race, but there was still the problem of a plane. On her small salary, saving enough to buy a plane would take half a lifetime or more. Nor would there be any prize money.

To complicate things, in late June, the cat was let out of the bag that the army had two guys en route to Hawai'i. News crews had grown curious when their giant Fokker plane had been spotted hopping from base to base on her way to California. The fliers planned on taking off from San Francisco sometime in the next two weeks. The military reported that their primary interest was testing navigation equipment for flying blind and that they had no use for a derby. But still, a flight to Hawai'i was a flight to Hawai'i.

Mahoney and the boys were sitting in the hangar lounge— which really was a ragtag circle of chairs around a card table off to one side—listening to the radio and placing bets on which plane would finish the journey first, when Livy showed up for work.

"My money's on the Fokker—that thing is a beast," said Louis Frank, another pilot who flew for the airlines.

Jim Penny, a mechanic, blew out a puff of smoke. "I'm with Ernie Smith. The guy has some mad piloting kills, determined as a badger that one is."

"How do you know him?"

"I met him a few times when I worked on the mail planes. A real piece of work."

It was always a dilemma for Livy, wondering where she stood with these guys. She never felt like she could just pull up a chair and join them shooting the breeze. No one was ever outright rude and they'd grown used to having her in the periphery, but there was always this invisible field they put off, like mosquito repellent, but for women.

Today, she couldn't resist jumping in. "Both planes have the same engine, so it's going to boil down to navigation skills and mettle. From what I hear, the army fellas are top notch, but so are Smith and his guy."

Jim shook his head. "The Fokker has three engines to his one. Big advantage there."

The Wright J-5 Whirlwind was exactly the engine you wanted for long distance flights.

"But Smith's plane is a lot lighter. And faster," Louis said.

"Hell, it's not speed you want over water, it's peace of mind. The more engines, the more peace of mind."

Livy looked at her watch. "The way I hear it, it's extra fuel that really gives you peace of mind. That and knowing your sextant like a lover."

Louis smirked. "And what makes you such an expert all of the sudden, Miss W?"

He'd adopted that nickname for her seemingly just to point out that she was a woman, that she didn't belong, and many of the others had followed suit. It annoyed the hell out her.

"I still plan on making the flight, so it's my job to know

everything I can. Any of you boys want to be my navigator?" she asked.

That got a laugh out of the bunch and Louis slapped Jim on the back. "I'm sure Jimbo here would love to spend twenty-six hours alone in a cockpit with you."

Jim knocked him in the arm, his face suddenly tomato red. Jim had invited her to the horse races on several occasions, and he wasn't a bad chap, but Livy had always politely declined. He wasn't the only one, either. But the way Livy saw it, having a man would interfere with her need to be in the sky and clamp down on her freedom.

She placed a hand on her hip. "Oh, really? How well do you know your way around a bubble sextant? And how's your dead reckoning?"

Mahoney finally sounded in. "Give it up, Slim."

His words seared through her. "Last I checked, giving up wasn't part of my vocabulary. Good day, gentlemen, I have a plane to fly."

She turned and walked out the door, flustered and frustrated but unwilling to give them an ounce of satisfaction.

In the next few days, Livy became obsessed with following the news of *Bird of Paradise,* the military Fokker to be flown by First Lieutenants Lester Maitland and Albert Hegenberger, and the *City of Oakland,* Ernie Smith's smaller plane. The media had been hyping up the rivalry between the two, and Livy had been eating up every word, measuring her own skills and experience against both of these crews as well as the entrants in the Dole Air Race. Did she really have what it took, or was she fooling herself?

She had been flying now for close to six years, starting off with the air tours, then graduating to passenger service from San Diego to Los Angeles, with the occasional jaunt to San Francisco, all along the West Coast and even going as far as Texas.

Sometimes ferrying passengers, sometimes ferrying planes for Mr. Mahoney. She had no time for a personal life, but that suited her just fine. Give her an empty beach, an open sky any day. It was unconventional, to say the least. Even scandalous.

In all those years, her mother had hardly warmed up to the idea. "Being a pilot is not a womanly thing."

"Says who?"

"Says your mother, the woman who carried you for almost ten months in her womb, who raised you and nurtured you and wants only the best for you."

"I can be a pilot *and* a woman, Mom. The two aren't mutually exclusive."

The conversation always went the same way. Ending with her mother shaking her tightly curled blond hair and smacking her lips together, and Livy leaving in a huff. She was so much more like her father. Free-spirited and adventurous. Anything he was doing, she'd wanted to do, too.

Which was why growing up on the water, navigation had become second nature. But there was a big difference between navigating in a boat at sea level, and in a plane, high above the earth's surface. On the ocean, you always had the horizon to sight your sextant off of, but up in the air, that familiar blue line was gone. Flying by sun, moon and stars, or determining wind drift were all fine and dandy, until the weather went south—or dark.

Livy's first *real* test in navigation had come when a headwind had slowed her down so much that the last half hour of a flight back from San Francisco had been at night. She had picked up two of Mahoney's prospective clients, both of whom had no idea about airplanes or flying, or women pilots for that matter. These fellows came into the hangar wearing well-cut suits and carrying leather briefcases, all business. They reeked of money and self-importance.

"We're looking for B.J. Mahoney's plane," one said, curtly.

Livy, who had been checking the propeller, smiled and said, "This is it. Are you Morgan and Finkelstein?"

The taller one with a narrow mustache nodded. "Ah, good. I'm John Morgan and this Bud Finkelstein. Where's the pilot?"

"You're looking at her."

Finkelstein chuckled. "Funny, lady. You must be the secretary. Can we get a cup of coffee before we go?"

There was no coffee around—she had looked—but there was a brown bottle sitting on the table.

"How about some moonshine instead? Calms the nerves, I hear, and it could be a rough flight to San Diego," she said.

Morgan glanced out the window. "What makes you say that? There's not a cloud in the sky."

"Just a sense." She looked at her watch. "Come on, we should get going."

They followed her to the plane, and as she slid on her jacket and snapped her cap, Finklestein said, "Hang on a sec, you weren't kidding back there?"

She smiled. "I would never kid about something like that. Now watch your head on the wing."

The two men exchanged a nervous look, but said nothing more.

Before takeoff, she'd noticed the weight of the atmosphere, much like any other person would notice rain or snow. There was a particular metallic taste to the air, and while it might be lovely outside now, something was brewing.

The first part of the flight was a breeze, and the air tasted sweet and dry, but when they'd neared Santa Barbara, the weather turned. A cluster of cumulonimbus clouds blotted out the whole sky. They were thick as vanilla ice cream and impossible to avoid. Knowing there were mountains on the Channel Islands, she climbed in search of clear air. The clouds were even thicker above, with buffeting winds. Soon they were getting tossed around like a badminton birdie. Finkelstein, immediately behind her, yelled every time they hit a big drop. Livy lowered airspeed and dropped the nose.

Livy was usually calm, even in difficult conditions, but now she began to sweat. Turbulent air rarely intimidated her, but these bursts were violent enough that the wings felt ready to snap off. In the east, flashes of lightning lit up the clouds. Should she try to land in Los Angeles, a familiar runway? Not in this storm. Then, up ahead, she caught sight of a dim patch of sunlight. She steered toward it, even though it took her out to sea slightly. When they broke out of the clouds, the sun was lower than she'd thought, and they were over open ocean.

The turbulence had subsided, but the wind was still howling, and she had to crab into it to keep from heading even farther out to sea. Being able to see the position of the sun gave her some assurance. She kept it over her right shoulder and followed a southeast line. It was all she could do. There was no one else to rely on now, certainly not these two gentlemen. Uneasy and full of self-doubt, she had no option but to trust her instincts and hope to God that Heath had taught her well.

"We there yet?" Finkelstein said.

"Soon."

When they finally caught sight of the coast again, the sun had set and stars were popping up in a darkening sky. Much to her relief, there in the distance was the Oceanside Pier, lights twinkling. Those headwinds must have been something fierce, though, because they were much farther north than she expected.

Finkelstein tapped her on the shoulder. "Tell me you can fly this thing in the dark."

The truth was, she'd had little experience flying in the dark up until this point. Actually, none.

"Relax and enjoy the ride," she yelled back, words swept away by the droning engine and rush of wind.

Between the stars and scattered lights along the coast, she

was able to roughly stay on course. Her heart was in her throat the entire time, as she kept an eye out for the lighthouse at Point Loma. As long as the weather held, that long beam of light would be impossible to miss. Ten minutes on, she saw its beautiful flashing. The men saw it, too, and began cheering.

Mahoney was waiting for them outside the hangar and gave each man a hearty slap on the back. "How was the flight, old sports?"

"A little rough here and there, but we made it, didn't we?" Morgan said, and Livy swore he winked at her.

Finkelstein, who looked pale even in the semidarkness, said, "I'll take a shot of that moonshine if you still got it, miss."

And God bless Mahoney, because he added, "Captain West is the cream of the crop. My finest pilot."

5

WANTED

Olivia

As luck would have it, both the *Bird of Paradise* and the *City of Oakland* made it to Hawai'i. Hegenberger and Maitland landed at Wheeler Field early on the morning of June 29 after circling Kaua'i for a few hours waiting for the sun to rise. Ernie Smith, having abandoned his first attempt and navigator, tried again two weeks later. He and Emory Bronte made it to Moloka'i but then ran out of gas and crash-landed in a kiawe tree. Miraculously, they both walked away unscathed. The way Livy saw it, the success of these two flights only bolstered her cause.

On Sunday morning, she was enjoying a lazy morning at home. Their little white house was tucked back several blocks from the shore. Pepper trees hung their weepy branches over clumps of lavender and rosemary. It was a clean, if modest, neighborhood, where everyone took pride in their yards. Livy still lived with her folks, mainly to save money for her own car—or airplane. A ridiculous notion, but one she couldn't shake.

Before the *Lady Bee* sank, there'd been four hundred and sixty-six dollars in her piggy bank—enough to buy a car with. Now the piggy bank was empty. Every penny earned, she gave to Pa. She would leave the money on the kitchen table in an envelope. At first she was worried he would put up a fight and refuse to accept it, but that first afternoon, when she returned from work the envelope was gone. Not a word about it.

Today, the whole house smelled like cinnamon. Bee was elbow deep in flour, making her famous cinnamon rolls like she did every Sunday before church. Pa was sitting across the table from Livy, holding up the newspaper as he always did. All you could see were his gnarled fingers, which was fine by Livy because she was in a bit of a funk, denied airplane funding yet again after a visit to Mr. Balfour, the man responsible for bringing a series of shiny new automobile dealerships to San Diego. He hadn't laughed as a few others had, which earned him a few points, but she'd barely got her foot in the door before she was back out on the curb fighting back tears. She'd often wondered if each person had an allotted number of tears, and hers had all been used up when Heath left, but her current situation proved otherwise.

Sun shone through the cracked windowpane, spilling light across the room. Livy downed her coffee and stood, determined to go for a beach walk and forget about flying to Hawai'i. It was only a few weeks away now, and time to face the fact that the race would go on without her.

Pa lowered the paper. "Hang on there, Liv. There's somethin' in here that might interest you."

"Later, Pa."

He began to read aloud. "'Wanted—fearless navigator to fly to Hawai'i with pilot. Aviation experience required. Sense of humor a plus. Reply to Felix Harding, San Francisco, CA, Western Union, no later than Monday at 5:00 p.m.'"

Livy went very still. "Read it again."

As he did, she mentally went down the list. Skilled, check. Fearless, check. Navigation and aviation experience, check.

Even the sense of humor. She might not be the funniest girl in town, but she could appreciate a good joke.

By now, her mother had set the last tray of cinnamon rolls in the oven and was hovering over Pa's shoulders, a sour look on her face.

"Can I borrow the truck?" Livy said to Pa, her pulse skipping along at full throttle.

Bee moved so she was blocking the door. "You two are too much. Have you lost your minds? You have no idea who this man is and you want to fly across the Pacific Ocean with him in a flimsy piece of machinery?"

The name Felix Harding meant nothing to her, but maybe Mahoney or one of the guys would know him. The aviation world was small and everyone knew everyone, it seemed.

"I'll check tomorrow at the airfield. Someone is bound to have heard of the man."

"As if that will make any difference. What kind of fool are you?"

Livy stood her ground. "You don't understand. I *have* to do this."

"Why? Why do you have to do it, Olivia?"

"Because if I don't, who will?"

"Loads of people. Heaps of them, all around the country."

"Flying is part of me, Ma, and if you don't get that by now, then you don't even know me. Not one bit," Livy said.

Her mother's face crumpled. She stepped aside, clutching her apron and shaking her head.

Pa tossed Livy the keys. "I'll be damned if that job description wasn't written just for you. Go on, get."

Livy skipped the beach and headed over to the Western Union, knowing they weren't open yet, but hoping Señor Morales would be on duty today. He usually came in early and could often be persuaded to send a message off the clock.

While on the outside he seemed terse, he was a softy at heart, and had commiserated with her all those years ago when she used to haunt him in hopes of a message from Heath. No message had ever come. When she arrived, the doors were closed and locked, but she could hear someone banging around inside.

She knocked. "Hello?"

No answer.

"Hello, is that you Señor Morales?"

Things quieted down, then a voice spoke, "Sorry, we're closed."

"Please, it's me, Olivia West. I have some of that smoked mackerel you love from my pa."

A moment later, she heard the click of the door unlocking, and it swung open.

Señor Morales was standing there, one hand twirling his waxy mustache, the other waving her in. "Either something really good happened, or something really bad. Which is it?"

Giddy with excitement, Livy gave him the jar of fish and told him what she needed.

His brow pinched up at the mention of the Dole Derby but he handed her a pen. "Make it snappy."

Because you got charged by the letter, writing telegrams had become an art in itself. Livy constructed her response to Harding carefully.

```
RYAN AERONAUTICS PILOT WITH EXTENSIVE NAV
SKILLS READY AND WILLING STOP CAN GET YOU
TO HONOLULU WITH EYES CLOSED STOP CONFIRM
ASAP AND WILL SEE YOU IN SF TUES STOP
```

She was about to write her name in, when a thought struck. What if she just used her initials? She'd already given Harding everything he needed to know. He hadn't specifically asked for a man, and she met all his qualifications, so what harm was there in leaving out the insignificant fact that she was a woman?

Absolutely none.

"O West" on its own felt a little flimsy, so she'd include her middle initial, too, boldly signing off "OM WEST." She told Señor Morales she would be back in a couple of hours. Now, instead of walking along the shore to forget about flying to Hawai'i, she would be planning her crossing.

The sand was cool underfoot, and kelp lay strewn in heaps along the shore. The sunny morning had given way to a thin layer of fog, as she'd known it would. Fog had a faintly sweet taste to it and Livy's mouth always watered just before the fog rolled in. It was a sure sign. Fog tasted different from sunshine, which tasted different from rain.

She walked and walked, pocketing a small granulated cowrie shell and a tiny perfect sand dollar. Seagulls pecking for crabs populated the long flat beach, and above, they swooped and flapped before disappearing into the white. She wondered how the fog affected them. To a casual observer it seemed to pose no problem. Then, a dark form appeared out of the mist. Silent, pure grace. Livy halted and her mouth went slack.

Albatross.

With a wingspan wider than she was tall, the bird was a perfect flying machine. The albatross was an open-ocean bird, rarely coming ashore, so she was surprised to see one here. Unlike most of the other gulls, this bird hardly flapped its wings, instead riding on air currents generated by the ocean. But what was it doing here? As it soared overhead, Livy spun around and watched until it flew to the edge of sight.

"Goodbye, beautiful," she whispered.

The bird banked, doing a wide turn out on the water, wingtip brushing a wave, and came back around. People called them Gooney birds because they were so awkward walking on land, but this bird was pure grace. Livy opened her arms wide. It did another pass, and from the white markings on its underbelly, she could tell it was a Laysan albatross. Home waters, Hawai'i.

"Take me with you!" she called.

On the way back to the truck, she formulated a plan to get herself to San Francisco tomorrow come hell or high water. Mahoney would not be pleased when she announced her sudden departure, but he'd had plenty of warning—even if he hadn't believed her. And if she couldn't find a ride on an airplane, she'd catch the train. Her mind spun on and before she knew it, she'd been out walking for two hours, hair damp, rolled-up pant legs soaking wet. She dusted off her sandy feet, hopped in the truck and drove back to Western Union.

Señor Morales seemed to be waiting for her, because the minute she walked in, he handed her a telegram. There was a thin smile beneath his black mustache.

```
CORNER OF UNION AND FRONT STOP LOOK FOR THE
ORANGE COAT STOP
FH
```

6

A ROAD UNTRAVELED

Wren

The big dilemma had been what to do about her tiny apartment, and how to pay rent before leaving town. If Wren asked her mom, Cindy, for help, that would open a new can of worms about Wren's *inability to grow up*. Her mom's words. Four years ago, Cindy had met Norman, a pharmaceutical salesman from Vegas with a big income and a bigger ego. As full of himself as he was, he loved her mother inside and out and she'd left the islands six months later to be with him. In a way, Wren felt orphaned, but she also felt a new sense of freedom with no one around to scrutinize the "nontraditional" way she was living.

Feeling fragile and not in the mood for a lecture, she put her key in an envelope with fifty bucks, shoved it under Mr. Fukuda's door and moved her very few belongings to the shop and studio she shared with Gina and a few other artists. It was cluttered with tools and tables and sawdust, but there was a small lounge area where she figured she could sleep until she found another job. At twenty-six, she was supposed to have life figured out, wasn't she?

* * *

The next morning, Wren pressed her forehead on the cool glass as they departed from Honolulu International Airport. Flying in the smaller plane was the way to go, she soon realized, as it was like a cheap sightseeing tour. The north side of Moloka'i, with all its cliffs and valleys, was even more stunning than she'd thought possible. She forgot about everything for a while as she watched for waterfalls and whales. On Maui, they stopped in Hana to trade out a few passengers, and she could see the Big Island in the hazy distance. It felt weird going to an island where she didn't know anyone, but she was excited for the change of scenery. And the more miles between her and Joe, the better.

Growing up with a single mother who taught at public school, money had been tight. Cindy had made up for it by organizing micro-adventures—as she called them—every weekend, and sometimes even after school. Camping at Peacock Flats and Koloa Valley, walking out to see the albatross at Ka'ena Point and sleeping in the lawn under the stars at the Honolulu Zoo, listening to the lions roar. Still, Wren felt like she'd drawn the short straw, missing out on all the island-hopping that some of her friends raved about.

Now, as they crossed the channel to the Big Island, she felt a ping of excitement. The de Havilland Twin Otter flew low over the whitecaps, the pilot so relaxed Wren was worried he might be sleeping. The plane began to bounce around violently, and a Japanese tourist woman screamed every time they dropped. Wren loved it.

"No worries, this is nothing. It gets a hell of a lot worse," the pilot said.

Flying into Waimea proved to be even more of a wild ride, in dense clouds and spitting rain, but they landed without incident. There was no bus service on the Big Island, and no rental cars in Waimea, but Bob Simms had been generous enough to offer her the company car for a day or two—a buttercup-yellow 1968 Dodge truck. After grabbing a map of the islands, she stepped out into the whipping winds of Waimea.

It must have been forty degrees, and all she had on was a spaghetti strap top with her favorite Daisy Duke jeans shorts. She dug around her backpack and found her flannel shirt, then hopped into the truck shivering. No one had warned her that it would be this cold. Luckily, the truck started right up without a hitch and she headed out, turning right onto Māmalahoa Highway. It was desolate country. No cars on the road, no houses, only cows grazing in chartreuse pastures that spread out as far as the eye could see.

She had traveled some with Joe, but he liked to go to Kaua'i and Maui to golf and hunt. Now, looking back, it seemed that they always ended up going where he wanted to go.

"Want to go to an outer island this weekend?" he'd say.

"Sure."

"Where do you want to go?"

"How about the Big Island, I still haven't been."

Then he'd nod as though considering it, and answer. "Or we could go to Maui. Supposed to be nice weather, and I think the Sandvolds are going to be there."

Every single time, it was some variation on this. They rarely went alone. It was always with this couple or that group. Wren wondered what Joe was doing at this very moment. The pressure to talk to him had been building under her skin like an active volcano, and yesterday, she'd almost caved. *Maybe just call him and let him know how well you're doing without him. Show him how strong you are!* She'd dialed six numbers before reason struck and she'd slammed the phone back down in its cradle. Joe did not deserve to have her heart, and she willed him out of her thoughts as she drove along.

When she hit the town of Waimea, she stopped for supplies for the day. A six-pack of Coke, Spam musubi, Saloon Pilot crackers and a bag of Fritos. People were walking around in cowboy boots with spurs on them and it looked like they actually used them. It felt like some kind of alternate reality, split between Hawaiʻi and Wyoming. There were Parker Ranch signs everywhere. Everyone in Hawaiʻi knew about Parker Ranch, the biggest privately owned ranch in the United States.

What Wren hadn't known was how adorable this little town was. Green houses with red roofs, red houses with white shutters with cutouts of roosters, and white houses with giant lawns and flower gardens. Behind the town were rolling green hills dotted with more cows, and in front, out beyond an expanse of flatlands, rose Mauna Kea. Tallest mountain in the world, if you counted from the bottom of the ocean. She hoped Hāwī was just as charming.

The road that cut across the Kohala Mountains only intensified in gorgeousness, adding on views of the ocean and Mauna Loa and Hualālai into the mix. At a lookout, Wren pulled over and got out her Polaroid camera, snapping a few shots. Quality wasn't great, but she liked the instant gratification. She managed to get three mountains in, and Mauna Kea and Mauna Loa were topped in a winter dusting of snow. Only one car passed, and she felt very small and alone.

After driving through a long corridor of ironwood trees, the road opened up again, this time descending toward Maui and Haleakalā, across the channel with the really long name she could never remember. Something *haha*. *Alenuihaha?* Directions to the property had been convoluted, so she pulled over again, just to make sure she didn't miss any turnoffs. Instead of going to Hāwī town, she was supposed to take a right fork before that, and then turn onto a long and winding road, which wasn't on the printed map and had no sign and no markings.

Turn right onto the dirt road past the big Norfolk pine.

Sounded easy enough, except that when she reached the area, there were a bunch of Norfolk pines. She found the tallest one, drove past it a ways, and didn't see any roads, just an overgrown driveway. Same thing after the next Norfolk pine, and the next. Frustrated, she went back to the tall one and pulled into the dirt driveway. She got out and walked down it a ways. The air was sticky and much warmer here. More like Oʻahu. There was no sign of a house and no sign of the road ending, just guava and sugarcane crowding in. Might as well see where it went.

She climbed back in and drove. The road meandered smoothly until it switchbacked down into a gulch. At the bottom, a stream trickled through remnants of an old rock bridge almost completely absorbed back into the earth. Thankful she had a truck with good clearance, Wren crossed the stream and drove back up the other side. The forest grew thicker, with kukui nut, more guava and clumps of ironwood, the branches reaching out and clawing at the side of the truck, squeaking as she passed.

As she bounced along, wondering how much farther she was willing to go, the road became more rutted and full of muddy potholes. Dense foliage pressed in around her, and when she slowed to a crawl, mosquitoes swarmed into the cab. Just her luck. Anyone who wanted to live out here would have to be either a mosquito farmer or a hermit.

Bob had shown her the site map on the deed, but she'd hardly paid attention. Her mind had been too busy trying to wrap her head around this unexpected inheritance. Now, she wished she had. When she arrived at a peekaboo view of open sky, she pulled over, climbed out and hopped up into the back of the truck. In the distance, she could see sweeping fields of sugarcane and blue ocean beyond.

As Wren got back in the truck and drove along, she tried to picture herself living here. Boonies and plenty of bugs. No social life. No men. That could be a bonus. And maybe if she could clear the trees and build a very tall house, she might get an ocean view or a view of anything at all. Bob had said there was a barn on the property. She began to imagine one of those New England–style barns painted red with neat white trim and punctuated with small windows, and rows of mac nut trees spreading out in all directions. If it had been a farm once, was there electricity? There were so many thoughts running through her head, she felt dizzy.

At long last, she hit a clearing in the trees, passing through a field of sugarcane. The red dirt road widened, but she still couldn't see beyond the tall, striped stalks. The smell changed from damp earth and rotting leaves to sweet grass and sunshine. A welcome shift that didn't last long. After driving through two more ravines, when Wren was just about to call it quits and turn around, she came upon a fork in the road.

Two roads diverged in the middle of bum fuck nowhere.

Frost would have definitely taken the one on the right, which was grassy and untrodden and more mysterious. She went that way purely because she liked Frost, crossing her fingers that there were no large branches hiding objects in the way. As soon as she started in, a feeling washed over her that she was crossing some kind of Rubicon. As if by entering onto this road, she had to keep going at all costs. Curiosity now piqued, she was committed.

After a few minutes of creeping along, brush scraping the undercarriage, she came upon a rotting wooden gate attached to two giant posts. Vines grew through the slats, and a rectangular piece of metal dangled from the center. She turned off the motor and debated what to do. If there was any indication at all that this was Aunt Portia's property, she ought to find it. As long as the land didn't belong to some gun-wielding *pakalolo* grower with trip wires set up to blow up all trespassers, she would be okay.

She decided to put on her camo pants because she recognized some of the grass as the same kind on the trails on Tantalus, that if you brushed up on them with bare skin, you'd come away full of fiberglass-like fibers. Hawai'i had no snakes, no bears or wolves or cougars, but there were wild pigs everywhere, and centipedes and cane spiders loved forests like this. Wren had once fallen asleep under a tree on a hike, only to wake up with a cane spider on her chest crawling toward her neck, no doubt heading for the dark cavern that was her mouth. That had traumatized her for life.

When she inspected the entrance gate, none of it appeared to have been touched in many years. She lifted up the dangling metal piece and saw that it was a sign with cutout letters. Ho'omalumalu. She had no idea what that meant. Bob hadn't mentioned a name for the property, which made her think she was in the wrong place. But there was only one real way to find out.

A big fat chain wound around one of the posts, and the gate looked rusted but still intact. The lock was one of those fancy European kinds designed to withstand a nuclear attack. Wren lost hope for a moment but when she fiddled with the lock, it came open in her hand.

She took it as a sign, tore off the vines, which turned out to be lilikoi, and pushed the gate in. Halfway in, the top hinge disintegrated and the gate dropped to the earth. With some effort, she pushed it the rest of the way. On the way back to the truck, she picked four fat lilikoi and squeezed one open, sucking the tart juice and seeds into her mouth. This one was full to the brim and the sweeter than most, and gave her a little pick-me-up.

The road from here on out was more gravelly, with rows of Norfolk pines that had obviously been planted by humans on both sides. Beyond, she reached an orchard of macadamia nut trees so tall and bushy, they were all grown into each other. Here was her first sign that she was getting warmer, and that maybe this wasn't some wild-goose chase after all.

When the orchard ended, she hit another ravine, this one with a wider stream full of rushing reddish brown water. The old moss-covered bridge looked sturdy, so she crossed it and drove up a rootsy and rutted section of road, where part of the hillside had slid off on the downslope. She hugged the other side closely. At the top, the land flattened and the forest thinned considerably, with only a few trees in a meadow of wild grass and weeds. At the far end, she spotted what she had been looking for all along. A man-made structure.

7

A MAN WITH A PLAN

Olivia

Mahoney, for all his grumbling, pulled through and found Livy a ride to San Francisco in the morning with Jed Johnson, the wealthy son of a banker who fancied himself an inventor. So far, none of his inventions had panned out. He was going to San Francisco to show off his latest, a whirligig that blended food in a big jar. Only problem was, the glass was prone to shattering and he'd had a near miss with his eye.

Livy politely listened to his jabbering the whole way there, but was relieved when they finally landed and parted ways. With an hour to spare, she took a streetcar to the designated meeting place and prepared to wait. San Francisco was bustling, and from the looks of it, there was a speakeasy on every corner. Men, women, and children were peddling every kind of fish imaginable—fish and chips, dried fish, smoked fish, fish sandwiches. There was a Wild West, freewheeling feeling to the city that appealed to her. People here were doing things and going places.

Near the corner where she was to meet Harding, she sat on a bench under a large jacaranda tree, which rained down small purple flowers. She sat and pulled out the blueberry scone her mother had packed for her and inhaled it in three bites. There was a chill to the air, and she wrapped her bomber jacket around her shoulders. Her eyes searched the crowds for the orange coat.

She'd decided to dress in her flying outfit to give herself an air of credibility—sleek pants, lace-up boots and the leather jacket that WWI pilot, J.D. Ostrander, had given her after a harrowing flight together from Los Angeles. She wore her hair shorter now, in a stylish bob, slightly longer in the front, that curled nicely around her ears. Before every flight, she dabbed a bit of rouge and red lipstick on, and she'd touched it up in the ladies room just after landing.

Two o'clock came and went, and Livy was about to give up hope when she saw a flash of color down the street. More rust than orange, definitely headed her way. She remained seated and when the man got closer, his eyes passed over her but didn't stop. He was clearly looking for someone, but Livy did not fit the bill. At the corner, he turned around and paced back and forth, scrutinizing everyone that passed, while Livy scrutinized him.

Everything about him was slightly askew. Tousled brown hair gave way to a five-o'clock shadow that nearly blended in with his skin. A short, thick mustache was the only part of him that looked well manicured. He had the air of someone street-smart and scrappy who was ready to take on the world.

Livy stood and he glanced her way again. This time, he took in her outfit and something like recognition flashed over his face. She hurried toward him, wondering if she had made the right choice in not being forthright. A rare case of jitters made her legs weak.

"Are you Harding?"

He went still as a rabbit. "Don't tell me you're O.M. West."

"My name is Olivia Mary, and I'm your navigator, sir," she said, holding out a hand.

To her surprise, he grinned and said, "Well played, my friend, but not so soon. I have three others lined up for an interview with the eximious Dexter Wittingham, a naval navigator and an old friend. You'll be number four and you'll need to more than pass muster. If you can believe it, I had over fifty people respond to my ad. Everything from Boy Scouts to Hollywood starlets."

The news was a blow, but she wanted to appear unflappable. "I would have expected as much, and that's fine by me. When do we meet?"

He looked at his watch. "Top of the hour. Come on, we need to get going."

They rushed along at a clipped pace, up and down hills, while Felix told her his story. He'd started off as a barnstormer and traveled the country performing daring flying maneuvers for paying crowds. After a stint in the navy, he made his way to Honolulu, where he worked for a tour company and flew between the islands. Soon after, he met his lovely wife.

"Tell you what, though, being out on the open water always gave me a bit of a sweat. If the weather made it so there was no sign of an island—up front or behind—I used to turn that plane around and call it a day," he said.

"What about your passengers?"

"Oh, they trusted me to do the right thing."

Livy had studied a map of the Pacific and knew that the islands were fairly close together. Eighty miles at the most, between Kaua'i and O'ahu. Nothing compared to what he was about to attempt.

"What makes you think flying from California is going to be any different?" she asked.

He shrugged. "The chance was just too good to pass up."

They found Dexter Wittingham and the others in a place called Pelican Coffee & Tea. It had the appearance of a bakery, big windows full of glass shelves of pastries and the warm aroma of roasting coffee beans pouring out the vents onto the street. But once they entered, with a whispered password, it became clear there was more going on. Groups of mostly men were huddled around tables holding mugs, but by the boisterousness of the place, chances were, it wasn't just coffee in the mugs.

"Wait here," he told Livy.

She watched as he went over to a man in a uniform sitting alone in a booth, exchanged a few words and then pointed her way. Just then, two other men approached Harding. They shook hands and chatted, and Harding pulled out a small leather-bound notebook and wrote something down. One of the men slid into the booth, while the other, wearing a tattered army coat, moved to another, smaller table and sat down. As he scanned the room, Livy noticed he only had one eye and hoped that would hinder his chances, then felt slightly guilty about it.

Harding came over. "These fellas are going to interview with Lieutenant Wittingham and me and then you'll get your chance. You can either wait outside or find yourself a table, maybe grab a bite to eat."

Rather than wait out in the cold, Livy found the only empty table, next to a bunch of cigar-smoking men in suits. A waitress in a starched white shirt and a pencil skirt came by and handed her a menu.

"If you want a kick, I recommend the double café au lait," she said with a wink.

The man who faced her at the table next door said something to his friends in a hushed voice, and one by one they all turned to look at her. Not used to being alone in a bar, her cheeks started heating up. Which bugged her, because she had plenty of experience being the only woman in the room. Nevertheless, she began to study the menu as though she'd be tested on every item on it.

Finally, one of them leaned back and said, "You waiting for someone?"

She nodded toward Felix and Dexter. "I'm here for an interview with those two. Just waiting my turn."

"What is it you're interviewing for?"

None of your business, she felt like saying, but instead answered, "Mr. Harding needs a navigator to accompany him on his flight to Honolulu. I'm here for the job."

A few of them chuckled, and one with what looked like a whole quart of oil in his hair said, "That crackpot? He doesn't even have an airplane yet. Best thing you could do is hightail it outta here and back to whatever ranch you came from," he said, eyeing her boots. "Besides, an airplane race is no place for someone like you."

She filed away the no-plane information for later, and said, "Someone like me?"

"A broad."

"Have you ever been in an air race, mister?" she asked.

"Well, no, but I've flown a few times." He tapped his greasy head. "You need to have a screw loose to want to cross the Pacific in one of those flimsy contraptions."

It was no surprise these men knew of the race, by now the Dole Derby was headline news.

"Actually, I have a couple of nuts, bolts and screws loose. Now, if you'll excuse me—"

She felt a hand on her shoulder and jumped, fully expecting it to be Felix. Relieved for the interruption and eager to get the interview over with, she went to stand up. But when she saw who it was, her rear end slid back into the chair. Every hair on her body stood on end.

"Olivia West, is that you?"

Heath Hazeltine was standing there with a slightly perplexed look on his face. Hair shorter than she remembered, but still messy, and that familiar almost smile that showed up mostly in the eyes and one side of his mouth.

She had imagined countless iterations of this moment over the past five years, and yet all she could say was, "Heath."

"What brings you to a speakeasy in this part of San Francisco?" he said.

By now, she had forgotten about the men next door, forgotten about Harding, the air race, why she was here. The singular desire to stand up and slap him across the face was causing her hand to throb, yet somehow, she managed to control herself.

"I'm here on business."

"Please don't tell me you're with Harding," he said.

Why did everyone seem to know Harding?

"So what if I am?"

He stared at her with his head cocked for a few moments. Those milk-chocolate eyes had been her undoing in the past. *Olivia, get ahold of yourself.* She forced her gaze back down at the menu, just as the waitress showed up.

"You ready?"

"I'll have the double coffee, whatever it was, the drink with the kick."

"Anything else?"

"No, thank you."

As the waitress turned to leave, Heath said, "Make that two." And then to Livy, he asked, "Mind if I join you for a minute?"

Yes.

Her foot began to tap. "My interview with Harding is any minute now, and I need to focus on that."

"Come on, Liv, we haven't seen each other in what, four years?"

"Five."

He laughed. "You always were smarter than me." Then his face turned serious, eyes pleading. "Please? Five minutes and I'll be out of your hair."

"Fine."

"Not in my wildest dreams did I expect to run into you here, and yet now that you're sitting with me, in the flesh, it makes perfect sense. You answered his wanted ad for a navigator, didn't you? For the Dole Derby."

She nodded.

He leaned toward her. "Why settle for being a navigator when you could probably outfly half the men in this race, myself included?"

She gasped. "You're in the race? Why haven't I seen your name in the papers?"

"I just made it official."

She closed her eyes, and could still see his backside, walking down the front steps of her house, hands in his pockets. Broad shoulders, narrow waist. Even then, after hitting her broadside with the news that he was leaving that very afternoon, joining the navy and not to wait for him, he still had the nerve to walk with that damn swagger of his. *Touch me and I'll break your heart*, it seemed to say. It had taken every ounce of strength Livy had to not run after him and get down on her knees.

First love is like wildfire, her mother used to say, *all consuming, dangerous and nearly impossible to put out*. She sure as hell had that right. Livy had been trying for five years to put it out, and had finally succeeded. She wasn't about to succumb to his charms now. Her heart had healed over, the fault lines stronger and reinforced with time and distance.

She pulled herself together, drew back her shoulders and said, "The only reason I'm not flying is that no one would even consider financing me or turning their plane loose with a female at the helm—stick, what have you. Trust me, I tried."

"Not even Mahoney?"

"Not even Mahoney."

They sat for a moment, eyes locked.

"I would have helped you had I known," he said.

She held his gaze. "I don't need your help."

"We all need a little help now and then, Liv. Nothing wrong with that. Say, how's your pa doing? I heard about his boat."

"He's fine. We're all fine and we certainly don't need your pity."

The edge in her voice was hard to miss, and something like hurt passed over his face. Meanness wasn't in her nature, but it was the only way right now.

"I understand," he said, pushing his chair out and stood. "I have a feeling you'll get the job, Liv. If you want it."

"If I didn't want it, I wouldn't be here," she said.

"This is a dangerous undertaking. How well do you know your pilot, the plane, the ocean out there? Are you ready to go down in the middle of the Pacific Ocean? Is the race worth your life?"

He spoke with a tone of real concern.

Suddenly Harding was standing next to Heath. "Excuse me, Miss West, we're ready for you."

"That was fast," she said.

Hardly any time had passed, or so it felt.

Heath nodded at Harding. "May the best man—or woman—get the job."

Lieutenant Wittingham was as dry as they came. He had a good navy buzz and a starched uniform with not a thread out of place. Meticulous in the way any good navigator should be. Livy was still confused about why the others were already done, but kept her questions to herself.

Harding spoke first. "You have one minute—give us your background in navigation."

She shifted in her chair, keenly aware of their eyes boring holes in her. "I learned how to box a compass before I could read a book. My father was a mariner and would take me out with him. He and his men also taught me how to read the charts, take a good departure, lay the course and fix a position. I understand the ocean, I can map the stars and I know weather like the back of my hand." She paused, thinking about how long it had been since she'd been out on a boat. "Later, when I learned to fly, I brought all of that knowledge with me. That was six years ago, and now I'm a pilot with Ryan Flying Company. Gentlemen, I know my way around a bubble sextant and I can dead reckon with the best of them."

She figured that was a good place to stop.

Wittingham took a sip of his water without a word. He set it down carefully and gave her a condescending smile. "Tell me, if you will, Miss West, the latitude and longitude of the Barbers Point Lighthouse on the island of Oʻahu."

Livy tapped a finger on the table for a moment, glanced up the ceiling as though racking her brain. "You said Oʻahu, right?"

Harding snorted.

"I did," Wittingham said.

She then looked him straight in the eye. "I believe it's twenty-one degrees, fifty-one minutes and seventeen seconds north, one hundred fifty-eight degrees, six minutes and thirty-two seconds west."

The two men exchanged a surprised glance.

"You can double-check, but I believe I'm correct," she said, knowing full well she was, as she had done her research. Barbers Point was notorious for a shelf of shallow shoals extending off the southwest point of the island.

"All right, now answer me this. What is compass error and how do you account for it?"

Livy thought for a moment. He was probably referring to variation, but there were others. "Are we talking variation? Deviation? Magnetic dip?"

Wittingham again tried to play down his surprise. "Let's go with variation, shall we?"

"Because magnetic north and true north differ, you need to account for that, depending on where you are in relation to the agonic line," Livy rattled off without a hitch.

"Tell us more about the agonic line."

"Well, it's where the two poles align, and declination is zero, sir. If you are west of the agonic line, the needle will point east of true north, and if you are east of the agonic line, the needle will point west of true north. So we need to stay on top of this on our way to Hawai'i."

Harding pounded his fists on the table. "Miss West, I'm doubly impressed! None of the others had even heard of Barbers Point. This shows me that you've done your homework. Bravo."

A feeling of satisfaction burned through her. "Thank you, sir."

"What do you say? Would you like the job?" he said.

"Wait, that's all?" she asked.

"That's it, my friend. For now at least. The race committee will have their own navigator test, and you'll have to pass that, but right now I need to get hopping." He handed her a card. "I'm staying at the Inn on Front Street. They have extra rooms—why don't you check in there and we can meet up in the morning, say about 0700 in the hotel lounge. Their coffee stinks but it's gratis."

She had so many questions, but he was off before she could get another word out. She looked at the hotel card. On the back he had scribbled his name and room number. *"Felix P. Harding, Aviator Extraordinaire."* She stuck the card in her pocket and let the reality of what had just happened sink in. She was going to Hawai'i!

8

THE QUESTION OF A PLANE

Olivia

DOLE DERBY CLOSING SOON

Oakland, California—There are just two days left to enter the daring race to the island of O'ahu in the beautiful Hawaiian Islands, some 2400 miles across the Pacific. All entrants must have their applications submitted before noon on August 2. The San Francisco Race Committee reports that 15 brave pilots have thus far registered. Entrants have come from far and wide, with a kind of verve that's causing a big uproar across the country. Think you have the mettle? Throw your hat in before it's too late. All you need is $100, an airplane and a love of adventure.

The hotel was a rickety old place with creaky halls and maroon carpet decorated with cigarette burns. The walls were thin, the blanket thinner. Livy spent half the night shivering, before finally getting up and putting on her sweater and flight gloves. Still, she flopped around like a dead fish, unable to get the encounter with Heath out of her mind.

She had never meant to fall for him. After almost a two-year hiatus, between that first flight and her return to the airfield at eighteen, Heath had been true to his word and taught her how to fly. His calm and steady manner in the plane appealed to her, along with his finely carved forearms and strong hands. Their friendship developed fast, though with a flirtatious undercurrent. It seemed like wherever one was, the other was always nearby. They joked and jabbed and skirted around the elephant in the room—that there was an attraction as big as the sea.

One day, after bringing the plane to a stop, Heath sat still, making no move to deplane. Livy was busy closing things up, rambling on about clouds and turbulence, when she finally glanced his way. He was chewing his gum furiously, and looking straight ahead.

"What are you waiting for?" she asked.

He answered her by leaning over, pulling out his gum and kissing her lightly on the lips. One of his hands went to her hair and his fingers slipped through her curls. Livy kissed him back, surprised but not surprised. A buzzing, like a swarm of bees, started up in her chest, and spread throughout her entire body. After a moment, Heath pulled away and pressed his forehead against hers.

"Damn, Liv, you drive me crazy, you know that?" he said, breath hot on her mouth.

She responded with another kiss, this one less delicate. His hands made their way down to her waist, and hers found his chest. They were fumbling and hungry and breathless in the small cockpit. No matter what she did, she couldn't seem to get close enough. His skin felt magnetic, and she wanted to touch every square inch of it. But eventually, they came apart for air.

"We should probably get out of here. They've gotta be wondering what's going on," he said, grinning like a mad fool.

For Livy, the moment had been a discovery of the true meaning of desire. Nothing had ever come close to it. *Ever.* Nor had anything come close to the shock and despair of his leaving when he up and joined the navy with no warning. Now, having him in the race complicated things, but she vowed to keep her distance. One of the most important rules in life, something she learned from her mother, was this: you never let the same man break your heart twice. It was a rule she planned on following to a T.

In the morning, bleary eyed but excited, she went down for an early cup of coffee to give herself a boost before Harding arrived. But Harding was already there, looking just as bleary eyed, though dressed sharply in a tailored black suit. His five-o'clock shadow was well on its way to becoming a beard. He waved and motioned her over.

"How'd you sleep?" he asked.

She chose positivity over truth. "Wonderfully."

"No offense, but you look like you were wrestling with the pillow all night. That's okay, I didn't sleep well, either. Too much on the mind." He dropped his head and looked into the mug. "My wife, Iwa, was admitted to the hospital last night. They say it was nerves. And now I feel like a real louse, because she's been running herself ragged all over Honolulu trying to drum up money to get me a plane."

He seemed on the verge of tears.

"I'm sorry to hear it, but I'm sure after a little care and rest, she'll be good to go."

"I hope you're right about that. That woman means the world to me. I couldn't go on without her," he said with such feeling that she wanted to reach out and hug him. Any man who spoke about his wife in such a way was a good man in her book.

"Speaking of planes, how is it that you've already entered but don't have a plane yet? Didn't you have to give them that info when you signed up?" Livy asked.

The place was empty, but Harding lowered his voice anyway. "I knew what I wanted to fly, and I knew I'd eventually get the money so it was just a matter of timing, you see. Just a small white lie."

"So do you or don't you have a plane?" she asked.

He scratched his neck. "That remains to be seen, but I'm hopeful. We have an appointment this morning at Vance Breese's factory over on Seventh."

"We?"

"You and me, of course."

She nodded, surprised to be included. "Of course."

She held her tongue on any more questions because, well, she wasn't sure she wanted to know the answer.

They took a streetcar through the morning gloom, with a whole lot of dinging and clanging along the way. The smell of the ocean and baking sourdough wafted through the windows, causing Livy's stomach to growl. Despite having a terrible sleep and wondering about the plane, she was thrilled to the bone to be there.

"This damn cold is worse than the deep of winter in Hawai'i," Felix lamented.

"The clouds should break by noon." It seemed obvious, but she reminded herself that not everyone knew weather like she did. "The wind will be filling in, you can tell by the way those high clouds are separating."

Before reaching Breese's place, they stopped by Western Union to telegraph Livy's folks the good news in the shortest message she could muster, though she knew it would not be good news for her mother.

```
I GOT THE JOB! MUCH TO DO BEFORE DEPARTURE
AUG 12 SO WILL NOT BE BACK IN SD BEFORE RACE
DAY STOP PA THANK YOU FOR TEACHING ME WELL
AND MA DON'T WORRY I PLAN ON MAKING IT BACK
IN ONE PIECE STOP WILL KEEP YOU UPDATED STOP
ALL MY LOVE LIVY
```

★ ★ ★

The airplane factory was small but tidy, with polished floors and high green tinted windows. There were three monoplanes in various states of construction. Harding led her to the near finished one, where a small crew was putting on the final touches.

"Ahoy, Mr. Breese! We've come to check on that plane of yours," he said.

A handsome man with a receding hairline came around to their side, wiping his hands on a rag and then shaking Felix's. "Today's your lucky day, Harding. My other client officially defaulted—lost everything at the races. I have his diamond ring, but that's only enough to cover one wing and a propeller. Fifteen grand and she's all yours."

Fifteen grand was a huge sum of money, but the look on Harding's face was one of pure relief and he visibly loosened, clasping his hands together. "Thank God in heaven and my darling wife."

Breese had his eye on Livy. "I thought your wife was in Honolulu. Or is this your daughter?" he said.

Harding patted her on the back. "Meet, O.M. West, my brilliant new navigator."

Livy smiled. "A pleasure, sir."

"Well, I'll be. A female navigator. I didn't know there was such a thing," he said with a wink.

Oh, brother. She ignored him, instead stepping toward the plane. "Is this our airplane, Mr. Breese? She sure is lovely."

"This one belongs to Sanford Laroux, he's picking it up tomorrow. Yours is over there." He pointed to a shell of a plane, missing most of the parts that made up an airplane.

"She's going to be perfect," Harding said.

No wheels, no propeller, no control wires and no canvas. Livy stood gaping. "But she's not even half-finished."

Maybe this whole thing had been a monumental mistake. In

being so eager to get in the race, she'd put herself in the hands of someone she hardly knew with questionable judgment. Heath's words came back to her. *Why settle for being a navigator when you could probably outfly half the men in this race?* His presumptuousness irked her, but she began to wonder if she had thrown in the towel too soon.

"But she will be. Come, have a look," Harding said.

They walked to the front of the frame. With every step, Livy grew more leery of the situation. More than anything, you wanted to be sure of two things: your equipment and your pilot. Here, she wasn't sure of either. In fact, there was hardly any equipment to be sure of.

"We're going to call her *Malolo*—it's a flying fish in Hawaiian waters. Beautiful blue things with iridescent wings they glide on for miles," he said, beaming at the plane as one would a newborn. "Main thing is, she has a stellar engine. A Wright Whirlwind J-5, same as Lindbergh."

Livy had to admit, the engine was impressive. She counted nine cylinders that radiated out like flower petals, glinting under the lights.

Breese, who was standing behind them, said, "This baby is the most reliable in the world. Her two hundred horses will easily get you to Hawai'i without a hitch. She breathes well and needs less fuel and pretty much just purrs along."

"How fast does she fly?" Livy asked.

"Top speed should be one-ten, cruising closer to ninety-four."

Not the fastest, but it would do.

Harding pulled out a check from his pocket and waved it around. "I told you I'd come up with the money, and here you are, my friend."

Breese took the check and shook his hand. "Congratulations, you won't be disappointed."

Harding smiled over at Livy. "Now, we get to work."

★ ★ ★

They went back to the hotel room, changed clothes and grabbed a bite. Felix sent a telegram to his wife in the hospital to give her the good news. Livy debated telling Felix she'd changed her mind. The fact that he hadn't been totally honest with her didn't sit well, and who knew if the plane would even be ready in time. But if he did pull it off, how would she feel sitting on the airfield watching the planes take off for Hawai'i?

There was also the matter of the prize money. Every time she meant to ask, she'd chickened out. Felix had had to raise fifteen thousand dollars for the plane, so chances were that twenty-five-thousand-dollar first prize would dwindle down to ten thousand or less. Would he give her some? It would only be fair and he seemed like a fair man. In the beginning, the money had seemed like such a big deal, and it was, but the truth was, she was already hooked.

They arrived at the factory before lunchtime. With the race coming up, there wasn't a second to waste. As soon as he'd handed over that check, Harding had been talking nonstop about how he wanted to modify the plane. Livy wondered how she could help and was willing to do whatever he asked of her, which turned out to be running around town picking up parts here and there. Mr. Breese lent her the old company truck, which she nearly crashed into a streetcar as it barreled down the crowded streets. Give her an airplane and an open sky any day.

They worked day and night for two days running. When she had run out of errands to do, Livy volunteered to help cut and secure the linen fabric over the steel tubing of the fuselage and wooden forms of the wings. No one batted an eye and they put her to work—they were that desperate to finish. It felt good to get her hands dirty and to have a part in building the bird that would carry them across the Pacific.

Once the wheels went on and the fabric covered the entire

plane, it began to feel like they really might finish in time. Felix, for all of his cursing and mumbling to himself, knew his way around an airplane. He always seemed to have the right tool and the right hardware for the job. Breese and his men appeared to agree with most of his alteration ideas, which set Livy at ease. Being a good pilot and being a good mechanic were not necessarily interchangeable, and in a race across the ocean, you wanted both.

The big conundrum was how to handle the fuel. Regular planes were not equipped with a tank large enough to carry as much of the flammable and heavy liquid as they'd need, but Breese was adamant that there wasn't enough time to fashion a new and bigger tank.

After much discussion, Harding crawled into the rear cabin with a tape measure, then asked Livy, "How much do you think you can you lift?"

"Why?" she asked.

"Because if nothing else, we're going to need to bring a bunch of five-gallon tins on board, and you'll be the one filling the tank."

All those years of hauling in fish, and now loading trunks and boxes twice a day had kept her strong. She might be small, but her muscles were well developed and well used.

"Then I guess my answer is however much a five-gallon tin of gasoline weighs."

He chuckled. "I knew you were the right man for the job the minute I saw you."

Rumblings around town began to circulate that the final entrants, all fifteen pilots and their navigators and crew, were beginning to arrive in Oakland. Flying in from as far away as Illinois, Oklahoma and Michigan. The press had its favorites, namely *Soaring Eagle*, *Miss Doran* and *El Encanto*.

Soaring Eagle belonged to William Hunt, the newspaper mag-

nate who owned half of California, and was a Lockheed Vega—
a swift, modern plane with a bonded wooden fuselage. Livy
had seen one take off from Los Angeles a few times and had
been surprised at its sleek design and high speed. Pilot Jack
Hunt, William Hunt's son, was known to be a seasoned pilot
and flight instructor with a penchant for bow ties and fancy
suits. Of all the planes in the race, she'd put her money on that
one. If she weren't flying in another.

The *Miss Doran* was named after Mildred Doran, the schoolteacher going along for the ride with a pilot, a navigator and a
Great Dane puppy named Honolulu, who had reportedly almost fallen out of the plane at least once on the long trip over
from Michigan. Talk about extra weight. In Livy's mind, people were enamored with the *Miss Doran* because Mildred had
managed to charm most of America with her hazel eyes, wavy
hair and flippant attitude. Livy was curious to meet her and
see what all the fuss was about.

The third favorite, *El Encanto*, Livy knew well. Good old
Norman Goddard, a veteran of the Royal Flying Corps, had
owned an airfield in San Diego up until two months ago, when
he'd sold it to pay his way into the race. He had been one of
the first people she'd approached, and he'd looked her in the
eye and told her to scram. The only person he had the time
and money to help was himself.

Having an airplane was critical to their success, obviously,
but equally as critical was the ability to locate a tiny island in
the vast blue sea. And that required intimate knowledge of
navigation. For Livy, this meant a deep understanding of this
complex skill, which was part science, part art, part learning to
listen to the wind and clouds and your own inner voice. This
morning, she was headed out to find the nautical charts that
would guide them across the sea.

For her seventh birthday, Livy had received a precious gift—

a brass compass with a long chain to wear around her neck. She took that compass everywhere she went, and never took it off, not even to sleep. Every time she went out on the boat, she picked up something new. She didn't realize it at the time, but a fishing boat was the best kind of classroom.

She learned the difference between true north—the geographical location of the North Pole, a fixed point—and magnetic north, which is where a compass points as it aligns with the earth's magnetic field. She came to understand magnetic deviation, and how the compass needle may not always point north, but that Polaris, the North Star, was always true.

When she turned ten, she got her very own sextant. Orlando, first mate and her favorite uncle, had been patiently showing her how to use one over the past year. Anytime the opportunity arose, especially on clear nights, they took sight of stars and planets, measuring their angles above the horizon, and from that, calculating a position line on the chart. That, he told her, would give you your latitude. Orlando always smelled like tobacco and tuna, but he had the most infectious laugh, and he treated Livy with such kindness.

As she walked down the street in front of her hotel, she thought of him, and wondered what he would be doing now if he were still alive. One thing she knew for sure was that he would be thrilled to pieces about this race. He thrived on new horizons, always seeking new fishing grounds and taking them farther south or farther out to sea. He'd been a born fisherman, just in the wrong place in the wrong storm. Livy shivered at the memory, hearing her name on the wind, just as a thick raindrop fell on her shoulder. Heavy rain was coming. She picked up her pace.

Olivia!

Dreams of that night still haunted her, but it was unusual to have them during the day. Probably just exhaustion and nerves. She rubbed her temples and tried to shake it off.

Up ahead, a black Ford pulled alongside the curb and slowed. The window rolled down a few inches.

"Hey, Liv, can I give you a ride?"

She knew that voice anywhere. When she ducked down to look in, Heath was at the wheel.

"Thank you but I'm fine."

"Where you headed?"

"Just off to run a few errands."

As soon as the words left her tongue, the skies opened up. She pulled her jacket tight and held the newspaper over her head.

In typical Heath fashion, he persisted. "From the looks of those clouds, the rain's going to hang around. Hop in."

He was right about the rain, and the last thing she needed was to come down sick before the race. So, even though she'd sworn off him, she jumped in the car. They sat there for a few moments in a watery cocoon, drops splattering on the windshield and running down the windows.

"Where to?" he finally asked.

"If you must know, I was headed to the Maritime Building to hunt down some nautical charts. Felix knows next to nothing about navigation so it's all up to me," she said.

"The Maritime Building it is, then."

They sped off, Heath with his left hand on the wheel, barely touching it, and his right resting on the back of the seat. His fingers were uncomfortably close to her shoulder, but she knew from experience, that that was how he always drove—with a casual coolness, yet always in perfect control. The same way he lived.

Inconveniently, her mind had suddenly gone blank. Heath seemed to be having the same problem, because they rode along in silence for a while. She uncrossed and crossed her legs seven times before something finally came to her.

"You never mentioned who's navigating your plane," she said.

"You're sitting next to him."

"What?"

"Don't sound so shocked. Charlie did it, so why couldn't I?"

"Hitting the European continent is a lot easier than hitting an island, as you already know," she said, even though she herself had wanted to fly solo.

"The best navigator I know is taken, and anyway, I think I have a better shot alone. Less weight and less chance for disagreement."

She risked a look and saw that he was grinning.

"Are you talking about Davis, Art Goebel's navigator?" she asked, though she knew he wasn't.

"I'm talking about you."

She tapped her fingers on the armrest. "I'm probably the least experienced of the whole lot."

"Maybe so, but I'd still take you over any of these boys. You might be green, but you have a special talent. You know that."

Their days of flying together were over, and the sooner he understood that the better. "Nice of you to say, but I'm sure every one of them is more than capable. You, too. Being in the navy must have taught you a thing or two. What happened out there on your last attempt?"

"I'm sure you read all about it in the papers."

"What the papers say and what really happened never quite match up."

Livy had to raise her voice to be heard over the rain, which was now coming down like marbles on the metal roof. The windows quickly steamed, and Heath wiped them with his sleeve.

"It's a long story. I'll tell you one of these days," he said.

As they drove along the waterfront, he pointed out buildings and docks and landmarks, keeping the conversation light and in neutral territory.

"What kinds of supplies are you two bringing along?" he asked.

She remembered Lindbergh lamenting over what to take on his crossing, and how he'd weighed every last item.

"We haven't discussed any of that. Every waking moment has been going into finishing the airplane and figuring out the fuel system—which is a real headache, but Felix has a cockamamie plan that just may work," she said. "What about you?"

"Oh, yeah, I have my list. Parachute? No point, over water. Life raft, flares, knife, canteens, thin wool sweater, flight suit, sextant, radio—"

"Lindbergh didn't take a sextant or a radio," she said.

"You ask me, Charlie got lucky. Where we're going, you can't rely on luck. I know he thought they were wasted weight, and he said he had no hands to spare, but I like the idea of having them along for the ride. It almost seems sacrilegious not to have either on board."

Livy had to agree. A sextant more than a radio.

"How about food and water?" she asked.

"Ten sandwiches, a chocolate bar cut into small pieces and a gallon of water. Nothing fancy, but the chocolate could help keep me awake, which I may need since I won't have anyone to talk to at night."

When they arrived at the Maritime Building, they dashed through ice-cold puddles, and Heath held the tall glass door open for her. Livy slid past him as fast as possible into a large foyer lined with old framed maps and paintings of ships. A woman at the front desk directed them to the room where maps of the Central Pacific were kept in large drawers.

"Can I help you?" a slick-haired salesman asked.

Heath deferred to Livy.

"Yes, please, a Mercator projection of the Pacific that shows California and the Hawaiian Islands would be great to start," she said, "Do you mind if we just look around?"

"You two Dole Birds, are ya?" the man said.

Someone in the press had coined the terms, and it stuck.

"We are," Heath said.

"But not together," Livy was quick to add.

He looked back and forth between them, but fortunately, didn't ask any more questions. He went over to a set of large drawers and soon produced two oblong sheets, one with both California and Hawai'i, and one just of the Hawaiian Islands, laying them out on a nearby table. The smell reminded her of going into the map store in San Diego with Pa, and the smell of fresh ink and paper.

"These are perfect," Heath said.

"What about gnomonic projections—do you have any of those, too?" Livy asked.

Heath shot her a look.

She shrugged. "May as well cover our bases, especially since we'll be at lower latitudes."

Gnomonic projections showed the great-circle lines as straight lines. She liked the grid aspect, but they became less accurate as you moved toward the poles.

A bell on the door rang, and two more men came into the room.

"Have a look in those drawers over there. I'll help these two and check back," the salesman said, nodding to another set of drawers.

Livy rummaged around, finding a map that showed the prevailing wind in the summer months. The find made her giddy, as it would greatly aid in the plotting of her course, and knowing what to expect with the winds could be the difference between living and dying. She laid that out, too. Then she went back to searching, eventually coming up with what she was looking for.

Heath had his back to her and was rifling through another set of drawers, oohing and ahhing. Finally, he came over with a smug look on his face.

"What is it?" she asked.

He produced a magnetic declination chart of the entire Western Hemisphere. Like gold. It resembled a topographic map, only the curved lines were color coded to show positive or negative declination.

"I could spend all day in here," she said.

"Me, too."

In her eyes, cartography was a form of magic. That someone could take the world, with all its mountains and valleys and deserts and tundra and rivers and oceans, and transfer that onto a piece of paper while keeping proportions true, made her head swim. As a girl, she would pull out her father's maps, spread them on the living room floor and trace every fine line with her finger, imagining herself as a surveyor one day, traveling the world and triangulating every nook and cranny of the earth.

After studying the declination chart, Livy dredged up a map of the Hawaiian Islands from a bottom drawer. It was an old map, and the words printed across the map were *"Sandwich or Hawaiian Islands."* She set it out on the table.

"Why are they called the Sandwich Islands?" she asked.

"From what I gather, when Captain Cook of the Royal Navy landed, he named the islands after one of his patrons, presumptuous chap that he was. The natives thought he was some kind of God, which he played up, but when they found out they'd been duped, they killed him. Eventually, the name Sandwich Islands faded away and they became known as the Hawaiian Islands, after the largest island in the chain," Heath said, finger tapping on Hawai'i.

"I don't suppose Cook and his boys asked the Hawaiians."

"I suppose not."

Also on the map was a box of Hawaiian words, with a pronunciation key: *"HA-WAI-I, Hä-wye-e. KIL-AU-E-A, Ke-low-a-ah."*

"Felix can pronounce all of these fluently. It's impressive.

His wife was born and raised in the islands, an actual Hawaiian, and she's drilled it into him."

"They look like real tongue twisters to me."

"But the words are beautiful, if you hear them spoken correctly."

They studied the rest of the map, absorbed everything they could from the parched and yellowed paper. There were eight main islands: Ni'ihau, Kaua'i, O'ahu, Moloka'i, Lana'i, Maui, Kaho'olawe, and Hawai'i. Beneath that was a box of text titled, *"The Hawaiian People, Islands and Statistics."*

"Oh, my word!" Livy said after reading a few paragraphs.

> *The people were classified as heathen of the worst type. Desperately wicked, and sensuality produced no shame. Child murder common and human sacrifice was protected by law. Cannibalism so common, that a mother would kill, cook and eat her fattened baby.*

"Anything written about Hawaiian people here should be taken with a monumental grain of salt. It's all coming through the lens of the Puritans, and those greedy bastards who wanted the islands for themselves," Heath added.

"Yes, but to have all this written on maps for all the world to see. It's awful."

"A tragedy is what it is."

None of what she read here matched the version of Hawai'i she had seen in postcards and advertisements. One showed a glimmering ideal, the other a wicked bunch of heathens. Both a fabrication, she realized. Even more reason to see for herself.

When they had finished taking notes, Heath pinned her to the seat with a stare. "So," he said, "I'd love to know how you plan on plotting your whole course out."

Livy frowned. "Why would I share my secrets with the competition?"

He took a step closer. "Is that how you see me now—your competition?"

"It's the truth, isn't it?"

Another step. She remained planted, determined to show him she wasn't afraid to be in his presence, and that any effects he'd had on her had long washed away.

"It may be your truth, but in my world, you and I will always be on the same team."

"Don't go there, Hazeltine, not now," she said.

This was not the place for any such conversation. Livy knew that. Nor was she even sure she wanted to rehash things with him anywhere. The past was the past was the past. She had moved on, thank you very much.

He nodded. "Sorry, I get it. But my last trip across the Pacific required little navigation, since we followed the ship radio signals the whole way. That turned out to not be as foolproof as we thought. I could really use any tips you can spare, Liv."

When plotting a great-circle route, it becomes a curve on a Mercator map, but a straight line on a gnomic. Livy knew that by plotting the great-circle points on the gnomic map, she could then transfer to the Mercator. He should know this already.

"Right now, I have to help Felix. And I know this isn't what you want to hear, but if you don't trust yourself, you really shouldn't be flying alone," she said.

A look of hurt flashed over his face and then he forced a smile. "Right."

It was a quiet drive back to her hotel, Heath tight-lipped and tense. Livy began to second-guess her decision as unsportsman-like, but then reminded herself, *You owe him nothing.*

9

A KEY TO THE LOCK

Wren

Wren didn't remember too much about her father, other than feeling warm and fuzzy in his presence. When he was around, the world spun in Technicolor. She had a vivid picture in her mind of waiting on the front steps for the sound of his old Volkswagen bug to turn onto their street, and the putter of its loud engine. The minute he got out of the car, she'd run up and jump into his arms, and he'd burrow his face in her neck and hair, blowing on her skin to make funny noises. She could still feel the roughness of his stubble on her cheek.

Kainoa Summers left when Wren was four, and she hadn't seen him since. As told by Cindy, he couldn't hold a job, had some real problems with certain substances and could not be trusted. Especially with young Wren, who had vague recollections of being alone on a beach and then later, raised voices and crying, even shattering glass. Then he was gone. A father evaporated. All Cindy would say was, *We are better off without him. He's on the mainland now.*

Over the years, Wren had gleaned only tidbits of information about him. He was an artist, like her, except he painted seascapes on large canvases or wood, even buildings, but those had since been painted over. He was a surfer and built his own wooden boards, he was an adventurer and a mean ukulele player and he hated convention. Hated being tied down, too. Some men weren't meant to have a family and he was one of them.

Cindy kept no photos, or so she'd led Wren to believe, but Wren had found a box in the garage when she was ten with a small plastic album full. Her father was tall and lean, with dark skin and eyes blue as the ocean off of Diamond Head. His nose was a little too wide, his eyes too far apart, but that gave him character. It was like seeing an older, male version of her own face, and she flipped through the pages for hours, taking in every nuance of this strange yet familiar man. His expression made her think he knew some universal secret that only he was privy to.

Wren always had this dream that she would run into him on the street or the beach or the airport and she would know him right away.

Dad? she would say.

He would look past her and keep on walking.

She would say it louder. *Dad!*

But he never turned around. She would yell so loud, trying to be heard, but he could never hear her. Whenever she woke from those dreams, she'd feel a strange melancholy that stayed with her for the entire day. Now, as she followed the overgrown road, she thought of him. This land had belonged to his aunt and his mother, and had bypassed him.

Up close, the wooden structure took the shape of a barn. It was bigger than she'd first thought, its green paint faded, its corrugated roof flaky and rusted but still intact. A fallen tree branch rested on one side. A chain whose links were as fat as fingers held together two giant doors. Wren pulled off to the side and shut off the engine. In the filtered light, she noticed steam coming from under the hood. She'd worry about that later.

This time, she had the key to the lock, but for some reason, she was nervous to open the doors and take a look inside. Instead, she followed a small path around back. Pig trail, maybe? Along the side were high windows with greenish glass panes, a few cracked. The barn stretched back into the jungle, and Wren swatted away mosquitoes and gnats. The soil was turned up under a nearby guava tree. More evidence of pigs.

In the back, windows ran across the upper reaches. The siding was covered in black mildew and a few of the boards had rotted out. Off to the side stood a small water tower that looked to be made out of steel, but was covered in moss. The hum of honeybees filled the air, and she glanced up at the trees but didn't see any. From what Bob had said, the place had been unused since the war days. No wonder it looked so dilapidated. She wished she had pressed him for more information, but it sounded like he had told her everything he knew.

A short distance away was a tin-roof shed. Wooden boxes were scattered nearby, some stacked three or four high. They looked like honey boxes, but Wren couldn't be sure. The red door was stuck shut, but with a little body weight, it swung open. Cobwebs filled the entire space and something small scurried out a hole in the back wall. Wren jumped back. Once she caught her breath, she took a step closer and peered in.

The shed was full of shelves and the shelves were lined with jars of all sizes, full of yellowish-brown liquid. Honey? It had to be. She remembered an article about King Tut and how he'd been buried with honey jars. Apparently it was still edible thousands of years later. Who knew how long this had been here. Certainly less than three thousand years. She took a long stick and batted away some of the cobwebs and snagged a big jar closest to the door, then shut it and continued on.

By the time she made it around the whole structure, and back to the front, she had made up her mind to get rid of it as soon as she could and maybe get a small house with a big garage—space to work on her light boxes. The barn was sure to be a teardown, but the land would be worth something. Or maybe not. This wasn't O'ahu. There was so much land on this island, and this place was the boonies. It could prove to be a tough sell.

She checked her watch, realizing she was famished. Somehow it was already two o'clock. The inside of the barn could wait a little longer. She ate her lunch on the tailgate, listening to the birds twittering and the wind rushing through a row of nearby ironwoods. It was peaceful and refreshing, and, she had to admit, a welcome distraction from her troubles back home.

Then, from off to the right side of the barn, came a rustling in the bushes. She lifted her legs up, expecting to see a pig or two, but instead a narrow, brindle-colored dog with big ears appeared. Wren froze, unsure whether or not to call attention to herself. The dog hadn't caught her scent yet, and it went straight to the barn, lowering itself down and scooting under the siding. So, the barn was inhabited after all.

She sat for a while longer, enjoying the warmth of the sun on her shoulders. There was another hour or so before she had to leave to catch her flight, and the sensations and sounds lulled her almost to a trance state. Eventually, she hopped off the tailgate, rattling the keys so the dog would hear her. Last thing she wanted was to startle a wild dog.

"Hey, there, I'm coming in," she said, picking up a nearby stick, just in case it came at her. Also good for spiders and cobwebs.

Here goes.

This lock was newer than the last, but took a few minutes of jiggling before it came free. With all the racket she'd made, the dog would surely have taken off. She took a deep breath, grabbed the black iron door handle and pulled with all her might. The doors wouldn't budge. Not even an inch. She tried again, talking all the while.

"Doggo, you still in here? Move along, I'm coming in."

As a girl, she'd been chased up a tree by the neighbor's angry black dog, who bit her calf before she made it high enough. Since then, she'd been wary of dogs. Cats were more her jam.

Wren moved to the right door and put all her weight into sliding it. Nothing happened. When she moved to the left door, it finally rolled back about two feet, then screeched to a stop. A shaft of light poured in, and a musty scent of old things and animal wafted out. It felt as though she were opening a tomb. Her whole body hummed with anticipation—and apprehension.

Between the high windows and the light from the door opening, Wren could see that the space was cavernous. It reminded her of one of those airplane hangars at Pearl Harbor with bullet-ridden remains of old fighter planes and bombers. She slipped through the doors, surprised at how empty it was. For some reason, she'd been expecting more farming equipment and stuff, more general clutter. Toward the back, there were two large pieces of machinery covered in canvas—tractors most likely, and off to the side, an old truck.

Being on the inside, she could see light streaming in the cracks in the walls where wood had rotted out. The roof, though, seemed solid. She walked across the cold concrete floor toward the truck, an olive green Ford with a stake-bed back laced in cobwebs. The truck was old, but appeared to be in decent condition. A work truck most likely. She wondered about the mac nut orchard. Who had planted it and farmed it? For how long? The questions about this place and her father's family were popping up faster than she could keep track of them.

Eager to keep going, she walked between the two big machines, and for the first time noticed wooden steps going up to a mezzanine. It looked about twenty feet deep and spanned the whole back section of the barn. There were no walls, just a railing. She tapped the first step with her foot, curious to go up, but skeptical of the integrity of the wood.

All of the sudden, she heard shuffling above and a *click-click-click* on the floor. She looked up. At the top of the steps, the dog stood staring down at her. They both froze, eyes locked. It was thinner than she'd first realized, brown eyes wide with fear. The dog seemed to be assessing whether it could make a run for it or retreat. Instead of turning to dash for the car, Wren remained in place. The poor creature looked starving.

"Hey, I'm not going to hurt you."

It cocked its head, one ear perking up.

Wren took a step back. "Sorry for the imposition. You know, I think I've seen just about enough here. I'm on my way out."

The dog began panting. There would be plenty of water in the streams, but as thin as it was, she wondered if it could make it that far. Maybe she should try to find some. Wait, hang on. This wild dog was not her problem. She had a plane to catch and a life to figure out. Being homeless, jobless *and* manless had never been part of the plan. But maybe that was the problem. There had been no real plan. Just a lot of moments strung together aimlessly.

Wren backed away slowly. The dog remained in place, eyeing her warily. Underneath the mezzanine was a door. She opened it to reveal a small bathroom with a black-and-white-checkered floor, a toilet and a sink. She turned on the faucet but nothing came out.

On the way out, Wren thought about pulling the canvas off of the tractors, but decided against it. They'd be covered in dust and cobwebs, and who knew what kind of critters might be living in their dark recesses. When she put the place on the market, she could sell them with it. This place was much too much work. The old truck was the only thing of possible value, and she could unload that separately. Her first order of business upon return was to find a realtor who could handle it all.

At the truck, she set her extra musubi and Fritos on the ground for the dog. Chances were it didn't drink Coke, so she finished that off, took a deep breath and turned her face to the afternoon sun. All that green around her started seeping in, filling her with a calm she hadn't felt in years. For a split second, she imagined staying here. Who would really miss her? What would happen? For one, she'd probably end up skinny as the dog. But this blissful feeling, if only she could hang on to it for a little longer.

Her watch said it was time to boogie, so she jumped in the truck, but when she went to start the engine, nothing happened. No turnover, no chugging, no rasping sounds. She ordered herself to stay calm despite tendrils of panic wrapping around her midsection. Bob had said the truck was temperamental. She gave it a few minutes and tried again. Nothing. She popped the hood.

She knew her way around cars thanks to Mr. Woodward, the one teacher at school who made her feel at home in his class. She and her friend Maureen only enrolled in auto mechanics because Alika Ka'aua was in the class, and they both had massive crushes on him. Then, unbeknownst to them, Alika dropped it the last day, and they were stuck. Mr. Woodward, though, proved to be patient and super cool, and gave them plenty of latitude as long as they completed the assignments on time. By the end of the semester, Wren could change a tire, change the oil and identify all the parts of an internal combustion engine.

Now, she checked the battery and its connections. Everything looked good. She moved along and inspected the fuel pump and fuel lines. Nothing seemed out of place, but it was hard to get in there and see everything. She used a leaf to wipe the dipstick and checked the oil. All good there, too. After assessing everything she possibly could, she slammed the hood shut and leaned back on the grille, groaning. Her hands were black and she had grease smears all over her top, and she felt like crying.

That was when the first raindrop landed on her shoulder and slid down onto her collarbone. She hadn't even been aware of the charcoal gray clouds building above. Grape-sized raindrops began falling by the barrel full, drenching her hot skin. Wren hopped in the car and shut the door, steaming up the windows within seconds. She might have walked out had it been dry, but with the downpour, no way.

According to the map, Hāwī town was at least fifteen miles away as the crow flew. Kapaʻau was just beyond that, and the road went on a ways and dead-ended at Pololū Valley. There was nothing else for miles. And she hadn't passed any houses the whole way out here. What about the fork in the road? If the rain let up, she could see where that led.

Rain pelted the roof of the cab, and only intensified in its fury. She took inventory of what she had with her. A jacket, a Tiger's Milk Bar, four Cokes and an orange, if you didn't count the food on the ground. In a pinch, she could forage for guava, or go back and pick lilikoi. But that depended on the rain, which showed no signs of letting up. She sat there, miserable, staring at the clock and wondering if her life could get any worse.

An hour passed and the sky darkened. Lightning flashed in the distance, eerily illuminating the face of the barn. Another hour, and night fell. When the rain lightened, enough so that she could hear herself think, Wren cracked the window to get some fresh air. From nearby, she heard a weird crunching sound, like someone munching on bones. The hairs on the back of her neck went up, until she realized it was the dog eating the Frito remnants. At least someone was enjoying dinner.

Would anyone come looking for her? Gina and her other friends knew she wasn't getting back until dark, so they'd probably just check in tomorrow. Joe, her person to call when things went wrong, had shed that role when he chose Julie over Wren. Now Julie got to call him when her car wouldn't start, when she couldn't get off the bathroom floor, sick with food poisoning or when she'd lost yet another job. Though Julie probably didn't lose jobs. Oh, God. Enough wallowing. The only other person who knew she was here was Bob. But unless someone planned on using the truck tonight, chances were slim that anyone would notice her missing.

Normally she enjoyed the solace of being alone, but now the darkness of the forest closed in on her, making her jumpy. Resigned to spending the night in the truck, she locked the doors and curled up in a fetal position, eventually drifting off to the pitter-patter on the roof. Morning could not come soon enough.

10

A ROOM FULL OF MEN

Olivia

August 8 dawned so sunny and bright that even the birds were celebrating. Grateful for a change in the weather, Livy walked to the Matson Building for a meeting with the head of the race committee, C.W. Lange, and the rest of the entrants. Having spent the past week holed up with Felix and the Breese crew, she was feeling jittery about meeting the officials and aviators—or for those still not here, their proxies.

Felix had demanded she go it alone, as he planned to put the final touches on *Malolo*. As luck would have it, the finished airplane had nearly identical specs to the imaginary plane he'd conjured up on the application—forty-one-foot wingspan, twenty-seven feet from nose to tail, same monoplane design and same engine. He took that as a good sign and Livy was inclined to agree. When everything came together like that, you had to wonder if it was part of some bigger design. Now, Felix said he had a secret he seemed very excited about, and told her it would be a surprise when she returned.

At the frosted glass door, she could hear the boisterous sound of voices. She took a deep breath, stood tall and walked in. Conversation ceased. All eyes turned her way.

A tall, bespectacled man with big ears and a clipboard said, "And you are?"

Livy held her hands behind her to hide the fact that they were shaking. "I'm Olivia West, proxy for Felix Harding. I'll be navigating *Malolo*."

"Why isn't Harding here? I know he's in town," Lange said in a most unwelcoming voice.

"He had other matters to attend to."

Like finishing their airplane, but of course she wasn't about to tell him that.

"You do realize, Miss West, the seriousness of this business, and that you'll be put through a rigorous in-flight test?"

"Fully, sir."

His gaze swept around the room, "We're on a tight schedule here, with qualifying the planes, the aviators and the navigators. I just wouldn't want you to waste anyone's time simply to suit your fancy."

She had half a mind to tell him where to shove it. "I don't plan on wasting anyone's time. In fact, I'm happy to answer any questions you may have about my inadequacies right now."

Lange looked flustered for a second, then said, "What is your plan, then?"

"I already have our course plotted out, and I'll be shooting the sun by day and the moon by night to keep us over the rhumb line. I know my night sky and have my nautical charts memorized down to the second, so I'm confident in my accuracy," she said, then added for good measure, "Oh, and I picked up a table of magnetic declination in the Pacific, so that shouldn't be a problem, either."

Behind her, someone said, "I'd take West over any of these guys."

Heath.

A big man across the room said, "Hell, Lange, you let her navigate, you gotta let my Connie navigate."

The minute he opened his mouth with that syrupy drawl, Livy knew it was Captain Bill Erwin from Texas, who everyone had taken to calling Lone Star Bill.

"We've been through this already, Mr. Erwin. Contestants have to be at least twenty-one, and your wife is only twenty. And pregnant I should add," Lange said, lowering his spectacles. "And from what I hear, you two almost ran into a mountain on the way here, so maybe it'll be in your favor."

That shut him down fast.

Lange was all business. He scribbled a note on his clipboard, then motioned Livy toward the desk where the boys hovered like vultures.

"Take your place, then. You can be Harding's proxy, and we'll see about the rest."

Livy felt a stone in her throat, but ignored it. If there was one thing she'd learned, arguing your case with men like Lange was a waste of time.

There was a wastebasket sitting atop the desk. Heath moved aside and opened a space for her, and she had no choice but to slide in, close enough so their shoulders almost rubbed.

He smiled. "Nice work."

The group was a ragtag bunch, from the darkly handsome Art Goebel in his three-piece suit and flight cap, to Auggy Pedlar, who had earned a reputation as a gregarious showman, unable to resist making bets with anyone and everyone that the *Miss Doran* would be first to Honolulu. Jack Hunt was a sturdy man, shorter than she'd imagined, who put off an air of great confidence. With him was his father, legendary William Hunt himself, newspaper magnate and millionaire. The others she didn't know yet, though she'd heard their names. They all seemed indifferent to her arrival. They were here for one reason only: to draw the best number.

A perky blonde in high heels and a powder blue dress pushed her way through. "Excuse me, fellas, I have your numbers here," she said, wedging herself in between Livy and the table as she dropped a handful of paper scraps into the wastebasket.

In a hushed voice, she said to Livy, "I admire your gumption. Good luck!"

The group pressed in around them. Everyone seemed to have their own idea about where they wanted to be in the lineup. *First to go gets a smooth runway. Last sees how everyone fares, and won't make the same mistakes. Just don't give me number fifteen.* Livy would take whatever number she got.

Lange raised his hand. "We go from Hazeltine, clockwise." Not surprisingly, that put Livy last.

Heath stuck his hand in and came up with number eight. Livy felt her heart lurch. Eight was her lucky number. She was born on the eighth of December at eight o'clock in the morning and was raised in their house at 88 Sandpiper Lane. Eights were prevalent in her life, and she always felt a dash of comfort when an eight came up in whatever capacity. When their eyes met, she knew he remembered.

Eager hands pulled out numbers, with some groaning and some hooting and hollering. The guys from Oklahoma pulled the one, and Hunt ended up with fifteen—the last to leave. From the look on his face, it was not what he wanted. By the time it came to Livy, the only number left in the trashcan was thirteen.

"Well, I guess we all know which number that leaves," she said, not at all pleased but trying to seem upbeat.

But before she could pull the paper out, Heath handed her his paper, closed her palm around it and said, "You know, most people think thirteen is unlucky, but for me it's the opposite. I'll take the thirteen, if you don't mind?"

As much as she didn't want thirteen for herself, she didn't want it for him, either. Never had he mentioned thirteen being a lucky number. In fact, she remembered quite well him being uneasy about flying on a Friday the thirteenth. Like fishermen, aviators were a superstitious lot. Some ate the same meal before every flight, while others always brought a mascot with them—a bird, a cat, even a lion.

"You don't have to do this," she said.

"I know, but I want to," he said.

Lange tapped his clipboard on the desk. "Accept his gracious offer and let's get on with it."

He then read the final lineup. The room suddenly quieted, and a sense of reality settled in among them. In just four days' time, every single one of these aviators would become part of history—one way or another.

Back at Breese's place, Livy could smell Felix's surprise before she even walked in the door, which was wide open. The strong smell of paint spread through the late afternoon, turning her nose inside out. They had painted *Malolo* red and stenciled her name in yellow Western-style block letters that covered the fuselage from nose to tail. They had also painted a Hawaiian lei around the nose, which Livy thought added a nice touch. Felix and a few of the boys were standing around admiring their work.

"What do you think, my friend? Isn't she the prettiest little bird you've laid eyes on?" he said, beaming.

"I love it. And she'll be easy to spot, that's for sure."

"We'll do a ceremony at the field once we qualify. Give the people something to talk about."

Livy then showed him her number, and he seemed pleased by the prospect of going smack-dab in the middle. Which didn't surprise her, because she'd been coming to notice that he was the kind of man who saw possibility in everything. Tell him no and he'd laugh with that toothy grin, and find a way around you. People like that were the doers of the world, the ones who accomplished the impossible. Because to them, failure was just a seven-letter word.

★ ★ ★

Bay Farm Island conjured up all kinds of things in Livy's mind—asparagus farms and hayfields and windmills—but she also knew that the city of Oakland had recently constructed a seven-thousand-foot runway, reported to be the longest anywhere in the world. Though she herself had never landed there, Felix had, and he was eager to show her where they would be taking off from come race day.

In the predawn hours, after checking out of the hotel—which had cost almost every dime Livy had—they had loaded *Malolo* onto a trailer and set out for the airfield, which was clear across the bay. Rather than risk putting the plane on the ferry, they would take the long way around. Breese had lent them the old truck with Breese Aircraft Co. conspicuously stenciled on the side. In the back of the truck was a canvas tent, a cot and two old army blankets. Livy's new digs: the field next to Bay Farm airstrip. Felix would be moving to an inn in Alameda, to be closer to the plane.

Felix's wife had improved over the last couple days, which gave him great relief, but now she'd gotten it into her head to catch the next ship over to California—which would arrive just about when the race was starting—so that she could be his navigator. He still hadn't told her he'd found someone.

"I didn't realize your wife is a navigator," Livy said when he'd told her.

"She's not, that's half the problem."

"What's the other half?" Livy asked.

"Oh, she knows she's the apple of my eye, but when she finds out I've hired a female navigator, there's no telling how she'll react. Either she'll love you or she'll want to scratch your eyes out. There's not a lot of in between with Iwa, you see."

"What *have* you told her?"

"Just that I'm still interviewing, and I have plenty of good candidates."

"Dishonesty only leads to heartbreak. Trust me, I know from experience," she said.

He side-eyed her. "You don't have a dishonest bone in your body, young lady. Want to know how I know that?"

Felix had a theory on everything.

"How?"

"You have a directness and a way of looking a person in the eye that gives it all away. I knew the minute I saw you that you were someone I could trust. I value that above all," he said.

She was flattered. "Thank you. And for the record, it wasn't me that was dishonest, it was him."

She had gone over and over it in her head. Was there a difference between withholding information and an outright lie? In Heath's case, she'd concluded that failing to tell her he was joining the navy and leaving San Diego the next morning counted as a lie of omission.

"So, where is this *him* now?"

She debated not answering, but Felix sounded so genuinely curious.

"*He* happens to be in the race."

"Our race?"

She nodded. "The one and only."

"Wait, let me guess." He drummed his fingers on the wheel for a stretch, then said, "Hazeltine."

He pronounced the name like Ovaltine, and Livy corrected him. "It's *tine*, like *time* with an *n*."

"So, I'm right, then. I had a feeling that first day at the speakeasy. You could see the atmosphere sparking between you two from a mile away. Attraction is alive, you know. It's a force all its own, much like electricity or gravity."

"Maybe at one time there was something there, but not now," she said.

"Ah, but do you think it's coincidence that you two are both here, in the race?"

"He taught me how to fly, and we're both pilots, so no, not particularly."

He chuckled, for some reason amused. "People make mistakes, especially young ones. Would it hurt to give the man a second chance? He seems like a nice chap—and quite dashing, I might add."

She was more than ready to move on to other topics. "Thank you for your worldly advice, but no. And anyway, now is not the time to think about Heath Hazeltine, or anyone else for that matter."

"Righto you are. We have a race to win!"

As they headed south, Livy was struck by the sheer number of buildings and factories and ironworks on land, and ships on the water. Everything from steamships to four-masted sailboats to sloops. Used to more of a bird's-eye view, the ride gave her a closer, more nitty-gritty perspective. The whole peninsula seemed ready to sink under the weight of it all.

Felix was on his second cigarette, trying to suck the life out of it, when he said, "So tell me, what do think our odds are?"

The question threw her. "I'm not much of a betting person. What do *you* think they are?"

"I feel confident, all right. Sixty percent says we make it, forty we don't. But even if we go down, the sea will be crawling with ships. Someone will find us, and we'll make it to Hawai'i one way or another."

Sixty-forty? Those were dismal odds. Not something she wanted to hear from her pilot, and she wished she hadn't asked.

"I prefer to stick to the idea that we *will* make it, and I refuse to waste my time thinking any other way," she said.

Felix glanced over at her, and she could feel him smiling. "Now that is the kind of attitude we need! I knew I took you on for a reason. As more of a waverer myself, I need someone to give me a good swift kick in the pants. Or on the *okole*, as they'd say in Hawai'i."

"Promise me something, will you?" she said.

"Say the word."

"No more talk of not making it or going down. It withers the spirit. We both need to be one hundred percent on this or I'm not going," she said.

And she meant it.

He nodded dramatically. "Very well. Very well, indeed! From this minute on, I will nip those thoughts in the bud. No more listening to those newspaper men, and all the bookies placing bets on us."

Ah, so that's where this had come from.

"I'm serious. Not another word," she said.

He zipped his hand over his mouth.

The runway at Bay Farm Island was something to behold, a wide ribbon of dusty earth that stretched as far as the eye could see. Low grass covered the surrounding area, and the bay waters lapped up along the edges of the island, serene and lovely. Aside from the runway, though, there was not much else. No airplane hangars or large structures to speak of. A few planes were parked at the far end of the runway, with canvas tents sprung up around them and hordes of people milling about. A wooden lean-to had been erected for the press, and cars angled haphazardly around it.

"Here we are, scene of the crime, where it all comes together," Felix said, staring wistfully ahead.

When they pulled to a stop near the planes, Livy closed her eyes and breathed in the salty air. In a few days' time, from this very spot, she would be setting out into the blue unknown. A tingle ran up her spine. Funny how dreams were dreams, and then one day, if you were lucky—or persistent enough, they became reality.

A crowd gathered around them, and she recognized faces of the other contestants, along with a whole slew of men in ties snapping photographs and men in greasy coveralls, eyeing the plane with looks of appreciation. The only thing missing, as usual, was women.

One of the reporters, a man dressed all in white with a red tie, honed in on Livy. "Miss West, is it? The rumors are true, now, that you'll be navigating?"

She flashed him a smile. "Looks like it."

"Do you think you're up for the job?"

"I know I'm up for the job."

"They're saying this will be the ultimate test of aerial navigation, and to fail means almost certain death—does that make you feel squeamish?"

He was right up in her face, and she could smell tobacco on his breath.

"Well, I guess we can't fail, then, can we? I was born and bred on the ocean, and I've spent the last five years in the air, piloting planes all up and down the West Coast. I trust my skills, Mr….?"

"Lee, J.P. Lee, the *Chronicle*. Now, did you say pilot?"

Livy was eager to break free and help Felix get *Malolo* off the trailer and ready for her maiden flight.

"I did."

He scribbled something on his pad, then looked her up and down. "Who would have guessed? Do you plan on flying during the race, too?"

"Felix apparently isn't much of a navigator, so no. Look, Mr. Lee, I'm happy to talk more later, but if you'll excuse me, we have a lot to do."

He smiled, all gums. "Sounds like a plan. I've got my eye on you, little pigeon."

Felix wasn't faring much better, with a ring of reporters standing round him, firing questions left and right. When he saw Livy, he waved his arms around like a conductor and said,

"How about this. I'm about to take her for her first spin, you can write about that. It should be a spectacle."

Once *Malolo* was on the ground, they rolled into an empty spot off to the south of *Woolaroc* and *Dallas Spirit*, with *Soaring Eagle, El Encanto* and Heath's plane, *Golden Plover,* just beyond. On the other side of the runway were *Miss Doran*—the only biplane of the bunch, *Oklahoma*, and *Pabco Pacific Flier.* Livy felt a sense of reverence to be in the company of so many fine flying machines. As much as she wanted to inspect each and every one of them, she was even more excited to get up in the air.

"No siree, you my friend are staying on the ground for this one. I would never forgive myself if something went wrong up there. Test flights are dangerous," Felix informed her.

"But I'm flying to Hawai'i with you. Isn't that just a wee bit dangerous?"

"I need eyes on the ground."

Sorely disappointed, she could tell he had his mind made up, so didn't push. Felix climbed in and asked her to hand prop the plane. Livy put her whole body into it, and the engine sputtered to life. He revved it a few times and then was off down the runway, starting and stopping, testing his controls. Camera shutters snapped all around.

She felt a presence next to her, and turned to see Heath standing beside her. "It's a good-looking plane. Nice color scheme, you almost need shades to look at her."

"All those spectators at Wheeler Field will have no trouble spotting her when she makes her approach," Livy said.

"That may be true, but more likely, they'll all be too busy swarming the *Golden Plover,* who is already on the runway," he said, half dimple making an appearance.

"Not a chance, Hazeltine."

They watched as *Malolo* sped up, grew smaller and smaller, wobbled slightly, then lifted away from the earth. A few nearby folks cheered, but Livy was holding her breath. Everything was riding on this little plane, and she prayed for it all to go smoothly.

When it began to level off, Heath said, "You can breathe now."

"I swear it's worse being down here watching. Why is that?"

She kept her eyes on *Malolo*, which was climbing steadily, engine humming along.

"Probably because you feel helpless, not in control. It's much easier when you're calling the shots. In the navy, I had a stint running the flight school and I can tell you that some of my scariest moments were on the ground."

She finally looked at him. "You ran the flight school? Why am I not surprised?"

"You know me, always wanting to tell people what to do," he said with a grin. Then more seriously he said, "Sure would be nice to catch up properly with you Liv. You two staying out here now?"

"I'm sleeping in the plane. But Felix likes his bed back at the hotel."

"Let me know if you need anything. I'm camped out next to my bird. It's not the Ritz, but being out here on the island reminds me a lot of old times, when we used to camp up the coast on those flats. Remember?"

How could she forget? The first time he took her there had been a surprise. It was her birthday, and she'd thought they were just going up for a spin, maybe spot some dolphins or rays out over the water. One of the farms up the way, just inland from the water, had a runway on it for crop dusting, and he'd somehow gotten approval to land there. When they set down, he pulled a big duffel bag out of the back.

"Wait 'til you see the stars up here, far from any city lights. You're going to fall in love," he'd said.

The trouble was, she already had.

They set up camp on the edge of the beach, walked for miles

and made sandy love under the shade of an old cypress tree. He was strong and tender, every inch of his body smooth, hard and extremely well-constructed. Livy felt as though she could never get enough of him, and the feeling seemed mutual. No man had ever touched her like Heath did, and it was likely no man ever would. She shook the memory off, galled that he would bring that up now. It wasn't fair, and he knew it.

She crossed her arms. "No, I don't, actually. It doesn't ring a bell. Excuse me, I need to go check in with the race committee," she said, walking off without another word.

The next morning, after another test flight, this one with Livy in it, a gray Ford came hauling down the runway at top speed right toward all the parked airplanes. She and Felix stopped what they were doing and watched. Livy had a bad feeling.

"What's this nutcase doing? Does he think he has wings or something?" Felix said, setting down his wrench and ready to dive out of the way as the car came skidding to a stop twenty feet away.

Livy recognized Lange right away, though she couldn't think why the head of the race committee would be here now. He walked up to them and said, "Go round up the others. I have an announcement. Meet me back here by the car."

He'd already got everyone's attention, and within five minutes, everyone who was there, gathered around. Including reporters.

"I just received word that Covell and Waggoner crashed into a cliff at Point Loma this morning, on their way out of San Diego. I'm sorry to report there were no survivors," Lange said, somberly. "May they rest in peace."

Livy felt as though she'd been knocked in the solar plexus. A cloud passed over the sun, darkening the sky, or maybe it was just the shadow of death, which now loomed larger over the group.

"Well, shit," someone said.

At the airfield in San Diego, Livy had met Lieutenants George Covell and Richard Waggoner, both competent naval aviators and good men. She also knew how thick the fog could be at Point Loma. But they would have known this, too.

Art Goebel stepped forward, holding his hat over his heart. "A damn shame, sir, but what about Davis, my navigator? He was to be catching a ride with those two."

"From what I hear, Davis didn't get clearance from the brass until after they left, so he missed the flight. Lucky for him, and for you, Mr. Goebel," Lange said.

Heath was standing opposite Livy and their eyes met. His were watery. He wiped his cheek. As a navy man, she was sure he'd known them. In that moment, she wished she could wrap her arms around him.

After a few moments of hushed murmurs and expletives, Lange went on. "Now I know how disheartening this must be for you all, but these things happen in our business. Neither of those two men would want this to have any effect on the race. They'd want you to get the hell back up there, and fly a few loops for them."

Heads nodded in approval.

"You got it!" Felix said.

"And let this be a wakeup call, a reminder to dot your *i*'s and cross your *t*'s. Triple-check everything and when in doubt, don't go out," Lange said.

For the rest of the day, the mood around the field was quiet and reflective, and everyone seemed to be tweaking this and tightening that. Mechanics made their rounds. Not that anything could save you from flying straight into a cliff, but there was something to be said for making sure your bird was solid and every piece of equipment in perfect working order. Especially for those who had already made long flights just to get to Oakland.

When Livy and Felix had finished their second flight up, and were ready to call it a day, Livy walked over to the rudimentary restroom shack and washed up as best she could in the sink. She had her head down, and was splashing her face, when she heard something snorting around her feet. She jumped about a foot in the air before realizing it was a puppy.

"You must be the navigator everyone's talking about. I'm Millie," said a pretty brunette with hazel eyes as she stuck out her hand.

Livy wiped her hands, then shook. "You scared the daylights out of me. And who is this little thing?"

A gangly Great Dane had its nose wedged in a crack in the wall, tail wagging at top speed.

"This is Honolulu, Lulu for short, she's our mascot, we brought her all the way from Michigan."

"Right, I've heard."

Millie smiled. "Of course you have. I seem to be the talk of the town these days—everyone wants to write about the flying schoolmarm. Or at least I was until that dreadful crash this morning. Those poor men and their families."

She was dressed in knee-high riding boots, bloomed riding pants and an olive-colored coat covered in fraternity pins of all things. The strange mix of military uniform and horseback riding attire didn't detract from her beauty, though in fact it gave her character.

"Devastating," Livy said.

"I have to tell you what a pleasure it is to have another female in the mix. This boys' club here has been getting dull. And you're gorgeous, to boot. Takes a little of the pressure off."

Livy laughed. "However I can help."

"Say, would you like to join us for a soda pop over at our plane? Auggy makes a mean Coca Cola," Millie said, drawing out *soda pop* so there was no mistaking her meaning. "And I can show you around, introduce you to a few of the guys. Some are nice, some are pills."

"I'd like that."

"Lovely, come by at six, then."

Millie and her team were posted up in a travel trailer and had set up a long table out front. She greeted Livy like a long-lost friend. There were bunches of roses, and gift boxes all over the table, presumably from admirers across the country. Their plane, *Miss Doran*, was a pretty blue-and-white Airsedan with Lincoln Oil painted on its side.

Millie tossed a stick for the puppy, who was all ears and paws. "I'm having second thoughts about bringing this little beast on board. I love her, but she never tires."

"Whose idea was it, anyway?" Livy asked.

"I don't know who thought of it first, but we all agreed we wanted a mascot. Do you have one? It's good luck, you know."

The thought had never occurred to Livy. She'd been too busy trying to get herself in the race. And anyway, mascots added weight.

"Says who?"

"Mr. Malloska, my dear benefactor, said so, so it must be true."

"Seems like more of a distraction than anything. But since there's three of you, I guess it'll give you something to look after," Livy said.

"Oh, I'm not worried about being bored, no siree. I've been on plenty of long flights and I'm happy as a pig in clover up there just seeing the sights."

Where they were headed, there wouldn't be much to see, other than ocean, sky and clouds.

"All that time up in the air, have you ever learned to fly?" Livy asked.

"Oh, heavens no. I don't know anything about airplanes, or flying them. I just love the thrill of being up in the air—it makes me feel…intrepid. And I want to be the first woman to fly across the Pacific, no offense to you of course," she said with a sweet and honest smile.

Livy didn't point out that she wouldn't actually be flying or navigating. She didn't seem to care, and neither did anyone else.

Millie grabbed her hand and pulled her toward the table. "Come on, let's get ourselves a drink. My nerves are frayed from all the hoopla and I'm tired of answering questions. Promise me you won't ask any questions, will you?"

Livy crossed her heart. Over heavily spiked Cokes, they swapped flight stories along with Auggy—who wore a crumpled straw hat that had seen better days—and a couple of the other pilots.

"Don't let that fresh young face of his fool you," Mildred said. "I have full faith that this man could get us to Hawai'i with handcuffs on. He's the best there is."

From the way Auggy looked at Millie, it was plain he felt the same way about her. While Livy had hardly made a dent in her drink, which tasted like firewater, Millie sipped hers dry and poured another. She spoke with a bold nonchalance about the upcoming flight, yet the way her foot tapped nervously, and how her smile stopped short of reaching her eyes, Livy sensed that some of it was show. If you weren't afraid just a wee bit, you were either a liar or missing a piece of machinery.

The sun lay low in the sky, orange and fiery and beckoning. Soon, they would all be following in its path. Every so often, Livy found herself glancing down the way toward Heath's plane. He and a man in overalls had been tinkering with the engine all afternoon, and from the looks of it were still at it. From what she'd heard, most of the planes in the race were using the same engine, the J 5 Whirlwind. Dependable as they came. So, why the need to tinker?

Eventually, he came over. Millie offered him a drink, but he declined. "Thanks but no thanks. I need my wits about me these next couple days. I'll drink when I'm in Honolulu."

"What's your poison, Lieutenant? I'll make sure to have one on hand for your arrival," Millie said with a wink.

"Don't think I'll really care much at that point, but I think you have it backward, Miss Doran. I may be checked into my hotel in Waikiki already and lining up my surfboard by the time you folks land," he said.

Millie rolled her eyes.

Irving Livingston, one of the other pilots going it alone, laughed. "The minute I pass into Hawaiian waters, I'll be listening for those steel guitars. Reckon I'm going to kick up my heels on the beach and watch those hula dancers as the sun goes down. Drink in hand."

Felix had now joined them. "I'll be sitting down to a feast, gorging myself one laulau at a time with my lovely Iwa by my side. Thank goodness she gave up on the notion of getting over here in time to be my navigator."

Everyone had their own idea of paradise, and everyone said they'd be first.

"What about you, Liv? What are your plans once you've landed?" Heath asked.

Honestly, she hadn't given it much thought. "I'll figure that out once I get there. I'm more concerned about what happens between here and Honolulu than anything."

Her answer seemed to stop the conversation, then Millie poked at her. "Why so serious all the time? If you can't have a little fun along the way, what's the point in anything?"

The words chafed. "The point is to arrive in Hawai'i alive, so that you then proceed in having the time of your life. Which is what I plan on doing," she answered.

Millie clasped her hands together. "Arrive alive! I love it."

"Touché, Miss West. A couple degrees off course and we

won't be having any fun at all. No beach, no drinks, no nothing," Irving said.

They all knew what was at stake. And yet Livy found it interesting how they each handled the knowledge so differently.

"Bah humbug. Everyone around here has been treating us as though we're condemned, as though these are our last hours of life or something. I myself refuse to succumb to such dreadful thinking. Believe that you can and you will, is what I like to say," Millie said, full of fire.

You had to give the woman credit. Maybe ignorance really was bliss in this instance. Not that she was wholly ignorant, but if you didn't know the sheer number of things that could go wrong, you were sitting pretty. In Millie's case, literally.

Auggy piped up, "Anyone hear the latest scuttlebutt on postponing the race? Seems they don't trust us much. Hell, if I want to risk my life, isn't that my problem?"

"Yeah, but they don't want to look bad," Goebel said.

"Maybe there's a reason that Lloyds won't insure any of us," Heath said.

"Can't say I blame them. Some of these planes look like they were assembled as an afterthought. And not everyone is qualified," one of the guys said, looking right at Livy.

"I guess we'll find out in the morning. Good night, everyone," she said.

Back in her tent, she curled up in the blankets and drifted off. It must have been something about being at the airfield, lulled to sleep by all the familiar feels and smells.

11

DOLE FEVER

Olivia

The morning sun dazzled, burning away a low haze, as a small flock of avocets took flight. All the birds in the area seemed a bit perturbed at the larger and much noisier newcomers. Spectators began arriving early, sitting on the roofs of their cars and spilling out into the fields. It felt like half of San Francisco was eager to catch sight of the Dole Birds and watch their test flights. There must have been thousands of people, and Livy got her first real taste of the Dole fever that was going around. Bets were being made, favorites picked.

Despite all this, word was still circulating that race officials were considering postponing the start and toughening requirements, which didn't sit well with any of the entrants. The thought of staying here longer, with the possibility of not even getting a shot, made Livy uneasy. It felt like the more they hung around here, the more likely something—or someone—would prevent them from getting airborne. And yet there was a familiar ominous tickle in the back of her neck, brought about by a shift in the wind and an ache in her bones. Some kind of weather was approaching, and if there was one thing Livy feared, it was a storm over the ocean.

They were up in the air testing out their makeshift fuel system, with Livy practicing filling the tanks—a cumbersome job in the cramped cabin—when they noticed a funny-looking plane making an approach over the bay. A huge triplane, it wasn't one she'd seen yet.

"That must be Hoot Gibson's plane, *Pride of Los Angeles*," Felix said, yelling to be heard.

Hoot Gibson was a rodeo champ and Western film star who had bankrolled the plane's entry into the race. Mahoney loved his movies and had instructed Livy to get an autographed photo for the hangar wall if she met him.

Felix changed course to get a closer look, banking to the right, causing the gas tins to all sweep to one side. In rough air, the empty ones were liable to be flying all over the cabin. Livy had doused herself to the point of being a walking firebomb.

Once they were near the triplane, they could make out Hoot's face painted on the fuselage. A remarkable likeness.

"Rumor has it that plane carries more fuel than a battleship, and if they make Hawai'i, Giffen and Lundgren plan to fly on to Australia and then hopscotch over to Paris," Felix said.

Livy was dreaming of faraway lands and admiring the unique lines of the aircraft when it suddenly took a nosedive. At first she thought they were just putting on a show for the hordes of people on the ground, who now looked like ants.

Felix yelled out, "For Chrissake, pull up, you fool!"

Pride of Los Angeles continued downward at an alarming angle, and Felix followed as best he could, runway coming up fast. Livy was unable to pull her eyes away, and yet terrified of the disaster they were about to witness.

Please, God, let them live.

The plane beelined it toward the runway, but it was clear they were out of control by the way it wobbled and dipped and plunged. On the ground, people who had been standing still now scattered in all directions. For a moment, it looked like

Pride of Los Angeles might make it, but the plane skimmed the runway, barely missing cars and tents and people lying prostrate on the ground, and then splashed sideways into the water just beyond. It was shallow enough that one whole wing stuck out.

By the time Livy and Felix buzzed over, two men had clambered onto the wing, and were pulling a third out of the water. One of the men waved and yelled something, but they couldn't make out his words. The crew was wet but alive.

Felix shook his head. "Today's their lucky day, but you can bet this won't go over well with the committee."

An hour later, Livy and Felix shook hands with Lieutenant Bob Watts, the man in charge of qualifying navigators. It hadn't escaped either of them that if she failed, their flight would be over before it began unless Felix could pull another qualified navigator out of his pocket. So far, only four others had passed. Watts was standing with Lange and when they both saw Livy, Lange gave Watts a subtle nod. The hair went up on the back of her neck.

The test required them to fly a fifty-mile course out and over the water, but before that, they'd have to reset their compasses on a large compass rose painted on the airfield. Each time they'd added something metal to the plane, or even moved stuff around, they'd have to wheel on over and make sure the needles were in sync.

Lieutenant Watts was dressed in uniform, with buzzed silver hair and a clipped face. He inspected the cockpit without saying a word, eyes taking in Livy's cramped space. She had made sure that every piece of navigation equipment was in its place—bubble sextant, flashlight for reading it in the dark, smoke bombs for dead reckoning, and her nautical charts. She hadn't realized it, but her hands were shaking.

When he had apparently seen enough, he climbed back out

and said, "Miss West, how confident are you in your abilities to get yourselves to Hawai'i?"

"Extremely confident."

He handed her a paper. "Good. Now here's the course. There are plenty of people who don't think you can do this. Show me you can."

She tapped her temple in a salute. "Yes, sir."

Once in the plane, Felix said, "I think he's secretly rooting for us."

"I hope you're right, because I have the distinct feeling that if Lange had it his way, I would be grounded permanently."

After compass adjustments, they flew the course with only half their gas tins loaded onto the plane. The scary prospect for everyone was not taking off with a plane full of fuel, it was landing one on the chance that anything went wrong. Thankfully, Felix had turned out to be an excellent pilot, and maneuvered well through the sky. He had a keen eye, a sensitive touch and he took directions well. When they came back in, Watts was waiting, stone-faced, clipboard in hand.

He bypassed Felix altogether and went to shake Livy's hand. "Congratulations on navigating a tight course, Miss West."

A rush of emotion flooded in. "So this means we're in?"

"According to this sheet of mine, yours is the highest rating of anyone so far," he said, a smile cracking his face.

Felix pumped his fist in the air and let out a big *whoop* as he twirled around. "Splendid! I've known it all along. This gal has what it takes, and then some."

Watts turned his attention over to Felix. "And you, Mr. Harding, promise me something, will you?"

"You name it."

"No matter what happens out there, you listen to her. Do that and you'll get there."

"Agreed."

When Livy turned around, there was J.P. Lee, taking notes.

He walked over. "Say, could I get more background on you. Place of birth, parents' names, spouse and kids, that kinda thing."

"I'm from San Diego and my parents are Bee and Cyrus West. My father is a well-known fisherman and my mother the finest baker in town. They are both fully behind me on this race and thrilled to the bone."

Livy imagined Pa picking up his newspaper and seeing her face plastered across the front of it, along with Felix and *Malolo*. The thought made her feel happy and rather important.

Then J.P. added, "The boss wants us to get all the dirt on you folks, in case, you know, we'll be writing your obit."

With the second plane crash in the same number of days, opposition to the race going on as planned had ramped up. Race officials had sent word to Dole that running the race now would be foolhardy at best, death inducing at worst. Lange had apparently been ranting that to go now would be a suicide mission. It hadn't helped that one of the navigators had come to the qualifying test drunk, planes were woefully ill equipped and pilots overly cocky.

But Dole wouldn't be swayed. The race would go on as planned.

That afternoon, the crews all decided to meet by the *Miss Doran* again to weigh in and see where everyone stood. A handful of the teams were ready to get on with it, but most could see that a few extra days would give them needed time to be better prepared.

Auggy was downright pissed. "This is an outrage. Those of us who want to go, should be able to go."

"Weren't you off your course by a long shot?" Felix asked.

"I'm still waiting to go up again. We were only off because of a mix-up."

"What makes you think race day will be any different? The

ocean doesn't care a thing about mix-ups or reasons," Livy pointed out.

Millie yawned. "This conversation is so dull. Either we go tomorrow, or we go in a few days. What's the big deal?"

"It's not for us to decide, is it?" Jack Hunt said.

Heath showed up just then, after a late test flight with Watts. Livy had kept an eye out, noting how smoothly he brought the plane down. Everything he did, he did better than everyone else—flying, wing walking, kissing, you name it. That obviously hadn't changed. Though the kissing part she wouldn't be able to speak to.

"If we all agree to postpone it a few days, Dole won't have a leg to stand on. I say we make the call. It's our lives on the line," he said, hair windblown and cheeks flushed.

He looked over at Livy and smiled.

Damn you, Hazeltine.

Everyone started talking at once, with Irving, Auggy and Jack Hunt shaking their heads and shouting out their disagreement. *No way. Let's get this race going!* But the others agreed with Heath. For Livy, leaving tomorrow would be more desirable, if it weren't for the lowering barometric pressure.

She raised her hand. "Can I say something?"

They all quieted and turned their eyes on her.

"I understand how badly we all want to just start this race already, but there's one thing we haven't even discussed, and that's the weather. The forecast might not be too bad for San Francisco, but offshore could be a different story. The barometric pressure is dropping fast, and if we wait a few days, we won't risk flying straight into a tempest."

"You a weatherman?" someone said.

"My father was a fisherman, so I understand weather."

Mr. Hunt, who owned just about every newspaper in California, looked at her coldly and said, "My meteorologist would have said something. We send up the radiosonde every day, top-of-the-line technology, which I would place my money on."

Livy stood her ground. "Sometimes they can miss a swiftly moving storm, or one with complex features. Weather prediction is not a perfect science, Mr. Hunt."

The radiosonde was in fact a useful tool, just not always reliable.

His gaze went up to the sky, and toward the ocean. "Not a cloud in sight. I say we continue as planned. But if you're right Miss...?"

"West."

"Miss West, come see me and I'll give you a job as a weather girl."

That got a few chuckles, but there was something dark around his edges that Livy didn't like. The way his gaze hovered over her chest, his air of self-importance and how he spoke over his son and others as if owning the world meant manners did not pertain to you.

No decision was made, and people trickled away, most of them staying in hotels in the city but a few camping out, like Livy.

And Heath.

The air was cold, stars dimmed from the city lights. The moon had yet to rise, and Livy sat on the ground, wrapped in a blanket, tracing constellations with her eyes. It was strange to her, how so many people knew nothing about what was up there. That the skies had their own laws, sun and moon and planets and zodiac all traveling the same path—the ecliptic. As her father explained it to her, the ecliptic was like a giant dinner plate in the sky, and it formed one of the planes used for celestial navigation.

She heard footsteps a second before a familiar voice said, "Crazy to think that tomorrow this will all be a memory, isn't it?"

Even though she'd heard him coming, she jumped. "Don't scare me like that!"

"I tried to walk loudly. Mind if I join you?"

She stood up. "I was about to call it a night."

He reached out and touched her forearm. "Are you going to keep trying to avoid me forever, Liv? If so, it won't work."

"Not everything is about you, Heath. In case you haven't noticed, I have a lot going on."

"Oh, I'm well aware. What we're about to do is a big deal. It's life-or-death. But still, I'd like to know that you and I can at least be friends."

She could at least give him that.

"Sure, we can be friends. Just like I'm friends with Felix and Millie and Mahoney. Nothing more."

"Friends it is, then," he said, disappointment dripping from his words. "But would it be too much to sit down and talk one of these days? Just to clear the air?" he pressed.

"How about we talk when we get to Honolulu?" she said, stepping back into the darkness.

"That's just the thing. What if we don't make it to Honolulu?"

The last thing she needed was Heath to cloud up her thinking. All those long-buried emotions were swirling around, just beneath the surface. But maybe she was going about this all wrong. Maybe she just needed to acclimate to his presence, and pretty soon they'd be old chums.

"I see. If you die, you'd like to do it with a clear conscience—is that it?"

He moved closer and she could hear his breath. "I don't plan on dying, but you know how real the risks are. What I really came here to say was I'm sorry."

Those last two words hung in the air between them, full and ripe and honest. They were the two words she'd wanted to hear for as long as she could remember, and yet now, she wasn't sure what to do with them.

He went on, "There are a million other things I want to say, but I couldn't take off tomorrow without you knowing that."

She could feel him, shifting around uncomfortably in the dark.

"I made a big mistake."

She still wasn't sure what this meant. Her whole life since Heath had been spent guarding her heart like a medieval fortress, and now this. All her bottled-up feelings threatened to spill out, and she resented his intrusion.

"Say something?" he said.

"There's really nothing to say. What happened between us was a long time ago, I hardly even remember," she said in almost a whisper. It was a screaming lie, but she wanted to give him a taste of his own medicine. Let him know he couldn't just show up and everything would be peachy again.

"Read you loud and clear, Slim. Now, get some rest and I'll see you in the morning," he said, turning and loping off into the night.

Later, she dreamed of a day with no sun and a night with no stars. Of lightning and blinding rain. And then darkness, all-encompassing.

12

FINDING GHOSTS

Wren

The road out was filled with puddles the size of bathtubs. Wren had no choice but to tiptoe around them or jump across as she made her way to the main road. She'd been walking for a half hour now and her legs were splattered with mud, boots soaked through. There was not a patch of dry ground to be found. At the fork, she opted to head to the main road, lest she wander deeper into the woods and find nothing there.

Every now and then she heard a commotion in the bushes and belted out Cat Stevens's "Morning Has Broken" to ward off any wild pigs. She knew they were more scared of her than she was of them, but she'd seen enough boar tusks to be nervous. The skies were by no means clear this morning, and the wind had kicked up a notch, but at least the rain had stopped.

Along the way, her mind had begun to fixate on a hot cup of coffee, scrambled eggs and buttery blueberry scones. Scones weren't part of her usual repertoire, so it was a bizarre craving, but her dinner had been meager and she'd woken up hungry. There'd better be some place to eat in Hāwī.

At the second stream crossing, the water ran clear and she

decided to risk a drink. You could only survive on Coke for so long. Since yesterday, the level had risen at least a foot, and the sound of swift-running water filled the ravine. Wren was sitting on a rock wiping the mud off her legs when she heard a rumble. It sounded like a car engine. Sure enough, a minute later a truck came barreling around the corner and into the ravine.

She rock-hopped back to the road and waited for the truck to approach, waving like a dork. Big and black and beefy, the truck pulled to a stop right next to her. Dark tint and tree shadows made it impossible to see the driver until the window rolled down.

A man in a cowboy hat and aviators said, "You lost?"

Wren was thrilled to see him. "My truck broke down a couple miles back, at Ho'omalumalu," she said, then threw in, "Do you know of it?"

"Yeah, Bob Simms sent me to find you. Get in."

Relief swept through her. "Oh, thank God for Bob! I'm a little wet and muddy, do you mind?"

He pointed with his thumb behind him. "Ride in the back with Scout, then, and hold tight to the rack. We'll go check your truck."

He didn't smile and his tone was flat, but she was grateful nonetheless. Scout, a gray pit mix, turned out to be much more enthusiastic about Wren's presence and kept licking her face as she tried to climb in.

"Back off, Scout," the man said.

Scout didn't back off, but Wren managed to swing herself up on one of the pipe racks to standing.

"All good, I'm in," she called.

The ride back went much faster than the way in because the man in question—she realized he never offered his name—had a heavy foot. Being high up in the bed of an F-350 with the fresh air blowing through her hair gave her a different perspective. She caught more ocean views, noticed groves of koa and 'ōhi'a, saw flashes of red birds flitting through the forest. She also swallowed a swarm of gnats.

When they reached the barn, the man opened the tailgate and let Scout out, but didn't hold a hand for Wren. Not that she needed it, but it seemed a little rude. Scout went straight to where she had left the musubi and Fritos and began snorting around like a feral pig. The man stood in place and did a slow three-sixty, as though taking it all in. He was a good four or five inches taller than her, with wavy brown hair and a '70s mustache. It was hard to tell how old he was, but she had to admit he had a nice profile.

"Do you have a name?" Wren asked.

He looked up at her and the sunlight caught his moss-colored eyes, causing a slight disturbance in her field. "Pono Willard."

He didn't look Hawaiian, but his name loosely translated to *upright* or *in harmony with all things*. In her Hawaiian language class in high school, her teacher, Mr. Spencer, used to drill into them to "live *pono*."

Wren hopped out and walked over by the yellow truck to put a little distance between them. "How do you know Bob, Pono Willard?"

"He and my old man go way back, and I fix his truck every now and again, keep it serviced."

"You're a mechanic?" she asked.

"Among other things. My family owns a ranch off Kohala Mountain Road, and I keep everything running smoothly."

"Well, thank you for coming all the way out here. If it helps, I already checked the battery and surrounding wires, and I don't think it's the starter or the fuel pump. But I'm sure you'll be able to figure it out," she said.

He raised an eyebrow but didn't say anything as he came over with a toolbox, took off his jean jacket and hung it on the rearview mirror, popped the hood and started poking around. Wren went to the opposite side and peered in, curious to see what he'd find. His hands moved fluidly, clearly comfortable in the confined space of a front end. He started pulling out the spark plugs and inspected them. Joe didn't even know what a spark plug was, and this somehow pleased her immensely.

"I replaced these not too long ago, but figured I'd check anyway," he said, holding one up for her to see.

It looked shiny and new.

"What else could it be?" she asked.

"Did you check the gas?"

She rolled her eyes. "Please."

"It's got to be the alternator, then, in which case we're screwed."

"Why is that?"

"Because I don't carry an extra alternator around with me."

Wren watched him work a socket wrench as though it were an extension of his hands. His forearms were smooth and wiry, with a long scar running up one. It made her curious. She also noticed no wedding ring. Which was a dumb thing to notice, but nowadays, ever since being dumped, it seemed like that was the first thing her eyes went to, automatically categorizing people into the married club or the single club, like she was.

A moment later, Scout, who had been obediently lying in a patch of sun, tore off down the side of the barn, barking furiously.

"Oh, shit," Wren said.

"What is it?"

She nodded at the barn. "A wild dog lives here."

Pono sauntered over to the side where Scout disappeared and let out a whistle you could have heard in Waimea. He waited a minute and then whistled again.

"Dammit, Scout never does this," he said, as though it were somehow her fault his dog had run off.

"The dog didn't seem aggressive. It was more scared than anything. Super skinny, too," Wren volunteered.

He called Scout again to no avail, then went down the path

after him. Wren followed. There was no sign of either dog, but you could hear a whining sound nearby. Around the other side, Pono stopped abruptly. Both dogs were there, the wild one on her back with Scout standing over her sniffing and wagging his tail. The moment felt very intimate, and Wren had the urge to turn around and leave them alone. Pono didn't make any sounds and they watched for a few moments, before the wild one caught their scent. The second she saw them, she split into the trees. Scout followed.

"Disobedient mutt," Pono mumbled.

"Boys will be boys," Wren said.

He frowned. "What is that supposed to mean?"

Such a sourpuss this guy was.

"It means that your dog appears to be smitten, and he's chasing his gal friend even if he knows he's not supposed to."

That elicited a shake of the head. They were facing the back of the barn, and Pono looked up, taking in the high green glass windows.

"What's inside there?"

"Not much. Just an old truck and two big tractors or something under tarps. There's a mezzanine in the back but I didn't go up because the dog was there."

"What are you going to do with it?"

"Sell it."

"What kind of truck did you say?"

"Ford."

"How old are we talking?"

"Why don't you take a look yourself? Maybe you can tell me what to do with it."

There was no sign of Scout, but he didn't seem too worried. She led him around and opened the door again. When it stuck, Pono slipped inside, examined the rail and said, "Grab the far corner and when I say lift, lift straight up."

Ten seconds later, he slid the door all the way open, allowing light to flood in. Right away, the barn felt warmer and more inviting.

"Whoa. Someone went through a lot of trouble to build this," he said.

"A long time ago, yes."

It was easier now to see the massive trusses that crisscrossed the ceiling, holding up the roof, and the two-foot-wide posts that they rested on.

"What do you think they did in here?" she asked, noticing for the first time faded lines painted on the concrete floor, in giant circles.

"You don't know?"

"I figured it was a mac nut factory because Bob said there was once a small farm here, but where's all the equipment?"

"Good question."

He shivered as if cold and made his way to the Ford, eyeing the two tractors as he passed. When he saw the truck up close, he whistled.

"Damn, you weren't kidding."

"What?"

"She's old, maybe even '40s," he said, walking around the truck and sizing it up.

"Is that good or bad?" she asked.

"Depends. It's not a daily driver, that's for sure. But fixed up, it could be worth something."

She liked the sound of that.

"Like how much?"

"No idea."

"I thought you were a mechanic."

"Everything I fix, we use. My old man hates to sell anything, so I just make sure things are running so we never have to. I'm not in the business of selling things."

He ran his hand along the back rail, kicked the tire, which looked low, and opened the door. It smelled like old leather and cigarettes. The dashboard and upholstery were in good shape. Pono climbed in and sat at the wheel. Suddenly he transformed from the thirty-something she'd just met, to a fifteen-year-old boy about to drive his first car. He was no longer grumpy, he was wide-eyed and enamored.

Wren watched, amused. "You're in love, aren't you?" she said.

One side of his mouth lifted up in a smile. "Maybe just a little."

"Well, I know the owner, and she'd probably cut you a deal."

That brought on an actual laugh, and in that moment Wren felt a shift, something lightening between them.

He climbed out. "Now I'm curious about what's under those tarps. They don't look like tractors."

"What do they look like?"

He shrugged. "Only one way to find out."

Scout showed up then, trotting in with his tail in the air as though he were the big man on campus. He went right to Pono and sat by his side, panting.

Pono rubbed behind his dogs ears. "Good boy. You stay put now, okay?"

Scout glanced behind him toward the barn opening and Wren followed his gaze. A narrow face was peering in at them, nose twitching.

"You can come in, we don't bite," Wren said.

The dog sized them up for a moment, then took a couple steps inside and lay down against the wall. You could see each rib outlined beneath her skin.

"Do you have any food?" Wren asked Pono.

"Two tuna sandwiches and two bananas."

"Can we give her the sandwiches?"

"What about you?"

"I'll take the bananas."

"I'll give her one now and see how it goes. We don't want to make her sick."

Pono walked out to get the sandwich, and Wren watched as he slowly approached the dog, speaking softly and holding out the sandwich. Wren held Scout, who started whining. Surprisingly, Pono managed to get within a couple feet of the dog, when her tail began to wag weakly. It warmed Wren's heart to see. He left the sandwich and walked back to the truck.

"Thank you for doing that," Wren said.

He shrugged. "Looks like a cattle dog, maybe came over the mountains. I don't think she's completely wild."

"Can you take her back with you?"

"Last thing I need is another animal to deal with."

"You have a lot already?"

"I live on a ranch."

"Right."

Wren wanted to push it, since it seemed like Scout really liked the dog, and she couldn't imagine just leaving her here. But Pono went to one of the tractors and started tugging at the canvas, then trying to lift it up from the floor. She stepped in to try to help, in turn getting smeared in cobwebs.

"We need to get higher up. You have any ladders here?" Pono asked.

There was nothing against the walls, but she took the opportunity to dash up the steps to the mezzanine and see if there was anything up there. When she reached the top, she stopped in her tracks. The area had been set up as a living space, with a four poster bed—all messed up and covered in dog fur, a leather couch and a rocker. Along the whole back wall ran a stainless steel counter. There was even an old fridge and sink, same era as the truck, if she had to guess.

"Everything okay up there?" Pono called.

"Someone lived here, or at least stayed here."

"Recently?"

"I don't think so."

"Any ladders?"

"No."

A moment later, she heard his truck start up, and watched him drive it through the massive doors. The upstairs could wait, though she wanted a closer look at everything, especially since the furniture appeared to be made from koa wood. She went back down and circled the canvas, searching for some kind of opening. With the light on it, she located two seams where the canvas had been snapped together.

"Beats me how they got this on here," Pono said, standing in the back of the truck and unsnapping.

Wren worked on the unsnapping the lower portion down to the floor, then peeled the flap back. It was impossible to see anything.

"Do you have a flashlight?" she asked.

"Under the driver's seat."

She fumbled around, pulled out a Maglite and climbed down onto her knees, shining first on the lower section. Two small-ish wheels. She was confused. Then she shone the light up and found herself staring at the underside of a wing held up by old wooden struts. It took a moment to register what she was looking at.

"Oh, my gosh!" she said.

"What?"

"This isn't a tractor."

13

RACE DAY

Olivia

When morning finally came, Livy felt like she'd been on a boat on rough seas all night, flopping around and tangling in her scratchy wool blanket. She felt out of sorts, remembering bits of the nightmare about Heath. Not only that, but she'd sworn she'd heard voices outside and the crunch of boots on dirt, but had been too tired to get up and see who might be out there.

The sun was still below the horizon, but the sky above lit up red. *Red skies at night, sailor's delight. Red sky at morning, sailor take warning.* This little rhyme had been hammered into Livy's head since she could walk. Now, the skies weren't bloodred and ominous, as she'd seen in the past, but they were red enough to make her uneasy.

She had just cleaned up and was setting out her flying outfit when Millie came over with a newspaper and a sour look on her face. She laid it down on the card table that had become Livy's central piece of furniture.

"That man is insufferable. I don't know if you *should* read this, but I think you're going to want to," she said, lips painted a bright coral, eyes lined in smoky gray.

The paper was the *San Francisco Echo*, owned by none other than Mr. William Hunt.

THE DOLE MISFITS
By J.P. Lee

The Dole Derby has been hailed as the greatest sky race the world has known. It is undoubtedly a daring, death-defying feat that few can fathom. With the healthy cash purse of $35,000 and the backing of airplane factories and business magnates, it has attracted a slew of top-notch pilots and navigators, many who are decorated military veterans. On the other hand, it's also drawn in enough incompetents and charlatans to give race officials cause to postpone the race to prevent unnecessary loss of life.

Topping this list of questionable entrants is Miss Olivia West, daughter of a San Diego tuna fisherman. Miss West was chosen by Felix Harding to navigate the monoplane Malolo, and purports to be well trained by her father. Yet this same father ran his fishing boat aground earlier this year and declared it a complete loss. Miss West is the only woman in the race with any responsibility, and the consensus among other entrants is that she should have stuck to wing walking or making sandwiches. Her counterpart, Millie Doran, seems to know her place and is content to be a dish and inspire the others in that feminine way. For she is an inspiration—

Livy stopped reading and threw down the paper as a feeling of rage came over her. "The bastard! What's it to him, anyway?"

Millie chimed in. "And I know my place? Someone needs to send Mr. Lee and Mr. Hunt off in their own airplane to Hawai'i, and see how far they get."

"They wouldn't even get off the ground."

Livy had the sudden urge to march down the airfield and

throw her sextant and maps and compass at the whole sorry lot of men. To walk away without looking back. Screw them all, chauvinistic bastards that they were. But that would mean they'd won, and Livy was never one to back down from a challenge. And then she thought of Felix and Heath and her father, even Watts, who all believed in her. That meant more than a bunch of shit-talking scoundrels.

"Let them talk all they want. We'll be busy making history," Livy said.

A slow smile spread over Millie's face. "I like your style, Miss Olivia West."

"Right back at you, Miss Doran."

Millie was not the doe-eyed, helpless female that the press had made her out to be. Not many other women would do what she was about to do, while maintaining a sense of humor and cheerful attitude. There would always be the mudslingers in the world, the ones who watched from the sidelines and tore apart those who were living to the fullest.

"Come on, we best be getting to the official stand," Millie said, holding her arm up.

Livy wrapped her elbow and together they went. The runway was lined with cars, more arriving by the minute. Felix and all the other pilots were there listening to Lange and another man ranting about how ill prepared everyone was.

Lange stood gravely in front of the group. "And it's not just me that thinks so. I got a late-night call from Jim O'Neil over at the Aeronautics Branch, who told me in no uncertain terms that we better call this thing off, give everyone more time."

Yet Dole had given the final word. The race would go on as planned.

Heath stepped forward. "If you don't mind my saying, most of us pilots and crew met last night, and agree with you. What if we say we'll fly on the sixteenth. That gives us four more days. More than that, and people are going to get restless."

"Call it a gentlemen's agreement," Goebel said.

Hunt and a few others voiced their opposition, "You think all these people came to see us back down? This is sending the wrong message to the world." He then looked over at Livy. "Not to mention we have as fair a weather as she comes."

Livy just shrugged. "Silly me, I guess I was wrong."

The day isn't over yet.

In the end, the majority ruled and everyone shook on four more days. Livy had been ready, and had spent a wasted restless night, but she was glad.

Later that afternoon, gunmetal clouds blew in from the ocean, dousing the airfield in rain and violent bursts of wind. A fast-moving storm, it caught everyone by surprise. Visibility was reduced to mere feet and everyone ran to their cars for shelter or huddled in one of the make shift lean-tos or tents. Felix had gone to pick up some parts and Livy huddled inside the small cabin. With a huge measure of satisfaction, she imagined the look on Mr. Hunt's face, and her telling him, *I have no interest in working for you.*

The next three days passed swiftly, as Felix and one of Breese's mechanics attached a new gas tank to *Malolo*. It was a great improvement, especially with Felix's propensity for cigarettes. He had promised he wouldn't smoke along the way, but one never knew. Livy sent another telegram to her folks, letting them know of the new start date. Her mom would not be happy with the extra waiting. They had sent word two days ago and it was easy to read between the lines and sense the concern beneath their excitement.

```
DEAR LIVY
OUR HEARTS WILL BE IN THAT PLANE WITH YOU
STOP WE KNOW YOU WILL FIND THOSE ISLANDS AND
CAN WEATHER ANY STORM STOP TRUST YOUR COM-
PASS AND RESPECT THE CLOUDS STOP
ALL OUR LOVE M AND P
```

Restless, Livy used the time to talk to the other navigators and learn their plans. Davis planned on following radio beacons the whole way, Irving was going to dead reckon and trust his gut and Jack Hunt refused to say anything on the matter.

The press continued to hover around, honing in on Millie, who drew them in with her bold statements, and then waved them away when she'd had enough. "Oh, whether we start today or next Tuesday doesn't matter, because we'll make it one way or another." Or, "I don't know about anyone else, but I'm only taking coffee and raspberries. I've never been much of an eater." When asked where the puppy would use the bathroom on the journey, she replied with a sly grin, "I'm not worried about that at all. I'm more worried about where I'll be going."

It was easier for men to use a funnel while sitting, and Felix had left it up to Livy to devise her own latrine. A simple bucket with a lid would have to do, and limiting liquids was key. It wasn't glamorous, but there was no way around it. She often daydreamed of airplanes with their own toilets. That would be something.

On the day before race day, Heath showed up early in the morning with two steaming mugs of coffee. His hair was plastered to one side of his head, and shot straight out on the other. Still in his pajamas, he looked boyish and disheveled.

"Come, I want to show you something," he said.

She had slept in pants and a sweater, but was still swaddled in a blanket.

"It's freezing."

"Trust me, you won't want to miss this."

He seemed so excited about whatever it was that she threw on her jacket and boots and walked with him through the cold and dewy salt grass, following a narrow path to the shoreline. The water was calm as polished glass, the storm having passed as fast as it blew in.

"Did you know the Indians used to call this Wind Whistle Island?" he said.

A high, eerie sound, she'd heard it during the storm.

"No, but it makes sense. I woke up in the middle of the night thinking someone—or something—was in trouble. It almost sounded human or animal."

He nodded. "I thought the same thing."

When they made it to the water, he veered along a coastal trail to a small sandy bay. The sky had turned a light violet, swallowing the last of the stars.

Heath stopped abruptly and held his arm out. "Shh." He pointed.

There on the beach was a big fat spotted seal, and next to it, a tiny replica. The mother's coat was a silver gray, the pup's almost white. In her eyes, there was nothing more adorable than a seal pup, and Livy's heart swelled at the sight.

"I found them yesterday evening and I was hoping they'd still be here. They reminded me of you," he said.

A memory of the beach north of La Jolla arose in her mind. Early on, while they were getting to know each other away from the airfield, Livy packed a picnic and brought Heath to a secluded cove that she knew about through patrolling the coastline on her father's fishing boat. It was a trek to get in by foot, and Heath had almost stepped on a rattlesnake, but once they made it, it was well worth the journey. She hadn't planned it, but the beach had become a seal nursery, with plump pups and their mamas everywhere. They didn't dare disturb the animals, even though they were dying to get in the water. Instead they found a spot under a grove of Torrey pines on a ledge above and watched the show.

"Makes me want to build a house on these cliffs so we can watch these little creatures grow up and then come back every year to start their own families," he said, wistfully. "Would you like that?"

We.

"They'd never let you build a house here, but we can dream, can't we?" she'd said, feeling a little light-headed at the implication.

"If not here, then somewhere overlooking the ocean, somewhere with a clear view of the horizon."

Livy still remembered those words. Now, on this beach on Bay Farm Island, there was only one mama and one pup, but their sweetness brought her feet right back to earth. Over the past months, she'd been so intent on getting in this race, and making the impossible happen, that she'd neglected the small and beautiful things that strung together a life. Or had the neglect actually gone on longer, to a time before, to when Heath left...?

Livy kept her distance as they watched the mother seal nudge the pup as it nestled into her side. It was lovely and heartwarming and just what she needed.

"Thank you for bringing me here," she said on the way back.

"I figured you could use a change of scenery. I think we all could at this stage in the game."

He sure was right about that. The uncertainty was beginning to wear on her.

That afternoon, Felix showed up with another surprise: a small troupe of hula dancers and an orchestra playing Hawaiian songs. He made a big fuss of getting the press over to *Malolo*, where he ceremoniously doused the plane with so-called seawater from Hawai'i and then sprinkled a little on himself and Livy, too. Livy kept quiet on the fact that she'd seen him go off down the trail to the water's edge earlier that day, holding the empty bottle. Standing below the wing, he read out messages of encouragement from the people of Hawai'i, and promised to be the first to cross the finish line—for them.

An informal gathering had been called at the Colonial Cafeteria to celebrate, though Livy would have preferred to stay at the airfield. She and Felix were the first to arrive, and as she sat at a long wooden table, she observed the colorful characters as they all strolled in. Other patrons in the place were all gawking, too.

At the table Livy ended up between and Millie and Juanita, the fiancée of Bennett Griffin, *Oklahoma* pilot. Juanita kept one hand on Bennett at all times, but she was friendly and chatty.

"How do you feel about this whole affair?" Millie asked her, once Bennett turned his focus on Art Goebel, sitting next to him.

"Oh, I vacillate between excitement and mild panic. We would have made things official this morning, but wouldn't you know it, California says you have to wait three days for a marriage license. As if we might wake up in three days from now and somehow discover that we aren't mad for each other," Juanita said, flicking her long ash into the tray and blowing smoke out her nostrils.

"Bastards! Since when is love anyone else's business than the couple at hand and the Lord above," Millie said.

"I was dashed at first, but Bennett went and booked me a cabin on the steam liner and now we'll be having a Hawaiian wedding. So now he has no choice but to arrive in one piece," she said.

Livy half listened as she ate a last supper—as some people were referring to the meal—of rich seafood stew with crunchy sourdough. She just couldn't bring herself to engage in small talk, so as soon as she finished, she went outside into the cool night and found a bench across the road. Out of the light, with her wool cap pulled down and her warm jacket wrapped close, she sat and counted stars.

Star counting had been her and Pa's thing. They would lie on the beach, on the boat or in the back yard, Livy nestled in the crook of his arm, and start with the brightest and work their way through the constellations. Before you knew it, Livy had fallen asleep and in the morning, she'd wake in her bed, sunlight in her eyes and her father's ocean scent still on her skin. Funny to think that she actually believed you could count all the stars in the sky. She believed anything her father told her.

Men's voices outside the restaurant brought her back to Franklin Street. They were standing off to the side, beneath the sign and away from the light. Livy strained to hear, though she wasn't sure why she bothered.

"This better not backfire."

"I don't give a fuck."

"Compasses."

"Keep your mouth shut."

One voice was familiar but she couldn't place it. There was something ominous in the way the men were huddled, and when the restaurant door opened, they scurried off into the alley. Probably just a moonshine deal gone bad. But, *compasses*?

Felix had offered to put Livy up for the night in her own hotel room, but she'd become accustomed to the tent and the familiar wind whistles and crickets. It reminded her of sleeping on the deck of her father's boat. The main difference was, tonight there were policemen set up around the airfield. He drove her back, window down, cigarette in hand.

"For such a ragtag bunch of misfits, we sure garner attention. It feels a little dishonest. Like I'm no different than I was a month ago when I was a true nobody," he said.

The press had been hovering at the Colonial, as usual.

"I know what you mean. Do you think when the race is over, we'll fade back into oblivion?"

"Everyone fades into oblivion someday, unless you're a king or a queen or a bandit. But I suppose if we win, this'll give us some measure of immortality. The firsts are always like that, you know? Like good old Charlie."

Livy thought about Lindbergh and how, overnight, he'd become the most famous man in the world. How people were saying it seemed like he'd walked on water, not flown over it.

"Everyone needs a hero, and Lindbergh sure fit the bill," she said.

"Tell you what, I know it seems like everyone is all about Millie right now, but you are quietly inspiring girls around the globe. Win or lose. They see you up there, doing your magic." He flipped a hand. "Voilà, they see themselves doing it someday. That's how progress works, and how heroes are born."

The words gave her a warm flush. She hadn't quite thought of it like that.

"It's not quite magic, Felix."

"Oh, but it is to some little girl in Dodge City, Kansas. They don't know that you've read the entire *American Practical Navigator* cover to cover. I consider myself a pretty sharp bloke, but that book terrifies the wind out of me."

She had to laugh. "It's not so bad."

"I beg to differ."

Somewhere around 10:00 p.m., Livy was in between wake and sleep, imagining in vivid color lying on a beach under the warm sun, coconut fronds rustling overhead. She'd nodded off and now there were people around her talking, but she couldn't open her eyes. Then she bolted upright, back in her cold tent next to *Malolo*. Someone was standing outside.

"Hello?" she said.

The voices quieted.

Livy stood up and looked out. "What are you doing here?"

There were three of them, one holding a small lantern, all dressed in black.

"We're with Ace Instrument Company, just doing some last-minute checks," the other said.

No one had mentioned anything about a last-minute check.

"Last I heard, everything was all set to go. What exactly do you need to do?"

The Ace Instrument Company had had representatives there all week, but Livy didn't know any of them because Felix only worked with Breese.

"There've been some issues with altimeters, and Lange wanted us to make the rounds."

"In the middle of the night? Sorry, fellas, but you'll have to come back in the morning when Felix is here."

They didn't put up a fuss, and slinked off into the darkness. Livy was left with a funny feeling. Something about the visit felt off. Yes, time was running out, but surely Felix or someone else would have mentioned to expect mechanics that night. She had trouble falling back asleep, a niggling worry that something was gravely wrong.

14

RACE DAY, TAKE TWO

Olivia

In the morning, when Livy climbed out of the tent, the first thing she noticed was something lying on the ground where her feet would land. She hopped to just to the side of it, bent down and picked it up. A white feather. *Snowy egret*. She looked around, wondering where it had come from, surely it had not just landed here on its own, had it? Only during mating season did the birds produce the white lacy plumes, and this was a perfect specimen. A good omen.

While the first race day had drawn masses of people, these four extra days had drummed up even more business. Throngs of spectators, thick as a river, lined the airfield. The other race entrants, even Heath, had all slept in hotel rooms, and arrived by police escort soon after breakfast. Horns blared as they came roaring in. While the runway was being watered and flattened, Felix and Livy loaded their fourteen sandwiches, water canteens and coffee into the plane. Excitement buzzed through her like a thousand airplane engines.

Then Vilas Knope, navigator of Millie's plane, showed up, tapping on the wing. "Knock, knock."

Livy poked her head out, surprised to see him so early. "Oh, good morning."

He came in close, and by the look on his face, someone may as well have died. "I don't want to alarm you, but you should know that two magnets were missing from one of my compasses this morning. They were there yesterday, without question."

Livy immediately thought of the men.

"Did you report it to Lange?"

"We decided to keep it among ourselves, lest they decide to postpone again. I've told all the crews. Just make sure to triple check your nav gear, and everything else."

Felix nodded at Livy. "I had my watchdog here last night."

Livy told Vilas about the guys in the night.

"Sounds like trouble," he said.

"Good thing you caught this now, or you'd be off to the North Pole. I don't like this one bit," Felix said.

The idea that someone among them was willing to kill off the competition in order to win did not sit well with Livy, and she was thankful she'd held her ground last night. But what about the others?

Winds were light, though picking up, and the fog had lifted. Test flights with near full fuel tanks had been done, and the noon starting time quickly approached. All the planes were now parked at the starting line, ready to go. Ernie Smith—the pilot who had landed his plane in a tree on Moloka'i a few weeks back—stood tall like a gunslinger, starting pistol at his side. His navigator, Emory Bronte, had been chosen as time-keeper. Seeing both men there in the flesh, gave Livy a boost of confidence.

The fliers all milled around under a large tent, dressed for the occasion in carefully chosen attire—suits, knickers, bow ties. Everyone wanted to look tip-top when they arrived in the islands. The whole lot of them also wore a flower lei around their necks, sweetening up the air, which was thick with airplane fuel and mud-packed marsh.

When Livy caught sight of Heath, who was late to the party, she smiled and shook her head. He'd somehow gotten hold of an aloha shirt with bold blue and green flowers, worn with white slacks and loafers. With his sun-tipped hair, he looked every bit a beach boy. Hawai'i would welcome him with open arms.

Felix took one look at him and said, "I hope you have a jacket in that plane of yours, my friend, or you're bound to freeze your nuts off," Felix told him.

"Sure do, Slim," he answered, but he wasn't looking at Felix, he was looking at Livy.

He walked straight over, never once breaking eye contact. "I guess this is it."

"I guess it is," she said.

"All the luck in the world, Liv."

At that moment, the magnitude of what they were about to do hit her hard, and there was a real possibility that they might not ever see each other again.

"Same to you," she said, almost choking on her words. Then more quietly, she asked, "Have you double-checked your compass?"

He brought her in for a hug and whispered, "Yes, I heard what happened."

His warmth flowed into her along with a sense of relief, and Livy suddenly wanted to hang on, but they were minutes away from the first takeoff, the whole world watching.

Before he pulled away, he slipped something into her hand. "Save this for when you're up in the air," he whispered in her ear.

A small envelope with *"Miss Olivia West"* written in his familiar scratch on the front. She stuck it in her pocket and watched him slip back in among the crowd. A small crack appeared in her armor.

When the clock struck twelve, a hush fell among the fliers as they watched Bennett Griffin and Al Henley of *Oklahoma* saunter out to their plane, waving and smiling. The crowd, however, had no use for silence, as whistles and hoots and hollers thundered down the airfield. The press boys were in a near frenzy trying to get the best shot. Then Henley hand tugged the propeller, hopped in, and a minute later they were on the line. The flag dropped. Ernie Smith fired his gun.

With almost twenty-five hundred pounds of fuel on board, they had enlisted a crew of mechanics to help push the plane forward. It took a while, but eventually, they accelerated down the runway in a cloud of dust. And just when it looked like they were going to outrun the runway, they lifted off and slowly headed out over the bay. Livy watched until the plane looked like a tiny bird in the sky, and then was gone—en route to Hawai'i.

It didn't matter in which order they took off, the first plane to Honolulu would be declared the winner, so they wasted no time. Next up was *El Encanto*, which was off to a faster start, but just as their wheels left the ground, a gust of wind knocked the plane sideways and it touched back down, looking a bit out of control.

"Oh, shit, this isn't going to be good," Felix said.

The plane bumped a few times, then careened off the runway and toward a clump of reporters and cameramen. The men all shot out in different directions, some diving to get out of its way. A second later, the plane spun around, tipping over onto one wing, which promptly crumpled, then took a nosedive, spewing dirt everywhere.

"Get 'em out of there!"

"All that fuel! She's going to blow!"

"Clear the area!"

Some people were running toward the plane to help, while others were running away, worried about an explosion. Livy herself was about to run their way, when Goddard and Hawkins emerged and scrambled toward safety.

"Poor blokes are out, I feel for them," Felix said.

Seeing such a close call made Livy's stomach curl into a twisted ball of seaweed. At least they were unhurt, but to not even get off the ground—that had to sting.

After a short delay, *Pabco Pacific Flier* faced a similar yet not so terrible fate, as Irving's overloaded plane ran out of runway and came to a stop, inches from the end of the strip. Another foot and he would have been mired in marsh. It was not the start to the race she had hoped for. Far from it, and the two mishaps cast a dark shadow on Livy's mood. But after that, *Miss Doran, Dallas Spirit* and *Woolaroc* roared off without a hitch. A layer of haze had thickened, blotting them out from sight long before the drone of their engines eventually faded.

While Livy was watching, a teenage girl rushed out from the sidelines and waved a newspaper photo her way. Livy glanced around behind her, thinking the girl was waving at someone else.

"Miss West, would you sign this for me? You're by far my favorite bird here," she said.

The photo was of Livy climbing out of the airplane a few days ago after a test flight, looking skyward at an incoming plane. Livy had seen the photo. It was taken at a pleasing angle, and the photographer had captured a dreamy expression on her face.

"I would be happy to! What's your name?"

"Annie, ma'am."

The girl beamed up at her, and Livy could see the adoration in her round blue eyes. Livy thought for a moment, then wrote a quick note. *"To Annie, the sky is no longer the limit. O.M. West."*

When Livy handed back the picture, Annie clutched it to her chest and ran off as though she was holding the rarest of treasure. Knowing that there were girls like Annie out there rooting for her more than made up for all the males who doubted her along the way. It was hard to imagine herself a hero, but maybe Felix had been right. Suddenly she wasn't just doing this for her father and herself, but for a whole ocean of young girls with big dreams.

No sooner had Livy set the pen down, when someone yelled. "Isn't that the *Miss Doran*? She's coming back!"

The plane didn't appear to be in any trouble, and landed smoothly. But when Auggy, Vilas, Millie and little Honolulu poured out, none looked pleased. Ernie Smith ran over and ushered Millie back to the roped-off area where fliers and mechanics and officials stood. She looked ready to collapse. Livy couldn't help but think of those men last night. Had someone been tampering with more than just Vilas's compass?

A dejected Auggy shook his head. "Damn engine backfired a few times and then nearly went out on us. The bugger was sputtering like a drunken sailor."

Millie sobbed as she set a wiggling Lulu down on the ground. She tried to speak but couldn't get a word out between her sobs. Livy went over put her arm around her, knowing how hard this must be for them. She rubbed her back gently, letting Millie cry on her shoulder.

Once Millie recovered some, she wailed, "We were off to such a fab start, that easy breezy takeoff and all those people waving madly at us. Oh, why did we have to turn back?"

"I'm so sorry," Livy said.

Ernie Smith jumped in. "Take it easy, Miss Doran. The day's not over yet. Once those mechanics have a look at the engine, you could be right back up there again."

She hardly seemed to hear. "What if they don't take me this time?" she cried, snot running down her chin.

"Why wouldn't they take you?" Livy asked.

"Oh, I don't know. You know men, they can't make up their minds, and they think it's dangerous, and I'm temperamental. You just can't believe anything they say."

She broke into tears again. Livy tried unsuccessfully to console her, until Felix pointed at his watch. Several of the planes who'd drawn numbers had failed to qualify, so their number eight takeoff was now number seven in a lineup of nine. They were next up. These mishaps were beginning to take a toll on her nerves, and she was ready to get on with it. When they were just about to climb into *Malolo*, more yelling erupted around them.

"It's *Oklahoma!*"

"She's on fire!"

A hush came over the crowd, as *Oklahoma*, trailing a big plume of black smoke, approached the airfield. You could have cut the tension in the air with a knife, but a few minutes later, the boys in *Oklahoma* landed safely and walked out of the plane with fire extinguishers in hand. Henley, the navigator, was in tears, while Juanita, who had been near hysterical, ran up and threw herself into a stoic Griffin's arms.

"That's it for us, I'm afraid. Melted cylinders will not get us across the ocean. But now we don't have to wait to get married. Hell, we can do it this afternoon if you want," he said, once they'd come back to the tent.

That got a cheer from those standing around, but the cheer soon turned to more yelling as all the heads turned back over the bay.

"Here comes *Dallas Spirit!*"

People standing on nearby cars were all pointing. Livy could just make out the green and silver, glinting in the early-afternoon sun. It was easy to see the problem, though—a large section of the canvas that covered the fuselage had torn free, and was whipping around behind the plane. Instead of beelining for the runway, Erwin made a big circle overhead. People ducked behind their automobiles, ready to make a further retreat if necessary.

Heath had come up next to Livy, hands in his pockets. His face was serious as he watched. "You sure you want to do this Liv? It's not too late to change your mind," he said.

"I could say the same to you," she said, knowing full well there would be no mind changing. They'd both come too far.

Breese's head mechanic stood to the other side of Livy, chewing his gum double time. "Cover your eyes, Miss West. There ain't no way in hell he can land this bird."

"If anyone can, it'll be Erwin," Heath said.

"For the love of God, look away!" the mechanic said.

There was a strange magnetism to watching a disaster unfold. Livy had a twisty, sick feeling in her stomach, and yet simply *had* to see what was going on. As the plane came down, they got a better look at how much of the canvas had stripped away. Most of one side was trailing behind the plane, a thirty-foot scarf flapping away.

"Easy, old boy, keep her steady," Heath mumbled.

When the wheels touched down, Erwin managed to keep the plane straight, and they rolled to a stop. Both men hurried to get out of the plane, and the crowd went wild. If she hadn't known better, she'd have thought they'd just won the race. But for Livy, next in line for takeoff, seeing that plane come unglued caused a new wave of doubt. It felt like danger was coming at them from all sides. These were all experienced pilots. But they were also pushing limits with planes overloaded, many of them jerry-rigged. They were attempting something that only a few short years ago would have been unfathomable. Maybe it still was. What if she walked away now? Would she? Could she?

But the thought passed as quickly as it came, and she knew— the sky across the ocean was her only path.

15

CRACKS IN THE CONCRETE

Wren

Pono popped up inside the canvas with Wren, as though he had to see for himself that she was correct—that the giant machines in question were not tractors, but airplanes. His shoulder rubbed up against hers, and he craned his neck up.

"You didn't believe me," she said.

"I'm just surprised, is all."

Being so close, she caught a whiff of coconut. It was not unpleasant. He looked good *and* smelled good. Wren ordered herself to stop that line of thinking immediately, and slid back outside. He followed.

It was a team effort to unsnap the entire canvas and drag it off of the airplane, and Wren and Pono worked carefully not to damage anything. When they had the whole thing in a heap on the floor, they stood back and surveyed what was in front of them.

"It's seen better days," he said.

"It looks ancient."

A single engine with a cracked propeller, faded red paint and two flat tires. Several of the wooden struts that held up the wing were broken, and one of the wings drooped down, nearly touching the floor.

"Do you know anything about airplanes?" she asked.

"Not a thing."

"Do you think they used this for crop-dusting?"

"Your guess is as good as mine."

Now she wondered if there had been an airstrip somewhere nearby. Maybe even on the property.

"Isn't your family from around here? Is there someone we can ask who may have known my great-aunt?" she asked.

He thought for a moment, running two fingers along his mustache. "My gramps maybe. And if he doesn't, he might know who would."

"Could we see him today?"

"Doubtful, but I can hook you up with his number."

Wren moved away a little and tried to make out the faded letters on the side of the plane. Whatever material it had been made out of had been eaten away by moths or bugs or something, leaving gaping holes in sections of the exterior.

"That looks like an *L* and an *O*," she said.

He pointed to the tail end, "And another *O*."

The letter up front was either an *M* or an *N*. The letters on the other side were no better, but they were able to piece together part of the name.

They both stood silent for a moment, then at the same time said, "Malolo!?"

Hers a question mark, his an exclamation.

Flying fish.

"As good a name as any for a plane," he said.

"It has to be."

"Exocoetidae," Pono said.

"Excuse me?"

"It's their Latin name."

"And you know this how?"

He looked at her as though she'd just asked the dumbest question in the world. "I fish."

"I know lots of people who fish, and I guarantee they don't know that name."

"Well, they aren't me."

Something about his self-assuredness threw Wren off balance, and she found herself wanting him to like her. Or if not like her, at least approve of her. He probably thought of her as some clueless city girl from Honolulu.

"I'm Hawaiian, you know," she said.

The words came out of their own accord, and right away she wished she could take them back. He looked genuinely confused. "What does that have to do with anything?"

"I just thought you might want to know. I know a lot about the ocean and the mountains. I even know some Hawaiian language."

"Yeah? That must be nice."

He turned away, so she couldn't see his expression. Next to the cockpit area, there was a small stepping stool, and Pono used it to pull himself up and look inside. His body was wiry and strong, with wide shoulders and lats clearly visible through his thin and faded gray T-shirt.

"Classic," he said.

"What?"

"It's just so dang simple. Just a few dials and a stick. Looks like something we could have built in shop class," he said.

"I loved shop class," she said.

Why did she keep volunteering pointless information? He obviously didn't give a rip.

He ignored her and said, "Should we see what's behind door number two?"

"May as well, if you don't mind me taking up more of your time."

"I'm out here. And as long as Scout is happy." He nodded

toward the door, where Scout had curled up next to the stray. Both dogs watched them intently.

They went through the whole rigmarole of getting the tarp off the second machine, and Wren broke out in a sweat. This time, they weren't too surprised to find another airplane. Quite a bit larger and painted orange with the words Air Hawaii stenciled below the wings.

"I've never heard of Air Hawaii. Have you?" she said.

"Nope."

"It looks newer than the other one."

He knocked on the side. "Sounds like wood to me."

They went up front and examined the engine and its pistons. Wren counted nine.

"Some serious pistons," she said.

He glanced her way, nodding and looking a little surprised that she knew what a piston was. Wren had the distinct feeling he was even more intrigued with the planes than the truck. Maybe she could unload them on him, too.

As if reading her mind, he turned back to her and said, "Now what are you going to do? I bet you weren't counting on this."

It was true, two ancient flying machines definitely complicated things. There was a certain allure to them, as relics of another era. But now, that sense of being overwhelmed she'd felt when leaving Oʻahu began to creep back in.

"Sell it as fast as I can, take the money, maybe buy a little house in Waimea. Waimea's cute, more my style," she answered.

"Have you even seen the whole property?"

"No."

He was now standing in front of her again, greasy hands on his waist. "Wasn't this your family's land?"

"On my dad's side. I didn't know any of them, though," she said, almost defiantly. "Even my dad."

He scratched his head and turned to her. "This may not be any of my business, but wouldn't you want to learn a little more before you get rid of it? From what I've seen, there's a lot to unpack here, and it's a pretty special chunk of land. Or are you that hard up for money?"

The sun began to peek through the high back window, illuminating a large swath of concrete around them. He was pressing her, and she found she couldn't look him in the eye. Instead, she found a crack in the floor and followed it to where it met a water-stained piece of wood in the wall.

"There's a lot you don't know."

His tone softened. "Yeah, well, I'm just calling it as I see it. This just doesn't seem like something you make a rash decision about, and to me, it feels like that's what you're doing."

Unfortunately, there was a certain amount of truth to his words. Even she could see that. But she was bone weary and emotional and on the verge of unraveling.

"You know what? I think I'm sleep-deprived and overwhelmed and I just need to get back home and think about things. Talk to my mom, too. I have ten thousand questions."

"Fair enough."

"What about you? Would you want any of these?"

"What do mean *want*? You just going to hand these over?"

"No, but we could trade. You could help fix them up, and we split the money. Vintage airplanes like this could be collectibles," she said.

He stared at the planes for a moment, and she could almost see the gears moving. "Tempting, but I have a lot on my plate." He checked his watch. "We should get going."

She wondered what else he had going on besides mechanic stuff. Ranching? Fishing? Family? There was that empty ring finger, though. His hands had been in front of her face several times and it was impossible not to keep noticing. They walked out, and Scout followed close behind, the whole back half of his body wagging along with his tail. The stray was nowhere in sight.

"I hate to just leave her," Wren said.

Pono whistled.

"Can you ask around if anyone is missing a cattle dog?" she asked.

"Yeah, but don't hold your breath," he said.

"Should we alert the Humane Society? Is there one here?"

"In Waimea. But they won't come all the way out here."

As they pulled out and drove down the weedy road, Wren felt a strange sensation deep in her abdomen. Almost as though someone was disconnecting the upper half of her body from her lower half. She leaned forward and placed her hand on her stomach.

"Are you okay?"

"I'm not sure. Maybe I shouldn't have drunk that stream water."

"Nah, it runs pretty clean."

She could feel the barn behind her, full of mystery, burning a hole in the back of her head. Or maybe it was something else. Wren had the distinct feeling they were being watched. She turned around for one last look. There, sitting at attention in front of the doors watching them go, was the stray dog. If Wren had been driving, she would have stopped the car, even though she knew the dog would have run off. But Pono was driving, and he had places to go, so she swallowed the urge to go back and instead concentrated on how the leaves danced in the breeze.

16

A GOOD CLIP

Olivia

At exactly 1:08 p.m. Livy and Felix climbed into *Malolo*. Two and a quarter tons of wood, metal, canvas and something undefinable, almost living. Over these past weeks, the plane had taken on a personality of her own. If she were human, Livy imagined she would be intelligent, thoughtful and dogged. The kind of friend you wanted by your side in a pinch. She'd be sweet and graceful and tough as nails.

Once inside, the entire world outside fell away. The overwrought mechanics, the thousands of men, women and children standing on the roofs of their cars, the other planes who were now over the Pacific and the crews still on the ground feverishly fixing their aircraft for another attempt. All the preliminary work was done. Engine finely tuned, wheel bearings oiled, fuel tanks loaded to the gills. Livy tightened her flying cap and cleaned her goggles, the air brimming with gasoline, hope and a big helping of fear.

Felix strapped himself in, sat for a moment in silence, then said, "Here we go, my friend. The moment of truth is upon us."

If they could get off the ground with all that extra fuel, fuel that cost more than her parents' house, they would be golden. That was the immediate concern, yet neither wanted to voice it out loud, especially not now. It was one thing to know that you should hypothetically be able to lift off, but another entirely as you sat in the plane, hearing the engine blast to life, having just seen the failure of so many other aircraft. Nor could she shake the fact that someone out there had stolen compass magnets, and might have done more to sabotage them—something they could have missed.

"Ah, listen to that purr!" Felix yelled.

Livy was just behind him, far enough that she could only hear two thirds of what he said. Better than some pilots and navigators, who had to communicate by devising elaborate pulley systems to pass notes back and forth. If she reached out on both sides, she could easily touch the wooden frame, held together in places with a steel band and rivets. Twenty-seven feet long, nine feet three inches high and with a forty-one-foot wingspan, the plane had little room to spare, but wasn't as cramped as some.

Ernie stood off to the side with the flare gun, and the second the starter swung his flag, he fired. They began to roll forward. Starters helped give their wing struts a push, but *Malolo* felt dead in the water, sluggish as all get out.

Felix leaned forward, as if by doing so, it would help. "Come on, old girl."

Livy imagined herself in his spot. What she would give to be at the controls, holding the stick in her hands. Instead, she sat in her tight seat and whispered a pep talk to the aircraft. "You can do this, little bird, just like the seagulls—light as a feather, full of grace. Carry us safely and swiftly and I will show you the way."

Slowly and steadily, they picked up speed, but by the time they hit the halfway mark on the runway, they still weren't near fast enough. Dust swirled up around them. Then the wheel

caught a small bump, and the plane bounced up, her tail slamming against the hard-packed dirt. Livy felt as though an entire
flock of seagulls was taking flight in her chest.

As they approached the point of no return, a trickle of sweat
ran down the side of her cheek. Felix would likely be drenched
by now, despite the cool temperature. She imagined pulling
the stick back slow and steady, as far is it would go. The wheels
came free for a second, then touched back down to the ground.
A hard slam.

Malolo was straining against all that weight, and yet Livy noticed a subtle shift in the engine, a smoothing out. She looked
outside, sea grass and ocean a blue-green blur. If they didn't get
airborne soon, they would end up in the marsh or in the bay.
Then all at once, the tail skid lifted and everything lightened.

"Hey, hey, hey!" Felix yelled.

A few seconds later, wheels left the earth and *Malolo* took
flight.

"Yes!" Livy cried, and she swore she heard the cheering of
the crowd over the sound of the engine, the rush of the wind.

But they weren't out of the woods yet. Gaining altitude was
always one of the most critical parts of a journey. Felix kept
the nose down to avoid stalling, just as she would have done.
She silently cheered him on, willing the heavy plane higher
and higher. They gained speed with no obvious signs of engine
overheating, no trouble at all really. Behind them and beneath
them, Bay Farm Island fell away as they flew over ferries and
boats and ships, jam-packed with people out to watch the race.
They were out over San Francisco Bay.

The next hurdle would be finding their way through the
thickening fog. When Livy woke that morning, she'd known
it was coming. As the day went on it would thicken, turning
the sky into a giant field of gauze. She'd told Felix and Heath
as much, but they all knew the race would go on. Now, they
flew straight toward the tall white bank along the coast.

"How we doing, Captain?" he called.

Livy checked her bearings. "We're north three degrees. Bear south slightly."

"You want to fly over this soup or under it?"

Though they were moving along at a good clip, *Malolo* was still not at full speed. She was simply too heavy. There was no saying how high the fog went, but Livy sensed it was thick, at least six or eight thousand feet.

"For now, fly below," she called.

That way, she could use landmarks until they were out to sea.

"We'll be skimming trees."

"You asked."

"Right."

Felix banked ever so slightly, and they turned toward the city of San Francisco. Another airplane showed up next to them, one of the several escorts. Livy waved and the pilot gave her a thumbs-up. Then another on the other side, this one much closer, with cameras pointed their way. What an event this was, and everyone wanted the inside story, the best shot, the unique angle. Livy was happy to be leaving them all behind.

They reached land on the other side of the bay about the same time as they entered a thin veil of haze, giving them a whitewashed view of the rolling hills and outskirts of San Francisco. When they passed over the forest the fog thickened into a near whiteout, and they rose higher to avoid slamming into any redwood trees.

"I don't know about you, but I didn't order any fog today," Felix said.

Livy counted the minutes until they passed over the rocky shoreline and were back out over the water, keeping an eye on the compass. With no more trees or mountains to run into, Felix took them lower, not far above the surface, where visibility was better—though scarcely. Livy thought of her father, and of his grounded boat, torn apart on the rocks in the fog. When it came down to man versus nature, nature usually won.

"Did I ever tell you I was scared of flying over open seas?" Felix called back.

"You did mention it."

"When I used to fly passengers between the islands, I would get real nervous, you know? A twitch in my eye. If I made it out into the channel, and couldn't see an island either behind me or ahead of me, I'd turn around."

When he'd first told her, Livy hadn't thought much of it. Now, his words carried more weight.

He went on. "As much as it scared me, it also called to me. I dreamed about it—crossing the whole of the Pacific—and figured some brave bloke would make the hop. Never once did I think that brave bloke would be me."

A hundred feet beneath them, the surface of the sea looked bleak and cold. They were close enough to smell the kelp and salty air, close enough to see the crests and troughs. They were far lower than they ought to be, but Livy wasn't about to start back seat driving this early in the flight. Despite her weight, *Malolo* seemed responsive to every move of the stick.

Livy's course would take them over the Farallones, a cluster of rocky islands and pinnacles twenty-odd miles from the coast. It was known for shipwrecks and sharks and birds, and Livy had flown around them once on an outing with Heath. After dropping off a passenger at a small airfield south of San Francisco, he'd turned to her with a sly smile.

"You up for an adventure?" he said.

"Always."

She would have flown to Antarctica with him if he'd asked her to. They had a few hours to kill before heading south again, so they grabbed a couple sandwiches and two bottles of Coca Cola and set off over the water. Livy knew better than to ask where they were going. Heath was the king of surprises and tight-lipped as a clam. He claimed it was because he loved to see the look on her face when they'd arrive at their destination.

The day was stellar, no clouds, no wind and an ocean full of sunbeams. Heath flew the Cloudster mere feet over the water, as Livy counted sea creatures—seals, a pod of dolphins, two gray whales and a giant sunfish. Soon, rocks rose up in the distance, with a plume of birds swirling around them.

"The Farallon Islands?" she said.

"You know of them."

"My father told me stories. The Devil's Teeth. They've been said to swallow boats whole."

"Right, I should have known. The fisherman's daughter."

He took them in low, close enough so that Livy could see a smattering of blue eggs dotting the cliffs, and seals basking in the sun, one on top of the other. As they passed by, the plane filled with the putrid smell of bird guano, which covered every square inch of rock below. A feathered frenzy of birds scattered at the sound of the engine. Cormorants, oystercatchers, petrels. Heath kept looking over at her, causing a slow burn across her skin.

"You're so beautiful when you're happy. You know that?" he said.

She shook off the memory as she checked her watch.

"Pull up to five hundred feet, we should be getting close to the Farallons," she said.

Those rocks were at least three hundred feet high, and slamming into them would put a quick end to their dreams.

"I can't see crap, and it's worse above us," Felix said.

"That's exactly why you need to. Those islands are solid rock."

Felix did as instructed and they flew into soupy clouds. There was no way to navigate in this mess, and Livy had been counting on seeing the islands to stay on course. Before takeoff, she had told Felix to head west at two hundred forty-eight degrees, and from there, they would slowly veer south.

The fog was ominous and gave Livy a claustrophobic feeling. *Malolo* seemed to be suspended in midair, unmoving. Just when Livy thought they had missed the islands entirely, Felix called out. "By God, there's land below!"

Livy peered over the side and caught a glimpse of a black, craggy pinnacle not more than fifty feet beneath them.

"What's our altitude?" she asked.

"Four hundred."

Altimeters were temperamental objects, and known to be off. They could be affected by atmospheric pressure, or any number of things.

"We need to be higher," she said.

He nosed them up, then leveled off. They continued for another seventeen minutes without spotting any more of the islands, then dropped back down to where they'd been before, around one hundred feet. Only now, the fog had thickened and swallowed the ocean in the process.

"I'm going down until I can see the water, or I'll lose my mind," Felix said.

Thank goodness for the turn and bank indicator that Breese had insisted on installing. The handy device was sensitive to the plane turning as well as pitching and rolling, so even if you couldn't see a thing outside, you could count on it for orientation. Never mind that Felix had little experience using it, he was getting a crash course in it this very moment. At forty feet, the slate gray ocean opened up beneath them again. Felix was of the mindset that the fog would soon lift, and it would be smooth sailing the rest of the way, but Livy knew better. They flew along blindly for another half hour, Felix calling out periodically to ask about their heading, and also cursing the blinding white.

"Someone turn this forsaken fog off," he grumbled.

Livy wished for horizon, sun, blue sky—anything to break the white monotony. She also suggested they try to rise above the fog, but Felix remained steadfast in his need to see the ocean.

All of a sudden, the plane shot up. "Hang on!" Felix yelled.

Livy, who had been double-checking her compasses, looked up in time to see the outline of a massive steamship looming in front of them. As wide as a runway, and taller than a small building, the ship appeared oblivious to their presence. Her smokestack and masts reached skyward like enormous trees. *Malolo*'s engine strained in the climb, and Livy braced herself on the frame of the plane. Colliding with a ship had not been something she'd accounted for in all of her darkest dreams.

"Bank right," she yelled.

It was their only hope.

Felix ignored her. Or maybe he hadn't heard.

Louder, she screamed, "Bank right! Now!"

The plane took a hard lurch to the right, and for a moment, she thought they were going to roll. The railing of the ship hurled toward them, and Livy watched two men dash for safety. She closed her eyes, waiting to hit. Then, by some strange miracle, they were over water, speeding away. Her stomach twisted in on itself. Up front, Felix stayed silent as a mouse. Neither spoke for some time, until Livy decided it was time to break the ice.

"Nice job, my friend," she said.

"Thanks, Captain."

17

A SMALL HICCUP

Olivia

Miles began to slip by. One hundred, two hundred, four hundred. That meant about twenty-two hundred to go if they were to stick to their expected route. All Livy had to go on was her compass, for there were no celestial objects to observe, and thus her bubble sextant lay useless in her lap. Felix had been unusually quiet after the near miss with the steamer, and she wasn't sure what to make of it. Over the past weeks, she had come to know him as the gregarious optimist, quick to laugh and never taking anything too seriously. Now, his silence felt preternatural—foreboding almost.

To make matters worse, they were still flying in and out of dense clouds. The rare patches of clarity never lasted longer than a minute. The monotony began to play tricks on her mind, and to combat drowsiness, she nibbled on a small piece of chocolate and obsessively surveyed her marine maps. Hawai'i was but a piece of sand in the vast ocean, and the notion of reaching it now seemed preposterous. What foolishness were they attempting on this voyage? She almost laughed at their hubris.

Smith and Bronte made it.

"Come again?" Felix said.

Livy must have spoken the words aloud.

"Nothing, just checking my calculations," she said.

"Did you say something about Smith and Bronte?"

"Just reassuring myself."

No answer. She could hardly blame him. Talking above the noise took energy, and energy was something they both wanted to preserve. They had a long night ahead.

In the hour before sunset, the strong smell of gasoline began to fill the cabin. At first, Livy tried to talk herself into believing it was just her sensitive nose. But soon, the smell became overwhelming and downright alarming.

"Do you smell that?" she asked.

"Smell what?"

"Gasoline."

"Probably just a little runoff. But check it if it makes you feel better," Felix said. Then he added, "While you're at it, take a look at the hoses. Pressure's dropped with both oil and fuel."

The last-minute jerry-rigged fuel system had more tubes than Livy was used to seeing, and without good light, it was hard to tell what was what. Despite that, it was plain to see—and smell—that something was amiss. She followed what appeared to be the gas line to where it fed off into the engine and found gas spilling out. Her body went numb.

"The gas line is shot," she said.

"How about the oil?"

"I can't tell by looking at it."

Livy fought back tendrils of panic working their way around her heart, then uttered the last words she ever thought she would hear herself say. "Maybe we should turn back."

Even if they did turn back, chances of making it were slim to none unless they could fix the line. They'd been in the air over five hours, but five hours gave them better odds than the twenty or more they would need to reach Hawai'i. Between

the loud rush of wind, the engine roar and the gas fumes, she
was having a hard time thinking straight.

"Engine's sounding rough, isn't she?" Felix yelled.

"Did you hear what I just said?"

"Loud and clear, Captain. We need to wrap some tape around
that hose, and get the oil running again. There's no turning
back."

Livy knew where every spare item in the plane had been
packed, and found the big roll of electrical tape. Whether it
would stick or not was another story.

"Why don't we go up, there'll be less pressure in the line,"
she said. "We're going to have to go up sooner or later, so why
not now?"

"Not 'til dark."

His obstinance made her furious. "Your pigheadedness is
going to get us killed, you know that?"

"I need to see the water," he yelled.

"Why, Felix, I don't understand?"

"I just do," he said, shoulders shuddering almost as though
he was crying. "What I wouldn't give for a fucking cigarette
about now."

For the first time, she began to truly worry about his state
of mind. A person of sound mind would have difficulty out
here, even in the best of circumstances, and these were as far
from the best of circumstances one could get.

She tried a different tack. "How about I fly the plane, and
you come back here and fix the hose."

"Just do as I say, and we should be fine," he said.

He instructed her to wipe the line down and administer the
tape. Livy's hands were shaking to the point where they hardly
worked, and she fumbled along, tape sticking to all the wrong
places. Finally, it stuck, and it seemed to do the job, though
how long it would hold was another story.

"Now, for the oil, I need you to put your mouth around the end of the hose and make sure it's airtight, then suck," he said.

"You want me to put engine oil in my mouth?"

"The alternative is much worse, I'm afraid. And once you draw the oil out, plug it with your thumb and reattach the hose."

Unfortunately, he was right. Without oil, the engine would seize. Livy pulled one end into her mouth, set her water canteen next to her and sucked until her cheeks burned. Nothing came up. She tried again, and was rewarded with a rancid, greasy taste in her mouth. She gagged and spit, but kept her thumb tightly on the hose. Attaching it back on was difficult, especially tightening the gasket, but she managed.

When all was said and done, Livy smelled and tasted like a gasoline station attendant. Her thumb ached and she feared the film of oil on her teeth would be with her the rest of the way. She took some water and a few bites of her first sandwich, not because she was hungry, but to wash away the bitter taste. Hunger had eluded her so far. There were too many other things to think about.

The clouds had darkened from ivory to silver to ash, and complete darkness was almost upon them. Felix had been quiet ever since the gas-and-oil fiasco. Every fifteen minutes, Livy checked their bearing. She was also in charge of logging their instrument readings—altitude, air speed, tachometer, oil pressure, fuel pressure, along with true course, magnetic course, deviation, compass course. On the hour every hour, she asked Felix to call them out to her, and this was the only time he spoke. Wind information was also to be noted. However, they hadn't been able to drop any smoke bombs yet to determine their drift, so she left those blank.

Even though moonrise was still hours away, Felix finally conceded that it was time to rise above the clouds. They were already flying in complete darkness, so his argument of being able to see the ocean no longer held sway.

The air is far less forgiving than the sea. Her father's words kept rearing up in her head. When she had first told him of her interest in learning to fly an airplane, he thought she was merely dreaming. But he knew she would no longer go on the boat after what happened with Orlando, so he had stopped trying to coax her back on and eventually realized she was serious about flying. *Just remember, if anything goes south, it's a long way down from up there.* What she would give to have him by her side right now.

"Make sure your strap is tight," Felix said.

The words were flat, devoid of emotion, yet they stirred a primal fear in Livy. Hours away from any land mass, flying blind with a pilot who was barely holding it together. Far less than ideal.

18

CITY LIFE

Wren

The next morning, Wren half woke to the sound of keys jingling in the door. She was face down, staring at a crack in a maroon cushion, drooling, trying to remember where she was. And then it hit her—the studio couch, wearing only a pair of underwear because it had been unusually hot and stuffy in the middle of the night. In a panic, she bolted upright, but not before Greg, the graphic artist who creeped her out, opened the door. The minute he saw her, his eyes dropped straight to her boobs, which she'd wrapped her arms around.

Yuck.

"Greg! Sorry, I'll get out of your way," she said, fumbling for her shirt and shorts and running off to the bathroom.

She splashed water on her face, which looked puffy and smooshed. Outside, the door slammed. From day one, she hadn't liked the guy. The way he looked at her—always a few beats too long—creeped her out, and he chain-smoked cigarettes to the point where his skin had a grayish hue. But he was friends with Kalama, and Kalama was the one whose name was on the lease, so he usually had the final say. He also had connections and brought a lot of work to the others, so Wren didn't have a leg to stand on.

The studio was in an old warehouse in Kaka'ako, surrounded by auto repair shops and strip joints and Korean BBQs. But it was cheap and huge and afforded them all enough room to spread out and have their own space.

When Wren went to get dressed, she realized she only had her shirt and no shorts. Her shorts must have fallen on the ground. She cracked the door and peered out. Greg was in his little alcove with his back to her, sitting at his drafting table. Wren tiptoed out across the floor, grabbed her shorts and quickly shimmied into them.

"I hear you're planning on moving in," he said, not even bothering to turn around.

The whiny sound of his voice grated on her already frayed nerves.

"No. I may stay here for a few nights. But I'm not moving in," she said.

All her stuff was packed in her truck.

"You can always stay at my place. I have a king bed."

They were the absolute last words she expected out of his mouth, and they made her feel dirty. As if she was that desperate. She'd always suspected his strange behavior toward her had to do with feeling shunned by Wren, and most other females of the human race. But those long, leering stares were not a plus when it came to wooing women.

"Thanks but no thanks," she said, grabbing her purse and hurrying out the door.

She needed to talk to Cindy, and she needed coffee. Not in that order. She drove to Ward Warehouse, ordered a steaming-hot mocha and went in search of a pay phone. In the open-air mall, she found a whole row near the middle of the shops. She called collect.

"Will you accept a collect call from Wren?"

"Of course I will."

"Hey, Cindy."

"Is everything okay over there? I tried your number but it was disconnected," Cindy said, a tone of concern in her voice.

In no mood to sugarcoat anything, Wren said, "I lost my job at Mama's and Mr. Fukuda kicked me out because I was late on the rent. But—"

"Oh, honey—"

"Let me finish." Wren told her about the call from Bob Simms and the barn and its contents and her trip over there, minus the truck breaking down and spending the night out there. "What do you know about the property?"

Wren could hear her mother breathing on the other end. An ocean between them. She waited and waited.

"Nothing. Your grandmother Lihau died not long after you were born, but she lived in California. Kainoa was such a free spirit, land would just have tied him down, like everything else did." Wren knew that the *everything else* referred to Cindy and herself. "And Portia, well she was Portia, eccentric as a bat and basically deaf. But you already know this. The third sister, I can't even remember her name, I think she was married to a pilot now that you mention it."

That was a tidbit Wren hadn't heard before.

"Dad never mentioned a property? You sure?" Wren asked.

"I would have remembered something like that. Kainoa was on his own program. If it didn't pertain to him, it didn't exist. It was sad, really."

"It seems weird."

"Yes, but it doesn't surprise me."

"Why not?"

"Because men don't pay attention to the details, honey. That's our job."

Wren laughed. It was such a typical Cindy comment.

"I guess I'm like a man, then."

"Oh, for goodness' sakes. Listen, you've been left a derelict property that no one cared about enough to even keep up, so I agree with what you said earlier. Sell it and move on. Use the money to buy an apartment."

Hearing her mother tell her to sell caused a knee-jerk reaction.

"What if I don't want to sell it?"

Cindy sighed. "Honey, you started this conversation by telling me you did."

If Cindy had her way, anything to do with Wren's father would be erased from all memory. She'd always underestimated the innate curiosity buried deep in Wren, wanting to know her lineage. The idea that blood was thicker than water.

Wren thought of all that land over there. The quiet, the space, even the remoteness, whispered her name. Being back on O'ahu, amid the buildings, the traffic and sirens and overall grime of city life, now felt jarring. There was also the matter of Joe and Julie.

"You know what, Mom?"

"What?"

"I think I'm going to go back and then decide. When I was there, I thought I needed to be here, but now that I'm here, I realize I need to be there. It sounds crazy, but thanks for the advice." Saying it out loud made it feel even more right, and Wren had never been more sure of anything.

Her mom laughed. "In case you didn't notice, you're going against my advice."

"Just talking it out with you helped. I'll call you from the Big Island."

"Be safe."

"Love you."

After hanging up, Wren went to the studio, packed every tool she owned and every scrap of wood and every roll of material into her truck. She'd have to find glass on the Big

Island. From there, she drove straight to Young Brothers. Her gas tank was already below a quarter full, the level required for shipping, thanks to having no money, and there was space on the barge. Her old Datsun truck would leave for Kawaihae the next morning. Getting it loaded would ensure she didn't chicken out. Because when she actually thought about what she was doing, the butterflies kicked up a frenzy in her stomach.

19

A VERY BAD IDEA

Olivia

The original flight date had been planned around a full moon. Now, four days later, they had a waning gibbous moon to look forward to, and Livy was counting the minutes until it rose. The moon was so many things to her—celestial body, illuminating guide, comforting friend. As a girl, she had spent countless nights combing the beaches under a full moon. And now, she loved flying by moonlight, following its yellow path in the quiet of the night.

Charting the moon was another story. Moonrise and moonset were relatively predictable based on the phase of the moon, but its position—or azimuth—was a little more slippery. Her father explained it to her in simple terms one clear night as they sat on the aft deck.

"Where the moon climbs over the horizon in the east is going to depend on our position around the sun. We're tilted at a twenty-three-degree angle, so she takes a different path every night. Understand that and you'll always know exactly where you are when the moon comes up, and when she goes down."

Tonight, the moon would rise at their backs, at a position

of about one hundred three degrees, if they were on course. *Malolo* had begun her climb, rising slowly as if feeling her way through the darkness, the only light, a tiny but blinding orange glow from the engine's exhaust.

Felix called out each time they hit another thousand feet. "Three thousand."

Air cooled against Livy's skin and she wrapped a wool scarf around her neck. The chill she felt was not just from the plummeting temperature. She still had an uneasy feeling about Felix, and now, he'd begun rubbing his eyes continuously. Keeping a plane level in the dark took concentration. Sure, his eyes were likely smarting from staring at the instrument panel all day in the glare of the fog, but that didn't change the fact that he needed to be at the top of his game.

"These damn dials are making my head swim," he said.

They had been up in the air now for nearly eight hours, but to Livy it had felt like forty. Then, a moment after they reached four thousand feet, the plane rolled violently to the right, and began accelerating downward. The force threatened to pull Livy out of her seat, and up into the ceiling. Nose down, they spun toward the ocean below. In her mind, she frantically ran through all her training. Never had she piloted in a spin like this. Then she remembered riding shotgun with Heath at an airshow in Los Angeles, where he rolled and spun and dove until her stomach felt permanently lodged in her throat. It seemed impossible that a plane could come out of these, and yet every time, they had.

"Chop the throttle," Livy yelled.

Felix should have known this from his barnstorming days, but they continued down at a dizzying speed, all the forces of nature conspiring against the tiny plane.

"Felix!"

Hearing his name seemed to rattle him into action, and he immediately cut the engine. They slowed some, *Malolo* shuddered and Felix hit the left rudder with everything he had. It was exactly what he needed to do. For a few moments, it seemed to be working as they hung weightless, but then the nose plunged again and down they went, gaining momentum with each foot closer to the ocean's surface.

Would it be better to die on impact, or to survive with the possibility of never being found, drifting in a lifeboat under scorching skies, circled by sharks while fighting off starvation? Aviation was a dangerous sport. She'd known the odds. And yet, wasn't it human nature to always believe that *it*—that terrible thing whatever *it* may be—would never happen to you. Livy remembered the letter in her pocket from Heath and how he'd wanted so badly to set things right between them. Sadness crept in and she wished she'd been more forgiving. His last memories of her would be of a cold, hard bitch.

Up front, Felix let out an unearthly sound somewhere between a growl and a scream. The plane seemed to lighten, and then leveled out.

"Yes!" Livy cried.

"For the love of God, I thought we were goners."

So did I.

It took a good ten minutes of cruising before Livy's nerves settled. Neither spoke. She thought of Heath kissing the ground that first day back in San Diego, and wished she could do the same about now. But the problem was, the lower they were, the worse their chances of surviving a graveyard dive became. Had Felix lost his bearings earlier, as they'd flown just over the water, they wouldn't be here now.

"I know it's tough, but we ought to go up again," she said.

"Roger that."

"Just watch your instruments."

Two thousand. Three thousand. Livy held her breath as they rose. All they needed was to climb above the godforsaken clouds and be able to have a horizon to level them with. Starlight, moonlight, any kind of light would do. An unsettled feeling came over her, and a moment later, the plane faltered, then entered another dive. Livy held tight to her flashlight with one hand, while bracing herself against a wooden strut with the other. This whole thing had been a bad idea, and she cursed herself for putting so much faith in Felix. This time, however, he was able to bring them out of the spin sooner, and they resumed climbing.

"I'm not sure how much more I can take," he said, after they'd crossed the two thousand foot mark.

"You don't have a choice."

Livy tasted salt on her lips. Helplessness tugged at her from all directions and she herself was on the verge of coming unglued.

"What if we land in the water and hope someone finds us?" he suggested.

He really had lost his marbles.

"Landing on water in daylight would be hard enough, and then what? This plane wasn't designed to float."

"I… I think we're fucked. Sorry, my friend."

As long as they were still up in the air, there was hope, slim as it might be. She shone her light over his shoulder, to help him see better, but was reluctant to unstrap herself.

Livy refused to let him give up, "I *have* to get to Honolulu," she said, leaning forward and tapping him hard on the shoulder to try to snap him out of his state.

"You and me both! My wife is counting on me."

There was no one counting on her. No one who cared like that, at least.

"Focus on the turn-and-bank indicator, don't look anywhere else," she commanded.

After flying level for some time, the old Felix seemed to return. The mood in the cabin settled. Livy patted perspiration from her face. She checked her watch: 2120. Not even halfway. *Malolo* was climbing at a good rate, engine purring along, when they banked again and began another nosedive. That was when Livy understood that they only had one shot at making it out alive—she had to get herself into the pilot seat.

20

A HUGE STRETCH OF TRUTH

Olivia

The human heart was not designed to live through three consecutive graveyard spins, of that Livy was sure. Once again, Felix managed to get them out of it, but how many more could they endure? The poor airplane was strained to the gills. Livy made a mental note to thank the builders of *Malolo*, because after that third dive, the little plane seemed no worse for the wear. She was astounded they hadn't lost a rudder or an aileron, with all the torque Felix had placed on them.

"I fear we won't survive another of those. Let me fly, Felix," she told him. He didn't respond at first, which made her think he was at least considering it. "Please!"

"What will they say?" he said, quietly.

"Who cares what they say!"

"We'll be disqualified," he said, voice cracking.

"But alive."

None of that mattered right now. Let them talk. Let them be disqualified. Livy just knew that Felix was in a dangerous state and ready to crack.

His back began to heave and loud sucking noises came out of his mouth, as he cried. "Oh, geez, I think I'm dying."

In five seconds flat, Livy undid her safety strap, grabbed her sextant, flashlight and charts, and squeezed around his seat. There was hardly room for one person up there, but someone needed to keep them from falling out of the sky.

"Get in the back. Now!" she ordered.

Without any further argument, Felix extracted himself, while Livy reached around him and held the stick. She anticipated another dive at any moment, but they held steady. Her entire body was wrapped around him, and he was wet with perspiration and smelled of fear and cigarettes. She could feel him shaking as he worked himself past her into the back. During the physical, no mention of heart trouble had come up. In fact, he'd boasted of perfect health, so she suspected it was more mental than physical.

All at once, Livy was in the pilot seat flying the airplane. It felt equal parts strange and familiar and terrifying. She took a few minutes to familiarize herself with the controls—phosphorescent numbers, lines and points upon whose accuracy everything depended. The stick was responsive, the engine powerful. Slowly, she began to climb, keeping her eyes trained on the dials.

In the back, Felix started groaning.

"Lie down and take some water," she called.

"Oh, God…oh, God…what have I done?" he mumbled.

It would be physically impossible to fly the plane and try to help Felix—or save him if he indeed needed saving. It would help to know what was wrong with him. Maybe the gasoline fumes had gone to his head. But if that was the case, she would have been just as sick.

"Hang in there. We're going to make it, I just know it," she said, turning her head so he could hear her better.

A huge stretch of truth, but desperate times called for desperate measures. Felix continued talking to himself, until his voice trailed off. There were a few minutes of quiet, while Livy checked all the gauges. Oil was okay, but they'd lost more fuel than anticipated with the leaking hose. The extra they'd been counting on had evaporated, along with any peace of mind. Livy would now have to fly *and* navigate a perfect course.

Then Felix started up again. A whimper that turned into a hiccup, then into flat-out wailing with the urgency of an exhausted child who'd just had his favorite toy taken away.

"Tell Iwa I love her, will you?" he cried.

"Save your breath, and tell her yourself."

"We'll never get there."

She had to shut him up before she went batty, too.

"Do you have any nerve tonic? Something. Anything?" she called back.

"No." But a little while later, he said, "Joe Dearborn handed me a medicine bottle this morning."

Joe was one of the mechanics. A wise older man with a penchant for reading people as well as he could read airplane engines.

"Did he say what it was?"

"No, just, 'If the pressure gets the best of you, drink up.'"

Livy had never taken nerve tonic herself—had never had any reason to, but she'd seen a bottle on her parents' bathroom counter recently. Jaspers Nerve Sedative. It explained why her father had taken to sleeping away the afternoons.

"Where is it now?" she asked.

"In my pouch under the seat."

Livy reached around under the cold seat, and her fingers located a small canvas bag. She handed it back to him. "Don't take too much," she said.

A moment later, Livy heard a bottle shatter on the floor.

When the first star appeared, Livy thought she was imagining things. But a moment later, they emerged out of the clouds into a wide-open sky, a web of stars beautiful and familiar. It was like coming up for air and sucking in a huge breath after a long dive to the bottom of a murky ocean. A small victory in the scheme of things, but she was so struck by such an intense relief that she began to quietly weep.

For as long as she could remember, the stars had been a connection to something greater. Beings of light visible from the plump grass in her backyard, from a kelp-strewn beach, a boat deck in the Gulf of Mexico or the evening skies between Los Angeles and San Diego. They were predictable in a way that life and death weren't, some more constant than others. The circumpolar constellations of Cassiopeia, Cepheus, Draco, Ursa Major and Ursa Minor never dipped below the horizon—if you were in the Northern Hemisphere. That made them useful for navigation, and her eyes sought them out now.

The altimeter read ten thousand three hundred feet, and Livy leveled off. A biting cold filled the cabin, and she realized her teeth were chattering. Her wool jacket was in the back with Felix, and she wavered back and forth on asking him for it. Not one peep out of him for the past fifteen minutes. On the other hand, without his nervous ramblings, she'd been able to concentrate and get her wits about her again. But it wouldn't do to become hypothermic, so she gave in.

"You still with me?" she said.

"I'm not sure."

"I need my jacket. It's stuffed in the left compartment back there."

A few moments later, he flung it over her shoulder. In the pocket were also warmer gloves. She slid them both on. Every little thing added weight, and Felix had given her a hard time when he saw them on the list. Thankfully, she'd held her ground.

"Are you warm enough?" she asked.

"I'm not sure."

He sounded loopy as hell, but she supposed it was better than hyperventilating or having his heart go out on him.

"That army blanket is under the seat. Use that if you need it," she told him.

The next order of business was to attempt a sighting with the bubble sextant. Whether she could manage while flying the plane still remained to be seen. There was no telling how far off course they were at this point, and even a few degrees could mean missing the Hawaiian Islands altogether.

Polaris would be her first guiding star, as it was steadfast in its northerly position. Next, she'd use Arcturus, as it was the brightest in the summer sky. But how to keep the plane level, have the charts out and sight at the same time? The cramped cockpit was no place to spread out her charts, her lap being the only dark surface to lay them on. But every time she looked down for any length of time, the plane began to fall off. And sure enough, with eyes back on the indicators, the turn-and-bank needle would be way to the side, altimeter dropping.

She continued on like that for some time, then finally gave up. The maps would have to wait. The one thing she had going for her was that she had studied them until her eyes blurred. The main thing was, they were headed west and inching south, following the great circle route. With wind drift, though, it was impossible to know how far they'd blown off course. In the morning, she hoped to drop the smoke bombs. But morning was years away. By flying west, against the earth's rotation, they were drawing out the night like a long story.

When the stars began to fade, Livy felt a strange giddiness. The moon was finally entering into the arena, sending light east to west across the heavens. Slowly, the skies turned from black to dark blue and the layer of clouds below formed a vast field of undulating silver. And a horizon at long last, something to help keep them level. Her eyes had grown tired staring at the dials, and looking out the window again was a wonderful respite. To be sure, the human eye was not created to stare at compact glowing objects for hours on end.

Felix was in the back snoring, oblivious to their transit across the Pacific. The transfer of responsibility weighed heavy on her. It was one thing to be a passenger, a guide even, but another to hold someone else's life in your hands on a journey such as this. Maybe Lindbergh and Heath had had the right idea. Going it alone seemed a brilliant move.

The letter still sat patiently in her pocket and she desperately wanted to know what he'd written. But it would be irresponsible to attempt to read it now.

"Where are you, Hazeltine?" she spoke into the darkness.

He could be anywhere in the sky, but perhaps he was nearby, soaring along above the clouds. Her eyes swept over the horizon, searching. Maybe they could follow each other the rest of the way. She shook her head. That was drowsiness talking. She'd be just as likely to see a bunny rabbit hopping across the clouds as to run into another plane out here.

Oh, how her eyelids wanted to close. Just for a few seconds…that would be allowed, wouldn't it? Her lashes touched her cheekbone. *Ahh.*

A feeling of restful calm came over her, as just ahead she saw a whole formation of airplanes. They were all here, every single one of the Dole Birds, and they were all ahead of her! *Malolo* went into a dive again. Livy pulled back on the stick, but it came off in her hands. *What the…*

Her body jerked awake.

Her clammy hands were still on the stick—thankfully still there. The altimeter said they'd lost five hundred feet, and the nose was down, left wing low. Instinct kicked in and she jammed the rudder and pulled back on the stick, toward her hip. The plane still felt sideways, as though free-falling through the dark on a wing. Now fully alert, skin tingling, Livy's eyes shot to the turn-and-bank indicator. The needle was right where it should be.

Trust the needle.

Heath's words. They'd been practicing flying by instrument on a moonless night out over the water.

"That way, if we go down, we have a softer landing," he'd said with a grin before taking off. Heath was a firm believer in learning more than you thought you needed to know. All contingencies should be covered because you never knew what might happen up there.

Wasn't that the truth! Livy had to battle with her mind, which held firm to the sensation of sideslipping into the abyss. She had to remind herself to breathe every so often and keep her eyes on the needle. It never wavered, and eventually, her internal system recalibrated.

Nodding off would not do. She pulled out a small jar of peppermint oil and inhaled deeply. The vapors went straight to her head, sharpening her senses immediately. It was also ten o'clock and time for a sandwich and more chocolate even though she had no appetite. Food would give her energy. Lord knew she needed some. Only problem was, all the food was in the back with Felix.

21

MAKING FRIENDS

Wren

Three days later, Wren hitched a ride from the airport to Kawaihae docks with a gnarled old man who talked about fishing the entire way. By the time she got out, she knew precisely when the *aku* and *'opelu* were running, and his top secret spots for bottom fishing. He'd made her swear she wouldn't tell a soul, never mind she only knew one person on the island.

Inside the gates at Kawaihae, her trusty orange truck sat all alone on the smoking-hot asphalt. Everything in the bed appeared to be where she'd strapped it, only now the truck and all its belongings were coated in a thick layer of salt, thanks to the rough wintertime seas.

She set out on the lower road to Hāwī, which paralleled the ocean, running through dry and rocky terrain with a very occasional kiawe tree. It was inconceivable that just up the mountain, and around 'Upolu Point, everything was lush and green. Hot air blasted in on her like she had the heater on. It felt as though she was driving away from one life and toward another. The cassette player was broken and the radio station from Maui played mostly commercials, so she rode in silence wondering what on earth she was doing.

Hāwī town, which she missed the last time around, was less of a town and more of a street with a few colorful old storefronts and galleries, and even more empty buildings. It had old sugar town written all over it. New ventures had been trying to gain a foothold ever since sugar shut down, but so far, nothing had come close. Despite the ghost town feel, it was charming, and Wren could only imagine what kinds of stories these old buildings could tell.

She arrived at the barn in early afternoon. The winds blew from the north, bringing a chill to the air and turning the sky a shocking cobalt blue. The fair weather was like a welcome hug from the island itself. She looked around for the stray, but saw no sign of her. The image of the dog sitting in front of the barn, watching them drive away, had been haunting her, so she'd picked up a bag of dog food along with supplies for herself at K. Takata Store, just beyond the main section of town.

"Hey, friend, I'm back. With real food this time!" she announced to the forest, which was humming with bees and the echoes of chirping birds. The dog didn't materialize. Maybe she was inside.

Wren pulled the truck into the barn and backed up beneath the mezzanine, taking her time to unload all her stuff and organize it in piles. Clothes, tools, toiletries and boxes of miscellaneous belongings. Before she moved anything upstairs, she'd have to give the place a thorough cleaning. A project that could take days or years, depending. But time was one thing she had plenty of.

For sleeping, she planned on setting up her tent inside in case of rain. She'd also picked up a cheap floaty air mattress from Longs, and had her three-season mummy bag. Too warm for O'ahu, but here it would be perfect.

Aside from sleeping, her most immediate concern was running water, or the lack thereof. The fact that there was a toilet and sink and a hose outside her gave her hope, but they were all dry for now, and until she figured out how to get them working, she'd have to find the nearest stream to bathe in—or find a beach park shower, and maybe create a composting toilet somewhere nearby. Eating was another story in and of itself. With no refrigeration, she'd have to buy ice if she wanted to keep anything cold.

All the comforts of modern life had quickly fallen away, and she was faced with the question of how long she could hack it. Growing up, they had camped around the island on their adventures, but usually only for a night or two. Existing indefinitely out here was going to take a whole different mindset. She hoped she was up to the task, which in theory seemed doable. In real life, who knew. Her decision to come now felt hasty. Then she reminded herself that being here solved her most immediate concerns: going cold turkey on Joe and having a roof over her head, even if it was an old and questionable roof.

The afternoon passed in a flurry of clearing and sweeping and dragging stuff outside to air out. She cautiously pulled the blankets and pillows off the bed, all the while praying for no cane spiders or centipedes. Right off the bat, when she moved a pillow, a mango-sized cane spider scurried across the back of the couch and up the wall. She screamed and jumped back. Mostly harmless, but creepy and lightning fast, cane spiders were the worst. She was glad for the tent to zip herself up in.

Against one wall, she spotted a sliding door that she hadn't noticed before. It was flush with the wood and blended right in. When she opened it, she found a zillion more jars and bottles, these empty. They ranged in size from gallon jugs to tiny mason jars and everything in between. There were old wine bottles, milk bottles, medicine bottles, clear, brown, sea blue, gold, leafy green bottles. Someone had been into glass. Cool. She closed the door and kept working.

When the sun dipped behind the mountains, she came up for air. Covered in sweat and grime and dust, she thought about searching for a closer stream than the one she'd driven over, but with daylight leaving, she instead went back to the first ravine, stripped down naked and let herself fall into the cold, swirling waters. The pool was small and only waist deep, but more refreshing than any shower. On the far side she found a smooth, mossy stone to sit on. Goose bumps covered her skin, and yet she didn't want to get out. From below, the roar of a larger falls drifted up.

Back at the barn, Wren boiled water on her camping stove and ate S&S saimin for dinner as she watched the sky fade from dusky orange to periwinkle to indigo. A picnic table would be nice, but for now, she sat on a big beach towel laid out over the tall grass and lumpy ground. Every so often, she'd call out for the dog, hoping to see her shadowy form emerge from the forest, but the dog remained elusive. Perhaps she should ask Pono to bring Scout back as bait. He hadn't given her any way to reach him, but she could easily ask Bob for his number.

He'd been so hard to read—guarded, kind of a badass and sexy in a could-care-less way. But beneath all that she detected a soft spot. She'd seen it in the way he spoke to the stray dog, and how he lit up when he saw the truck and the planes. He didn't say much, but what he said carried weight. And those arms. The truth was, he was the kind of guy women swarmed to. Which made her decide then and there that she wouldn't try to call him or find him. This was her deal. No male required.

It wasn't until later, when she was tucked into her sleeping bag in the pitch-black about to fall asleep, that she heard a scraping sound, then the clicking of nails on concrete. Her body tensed up, and she felt like a little girl again, alone in her room and scared of the dark. With such a vivid imagination, she'd always conjure up spooky scenarios based on the latest stories from the six-o'clock news Cindy watched religiously. If a strangler was on the loose, Wren would sleep with a baseball bat in her bed. Or a Peeping Tom or a rapist, she'd devise ingenious ways to ward them off.

The dog stopped just outside her tent, breathing heavily and sniffing. Her snout pressed in, right where Wren's head was and Wren felt herself loosen at their closeness. But when she rolled to her side, she caused a squeak on the air mattress and sent the dog running up the steps. Poor thing was in for a surprise with all of the bedding stripped away. Wren had felt bad and ended up folding a towel on the floor next to the bed. Now, the floorboards creaked as the dog circled around the mezzanine. Eventually, she lay her body down, the sound of bone on wood causing a pain in Wren's hip.

In the morning, Wren made a list of things she needed and things she needed to do: clean mattress or futon, plywood, bucket, propane, mosquito punk, mosquito net, find a plumber, find a job. She was going to have to get creative with this last one, because Hāwī was not the kind of place in need of waitresses. Nor were people here likely to need pricey light fixtures. The thought made her depressed. She loved her creations, but maybe it was time to wake up and smell the coffee. She'd been at it for years now, with nothing but a few design awards to show for it. You couldn't eat design awards, nor buy gas with them.

Before stopping anywhere, she took a drive through Hāwī town, and then onward to Kapa'au, taking note of shops and eateries that might be of use to her. One thing that stood out was how tidy and well manicured the yards were, with not a leaf out of place. A big chunk of the people who lived here were descendants of sugar plantation owners or managers or workers. Japanese, Filipino, Chinese, Portuguese, *haole*. And before all of that, Hawaiians. King Kamehameha himself was born nearby, and there was a giant painted bronze statue of him in front of the old courthouse.

Kapaʻau was only a stone's throw down the road from Hāwī, and though tiny, it had a public library, post office, police station and a hospital that looked more like a house. Wren drove up and down side roads, wanting to get a feel for the place. A few older folks in yards quit their weeding or trimming and stared at her as though she was casing the joint. She smiled and waved. On the way back, she pulled into the hardware store. A middle-aged Japanese gentleman behind the counter greeted her. The name Chester was embroidered on his blue button-up shirt.

"Can I help you?" he asked.

She told him what she needed, and he eyed her above his wire reading glasses, which had slid down his nose.

"You new in town?" he asked.

The question caught her off guard. She hadn't prepared any answers for nosy neighbors.

"I guess I am."

He chuckled. "As good an answer as any. You here with family?"

His words were tinged with pidgin, and *here* came out *hea*.

"Nope, just me."

He started walking toward the back of the shop, and she followed. They collected each of the items on her list, and he was so helpful, she felt as though she had her own personal shopper. At the last minute, she saw a jar full or rawhide chews, and she grabbed a few.

"Where you staying?" he asked.

For some reason, she was hesitant to say.

"Just up the road," she told him.

"You own a dog?"

She laughed. "You ask a lot of questions, Chester."

"Goes with the territory. You own a hardware store, you get to know people in your town."

"Well, if you must know, I don't own a dog, but there's a stray where I'm staying and I want to win her trust."

His face lit up. "Ah, I have just the thing. Hang on."

He went out a screen door in the back, and she peered over the counter. A covered deck connected to a house in the back. Another door slammed, then a few minutes later, he came back and handed her a bag.

"Ahi. One of my customers dropped way more than we need."

The bag smelled fishy, but if it won the dog over, she'd take it. "Thank you. And one more thing, do you know a plumber?"

"What do you need done?"

"I'm in an old...barn." May as well be up front—the man had just given her half a fish. "There's a sink and toilet and an old-fashioned water tower, but none of it has been used in years. I need running water."

He squinted at her. "My son, Glen, can help you."

"Your son is a plumber?"

"Not licensed, but he works on all the farms."

"Perfect!"

"Give me your address."

"There isn't really an address, as far as I know," she said, describing in more specific terms how to arrive at Ho'omalumalu.

"I'll send him this weekend—8:00 a.m. Sunday."

He helped her load the truck up, and for the first time in a long time, she felt hopeful that this crazy idea could actually work.

22

SALTWATER BLUES

Wren

Back at Hoʻomalumalu, Wren set out to explore the outer reaches of the property. The map she'd been given showed landmarks, one of which was a stream bordering the east end. There was no road and no real trail, save for a possible pig or dog trail that led off through the bushes. She followed it as it wove through knee-high grass, then guava and kukui, eventually reaching a line of towering eucalyptus. She checked the map. This must be the south end. She followed that for a while, then came upon a macadamia orchard. This one was much larger than the one she'd passed through on the way in. The branches drooped from the weight of the fruit. They were *covered* in small green-and-brown balls.

Beneath the trees, the earth had been turned up by pigs, but Wren picked up enough to fill her small backpack, excited at the prospect of having another food source. So far, she'd found lilikoi, guava, strawberry guava, avocado, thimbleberry and mountain apple, but mac nuts were her favorite. The landscape here felt like Oʻahu, and yet with its own flavor. More humid, but also more breezy. Bigger trees, bigger sky. Here she felt as though she were at the end of the world, and she was still try-ing to determine if that was a good thing or a bad thing.

A little farther on, she came upon a dilapidated shack about fifteen feet square with a small covered deck off of one side. Only half the windowpanes remained, and vines crawled through the jagged holes. In front of the shed, she noticed patches of asphalt. They hopscotched down in both directions, intermingled with meadowy grass. Few tall trees grew here. A road, perhaps? And then it hit her.

A runway!

She tried to push open the door, but it wouldn't budge, so she went around to the side and peeked in the window. A bench, rusted remnants of an old icebox and a small table were all that remained. But on the back wall she noticed a long sign on black painted wood with yellow lettering still easy to make out. Air Hawai'i, it said.

Wren kept going past the shack, and eventually came upon the stream, which was lined by smooth, car-sized boulders. The narrow waterway ran swiftly. With no visible way to get in, she turned around, ready to get back to work at the barn. There was so much to do, it made her head swim. Then, up ahead, there was a flash of movement in the trees. An eerie feeling permeated the woods in this section. Dark water and a shad-owy forest. Maybe it was just the wind, blowing things around.

"Hello?" she said.

There was no response. Not that she had expected one, but the feeling that she wasn't alone followed her back to the barn. Maybe she ought to get a shotgun or some kind of protection. They had three-pronged diving spears at the hardware store, even one of those might be better than nothing.

She worked all of that afternoon and the whole next day on cleaning the mezzanine, building the composting toilet and patching cracks in the walls. Fortunately, whoever had built the barn had made it bombproof, with heavy old-growth beams and thick, solid wood walls that had withstood the test of time admirably. The planes hovered in the back of her awareness, but there was nothing she could do about them until the place was livable, in the most basic sense of the word.

Once the place was clean, Wren stood in the middle of the barn floor and circled around, looking up. Right away, her mind went to work envisioning where to hang lights, making the place her own. Less industrial. None of her electric fixtures would work, but she had lanterns and a few candles she'd made. Maybe there was something she could do with all those bottles. They were vintage and funky and best of all, free.

She grabbed her notebook and started sketching. With such an expansive open space, the barn deserved something big. Something rustic and raw and bold. Those rafters practically begged to have something hanging from them. Candles were easy to make in sawed-off wine bottles, all she'd have to do was find a supply of beeswax. She drew up several designs, all variations of circular candle chandeliers. But none fit. Brain fried, she shoved her notebook aside. She'd come back to it when she had more energy.

When four o'clock rolled around, and Wren was head to toe in sweat, sawdust and mosquito bites, she grabbed her bikini, mask and snorkel and towel and hopped in the truck. Even if she ended up not needing them, she'd learned to never go anywhere without. Just in case. She'd been on the Big Island for two whole days and hadn't even jumped in the ocean and was determined to change that.

Along such a rocky coastline, beaches didn't exist, but Chester had told her that the landing at Māhukona Beach Park, an old sugar port, was an easy place to get in the water. She pulled up into a parking space with a view of the ocean anyone from the mainland would pay big bucks for. Even though there was a wind line outside, the water in the small rocky cove was smooth as blue glass. She had the entire place to herself, along with a family of little brown ground birds, who were squawking away.

In the water, she explored the vivid coral fields at the mouth of the bay, up to where the bottom dropped away into a blue-black abyss, glad she'd brought her mask and snorkel. If only she'd had more time, but the fading daylight made her turn around.

She was leisurely kicking toward shore, when she heard someone yelling. Before she could lift her head out of the water, a large creature smashed into her, churning up the water and scratching at her side. *Oh, fuck—shark!* A jolt of electricity ran though her body, but when she held her hand out to push the animal away, she felt fur instead of sandpapery skin. Wren wiggled away and came up for air, keeping her hand out for protection. A large dog circled her, making a big splashing commotion with its paws.

A man's voice firmly said, "Come here, boy."

"Get your dog off me!"

A big kerplunk later, and the man was also in the water. Wren's mask slid down her face, pulling her hair in her eyes. She couldn't see a thing, but was able to swim away toward the rusted ladder on the concrete landing. Underwater, she pulled the mask off before surfacing. When she turned around to see her assailant, she realized the dog looked familiar. As did the owner. Gray pit mix, mustached man.

"Pono?" she said.

At the same time, he said, "Wren?"

Out of breath, she grabbed on to the ladder. "He scared the shit out of me."

"Didn't I just put you on a plane to Honolulu?" Pono asked.

He was treading water, while holding on to Scout, who looked like he still wanted to drown her with licks and paws.

"I said I might be back," she said.

"You sounded pretty doubtful."

"Things changed."

His eyes reflected sunlight and something more mysterious. Pono dunked underwater for a moment, then came up and shook his head like a wet dog. "Sorry about Scout. Are you gonna be okay?"

"I'll live, but I think he got me pretty good."

Wren climbed out, feeling the burn of his eyes on her butt, which was now eye level with his face. On the landing, she dabbed her side with the towel and checked the damage. Long red scratches covered her whole right side, and she may as well have been mauled by a lion. Pono appeared next to her a moment later, and Scout came up, softly nudging her leg.

She patted his big head. "Hey, buddy."

He wagged his whole body in a way that was so endearing, Wren found it impossible to be upset with him.

Pono frowned. "Damn, that looks like it hurts."

Right around then, her side caught fire, burning in the salty air. "I'll get some Neosporin on the way home."

"Home?"

"The barn."

One side of his mouth went up. "Don't tell me you're staying there."

"Okay, I won't. But I am."

"Spiders and all?"

"I'm in a tent for now."

"I'm impressed. In all honesty, I didn't think you had it in you."

"That's not fair," Wren shot back, instantly annoyed. "You don't even know me."

His gaze swept back down to her side, and on the way up, they passed over her stomach and her chest before meeting her eyes again. Remarkably, there was no awkwardness to it because Wren was pissed.

"I've spent my life on a ranch. I know how to read animals, and people aren't a whole lot different," he said, stepping away and picking up his own towel.

After he dried off his hair, it stood out like he'd stuck a finger in a light socket, making him look boyish. But there was nothing boyish about his body. Now, it was Wren's turn to take a tour of his shirtless male form. Smooth, taut skin over wiry muscles, every notch visible. His wet shorts hung below his tan line, exposing a porcelain-white line against his otherwise sun-kissed body.

"I guess you were wrong, then, because here I am. Living in a spider-infested barn with no running water, and a wild dog and two antique airplanes for company," she said.

His face broke into a wide grin and he actually laughed. "You've got me there. Speaking of the dog, any luck?"

"I just got here yesterday. She only came in after I went to sleep. I put out a bunch of ahi, and it was gone in the morning, so either she ate it or a rat did."

"She'll come around. What about the truck and the planes, any thoughts on those?"

Wren remembered how starstruck he'd been while in their presence, and the words came out before she even considered what she was saying. "No, but maybe you could help me. I don't have any money, but a trade? If you helped me fix them up, I could pay you when they sell."

He whistled. "Maybe, if I had nothing else in the world to do."

"Is that a no?"

He fingered his mustache. "The truck maybe, but two old airplanes? Do you have any idea how much work that would involve?"

"No, do you?"

"Not really, but I do know it would be more than I should take on."

"When else would you have such a unique opportunity? Admit it, you're tempted," she said.

Pono seemed more relaxed today, though still guarded. He stared out to sea for a while, chewing on his lip. "Check it out," he said.

Wren turned, just in time to see the sun slip beneath the clouds. The entire horizon had turned a psychedelic orange with a long gold seam running through it all. This wasn't how she'd envisioned watching the sunset, but it was beautiful nonetheless.

Then Pono surprised her by saying, "How about we come over tomorrow afternoon around four and look things over more thoroughly?"

We?

He was quick to add, "No promises."

Wren felt like cheering, but kept her cool. "I would love that. And by *we* do you mean Scout?"

A slight nod. "He goes wherever I go."

Her heart melted, just a little.

The next day, Wren spent the morning filling buckets and doing a final deep clean of the mezzanine. Every nook and cranny, every surface shone when she finished. Yesterday, she'd found a two-drawer metal file cabinet under the counter that was either stuck or locked shut. She banged on it with a hammer and tried to pry the lock with her Swiss Army knife but nothing budged.

At lunchtime, she drove back to town to search for a mattress or futon, the last and most important item on her shopping list. Money was precariously low, but she managed to find a Japanese futon for next to nothing in the secondhand store. Its red cherry-blossom print was faded and torn, but the foam had kept its form. It was a double, too, and would cover most of the bed platform. She could hang the mosquito net over the four posts on the bed and feel mostly insulated from the barn's interior wildlife.

On the way home, she did a little more exploring of side roads, and came upon a ramshackle old sugar plantation house, painted turquoise with rust-red trim. The yard stood out because it was a little unruly, but you could tell the place had once been something. Maybe the manager's house, or the company store. Today had been cloudy, with bursts of rain, and you could almost smell burnt cane. Chester had said there were once five mills in Kohala. Sad that they were all gone. With them, half the island's livelihood.

A sign hung above the gate that said, Malama Care Home. Wren almost passed on by, until another sign, nailed to the telephone pole out front, caught her eye.

Help Wanted.

Her foot pressed the brake pedal, almost of its own accord. Someone needed help, and she needed a job. Maybe she ought to investigate. From this vantage point, she could see another wing of the place, and a big yard with a covered trellis in the back. She contemplated going in and inquiring as to what kind of job was being offered, but thought better of it when she remembered she was in a short dress and combat boots and looked highly unprofessional. She'd come back Monday morning in more appropriate clothing.

Never mind the fact that she had zero experience working with old people. This could be a good fit for the new and improved Wren. Off on her own, thinking less and less about Joe and what he was doing at that very moment, and more about what it was she wanted to do with her messed-up but still precious life.

23

THE LONGEST NIGHT

Olivia

Livy spent the next thirty-odd minutes obsessively thinking about the sandwiches stashed in the back. They were so close and yet so far away. She debated strapping the stick in place or waking Felix, but in the end came to terms with the fact that she may not eat for the remainder of the night or possibly even the race. But Felix was bound to wake sometime, at least by morning. Whatever had been in that bottle sure did a number on him.

As the moon rose higher, the stars disappeared. The otherworldly beauty of the cloudscapes resembled waves in the sky. Livy felt small and insignificant, yet alive in a way that she only ever felt when out in nature. She picked out constellations and followed them again and again to keep herself awake.

Pa would be so proud, and she wished it was him in the back instead of Felix. Cyrus West was the man you wanted on your lifeboat or that deserted island you were marooned upon. He was the man who could fix anything, and who never wavered in his belief that every problem could be solved. Which was why it had been so hard to see him unravel. A part of him was still out on that sandy shoal and it broke her heart.

Over the next couple hours, Livy's mind bounced around like a float in the shore break, making forays back in time and then rushing to the future to a hundred and one scenarios of how this race might end. In one version, she saw green mountain peaks rising in the distance, and as they closed in on O'ahu, she swung *Malolo* in low over blue lagoons, landing before anyone else in the race. The crowd went wild when she and Felix emerged, burying them in flower lei.

In another, she made a forced water landing in the darkest hour of night, amid a sea of phosphorescent whitecaps. She managed to get the life raft, but Felix was unconscious, and she couldn't pull him out. As she climbed onto the flimsy rubber raft, she heard creaks and snaps as *Malolo* disappeared beneath the waves.

A moment later, those thoughts gave way and she was back in the cockpit, checking gauges and measuring the position of stars. Promising God that if she made it to Honolulu alive, she would never ask for another thing in her life. Livy began to talk to herself out loud. The mind fatigue was starting to take a toll, compounded by lack of food and sleep, and she realized she had to do something about it lest she end up like Felix. For some reason Mrs. Batha, her eighth-grade English teacher, came to mind. The old woman had lived in India for many years, and used to expound upon the importance of being mindful. *Notice every little thing around you. The song of the finches outside the window, the feeling of the warm breeze on your cheeks, the scent of freshly peeled orange.* Livy tried it. She noticed the drone of the engine and thunderous wind, the frigid air on her cheeks and the faint smell of clouds. It worked—for a while.

As the night wore on and her surroundings stayed the same, she began to feel a complete dissociation from her body. She had a distant awareness of her arms and legs, her rear end in the seat, but nothing more. She was merely a speck of an all-encompassing mind, and something bigger. Made up of light from distant suns, built of air and water and the spaces in between. She was all of life and she was untouchable. Hunger faded, cold vanished and only the night remained.

At half past four, Felix came out of his stupor. "Good God, where are we?" he yelled.

Livy was hugely relieved. "Somewhere over the Pacific."

"How long was I out for?"

"Most of the night."

He moaned. "Feels like someone smashed my skull open with a sledgehammer."

Livy had already planned on flying the rest of the way, so the news didn't worry her much. Felix could not be relied upon anymore, and she'd been hoping that if he woke, he wouldn't want to switch places again. But she also craved someone to talk to, another human voice to tether her mind into the airplane.

"Hand up a couple of sandwiches, would you, please?" she said.

A minute later, she took her first bite. Soggy bread. Crunchy pickles. Tangy tuna. It was the best sandwich she had ever tasted, and she gobbled it down in thirty seconds flat. Soon, Felix let out a belch that smelled like sea lion breath, then began to rummage around. She could hear things banging around in the back.

"What are you doing?" she called.

"Getting the life raft ready."

"We're in fine shape, Felix."

"I'll feel better if it's out."

"Have at it," she said, more to herself than anything.

There was no point in arguing. The raft was nothing to write home about, an inflatable rubber affair designed for one person that allegedly could hold two, its seaworthiness questionable. The thought of floating around in such a flimsy thing offered little consolation, but it did have a pump and repair kit, so there was that.

"What's our altitude?"

"Ten thousand."

"Bearing?"

"Two thirty-eight."

"Lucky thing you can fly this bird, my friend."

Luck hadn't had much to do with it. Livy thought back to the brutal hours of training, of bending over backward to prove herself worthy and of the countless near misses she'd endured. Some were her own doing, others were due to faulty equipment or inclement weather. Everything led to this moment, and she wasn't about to go down now because Felix hadn't known his own limitations. She was aboard *because* she knew how to fly a plane—expertly.

An hour or so later, after the longest night in history, the sky above the clouds slid from black to powder blue. Livy had passed to a place beyond exhaustion, but knowing that the sun was on its way up gave her a much-needed morale boost. They had traveled eighteen hundred miles, and still had another eight hundred to go. But with the night behind them, Hawai'i seemed just a jump, skip and a hop away.

The clouds that had followed them the whole way were still there, thick and relentless, and once again, would make daytime navigating difficult. But they sure were lovely in the predawn light. Soft and feathery fields of pink, shot through with sunbeams. When the sun finally rose above the clouds, Livy was thankful it was at their backs. Flying into a sunrise was difficult on the eyes, and hers were already strained and burning.

Felix made no mention of flying again and he was useless with navigation. His singular focus seemed to be on recording their flight information in the logbook, and he'd taken to calling out the questions and then answering some of them himself.

"Wind direction, unknown. Wind velocity, unknown. Visibility, unlimited. Ceiling, cloud tops approximately nine thousand. What's our airspeed?" he asked.

"Ninety-three miles per hour."

"Tachometer?"

"Sixteen hundred seventy-three rpms."

"Fuel?"

"Tank one is empty. Tank two half-full."

"Throttle down. We're lighter and we need the range."

She did as instructed. They had three tanks, so all was good in that department, as long as they were on course. The early fuel scare had almost faded from memory, but it was something to keep an eye on. There were so many things that needed to be monitored, and failure to notice any one of them could spell disaster. Livy felt a new detachment, after having flown in the face of disaster for so long now. Maybe that was just the way of humans, to adapt to just about anything.

At half past seven Hawai'i time—three hours behind Oakland—Felix shouted, "Two o'clock, a break in the clouds!"

Ahead and off to the right, it sure looked like a hole. Five minutes beyond that, the clouds grew intermittent enough that Livy caught glimpses of blue far below. Finally, the skin of the sea. She peered down, and there was space enough to see whitecaps on the surface before they hit more clouds. As they continued on, the clouds thinned and she decided to head down. Salt air would do her mind good.

"I'm taking us down," she called.

"About time."

Malolo seemed to enjoy the descent, or at least Livy imagined she did, engine relaxed, wings light. The first thing she noticed as they dropped through the spotty clouds was warmer air. She unbuttoned her jacket and peeled off her scarf. Where they were headed, she wouldn't be needing them. That red polka dot swimsuit she had sent on the steamer with her other

belongings called her name, waiting patiently on the shores of
Waikiki.

She pinched her cheek. *Focus, Olivia. You aren't there yet.* She
called out every thousand feet of descent, as Felix had done
yesterday when climbing. *Yesterday.* It was hard to fathom that
she had been in the air for almost a full day now. There would
be no more darkness between here and Hawai'i. What a mar-
velous thought!

As they drew nearer and nearer to the ocean, the clouds disappeared altogether, save for a small cumulus cluster here and
there. Seas were calm, and blue as a robin's egg. White trails of
foam were becoming more sparse, air dense and full of moisture.
Livy unbuttoned her shirt and fanned herself. The fair weather
should have made her happy, but instead caused her skin to itch.
It was August in the tropics, the time of hurricanes and tropi-
cal storms, and they were still a long way off from the islands.

For the first time, she caught sight of their shadow, leaping
from wave to wave like a playful dolphin. So much blue. Livy's
apprehension began to fade, won over by the sheer beauty and a
surge of gratitude. The most wonderful part of it all was seeing
the wind on the water——tailwind, you could tell from the stri-
ated patterns on the surface. The northeast trades were blowing
as they should be. Blowing them toward Hawai'i.

24

DEGREES OF ERROR

Olivia

The lack of any real opportunity for navigation over the past eighteen hours had Livy concerned. They could be hundreds of miles off course, and wouldn't even know it. If anything, they were likely south of the line she'd wanted to follow because the stars inevitably drew you along with them as they traveled through the skies. And during the long stretch of night, when her eyes had wanted to close and her mind wandered to those far-off places, she'd snapped back to find the compass needle off of the lubber line.

Wind drift was another factor. Wind is air in horizontal motion, created by differing atmospheric pressures, which in turn are due to changes in temperature. There are belts of high pressure circling the earth in each hemisphere. At lower latitudes air generally flows to the equator, and at higher latitudes, toward the poles. Add in the earth's rotation, and you end up with the concept of prevailing winds. Pa used to say, "Understand the prevailing winds, and you've won half the battle."

In her mind, Livy did her best to calculate degrees of error from flying for eighteen hours, averaging ninety-four miles per hour. Though the surface wind was prevailing northeast, aloft, it could have been different. In the end, she made her correction based on the most probable scenario—a strong tail-wind pushing her southwest—and veered north by six degrees. If she was correct, they'd see islands in less than half a day. If not, well, she didn't want to think about it.

No longer tied to the instruments for survival, Livy checked the charts again. She had them memorized, but wanted to be safe. Because aiming for the middle of the island chain gave one the greatest chance of making landfall, Maui was their target. Felix had told her about the two most southern islands in the archipelago, Maui and Hawai'i, and how they were home to towering volcanoes with summits high above the clouds, the perfect beacon for a bone-weary pilot.

To keep her mind alert, Livy sipped on cold coffee from the thermos as they flew along over the sparkling blue ocean. They were only five hundred feet up and had still seen no sign of life. No dolphins, rays, sharks or birds. Birds were a navigator's best friend, especially land-based birds. She'd been told to keep an eye out for terns and great frigate birds, who never flew far from the Hawaiian Islands. They were still too far out for those, but she'd been hoping for an albatross, a familiar friend in the skies.

Felix's state improved to the point where he began to seem like his optimistic old self, and eventually, the moment she had been waiting for came.

"We're going to have to switch places before we make our final approach," he told her.

It made perfect sense. With Livy piloting the plane, they very well could be disqualified. She was not listed as the pilot, nor had she been cleared by the race committee. Instructions had been clear. Yet having flown for more than half of the way, she craved that landing. To feel the wheels touch down on Hawaiian soil.

"Not yet," she said.

"When we sight land."

"Roger."

Time moved differently in sunlight, and for a while everything felt right in the world. The old Felix was back, *Malolo* continued to perform well, and Livy felt better about their course. Heath's letter was still burning a hole in her pocket and she pulled it out and set it in her lap. Felix would probably read it for her in a heartbeat, but it felt too personal to share. Or maybe it wasn't. Maybe it was just a good-luck, wish-you-well letter.

She was about to pick it up, and read one line at a time, when Felix yelled, "There's something up ahead. Sweet Jesus, a mountain!"

Livy's head shot up. In the distance, off to the left and at the edge of sight, a tall form loomed. She checked her watch, which she had rolled behind to be on Hawaiian time: 9:22 a.m. That put them just over twenty-three hours. It was too soon. Estimates had been at least twenty-six hours and probably closer to twenty-eight to reach the islands. Unless the tailwind aloft had been stronger than she'd thought.

"It can't be," she said.

"That's a mountain as sure as I'm Felix Harding."

Tall and craggy, it sure looked like one. But from everything she'd heard, the volcanoes in Hawai'i were broad and smooth.

"It's green. There's a valley," Felix said.

There were no other islands for at least a thousand miles. Livy rubbed her eyes, hoping to God it wasn't a mirage. When she opened them, the mountain remained.

"Do you see any others?" she asked, still hesitant to believe their good fortune.

"Negative."

A couple minutes on, the mountain began to change shape before their eyes, its outline blooming up into a giant cauliflower-shaped mass. A wall of blue gray filled in below. Livy's heart dropped to the floor of the plane just as she saw the flash. Now, that nagging feeling made sense. And the humid air.

Thunderstorm.

Felix must have seen it, too. "Oh, dear."

Fog and clouds were one thing, and despite the poor visibility the whole way, they'd been blessed with calm air. To make it this far, only to have a thunderstorm rise in their path, felt like a cruel hand being dealt. The storm blocked out everything in their path. Their best bet would be to fly above it, though Livy well knew that those cloud tops could be higher than ten thousand feet. Or even twenty.

"What's your plan, Captain?" Felix said.

"What do *you* think?"

Having lived in Hawai'i, he ought to know these storms better than she did.

He pointed up. "I don't like the looks of that black curtain."

"Do we have enough fuel to fly around it?" she asked, though she already knew the answer.

A sardonic laugh. "Not this time."

Moments later, the plane hit an air pocket and free-fell. A warning from the storm. Livy began another climb, as dread slid through her veins. Already in a near altered state of consciousness, she needed every wit about her if they were to make it out unscathed.

Or at all.

At nine thousand feet, all hopes of flying over the storm were dashed, and they entered the ominous gunmetal clouds. Immediately, *Malolo* began to buck, wings straining against the force. It had taken Livy some time to get used to flying in turbulent air. To be flying at all seemed to defy all laws of gravity, and lurching around thousands of feet up, at the whim of excitable air currents, gave one pause. Thunderstorms raised it to another level.

How had she not seen this coming?

Darkness closed in on them—an eerie twilight with bright flashes ripping through the clouds. Above the roar of the engine, thunder boomed, rattling her teeth. The tiny plane began to violently bounce around. Loose objects were tossed about, and Livy's light hit her in the side of the head. She fought to keep her eyes on the turn-and-bank needle. Any kind of stall or spin and they were toast.

The air is far less forgiving than the sea. She heard those words again, and was pulled back to the moment on her father's boat when Orlando had been swept over. This storm had the same ferocity, but instead of kicking up waves of water, it was kicking up air.

Olivia!

Beads of sweat broke out on her brow. In her mind, she saw herself running through the spitting rain, the boat listing badly to port. Orlando had somehow managed to hang on to the rail, and she grabbed hold of one of his hands. But he was a burly man, his weight too great for her to haul back in. She held on for dear life—almost swept over herself, and then his rough fingers slipped away. He was taken by an ocean who stole things with impunity.

Olivia!

The image disappeared as quickly as it came, and she realized it was Felix yelling her name. "Throttle down!" he cried.

Heath had taught her to slow down in severe turbulence because it reduced the load on the airframe and lowered the risk that the plane would come apart. It also helped the pilot keep control, rather than getting rag dolled around the cockpit.

Livy dropped their airspeed to eighty-five miles per hour, and climbed slowly again in hopes of finding a smoother flight level.

But a hundred feet up, hailstones blasted the airplane, sounding like a thousand rounds of buckshot. The air tasted metallic and the hair on her arms stood on end. Livy held on, hand melded to the stick, slowing the airspeed even more. In the back, Felix was yelling, but she couldn't hear a word he said.

She thought of his wife waiting anxiously for him. Who did she have waiting back at home? Only her parents. The thought dredged up the sad realization that maybe she had been too singularly focused on flying. A part of her knew that after losing Orlando, she'd closed her heart because it was easier that way. Life had progressed along relatively smoothly until she'd met Heath. He had started to open her heart back up, in ways she'd never anticipated, but when he walked away, she'd buttoned it up tighter than before and tucked it away where it couldn't be touched. Flying gave her a thrill, but it also protected her. She saw it clearly now, written in the clouds.

Chances were good the other planes would be facing this same storm, and the thought sent a shiver down her spine.

You are not going down in this storm, Olivia. Another man can't die on your watch.

With a new reserve of energy, her mind spread out beyond the confines of her body, the plane, the storm. All those years of watching birds in flight, and now she had become one. At least that's how it felt. Soaring through a thunderstorm on wings of wood and cloth. The storm was no more her enemy than the clear blue sky.

She lost all sense of time, and ten minutes or an hour later—she couldn't be sure—they were out the other side. Air calmed, skies opened. An ocean as wide as the world spread out before them. Livy felt lighter than the clouds. She opened the small window and held her hand in the slipstream. At the same moment, she felt a hand on her shoulder.

"You're a hero, my friend."

25

OLD SPICE, NEW LIFE

Wren

That afternoon, Wren changed her outfit four times before Pono showed up. Crazy behavior, she knew, but couldn't help herself. Once again, she found herself wanting to impress him. *You worry about being you and everything else will fall into place.* Gina always said that when Wren was lamenting about her mother or Joe or how she wasn't turning out like she *should*. Still, at this moment she wanted to appear confident and capable. And also casually feminine, despite feeling the opposite.

He arrived on time in a dark blue International Harvester, with Scout half out the window, smiling wide. The sun reflected in the shiny paint job, and every piece of metal gleamed as though freshly polished.

"Nice car," she said, when he got out.

Scout tore off behind the barn again.

"Thanks. It's taken a while to get her looking like this."

"You did all this?"

He took off his glasses and eyed the vehicle with tenderness. "Over a period of six years or so. My side gig."

It all made sense now. Wren had taken a leap, and now the

universe was handing her a gift. Pono was the perfect man for the job, even if he didn't know it yet.

"You're good at what you do," she said.

It wasn't a question.

That earned her a thin smile. "I try."

She led him inside.

"Any intel on the planes?" he asked.

"No, but I found signs of an old runway on the property, halfway between here and the big mac nut orchard."

"There's another orchard?"

She nodded. "A huge one with giant old trees. I brought some back if you like raw mac nuts."

"Love 'em. I can ask my gramps about the runway when I ask about the planes. Did you ask around in town?"

"No. Chester Miyashiro is the only guy I really spoke with."

"If it happened in Kohala, Chester would know about it."

"I got that feeling. Which was why I didn't ask," she said.

"You have something to hide?"

"No, but this is all new to me. I'm doing things on my own time. Still processing, you know?"

He nodded. "Yeah."

Wren sensed a sadness just beneath his skin. Trouble was like that, she'd noticed. It clung to you and weighed you down and gave off its own scent. As much as you wanted to kick it, there was only one true remedy: time.

He set down his beefy toolkit on the ground and opened the hood of the Ford. "This old lady is probably a 1940. Original tires, from the look of it. Have a look inside and tell me what the odometer reads."

"They had odometers in 1940?"

"You'd be surprised. Vintage cars had all the bells and whistles."

"What about AC, when did that become a thing?" she asked.

"Mid-fifties, I think?"

"I'm behind the times by about thirty years, then."

He leaned against the grille, and she noticed his Levi's were legitimately ripped and faded and streaked in grease. "On this island, you're going to want AC."

"Getting AC in my truck is pretty low on the list. Have you looked around here lately?" she said before opening the door and sticking her head in to check the odometer. "Eight thousand eleven miles."

He stopped tinkering. "What?"

"That's what it says."

Before she knew it, he had squeezed in next to her to see for himself. "Unbelievable. And you say you know nothing about your aunt or why any of this is here?"

He didn't move to get out.

"All I know is that there were three sisters who inherited the land from their father. One was my grandma who died after I was born, and then Aunt Portia left it to me. I don't know how their father, my great-grandpa, ended up with it."

She told him about Portia's note.

"Do you know their maiden name?"

"Kahawai."

"Hmm. Don't know it."

Pono's shoulder was warm and hard, and he smelled like Old Spice, which was strange because it was the one smell she associated with her father. Suddenly, she was sitting on her daddy's lap, hands on the steering wheel, him holding on to her waist with big, strong hands. A feeling of joy surrounded them. This was a new memory and she wanted to cling to it, but it slipped away as quickly as it came.

"Are you free tomorrow? I can take you to meet my gramps and maybe you'll get some answers," he said.

"After Chester's son comes to look at the pipes."

"I'll set it up."

He went back under the hood and nosed around for a while,

then slid under the truck. He made a few muffled comments to himself, while Wren sat on a wobbly stool and watched his scuffed boots. When he finally came up, he looked excited.

"Far as I can tell, this baby wouldn't be too hard to fix up. She was hardly even driven."

"Why are cars and planes and boats always *she*?" Wren asked.

"In the old days, having a woman on a boat was said to be bad luck, and would, you know, anger the sea gods. So to appease the women left back home for years on end, sailors named their boats after them," he told her.

A small laugh escaped. "You can't be serious."

"Just a theory."

"So, will you help?"

He bit his lip and shrugged. "I guess I could."

Wren felt a smile spreading through her, warm like honey. She wanted to walk over and throw her arms around him, but didn't want to scare him off. Instead, she made prayer hands and bowed.

"You have no idea how much this means," she said.

To have a coconspirator in on this made her feel so much less alone.

Pono wiped a smudge of grease from his forehead with his shirt. "Now, let's look at those planes again."

They pulled off the tarps and folded them up. A layer of mildew coated the insides, and you could smell it coming off the planes, too. Dark splotches of black spread over both exteriors.

"Nature's paint job," she said.

"Covering them may not have been the best thing in this climate."

They examined both planes more thoroughly this time, Pono pressing down on the wooden propeller, which was frozen in place. Wren climbed inside the smaller one, amazed at the rudimentary but well-crafted frame.

"They might appear simple, but the engines are impressive, and the aerodynamics are more sophisticated than you'd think," he said.

"Do you think these are the same era as the truck?" Wren asked.

"Older. Probably twenties."

"How do you know?"

"Because they aren't made out of metal."

"My mom thinks Portia's sister was married to a pilot. Maybe he was in the war," Wren said.

"No way these are WWII planes."

"But maybe they were his."

"No names?"

She hopped out and walked over to where he stood. "It sounds like you have an intact family, and you work for your dad and you're close with your grandpa, but my family isn't like that. It was always just me and my mom—who I called Cindy not Mom—and our Siamese cat, Olivia Newton John."

He smirked, and she saw his dimple deepen. She gave him the rundown, including more information than he probably wanted to know. If he was going to help her, he may as well know as much as she did. Plus, once she started, the words just poured out.

"And you have no idea where your dad is now?" he asked.

"Zero." Wren shook her head. "My mom is a grudge holder extraordinaire."

They were standing face-to-face now on either side of the engine. She was surprised what a good listener he was. In her experience, good-looking men were usually better talkers than listeners.

"Sometimes grudges are justified," he finally said. "Have you ever tried to find him?"

"I used to look for him everywhere I went, once I discovered a hidden box of photos of him. But no, I haven't. I guess it made me mad that he never fought for me or never came looking, and Cindy said he moved to the mainland," she said.

"You only know one side of the story. Keep that in mind."

She noticed for the first time that his nose was slightly crooked, and that his lashes were so long they nearly touched his cheek when he blinked. He had such an interesting face, Wren wanted to study every detail, but that would be weird and would probably make him uncomfortable. She needed him here, and not as a love interest. Love interests were on the back burner for the foreseeable future. Her heart couldn't take another sucker punch.

"Maybe I'll find out more when I get that file cabinet open," she said, turning toward the front door when she caught movement out of the side of her eye.

Scout came trotting in, and came straight to Wren, rubbing his dirty, leaf-covered side against her leg and almost pushing her over.

"Nice to see you, too," she said, laughing.

Pono nodded toward the door. There was the stray, sitting just outside, watching them. "Just ignore her. Keep doing what we're doing."

"What are we doing?"

"You were about to show me that file cabinet."

"Was I?"

He looked her in the eye and said in all seriousness, "May as well use me while I'm here."

Oh. My. Gosh.

He followed her up the creaky steps. Wren felt proud about what she'd done in such a short time in the mezzanine, draping the mosquito net over the four posts of the bed, covering the couch with a clean white throw, laying down a lauhala mat she'd found at the secondhand store and even going so far as hanging one of her newest light fixtures from a beam. No light in it yet, but she could dream. Tonight she'd actually try to sleep up there.

The minute Pono saw it, he stopped. "Whoa. That light is cool. Was that here already?"

Wren had fashioned it out of an old bench top, drilling holes and hanging glass spheres of light on cords below. The whole thing hung from four wrought iron chains wrapped around the beam. Wren had been extremely pleased with the finished product, but no one had seen it yet.

"No, this is mine," she said.

"Somehow it fits with the whole vibe."

"Thanks. I was going to try and sell it on O'ahu, but I finished it a couple days before I got the call from Bob. And now, I don't know if I even have the heart to sell it. To tell the truth, I've been a bit discouraged."

He looked surprised. "You made this?"

"Yeah. I make lights. If we were in France, you could call me a chandelier."

"You mean a chandelier maker?"

Wren shook her head. "A chandelier is actually someone who makes candles. Or lights. I make both, so there you have it. Although now, I'm not sure about materials. I partnered up with a glass blower in Chinatown, but I doubt there are any here in Kohala."

"I know there's one at Volcano. But that's far."

"How far?"

"Close to three hours."

Then she thought of the bottles downstairs. "I might be able to make do. Remind me to show you the old bottles downstairs."

"I thought the bottles were full of old honey."

"Different bottles. Speaking of honey…" She nodded to the counter where the jar of ancient honey sat, still unopened. "You want to take home a few jars?"

"What, are you trying to poison me?"

When he laughed, his nose scrunched up, almost childlike.

"God's honest truth, it's supposed to last for thousands of years," she said.

"Have you tried it yet?" he asked.

She picked up the jar and turned it upside down. The honey seemed to have crystalized, hard as stone, though maybe that would change if she set it out in the sun or heated it. "Not yet."

"Report back when you do, and then we'll talk," he said.

She grinned. "Deal."

They turned their attention back to the file cabinet. Pono was unable to get the drawers open at first, and had to go back down and get a screwdriver and a hammer. Eventually, with enough prying and hammering, it sprung open. Inside sat a wooden box.

Pono glanced up at her. "You want to do the honors?"

Wren stared down at the box. Musty and full of secrets about to be discovered. The past catching up to the present.

26

MILE MARKER 12

Wren

Anticipation floated in the air as a gust of wind tickled the back of Wren's neck. In just a couple short days, she had gone from mild curiosity to being fully invested in uncovering the barn's history. She also could feel between the walls a sense of romance, a nostalgia for things and people past. And also the presence of heartbreak. Why else would the place have been left alone to decay for all these years?

She opened the box, with Pono looking on. In it was a pair of goggles, a silver dollar, a compass contraption—the kind you saw on ships in old movies, an ancient set of binoculars and a fleece-lined leather flight cap. Beneath those lay a yellowed envelope. She held the coin up in the green filtered light pouring in through the window.

"It's from 1927," she said.

"That sounds about right."

"Did they even have airplanes in Hawai'i back then?"

History had been her worst subject.

Pono shrugged. "I have a feeling we're about to find out."

They laid out the box's contents on the counter. Priceless

artifacts from another lifetime, each piece with its own story. These must have been important to someone. Someone in her family.

She picked up the envelope, and from the weight of it, guessed it contained photos. "Let's go outside where there's more light."

Sunset fast approached, sending long shadows across the clearing in front of the barn. Both dogs were lying in the grass a little way off, catching the last warmth of day. They sat up and watched but stayed where they were. Wren was pleased the stray didn't run off this time.

She opened the envelope carefully. On top was a grainy photo of a tallish man standing in front of a bright red plane with the word Malolo painted on the side.

"Our plane!" she said.

The man was the classic picture of an early aviator. Cap and goggles, leather boots, squinting into the sun with an ear-to-ear smile. He was haole, and she didn't recognize him.

"Did your grandma and great-aunt have a brother?" Pono asked.

"Not that I know of. This has to be the pilot my mother mentioned. The other sister's husband."

It was kind of embarrassing that she didn't know the third sister's name, but whatever, Pono knew her story now. It wasn't her fault.

Behind the plane, in the distance, stood a line of people in dark-colored coats. Some wore hats.

"That doesn't look like Hawai'i, does it?" Wren said.

"Not a bit."

Pono stood an inch or two away, arm to arm. She tried to flip to the next photo, but they were stuck together. He reached out and held the lower ones in place, while she pried them apart ever so slowly. The next few were of the man with a woman, also dressed in flight garb. She was small, with wavy hair and a sunny smile. Even with the poor quality of the photo, you could see a glint in her eye.

"Your great-aunt?" Pono asked.

"She doesn't look anything like Aunt Portia. Remember, they were half Hawaiian and this woman looks white as milk."

"I know plenty fair-skinned Hawaiians."

"Like me?"

"I didn't say that, you did. And anyway, it's what's inside that counts," he said, matter-of-factly.

Aside from Wren's nose, and her root-deep love for Hawai'i, you'd never know she had a drop of Hawaiian blood. She sometimes wished it was otherwise, but why waste time worrying about something you had no control over?

She examined the photo more closely. "I still don't think it's her."

She slipped this one to the back. Next was a similar photo, but the man and woman were both up to their chins in lei, their faces a skewed, haggard version of the previous shot. *Malolo* was in the background. In the next, with them stood a man in a tall hat with a solemn expression on his face. No smile. Another shot had four of them, two other men buried in lei. Then finally, the same man with a different woman. Darker skin and lighter eyes. Her head was tilted in, leaning on his shoulder, with a smile bright enough to light the night sky.

"That's got to be her. She looks like you," Pono almost yelled in her ear.

Wren had the same thought. Something in the shape of the eyes, and the high smile that showed a little bit of gum.

"Gotta be. But what do you think all these lei are for? It looks like some kind of event," she said, more to herself than anything.

"Maybe an air show. Or a race."

She leaned in. On the bottom of the last photo, in faded pen, someone had written *1927*. Same year as the silver dollar. Wren wanted more. It felt like she'd just started reading a book, but someone had torn out the rest of the pages. They went back inside and checked the drawers again to see if they'd missed anything, but they hadn't.

"Those planes, or at least *Malolo*, may be more valuable than we think. Are you in?" she asked, though she suspected she already knew the answer.

He looked up at the high windows, having some kind of internal exchange, then looked at her with a smile in his eyes. "I'm in."

After Pono and Scout left, Wren filled a bowl with kibble and fish, and left it on the middle step. That way the dog would be forced to come partway up, but could still have her privacy to eat in peace. Candlelight turned the green glass a burnished gold, and for all of its open space, the mezzanine actually felt cozy.

Wren lay on the newly constructed platform bed and futon, and read by flashlight under the mosquito net. She was halfway through *Lonesome Dove*, and kept picturing Gus McRae as an older version of Pono. She couldn't help it. Even though Pono claimed to just keep all the machines on the ranch running, he was probably a badass paniolo in his own right. The bow in his legs gave him away.

When her eyes finally rebelled, and she found herself spending more time thinking about Pono in the saddle than Gus and Call, she closed the book and turned off the flashlight. A shadowy darkness filled the barn, but light from the almost full moon bounced across the walls. She listened to the rush of wind through the trees, and the loud chirp of crickets rubbing their legs together in a nighttime symphony. She had never felt so alone, yet strangely, she didn't feel so lonely.

Not until Wren was almost in dreamland did she hear the steps creak. Immediately, she was wide-awake, listening. A few moments later, the sound of slurping and crunching broke the quiet. The dog inhaled the food in about three seconds flat, then there was silence again.

Come on.

Wren held her breath, hoping to hear the dog coming up the steps instead of retreating. She heard no movement for almost a minute, and then a light tap, and another. Slowly creeping closer.

We can both live here.

When the dog reached the top, Wren sensed eyes on her, watching. Light sniffing. More silence, and then the sound of nails over towel, scratching on wood. Pawing, nesting, making her bed her own. Then, a big, long exhale.

"Good night," she whispered.

The dog had already begun to snore.

In the morning, the dog was gone before Wren woke, and she lay in bed trying to come up with a suitable name so she didn't have to keep calling her *the dog*. Though she didn't know her well, she admired the animal's reliable nature, and how she could always count on her to come back to the barn at night— even if she wanted nothing to do with Wren. The Hawaiian word *pa'a* came to mind. As in Hokupa'a, aka the North Star.

Wren said the name out loud. "Pa'a."

Pah-ah.

It rolled off the tongue nicely, and anyway, Wren could use a guiding star in her life right now. Everything felt so off the cuff, so random and unplanned. So far she'd been lucky at how things had fallen into place, but she knew how quickly life could unravel.

So, Pa'a it is.

Glen showed up right on time and after a quick check of the water tower and the plumbing fixtures told her that her problem was most likely due to a crack in the main pipe coming off the tank. Fix that, problem solved.

"I can replace it with PVC for now, if you like?" he said. "Copper gonna cost you plenty."

Less than two hours later, the barn had running water. The tank was nearly full, and they let the faucet and the hose flow for a while to clear out decades of disuse. A centipede shot out of the hose and flipped around on the ground before scurrying away. Wren jumped back and screamed.

Glen laughed. "Cane worms. No boddah them, they no boddah you."

"Cane worms?"

"Dats what Grampa when call um. When da cane burned, da centipedes come out of da woodwork. Make house wit you."

She felt faint at the thought.

"Did your grampa work on the sugar plantation?"

"My whole family did."

"Is he still alive?"

"Nah, he stay gone. Both him and my tutu. Hard life, you know?"

She didn't really, but wished she did. Hawai'i was what it was because of people like his grandparents. In the end, Wren paid him in mac nuts because he wouldn't take anything else.

"In Kohala, we take care of our own."

When he said that, Wren stood up a little straighter. At public school, she never quite fit in. Not with the rich haole from Kahala, not the *mokes* and *titas* who tolerated her—but just barely, and not the Japanese in their low-rider Honda caravans. It often felt like her Swiss, Norwegian, Scottish, Korean and Hawaiian blood could never quite make up its mind. Who was the real Wren Summers?

Along Kohala Mountain Road, driving through the corridor of ironwood, Wren caught glimpses of rolling green hills and brown dots of cattle, a few horses here and there and the infrequent house on the *mauka* side of the road. She slowed as instructed at mile marker twelve, then turned left at a gap in the trees. Two lava rock posts held a sturdy wooden gate decorated with lacy white-green lichen. Pipi Ranch.

The gate was open, and she followed a paved road through tall grass. Green every which way you looked. Even the clouds seemed green. Wren breathed it in, along with the dusting of fog that had crept down the mountain. As instructed, she veered right at a fork and drove until she came to a red-and-white cabin tucked in a grove of ʻōhiʻa trees. Two horses grazing out front swished their tails, glanced up at her, then put their noses back to the grass.

A few minutes early, she walked up the steps onto the lānai. "Hello?"

No answer. She turned to admire the sweeping views of the ocean and of Hualālai rising in the distance. The air felt icy, and she wondered if it had ever snowed on the Kohala Mountains. It sure felt like it could. She pulled her sweater in close, happy to be in jeans, but wishing they weren't ripped up the whole front.

"Terrible, isn't it?" a voice off to the side yard said.

Wren jumped, slightly. Not one but two old guys came around the house, walking up the steps in boots and real cowboy hats.

"I was just thinking that if I lived here, I'd never want to leave. I'm Wren…" She wasn't sure how to introduce herself. "Pono's friend."

"I know who you are. The pretty girl with the truck and the airplanes," the haole one said with a wink. "I'm Dodge Willard and this old cowboy is Blue. Blue Pohaku, but I just call him Boss."

Blue took off his hat and nodded, eyes bluer than the sky. "Aloha." He seemed older than Dodge, dark skin carved by the elements.

There were four wooden chairs with red palaka cushions, and Dodge motioned for her to sit. "Make yourself comfortable. I'll get us some bottles."

The men had seemingly come from out in the pasture, and she wondered what they had been doing. "So, you're in charge of the ranch?" she asked Blue.

He wiped his face with a worn bandanna. "Used to be. Too old now, but I make myself useful one way or another. Today we was walking the fence lines."

"How many acres is the ranch?"

"Two thousand, give or take."

"That'll keep you young," she said.

He nodded. "Even if I wanted to, I could never leave this mountain. She's my mother, wife and granddaughter all in one."

"I can see why. The land here is so raw, so beautiful, it's humbling."

She heard a phone ring, then Dodge rejoined them on the porch a moment later, holding three Budweiser bottles and passing them out like Popsicles.

"Boy gonna be late. *Cheers*," he said, clinking his bottle against hers and Blue's. "In the meantime, tell us what you need. Pono told me some, but I want to hear it straight from the horse's mouth."

Horse came out *hoss*, his words tinged with the pidgin of old-timers.

Wren gave an abbreviated version of how she ended up here, then added, "I want to know about the planes, but also about my roots. If my great-grandfather was from here, or my grandma, I figure someone would have known them."

Dodge was handsome in a rugged, silver-haired way, with sun-baked skin and olive-colored eyes that had seen a thing or two in their years. "I didn't know them, but Blue remembers the family," he said, in a gravelly voice.

"Kahawai." Blue's hand shook as he set the beer on the armrest.

Wren's whole body went still, waiting for his words to drop.

"I remember the three girls from church, little-kid time, when my aunty would take me. Good-looking wahine, every single one. Their mother Sassy—that was the name she went by—dressed them like triplets, head to toe, fancy kine'. I used to wonder how they stayed so clean. All us other kids was dyed red from the dirt."

He took a swig, then continued. "Sassy's father worked for the plantation. Scottish, engineer or something like that. She was known small kine' *pupule*—little bit off. Next thing you knew, they was outta there. Some *pilikia*—trouble—went down and she left for O'ahu with the three girls in tow."

Wren had to ask. "What kind of *pilikia*?"

"Kohala was rough those days, a hard life. She acted all high on her horse, but the husband wasn't that way. Nice man, hard-workin' Hawaiian, a bit older than her. Word on the street, Sassy was messin' around with the plantation manager's son. His wife found out and showed up at the Kahawai house. Sassy almost shot the lady's foot off with a hunting rifle."

So Wren had a great-grandmother named Sassy who was not a nice woman. She was at a loss for words, glad Pono wasn't here to hear this.

Blue covered her hand with his age-spotted, leathery palm. "Couple years later, the girls came back, their mother dead. By then I was living Waimea side with Uncle and working Parker Ranch, but I saw them when I went home. The youngest, she was the prettiest, and now she was red like the rest of the kids. Wild hair, free spirit, *keiki o ka 'aina*. The older one, she good, too. She helped her father keep house, I think. But the middle one, she little bit *pupule* like the mother."

Portia. Wren was sure she was the middle one.

"Do you remember how the mother died?" she asked.

He squeezed her hand when the words came out. "Hung herself from a tree. Honolulu side."

A knife twisted in her heart. So much to digest and so many more questions bubbling up. Ask now, process later.

"Do you remember their names?"

"Lihau, the youngest. Oldest Iwa, I think? I don't remember the middle one. Father was Mr. Kahawai to me, but his first name was Clyde. He was a surveyor for the territory."

Lihau. Iwa. Clyde. Lihau was her grandmother. How messed up was it that until this day, she'd never even known her grandmother's first name? Or her great-grandfather's. Chunks of her history were locking into place, causing a strange fullness below her navel—her root chakra in yoga speak.

"Do you know anything else about him or the land I was left?" she asked.

"I know he loved his daughters. He bought a big piece of land, you know the surveyors, they always got the best land. Sad thing, he *make*—died—from the plague. Dang rats. The daughters moved back to O'ahu, I think they got the city life bug when they were there before."

"Do you know what they did on O'ahu?" Wren asked. "Especially Lihau, she was my grandmother. All my mom ever said, was she was the youngest."

"Hula. Bunch a girls from here packed up and went to work at the Royal Hawaiian Hotel. Wasn't long before they all landed husbands. Haole boys, every single one. A musician, I think hers was."

At the sound of thundering hooves, Wren turned to see a splotchy black-and-white horse galloping their way across the field. A big dog tromped behind.

"Boy. About time," Dodge said.

Wren sipped the ice-cold beer, enjoying the fizz of the cool liquid sliding down her throat as she watched Pono and the tall horse approach. He was a natural in the saddle—of course he would be, and he came right to the deck and swung off in one swift and graceful move. Wren smoothed down her bangs, which had been disobeying all afternoon.

"Sorry I'm late. The backhoe needed some love," he said, looking directly at her.

Scout came over and tried to climb into her lap. She laughed, pushing him away.

"No worries, I'm in good hands," she said, nodding to the two men beside her.

Pono went inside and got himself a beer, then sat in the empty chair at the end, next to Wren. He pulled it forward and a little closer, knee bumping hers slightly. She didn't pull away. Neither did he.

"I would never intentionally leave a woman with these two, unsupervised," Pono said, with a grin. "You sure they're behaving?"

"Perfect gentlemen."

Blue chuckled.

"Someone's gotta do it, boy," Dodge said. "Blue was just filling her in on her family."

Wren was having a hard time getting the image of Sassy shooting at the other woman's feet out of her mind. That she shared the same blood as this whole branch of people, whose names were now on her tongue, felt surreal.

"I knew if Gramps didn't know, Blue probably would," Pono said.

"You guys have no idea how much this means to me. It's everything," she said, eyes misting up.

"I don't know anything about your father, but minus Sassy, the Kahawais were good people," Blue said.

The words settled in on her shoulders like a warm shawl.

"Do you know anything about those planes and why they might be there?" she asked.

"I was working 'Ulupalakua on Maui, but I remember the husband of Iwa was one pilot, flying people around, sightseeing. They would buzz us sometimes, spook the horses. I gave him a piece of my mind when I saw him Waimea side one day."

"You knew him?"

"Just that one time. Told him my mind. He listened, apologized." His loose lower lip jutted out and he looked up at the clouds, as though recalling. "There was a race, he was in it, if I remember correct."

"What kind of race?" Pono asked.

"Airplane. Mainland, Honolulu. Big news, choke people."

Wren had never heard of any airplane race to Hawai'i, but that was a long time ago. Not the kind of thing they learned in history class. Textbook, or it never happened.

"Any idea why the barn and the planes seem to have been abandoned?" she asked.

"The war, is my guess. Plenty people left, never came back."

They sat with that thought as the fog moved in and whitewashed everything around them. Trees disappeared and the horses became large, gauzy shapes. The air quieted, as if remembering all those souls. On Cindy's side of the family, Wren's grandparents were living near Punchbowl during the attack on Pearl Harbor. They still talked about it as though it had happened yesterday. A bomb had taken out the house down the street, a baby killed. No one in the islands was unaffected.

"I'll do more digging, but you've given me a great start. Thank you, Mr. Pohaku."

They finished their beers, and Wren excused herself to use the bathroom. On her way, she passed a wall of photos. Grainy black-and-whites of cowboys and cattle. Of Mauna Kea, Mauna

Loa *and* Hualālai topped in snow. A large frame of a much younger Dodge and a pretty brunette standing in the ocean holding a fat baby. An old wedding shot of them shoving cake in each other's mouths, edges yellowing. But the one that stopped her in her tracks was not of Dodge, but of Pono. This one, also a wedding picture. The woman by his side looked part Hawaiian, with round eyes and a smile big enough for the both of them. Wren stared quietly. Pono looked younger but not young. The picture couldn't have been more than five years old, so where was this woman?

Not wanting to appear *nīele,* she forced herself to keep walking. But while she peed, she couldn't get the picture out of her mind. You could feel the love between them sure as the grass here was green. Pono wore no ring, so that left only two possibilities.

Back on the lānai, Dodge filled Wren in on the ranch history. It was started in 1928 on eleven thousand acres by his father and a buddy from Maui. Cold in the winter and dry in the summers, they had weathered all that the island could throw at them, and still managed to stay afloat. He was a colorful storyteller, and Wren enjoyed getting lost in someone else's life for a time. She appreciated their sense of family, envying Pono his roots.

"You gonna show this wahine around, or do I have to?" he said to Pono when done.

The surrounding fog had thickened into rain, pitter-pattering on the roof like falling pins.

"I'm sure he's busy, and I'm not dressed for this weather, anyway," Wren said, hoping to save him the trouble.

"We got gear," Dodge said.

Pono shot him a look. "Next time."

Wren had half hoped he'd say yes, and maybe they could sit in his house, wherever it was, and sip hot chocolate by the fireplace. Maybe she could learn a thing or two about him. Maybe something more would happen.

"I would love that," she said, with her most dazzling smile. The look he gave her made her skin tingle.

27

EASY THERE

Olivia

Smith and Bronte had made it to Moloka'i twenty-five hours and two minutes after leaving Oakland. Now, Livy and Felix had been in the air for twenty-six hours with no land in sight. The weather was balmy, with gentle rolling swells below. Sun-filled minutes ticked away. On any other day, Livy would have skimmed the water and looked for dolphins or other sea creatures, but this was no ordinary day. They had reached the critical point in the trip, where intercepting the islands would either happen or it wouldn't, and they'd end up on land or in the water when the tanks ran dry.

"How are we on fuel?" Felix asked for the eight hundredth time.

After the thunderstorm, they'd smelled gas fumes again, but Felix couldn't find a leak. He'd also become convinced that they'd passed Hawai'i and were headed for a watery grave.

"We should be okay for another couple hours, maybe less."

The needle on the fuel gauge moved quite a bit depending on if they were climbing or descending, and she didn't entirely trust it.

"Should we turn around, swing a wide loop, fly a grid?" he suggested.

"That would burn too much."

"Better to die trying."

His uncertainty chipped away at her nerves, which were already on shaky ground. Next time she did something like this, some hairbrained foolish misadventure, she wanted someone more steadfast as a partner. Someone like Heath. Cool under pressure was the name of his game. His letter had disappeared in the thunderstorm, and now she'd have to wait to read it.

Behind her, Felix had out the binoculars and was scanning for islands. They were cruising along at seventy-five hundred feet, allowing them to see farther than they would at a lower altitude. As with the green mountain that turned out to be a storm, they had a few more false alarms. It amazed Livy to no end how the mind could play tricks on you to such a degree of sureness.

"Volcano!" Felix yelled. "Ten o'clock." Livy wasn't counting her chickens, but he handed her the glasses and she took a look. "See for yourself," he said.

In the distance, above a layer of clouds, she saw a dark pyramid of earth and rock. She blinked. It was still there. Blinked again. Still there, much higher than their flight level, majestic and real as the ocean below. It couldn't be. And yet it was.

Hawai'i.

"Mauna Kea!" Felix cried. "I'd recognize that peak anywhere."

Beyond that was another summit, nearly as tall, but broader. Livy's mind screamed, *You've done the impossible!* They had reached the Big Island. Against all odds, they had made it. Worn-out, delirious and dying to crawl onto any piece of solid ground and pass out. Even if they ran out of gas now, they'd at least have a fighting chance.

Livy banked to the west and soon they caught sight of Haleakalā on Maui, not as tall but just as striking. She dropped down for a closer look. Green and lush valleys. Waterfalls. Black sand beaches lined with white foam. When they reached Molokaʻi, they saw their first birds—what must have been small black terns riding the thermals along the dizzying cliffs.

A large peninsula with coconut trees and a tall white church jutted out, and Felix called up, "The leper colony. Those unlucky bastards are banished here when afflicted. Breaks the heart."

Hundreds of people streamed out of long wooden houses onto a large grassy areas, pointing up and waving. She dipped a wing, grateful for the fortune of her own good health. Seeing them so full of life and yet sequestered away like that broke something loose inside of her. Already emotional, she began to weep.

By the time they reached the tip of Molokaʻi, and she could breathe again, Felix tapped her shoulder. "Time to switch places."

It was as though her body developed a sudden inertia, legs heavy, rear end lodged in the seat, arms turned to lead. How could she come this far, only to climb in the back seat? She needed to see this through to the end. In the pilot seat.

"Come on there, we don't want to be disqualified," he said.

Who cared about getting disqualified? Not Livy, for one. But then she thought of her father, and the money. The whole reason she'd embarked on this journey in the first place. Those early days seemed so distant now, even though she'd only left San Diego a little over two weeks ago. She'd been another person, starry-eyed and naive.

Felix had slid up next to her and was ready to take the stick. The sight of him close up shocked her. He'd aged ten years overnight. Eyes puffy, hair wild, a bruise on his left cheekbone and still wearing his life jacket. She probably looked as bad or worse.

"Easy there," he said, as Livy disconnected herself from the seat.

Letting go felt like tearing off an arm or a leg. *Malolo* had become an extension of herself, a dear friend that she'd been to hell and back with. In the back, stuff was strewn everywhere, the life raft ready at hand.

They came to shore at Diamond Head and flew just off the long white ribbon of Waikiki Beach. The coconut trees, turquoise water and a sprawling pink hotel were just as Livy had imagined.

"The Royal Hawaiian," Felix said, nodding to the right.

He'd brought them in low, two hundred feet. For all of its allure, the beach was remarkably empty. She'd expected more people. There were a couple canoes in the water, and long wooden surfboards riding the waves, but few inhabitants. The only indication that anyone knew they were coming was a large banner in front of the hotel that read Welcome, Dole Birds.

Livy couldn't believe they would soon be landing on Hawaiian soil and swimming in these same turquoise waters. Pretty soon she was laughing and crying at the same time. Delirious, but overcome with emotion. *It felt so damn good to be here!* They flew over a large inlet called Pearl Harbor, lined with an intricate coral reef that opened into several giant back bays. Felix then guided them over the land, between two razorback mountain ranges across a high plateau, wholly competent again now that there was land in sight.

"Here they come," Felix said.

Two military pursuit planes approached from the opposite direction, flying in formation. Before they reached *Malolo*, the Boeing PW-9s split up and banked away, looping around until they were flying alongside them back toward Wheeler Airfield. Livy glanced over and the pilot closest held up one finger and then two, a wide smile on his face.

Second place.

Livy saluted him, then blew a kiss.

"What is it?" Felix yelled.

"We're second!"

They'd go down in the record books. Changing the face of flying. Changing the face of the world.

"No!"

"Yes!"

Felix hooted and pumped a fist in the air. Both of them had long ago given up any pretense of winning the race, they'd just wanted to survive.

Below, moss green fields—pineapple, according to Felix—cut through with reddish dirt roads, spread out in all directions. They bumped along through a rough patch of air, and a long strip came into view. When they drew near, Livy realized why there had been so few people on the beach at Waikiki, and such empty roads along the way. The whole population of O'ahu was at Wheeler, waiting for them. There must have been tens of thousands of people, more than Livy had ever seen in one place.

Felix swung around toward the mountains to the west, and landed into the wind. A blue-and-yellow plane sat to one side of the runway, near a viewing stand. Art Goebel and Bill Davis, the Hollywood stunt pilot and the navy lieutenant, had made it first in *Woolaroc*.

"Lucky bastards," Felix said.

"Good for them."

It took almost the whole airstrip to come to a stop, but they were on firm ground and it had never felt better. Touchdown time: 1:11. Soldiers on the ground guided them and helped push *Malolo* alongside *Woolaroc*. Felix shut down the engine, and the propeller slowed to a stop. He leaned forward with his head on the dash, back heaving up and down like he was trying to start a fire by blowing on it.

"Like I said earlier, you're the real hero here," he said.

And no one would know it.

"It took the both of us," she said.

"Someday, I hope to make it up you."

"Let's go, they're waiting."

She had so much to say to him, but that would have to wait. Right now, she wanted to bask in just being here, and coming in second.

He sat up, and stretched his neck. "I'm not sure I can walk."

"Neither am I."

He laughed. "I owe you my life, you know that?"

He then climbed out and stepped down onto the hard-packed dirt. She saw his legs almost buckle, but he caught himself on a wing strut. A swarm of people surrounded him, tossing flower lei over his neck. Livy came down next, and was greeted by a burst of warm Hawaiian breeze. She was acutely aware that Heath was nowhere to be seen. How was it that she and Felix had beat out so many of the favorites?

When her feet hit the ground, she knelt down on shaky legs and kissed a chunk of rock. Felix was suddenly next to her, doing the same. Cameras clicked and people cheered. He smiled when they both came up, lips dusted with the rust-colored dirt. A look of knowing passed between them. No one else would ever know how close they'd come to being yet another casualty of the Pacific Ocean.

Above the sea of voices, a woman screamed, "Felix!"

Livy looked toward the commotion and saw two armed soldiers escorting a pretty brunette, parting the crowd as they approached. When the woman caught sight of Felix, she picked up speed and fell into his arms.

"Felix Harding, what took you so damn long?" she cried between kisses.

Livy and the others around them stepped back to give them space.

Felix shrugged nonchalantly, as if he'd just come back from picking up milk at the grocery. "Sorry for the holdup."

"I've been beside myself with worry, tormented and tortured."

"I'm here now, aren't I?"

"Promise me you won't do that again. Ever."

"I swear on a stack of Bibles up to the moon, babe. You needn't worry about that."

Felix was still yelling, but after twenty-seven hours behind a droning engine, his ears had to be ringing as loudly as Livy's were. He bent over and kissed Iwa tenderly, pulling her in at the waist as though he couldn't get close enough. The crowd went wild. A bespectacled man in a white suit patiently waited until they came apart, then shook Felix's hand. Cameras snapped and reporters nudged their way in. If only J.P. Lee could see her now.

Felix grabbed ahold of Livy's arm and pulled her over. "This woman is one hundred percent responsible for getting us here, Governor."

Governor Farrington turned to Livy. "A day for the record books, Miss West. You outmaneuvered all of the other navigators in this race, save Bill Davis. How do you feel?"

You have no idea.

Livy smiled. "Tired and happy."

"My hat's off to you."

Soldiers with bayonets ushered them back to *Malolo* for more photographs, which took forever because everyone wanted to shake hands, get a photo with them, or an autograph. Mr. Dole introduced himself, and shook both of their hands tensely.

"I thank you both. Hawai'i thanks you both. Now, where are the other three planes?" he said, lines of concern on his face.

That, Livy could not answer. "Which three are we waiting for?"

But he didn't hear her, turning away to answer more questions. Her legs felt wobbly and her equilibrium was off, similar to returning to land after days at sea. She kept having to reach out and steady herself on things. When she and Felix had had enough, they were whisked off to the viewing stand and given glasses of champagne and all the sweet and juicy pineapple they could eat. Goebel and Davis were there, looking as haggard as Livy felt.

There was also a dapper man with a notepad in hand, and at first she thought he was a reporter, but he took down her parents' information and said he would be personally sending telegrams just as soon as he could.

"Thank you kindly, my mother is likely to be prostrate on the floor with worry."

Goebel then turned to them. "Did you hear? The only other planes that made it out of Oakland were *Soaring Eagle, Miss Doran* and *Golden Plover.*"

Good for Millie, they must have had a second go at it.

"Any word?" Livy asked.

He shook his head. "Only Hazeltine had a radio, but no transmitting capability."

Livy had stopped listening. The letter! It was still in the plane. She excused herself and ran back, shouldering her way through the dense mass of bodies. The smells here were different from California: sweet flowers mixed with burnt cane, and far-off rain. She found the letter smashed under one of the life raft oars, a corner ripped off. She couldn't open it fast enough.

My Dearest Olivia,
I wanted to say these words to your face, and see the look in those bottomless eyes of yours, but I knew how selfish that would be. I know this race is everything to you, and I don't want to interfere. The only thing that would make me happier than winning, is to see your plane on the ground when I get there.

So here's the thing. I still love you. I never stopped, not for one second. When I left, I told myself what I was doing was for your own good, when really it was just chickenshit. I'm going to be having a conversation with God along the way, asking that when I get to Hawai'i, you will give me another chance. I hope this doesn't sound too presumptuous, but I promise to make up to you all the hurt I caused if you would see it in your heart to let me back in, not just as friends. We could stay an extra week or two, learn to surf, see the volcano. Give it some thought, will you please?

As you read this, you're somewhere over the Pacific, maybe ahead of me, maybe behind. Just know that I'll be thinking of you the entire way across.
Yours always,
Heath Hazeltine

Livy read the letter hungrily, and then again. She took her time, savoring every word, his slanted handwriting so familiar. She held the paper to her chest and closed her eyes. Her heart flooded with so many emotions, it was hard to know what was what. How could she have been so hardheaded back in Oakland? The signs were all there, but she had turned a cold shoulder, too scared to let herself love again. Heath had tried, and she had blocked him every step of the way. It was a wonder he hadn't given up entirely. These strange games that humans played.

Now, her icy cool was melting away, and the underlying feeling was one of deep contentment and wonder, the way you felt watching a newborn animal taking its first breath, or a summer sunrise as it blazed over the horizon.

Heath Hazeltine, where are you?

28

PLEASE, PLEASE, PLEASE!

They waited and waited and waited for the other planes to arrive. Minutes, then hours ticked by, and the crowd slowly dispersed. Livy and the other fliers sat in the stands with several of the sponsors and a mishmash of race officials. William Hunt was off on his own standing by a shiny black Studebaker, pacing back and forth and chain-smoking. No one wanted to leave until the whole gaggle was in. They were all trying to console each other, and all failing miserably.

With so little information, they kept repeating the same few facts over and over again, trying to convince themselves of the chances of survival. *Miss Doran* had been spotted passing the Farallones sometime around 3:00 p.m. yesterday, flying low over the water and looking good. There had been no other reports of sightings from ships and schooners across the ocean, but with cloud cover as it had been, that would be expected. Livy and Felix had certainly seen no ships. Will Malloska, *Miss Doran*'s sponsor, insisted that their plane was designed to float and had waterproof wings.

"They're going to come out of this alive, you wait and see," he kept repeating, trying to convince himself as much as anyone else.

Art Goebel chimed in. "*Soaring Eagle*, too. From what I understand, she has some kind of state-of-the-art inflatable bags that'll keep her from going down."

Felix put a hand on Livy's forearm as he spoke. "And Hazeltine. He was with Rogers when they sailed that P-9 to Kauai. If he got into any trouble, he'll know what to do."

The glaring difference there was that the P-9 was built to land on water, but Livy kept her mouth shut. People needed hope right now—herself included—and she wasn't about to dash it.

Two young women who worked for Mr. Dole kept bringing over plates of sandwiches and drink, but no one was much in the mood. Theories were tossed around, and praises sung of the skill of the missing airmen, all experienced, all top-notch. Livy heard only half of it, as her mind was busy pleading with Heath, begging him to come flying over that mountain this very minute. The waiting was tortuous, and yet she could not peel her eyes from the skies. There were things she needed to say to him. Important things. Life-altering things.

Come on!

What she felt like saying, but didn't have the energy, was how much of it all boiled down to luck. Yes, experience and skill and preparation were important, but there were so many variables, so many things that could go wrong along the way. She'd seen it firsthand. Life was all about luck. Either you had it or you didn't, and that could fluctuate wildly. In her case, she'd been lucky as hell to make it, and now unlucky as hell to love a man who was still out there somewhere. Because the truth of the matter was, if those planes hadn't landed by now, chances were, they wouldn't.

Ever.

Iwa had not let go of her husband's hand since his arrival. "You two Dole Birds are going to need to get some rest one way or another. How about I set up a blanket on the grass over there?" She nodded toward a grove of spindly trees.

"Thank you but I couldn't."

Livy was too worried to care about sleep. Was it possible Heath was still up in the air? Maybe the *Golden Plover* was extraordinarily fuel efficient, more than anyone expected. Especially with the weight of only one man. She knew it was wishful thinking, but that was all she had at the moment.

Please, please, please, let him be alive.

As the sun lowered in the sky, the group gathered tidbits of information from a soldier named Lieutenant Varney, who assured them that the military had planes and vessels out looking for the overdue aviators.

"If they're in our waters, we'll find them," he said.

Felix stood up. "If our friends aren't in by morning, I'm going up to look for them."

Iwa tugged at his hand, not looking pleased. Livy liked the idea, though. *All hands on deck,* her father would have said. And he would have been the first to volunteer.

"Find me a plane and I'll go, too," she said.

"You're on, my friend."

The thought of getting in an airplane so soon again made her queasy, but sometimes life demanded you do things that rubbed you the wrong way. This was one of those times.

As promised, the top two finishers were awarded complimentary rooms at the Royal Hawaiian Hotel for a week. They arrived in the dark, and Livy dragged herself up to her room. She was tempted to take a hot bath but decided she would most likely drown in the bathtub if she did. Instead, she fell onto the bed in a heap of exhaustion and passed out cold.

She spent most of the night back in *Malolo,* living out a series of bizarre scenarios. Flying underwater. Landing on a cloud and finding that she could actually walk on it. Running out of gas but somehow gliding the rest of the way. When they approached Wheeler Field, Heath stood off to the side of the runway with two big seals next to him. He was waving but they'd lost their wheels and couldn't land.

She woke to the sound of a metronome. Wait, no, that was someone knocking on the door. It took a moment to register where she was. Light poured in from a window, and her eyes burned when she tried to look around.

"Open up, it's me, your cowardly captain."

All at once, awareness flooded back. Heath and Jack Hunt and Millie and her crew were all missing, while Livy was stretched out in a luxurious bed in Matson Line's new pink hotel. After disentangling her aching body from the sheets and slipping on a hotel robe, she let him in.

"What time is it?" she asked, rubbing her eyes.

"Half past seven."

Felix looked remarkably refreshed.

"Any word?" she asked.

"Nothing. Iwa and I are headed to Rodger's Field if you want to join us. The award ceremony is planned for three o'clock this afternoon, so that gives us plenty of time beforehand."

"Give me ten minutes," she said.

The airfield on the outskirts of Honolulu bustled with activity. Volunteers had come out of the woodwork to offer their services, and Felix had lined up a plane for himself to go out looking for the others, and another for Livy. A Curtiss Jenny, just like the one Heath had taken her up in so long ago. She fought back tears at the memory. Funny how now the floodgates had opened, she was crying every other minute.

Iwa noticed and put her arm around Livy. She smelled like lavender cream and coffee. "Don't lose hope, Sweets. Don't you know that *hope is the last thing ever lost.* A proverb to live by if there ever were one."

Iwa was a mother hen, that had been obvious right off the bat. The kind of woman who always made sure everyone was taken care of. She would bleed for you, which was probably why she'd ended up in the hospital. The love she had for Felix was nonnegotiable.

The owner of the aviation company was there, a man named Kama Asis, who wore an aloha shirt and safari shorts, most likely his tour guide attire. It turned out he would be joining the search. In the hangar, they huddled around a big map of the Hawaiian Islands and Livy downed two cups of dangerously strong coffee as he outlined the plan.

"The more eyes up there, the better," he said, finger tracing the faded lines. "I'll skirt to the north. Miss West, why don't you island hop over to Moloka'i, buzz just south of Maui to Kailua Kona and back. This fine weather is supposed to hold, and on that route, you can't get lost. Harding, you travel south of Lāna'i and Kaho'olawe. If there's a plane down, between the three of us we should see it."

Other fliers would be heading toward Kaua'i and Ni'ihau, in case one of the planes had overshot O'ahu, and some were flying a grid north and south of the islands. Kama had been in touch with Lieutenant Varney, who said they'd had several reports of sightings, but none had checked out. On the California end, planes and boats were also searching. Radio broadcasts had been sent across the Pacific, and any vessel with a radio was alerted to keep an eye out.

"You ever flown a Jenny?" Kama asked Livy.

"Yes, sir."

"Good, because I'm trusting you with my baby."

Felix cut in, "Your baby is in good hands."

The plane had been well cared for and had a splashy green paint job. There was no radio, but everyone carried a bundle of flares to drop if they found one of the planes. After *Malolo*, the Jenny felt clumsy and sluggish. Soon, Livy was airborne, traveling southeast toward the Big Island. It was nice not to worry about compass heading, because she could see the shadow of Moloka'i in the distance. Her eyes felt as though someone had thrown acid in them, and flying into the sun didn't help.

Since yesterday afternoon, her emotions had vacillated between despondency and hope. It had been hard to listen to her own voice while surrounded by so many people, so being alone with the sky and the ocean helped clear her head.

"Always assume the best, and the forces of nature will conspire to make it happen," Pa often said.

Her mother would roll her eyes and correct him. "No, honey, God will make it happen."

And Pa would answer, "Nature and God are one and the same, my dear."

Either way, Livy wanted to assume the best. She *had* to assume the best, because she *had* to see Heath again. The chafing feeling that this was somehow her fault began to cut into her skin. Heath had asked for her help in navigating, and she had refused to give it to him. What kind of coldhearted person did that?

Aside from clouds bunched up along the mountaintops, the endless skies were a dreamy blue. A little bumpy on the climb out of Honolulu, but that was to be expected. She passed several fishing vessels and a big schooner, and saw a few other planes ostensibly on the same mission as she was. Seabirds were also out in force, and she passed over a tornado of frigate birds diving and circling for fish. The flying was easy, almost mindless, and the peace and quiet soothed the ache in her chest.

She flew along the southern coast of Moloka'i and the northern coast of Lāna'i, then right over Kaho'olawe, an island whose name she would never be able to pronounce. She followed the contours of the islands, passing over sandy coves and rocky inlets, mostly deserted, all stunning. On the lee of the islands, the water was smooth and shiny. It would have been easy to spot a downed plane had there been one to spot. Crossing the channel to the Big Island was another story, with winds whipping up whitecaps and tossing the plane around. If someone had gone down here, chances were far less favorable.

As she neared 'Upolu Point, she saw something up ahead in the water. A small boat, perhaps? Her pulse ramped up as she dropped down to a hundred and fifty feet above the surface. It was too small and flat to be a boat. The object looked long and rectangular. *A wing?* When a swell lifted it up, she caught a quick glimpse of red, and then it disappeared again. None of the missing planes were red, but *Miss Doran* had some red on her. The next time it lifted up, she saw white.

Another five minutes on, the whole object came into view. Livy wilted when reality set in. She knew exactly what it was: an icebox off a fishing boat. Still, she continued on, following the coast to Kailua and then turning around for the return to O'ahu. She flew an opposite zigzag from her flight over, and saw nothing else of interest. But she was eager to land in hopes of good news. Someone, somewhere, was bound to have seen something.

29

PAU HANA TIME

Wren

The whole house creaked as Wren walked up the steps of Malama Care Home. No one was around, so she let herself in the front door, into a great room much larger than it appeared from the outside. That room opened to another room, which opened to another room. At the far end of the first room, several old folks sat on a couch watching *The Price Is Right* on TV. *Come on down!* All but one turned and stared at her. She waved self-consciously. They smiled somewhat vacuously and went back to their show. The air in the house carried hints of teriyaki chicken and Pine-Sol.

She knocked on a turquoise door with a crooked office sign off to the right of the main doors, but no one answered. Then she saw a small bell on a shelf. She rang it, and soon a middle-aged Filipino woman came hurrying around the corner, arms full of toilet paper rolls.

"Felicity, is it?" she said in a singsong voice. "Boy, am I happy to see you! We have two new residents and I've been running around like a chicken with no head. I was on O'ahu last week visiting family, but Helen spoke highly of you. I'm Myra, welcome!"

Wren hated to disappoint her. "Sorry but I'm not Felicity. My name is Wren and I came to inquire about a position. I saw your help-wanted sign."

The woman looked disappointed. "Oh. The position has been filled." She glanced at the clock with giant numbers on the wall. "Felicity should have been here two hours ago, though."

"What exactly is the position for?" Wren asked.

"Nurse's aide. You got experience?"

"Um. No."

"Do you like old people?"

In all honesty, she hadn't spent much time around old people, besides Cindy's parents on their once-a-year visit from Florida when they came to lie on Waikiki Beach and read under an umbrella all day. But she liked Dodge and Blue.

"Love them!"

"I'll show you around. We can talk."

If you had told Wren a month ago that she might be applying for a job as a nurse's aide in an old folks' home, she would have laughed in your face. Now, she was saying a silent prayer that Felicity never showed up. Myra led them past the TV watchers, through a small dining area and into another room with a piano, art supplies, games and a couple ukuleles. Four residents, one haole man and two Japanese and one Hawaiian woman, were playing cards.

Myra hurriedly introduced her, and moved on to show her a long hall with small bedrooms off each side. Two beds per room, twelve residents total. Several were occupied, with residents lying in bed, slight figures under thin green blankets. A nice breeze blew through the open windows, which helped bring life to the place. A sense of melancholy filled the house, and yet Wren felt strangely honored to be here.

Myra then took her onto the back lānai, which overlooked a big yard scattered with trees and benches. A lone woman sat on one of the benches, watching two fat hens with lacy feather stockings pecking in the grass.

"Fresh air is good for them, so we encourage time outside." Wren nodded.

"If we hire you, you would help with showering, brushing teeth, getting them up and dressed, helping eat, walking, that kind of thing. They're all at various stages. Some are senile, others sharp as tacks but their body's given out. Some are easy and compliant, a few are *kolohe*, harder to manage."

A loud thump came from one of the bedrooms. Myra shook her head. "Mr. Larsgaard, he keeps trying to walk, even though we tell him to wait for us or use his walker. Come."

Wren followed her, and sure enough, a man half lay, half sat on the floor, mumbling to himself. "Fucking useless appendages. No point in even having them anymore."

Myra kneeled down, and in a kind and soothing voice said, "Mr. Larsgaard, remember what I said about patience? Your legs work, you just need a little help in the form of a walker."

"Cursed thing." He looked up at Wren with remarkably clear eyes. "What are you gawking at? Give me a hand."

Wren hopped into action, and helped Myra lift him up so he was seated on the edge of the bed.

"Are you hurt?" Myra asked, checking his arms and legs for signs of a break.

"Only my pride." Then to Wren he said, "I haven't seen you before. What brings you to this crypt?"

"I'm applying for a job—"

"Do you play cribbage?" he asked.

"It's been a while, but yes."

He mock smacked himself in the forehead. "You're hired, then. Myra, tell Mrs. Oshiro I said so."

Myra smiled and fetched his walker, and set it directly in front of him. "If you say so, Mr. Larsgaard. Now, listen up. Use your walker or I'm going to have to strap you to the bed."

He laughed. "Good sense of humor, this one."

"I'm not kidding."

Wren hoped she was kidding, and sensed that she was, but you heard horror stories about places like these. Poor people drugged to oblivion, abused or left alone in their rooms all day. This place didn't feel like that at all.

Mr. Larsgaard switched his focus to the walker, and pulled himself to standing, muttering obscenities under his breath. Once he was up, he moved with surprising ease, feet shuffling, but arms strong.

"Good, now if you'll excuse us," Myra said, giving him a pat on the shoulder. On the way down the hall she said, quietly, "He's one of the *kolohe* ones. A real sweetheart, but stubborn as a bull. So, when do you want to start?"

Wren was taken aback. "What about Felicity?"

"Felicity missed her first shift, so she's out."

"Don't I need some kind of training?" Wren asked.

"Think of it as on-the-job training. We need help ASAP, and as long as you like people and aren't afraid to wipe someone else's *'ōkole*, you're hired."

That part freaked her out a little, but if Myra could do it, so could she. They worked out hours—twenty-four a week to start, two mornings and two afternoon shifts, and when Wren left, she was a proud new staff member at Malama Care Home, starting tomorrow. Never mind that she had no idea what she was doing. How hard could it be?

In that first week at work, Wren cycled through every emotion that could be found in the English dictionary, and then some. Touched at how warmly some of the residents welcomed her into their home, happy to see the look on Mr. Larsgaard's face when she finally had a moment to sit down and play cribbage with him, anxious about her first bath assist with Mrs. Yim, though it went better than expected, felt gut-wrenching sadness when Molly Anderson kept asking where her husband was. Wren had been instructed to say he was out with the horses, and each time, Molly would break down in tears, worried he wouldn't come back. The poor woman spent her whole day repeating the same question, genuinely wondering, and it broke Wren's heart.

At the end of each shift, she'd leave feeling as though she'd run a marathon but also remarkably satisfied. In just a matter of days, she could feel the love and appreciation from the old folks. They didn't need much—to have a warm hand to hold, or an ear to hear their stories, made them ever so grateful. The work was so different than anything she'd done before. Shitty pay, but Wren suddenly felt rich in warm fuzzies.

The only woman who Wren had not interacted with was the one she'd seen in the yard that first day, sitting on the bench under the mango tree watching the chickens. The woman spent all her time out there, and Myra said she liked to be left alone with the birds. Wren caught sight of her through the windows as she was helping others, and every now and then, it felt like their eyes met, but the woman's blank expression never changed. It was easy to imagine she'd once been beautiful, with thick, wavy hair and fine bone structure. Even now, she exuded a quiet grace, but she was thin as a koa leaf, and looked ready to blow away in the next storm that whipped through.

On Friday afternoon, on a whim, Wren decided to walk out and say hello under the guise of feeding the hens, Cookie and Brownie. The woman faced away from her, and up close, she seemed so small.

"Gorgeous afternoon, isn't it?" Wren said.

It was true, sunlight shimmered through the web of mango leaves, the sky a startling blue. No response. Wren stood next to her for a moment, taking in the afternoon peace and wondering if the woman could even hear. She'd forgotten to ask about that.

"Don't look now, but a plover just landed off to your right," Wren whispered. "Maybe if we're very still, he'll come over here."

The woman didn't look anyway, deaf or not deaf. Wren watched the plover out of the side of her eye as it darted after insects or worms. When it noticed her, it bobbed its head a few times, then took off in the other direction. She noticed the woman was looking, too.

"Well, I just wanted to introduce myself, in case you ever want company out here. Other than the birds, that is. Though I must say, I don't blame you for being out here. I prefer birds over people any day." She turned to leave, then added, "By the way, I'm Wren."

When she was halfway to the house, the wind carried a sound to her ears. *Lovely name.* Wren spun around and was going to respond, but the woman had her eye on the plover. Maybe Wren had imagined it? Maybe she hadn't.

Pono showed up at five o'clock, unannounced. She heard the rumble of his engine while sitting outside on the old Adirondack chair she had picked up on the side of the road earlier in the week. She'd stripped the cracked and peeled red paint, sanded and oiled the wood, and now it was good as new. Her body felt like weighted stone as she lay back and watched a Hawaiian hawk circling above, riding the air currents. Too tired to get up, she waved at him as he pulled to a stop.

He jumped out and let Scout out of the back. "You okay?" he asked.

Scout ran off without so much as a crotch nudge.

She sighed. "Did I tell you about my new job?"

She honestly couldn't remember, too much had gone on since arriving here.

He hovered near the truck, awkwardly. "At the old folks' home? You said you were going to check it out."

"Well, I got the job, and now I'm working."

"Looks like you could use a *pau hana* beer," he said.

"If only I'd had the foresight to stop at the store."

He reached into the truck bed and produced a small cooler. "Beer and pipi kaula. You want some?"

She wanted nothing more. "Are you for real?"

"If not, no worries. I had both in my fridge and I figured you and the dog might be over here starving to death in your remote outpost," he said, still hesitating by the truck. "No pressure, though."

Was he actually nervous?

She laughed. "Get over here with that before I pass out from thirst."

Wren forced herself up and gave him a peck on the cheek, local style, and grabbed the only other wooden chair from inside the barn. He pulled out an icy Budweiser, popped the cap with his belt buckle and handed it to her. Then he did the same for himself as he straddled the chair backward.

"Tell me about the job," he said.

So she did, surprised at how much she had to say.

"I would have never, not in a million years, thought about getting a job in a place like this. I'm an artist, for Chrissake, and all my side jobs have just been to make money, but being there is so grounding. Seeing these people cuts right to what's important."

"Old people rule," he said.

Wren laughed. "Did you make that up?"

He shrugged. "It's just the truth. I spend more time with Blue and Dodge than people my own age for that reason. They *know* things. They've lived. There's no bullshit."

"Cheers to that," she said, raising her bottle.

He tapped it with his, catching her eye and holding it.

"Any luck with the dog?" he asked.

"We're coexisting. She comes in after I go to bed and leaves before I get up. But she eats the food I put out, and sometimes I feel her presence beyond the trees, like she's watching me."

"That reminds me. I brought you something." He went to the truck and returned with a hunting rifle. "You shouldn't need this, but it's good to have, alone out here and all. You know how to shoot?"

"I'm from O'ahu. What do you think?"

Wren had never even held a gun.

"I can show you. Not much to it."

"What should I be worried about?" she asked.

"You shouldn't be worried, but you should be prepared. It's a small town, and when word gets out that you're out here all alone, you never know. This island has its share of bad seeds—druggies, nut jobs, etcetera. Ninety-nine percent chance you all good here, but hey, why not?"

"Okay."

He nodded. "Come over here."

Wren obeyed.

"This is a .22. It's not loaded, give it a feel," he said, handing it over gently, as though it was a newborn baby.

Heavier than expected, the metal was cool to the touch, and deadly. She couldn't imagine pointing it at someone. Pono walked her through how to load, aim and shoot, and she found herself spending more time looking at his arms than at the gun. He was quite possibly the smoothest man she'd ever met, but he was so busy doing his thing, he didn't appear to have any idea. Working alongside him was going to prove difficult.

"We can do target practice another day in an open space when the dogs are secure. Maybe the orchard," he said. "Meantime, keep this by your bed. It's loaded, so make sure the safety is on."

She was touched by his concern. He'd somehow gone from aloof mechanic dragged out of his way to help the dumb city girl, to hot friend who showed up with beer, guns and pipi kaula. She could still sense a wall around him, but it had begun to crumble in places. After the gun lesson, she helped him unload a Honda generator that weighed a ton, and two cans of gas to run it.

"You don't work this weekend, do you?" he asked.

"Nope, just Tuesday through Friday. Six-hour shifts to start."

"Good, because I have free time, let's try to bang out as much as we can."

He walked inside, then stopped when he saw the lamp she'd been working on. "You've been busy, I see."

Wren had finished her new candle chandelier and hung it up last night. Chester had brought in a bunch of beeswax from a local beekeeper and sold it to her on store credit. She had then cut and wet sanded the old wine bottles and filled them with wicks and wax. Each one was a different shade of glass, but that added to the charm. Then, same as the lamp upstairs, she had set them into an old plank, and attached four wrought iron chains. She had yet to hoist it up and light the candles.

"Light is everything," she said.

"You should sell these."

Wren eyed the piece. "That's been the point, but I never could seem to quite make it work. Like, really work. Orders were trickling in, not flooding in."

"I'd buy one in a heartbeat," he said.

"Really?"

He shoved his hands in his pockets and smiled. "Yeah. Can I put in an order now?"

The barn really was a perfect wood shop. Miles of space, soft light and the sound of honeybees tapping at the tall windows.

"I'll add your name to my very long waitlist," she said.

"What number am I?"

"One," she said. "Oh, and with every purchase, you get a free jar of honey."

The corner of his mouth lifted. "I'm serious, Wren. These

are one of a kind, and they have this whimsical quality about them. Homemade, handcrafted. None of that manufactured shit pumped out of some factory in China."

"I'm honored you think so. Using the old wood and the used wine bottles gives them a different feeling than my others."

It was strange how over the past week, more and more ideas had been coming to her, as though someone had turned on a faucet in her brain. She couldn't wait to try them out.

From the side came the thud of heavy footsteps, just as Scout bounded up to them with muddy paws and dirt on his fur. The stray stood at the fringe of the woods, panting.

"Come here, girl, we've got something special," Pono said.

Wren liked how his voice turned all sweet and buttery when he spoke dog.

"I've named her Hōkūpaʻa, Paʻa for short," she said.

"Does she know that?"

Wren shrugged. "I don't know, try it."

They both called her name. Pono waved a strip of the dried beef. Her nose pointed in the air as she sniffed. She stepped forward gingerly with her dainty, narrow legs and small paws. Wren was surprised that she kept creeping toward them in slow motion. When she got about six feet away, she stopped and sat. Pono moved toward her slowly. Paʻa started shaking, but didn't back away. Pono set the meat on the ground halfway between them and retreated.

"That's for you, girl… Paʻa. Go on, we don't bite," he said.

Paʻa crawled to the meat and swallowed it whole, then looking at them as if to say, *Is there more?* Scout, who had been told to stay and had been such a good boy watching this all go down, finally couldn't take it anymore and barked and wiggled.

Pono eyed him. "Quiet."

Scout quieted, seemingly aware that something important was happening. Then Pono knelt down on the ground and held his palm out, two more strips of pipi kaula resting atop it. Paʻa looked at Pono then to Scout, then back to Pono.

"I'm not going to hurt you," he said, in almost a whisper.

The whole time, Pa'a kept her eyes glued to Wren, not Pono, as if Wren was somehow the bad guy. Seeing her in the light, Wren thought that maybe, just maybe, her ribs were slightly less exposed. And her tail, which had been permanently tucked between her legs, was now more relaxed.

"Pa'a," Wren called softly, holding out her strip.

Pa'a came over and sat a few feet away, holding her ground. Wren gave in and tossed it to her. This one she chewed more thoroughly, then backed away and sat, staring down Wren for more. A thin line of drool hung from her jaw.

Wren felt her whole body smile. "You like that, huh?"

A barely perceptible wag of the tail. But when Wren moved toward Pa'a, the dog spooked and jumped back, circling around and standing a safe distance away.

"Let her come to you, not the other way around. It's how it works with animals," Pono said.

The same could be said about men.

She felt a little silly. "It's a start, at least."

Pono looked at Scout and nodded, releasing him from some invisible bind. Scout trotted over to Pa'a and started licking her mouth. Pretty soon, they were rolling around and wrestling on the ground, a mash-up of fur and teeth and tails.

"I've never seen him this way," Pono said, crossing his arms and watching.

"He's smitten."

He slid her a look. "He is."

Wren had the distinct feeling he wasn't just talking about the dog.

Pono showed up with the sun the following morning, buzzing from a giant thermos of coffee, and ready to get to work. Wren had been in bed when his truck door slammed, and she dragged her tired ass out from under the spider net and into her blue mechanic suit. She tamped down her bedhead and hopped down the steps two at a time. There he was, standing next to *Malolo* with a toolbox in hand.

"Are you sure you didn't sleep in the truck? I feel like I just closed my eyes," she said, gritty eyed and in need of coffee herself.

Pono looked amused. "Nice suit. Kyle?"

She looked down at the embroidered name tag on her suit: Kyle.

She put her hands on her hips. "What, you don't like it?"

"I love it. Do you have a mug? I brought coffee."

"Not so fast. This suit came from my high school teacher's son's auto shop in Kaka'ako. I won it in a competition for who could design the best car. I beat out everyone, even the guys."

His mouth lifted on one side. "You're full of surprises, aren't you? What did your car look like?"

"A cross between a station wagon and a tank."

"Sounds like my truck."

"Mine was amphibious."

He laughed. "You've got me there."

She poured coffee into her Kliban Cat mug, while Pono walked around the planes. She watched him reach out and feel one section of the larger plane, peeling away a chip of paint.

"There's white paint under the red."

"White's not that exciting a color if you want to stand out," she said.

"So, what are we working on first, the truck or the planes?" he asked, voice bouncing off the rafters.

"I thought you wanted to do the truck and see how much we could get for it."

Pono couldn't seem to keep his hands off the airplanes. "I asked around. These birds could fetch a lot more money. Es-

pecially if this one was in a race. It could be historically significant."

She added to her mental list: *look into air race.*

"How much are we talking?" she asked.

"Hundreds of thousands. Maybe more."

She tried to appear calm, despite the numbers. "It's your
time, so you tell me."

He hopped in the smaller plane again, which made her think
she had her answer.

"I could work on the engine and you work on the body.
Start with this one?" he said.

"A plane is a lot different from an automobile."

"All the more reason. I've worked on just about every kind
of engine there is, with the exception of a plane. How often
do you get a chance like this?"

Wren had to admit, the planes had an allure. Vintage, mysterious and all-around cool. Even if she had no idea what she
was doing, that seemed to be the new theme of her life. May as
well go with it. The hard part was going to be affording materials, but now that she wasn't paying rent, she could use her
salary, whopping as it was. And the fruits would more than
pay off later. If they could actually pull it off. She hardly knew
Pono, but he seemed competent.

After coffee and scones—he had brought blackberry scones
his mother had baked—they mapped out what work needed
to be done. Wren opened one of her light fixture notebooks,
and took down notes as he rattled on. *"Wiring, pistons, fasteners, wood panels, gauges, canvas."*

"Finding the right canvas is going to be the hardest part, I
think," Pono said.

The job began to feel overwhelming before it had even
begun.

"Are you sure we shouldn't just do the truck?"

"Not feeling up to the challenge?" he said.

"It's not that. I just don't want to take up your whole life."

He set his coffee down on the wing, and came over to her, a foot away, close enough that she noticed a new crop of freckles on the bridge of his nose. "If I didn't want to do it, I wouldn't be here," he said, voice low and hoarse.

Wren quieted, and they continued on, but now she couldn't stop thinking about what exactly was happening here. By now she'd deduced Pono wasn't attached, but neither of them had broached the subject or made mention of significant others. It felt like the boundaries had begun to blur between them. Whenever she got within a few feet of him, she got a light-headed, dreamy feeling. A sunshine-on-your-shoulders warmth, but more diffuse. Then, thankfully, the voice of reason came, in the form of Gina's favorite line. *You don't need to name it, just keep on keeping on, and life will work itself out.*

30

MORE QUESTIONS THAN ANSWERS

Wren

It took a good part of the morning just to figure out what worked and what didn't on the airplane, and making more lists of everything that needed to be done. At lunchtime, they stopped and ate tuna sandwiches—Pono had brought four—with sliced pickle and Fritos outside under a cloudy, humid sky. Wren provided lilikoi and guava juice she had made herself from the overabundance of wild fruit on the property. The weather had gone from sunny trade winds to still, thick air full of mosquitoes and moisture, and they both wore a glossy sheen on their skin. By the end of the day, they realized what a long haul the project was going to be, but both were one hundred and twenty percent in.

Pono left just after four that afternoon, and Wren took a walk to the stream to rinse off the grime of the day. The cold, rushing water held its own special appeal and she found herself looking forward to it. Though it hadn't rained at the barn, tar-colored clouds bunched up near the top of the mountains, adding a moody vibe. Once again, her skin pricked with the feeling she was being followed. Every gust of wind or squeal of a branch made her look, but no one came out of the shadows. When she reached the stream, it was running much higher than yesterday, with white water bubbling over the mossy rocks.

Excited for the icy plunge, she sat down and untied her boots, pulled off her jeans, then slipped her G N' R T-shirt over her head. With only the birds around to see, skinny-dipping had become second nature. When she looked up again, Pa'a was standing on a rock between her and where she usually entered the water.

Wren fell back in shock, one hand over her heart. "Holy crap, you scared me."

The dog didn't flinch.

"What are you doing here, girl?"

The roar of the water swept her words away. Wren stood up, unsure of what to do. She wanted to get in, but the dog remained planted in place. She looked around for another way, but could see none with the water level higher on the rocks. Pa'a sat down, eyes driving into Wren, the same way she'd seen those border collies staring down sheep on the Discovery Channel.

"Are you trying to herd me?" she asked. "What is it?"

Pa'a let out a high-pitched sound, somewhere between a whine and a howl. A shot of static electricity traveled down Wren's spine, just as she heard the sound of heavy rain upstream. *Unless it wasn't rain at all.* Reality hit swiftly, and Wren grabbed her clothes and scrambled back up the embankment toward higher ground as fast as she could. Pa'a flew past her, tail between her legs, as the sound of rushing water thundered toward them. By the time Wren reached the top, her lungs burned. How dumb of her not to pay attention to the signs. Black clouds up *mauka*, full stream. *Flash flood.*

Below them, the sound of crashing tree trunks and moving boulders roared, as a wall of brown water tore through the gully where they had been standing not two minutes earlier. Wren leaned over, both hands on her knees, trying to catch a breath. Pa'a stood off to the side, tongue out. No big deal.

Wren turned to the dog, "You just saved my life, you know that, right?"

Pa'a looked away, then loped off down the road.

That night, Pa'a showed up as Wren was eating dinner—a peanut-butter-and-*poha*-jam sandwich. It was the first time, other than when Pono and Scout were there, she had come while Wren was still awake. Wren got up and grabbed the rest of the pipi kaula out of the cooler. She would have eaten it herself, but was saving it for Pa'a. It was the least she could do.

Her table consisted of two sawhorses and a big piece of plywood, and her light, candles in wine bottles with the tops sawed off—her latest creations. Pa'a sat at the bottom of the step and wouldn't come closer, so Wren put the meat in a bowl and set it down between them. Earlier, she had moved Pa'a's bed a foot closer to her own. Little by little, she hoped to get the dog next to her at night. Even though Pa'a snored, there was something soothing and soul satisfying about listening to the animal sleep peacefully, as though everything was right in the world—if only for that moment.

Pa'a gobbled up the pipi kaula, licked her chops, then went over to a towel underneath *Malolo* and curled up, one eye on Wren.

"Hi, Pa'a," Wren said, then repeated her name a few times to try to get the dog to associate the word with herself. Was that how you did it? Pono seemed to think so.

When Wren went upstairs, Pa'a followed five minutes later. If she noticed her bed had been moved, she didn't let on. Wren thought about how much had happened in her short time here, and how she'd been so focused on living, she hadn't had time to be miserable, or dwell on Joe. They both went to sleep to the sound of light rain on the tin roof. Tired, full stomachs, and for the first time in a long time, hopeful.

At lunchtime the following day, after hammering it out all morning, Wren took Pono to the shack with the Air Hawaii sign. They both were streaked with grease from taking apart the plane engine, and Pono had grown frustrated, unsure he'd even be able to repair the thing.

"We may need to scrap it and get a new one."

As if Wren could afford that. "We'll do what we can, and go from there. At least get her looking pretty again."

He was of the mind they needed an airplane mechanic, and she didn't disagree.

"I can go to ʻUpolu Airport tomorrow and ask around. Fish for more information, too, on *Malolo*'s history," she offered.

"It wouldn't hurt."

As they tromped beneath the green canopy of kukui nut trees, Scout and Paʻa ran ahead of them, noses to the earth, covering at least twice as much ground as the two humans. Wren told Pono about the flash flood.

He frowned. "I should have warned you."

"How would you have known?"

"I've lived here my whole life. I saw those clouds as I was driving out, but I forgot you were feral. Otherwise I would have turned around."

She laughed. "Well, Paʻa and I survived, so no harm done."

"Animals know. They're so much more intelligent than we give them credit for," he said.

"You hear those stories of dolphins saving people from sharks or dogs saving kids from bears, but to see Paʻa in action. Her stare could have moved mountains. It's something I will never forget," Wren said, a catch in her voice.

She watched the two dogs, wondering what kind of particles those sensitive noses were picking up in the way of pig pheromones, decaying leaves, mongoose urine, rotting fruit, fungus, dragonfly wings and a whole ecosystem of smells undetectable to humans.

When they reached the shack, Pono jimmied the door open after tearing out a clump of vines, and they went inside, careful not to fall through the floor. Wren held a stick out and wiped away a spiderless web that held a few unsuspecting moth skeletons and a dead beetle.

"I wonder how long this place was in business. Seems pretty off the beaten path," she said.

"You'd think so, but have you ever flown along this coastline?" Pono said.

"No."

"These valleys with their black sand beaches and waterfalls are like an eighth wonder of the world. On a sunny day, you've never seen anything like it."

Wren had seen pictures.

"Maybe one day we can go," she said, surprising herself.

"You're on."

"Maybe in *Malolo*."

He laughed. "That might be pushing it. But you never know, we might surprise ourselves."

We just might.

They nosed around, and Pono picked up a fountain pen off the floor. He held it up to a stream of sunlight pouring in.

"IKH. What do you think?" he said, holding it out for her to see.

"Looks like it. Iwa Kahawai something or other."

She set it down on the desk. The entire surface was rusted, but from this new angle, Wren noticed a drawer. She opened it. The only thing inside was a folded-up newspaper article, yellowed with age. She carefully unfolded it and spread it out on the desk. Pono came up behind her, leaning into her hip.

Her heart beat wildly when she saw the title of the *Honolulu Advertiser* article: *"Dole Race Disaster. No Sign of Missing Fliers."*

Wren began to read aloud. "'Three planes and five souls are still lost at sea, as the massive search continues for the Dole Derby fliers. Out of nine airplanes to line up at Bay Farm Island on August 16, before a crowd of two hundred thousand, only five made it out to the great blue yonder. Two crashed on takeoff and two turned around due to mechanical issues or equipment failure. A very inauspicious start to a race that had already claimed three lives before it even started.'"

"Damn," Pono said.

"Devastating."

She went on. "'A reorganization of the search will take place today, with military and civilians cooperating in one of the greatest searches this side of the Pacific has ever seen. Dole planes will be aiding in the search, and grounded race participants Captain Bill Erwin and Alvin Eichwald will be setting out again from Oakland, determined to participate in the hunt. Race winners Arthur Goebel and Lieutenant Bill Davis, as well as second-place finishers Felix Harding and navigator Olivia West, have also been active in the search.'"

Wren paused. "A woman navigator. How cool is that?"

"In 1927 no less."

She continued reading. "'A US navy spokesman reports that all rumors of finding any of the fliers are false, but that two submarines have been dispatched to investigate floating objects in waters several hundred miles off O'ahu. A search plane circled, but did not see any survivors, nor were they able to positively identify it as relating to the Dole Derby.

"Hope is fading fast for the safe return of any of the missing, and many are questioning the sanity of such a race. With such poor odds and a hasty timeline, an undertaking this monumental has been labeled reckless by some, suicidal by others. Goebel and Harding have both acknowledged that they would give anything, even the financial gains and hero worship, to have their fellow fliers back on land safe and sound.'"

By the time Wren finished, a grapefruit-sized knot had formed in her stomach. Her gaze dropped to a line of photographs below the article. Black-and-white smiling faces of sunburned men with a name underneath: *"Arthur Goebel, Felix Harding."* Felix Harding was the man from the photos in the box. The curly-haired woman in the other photos must have been Olivia West, his navigator.

"Looks like Felix Harding is our man. And this plane of yours has quite a history," Pono said.

Wren looked closely at all the photos, two with planes in the background. Funny to think that this famous little plane belonged to her now.

"I wonder about the other plane, though," she said.

"We know it's not *Woolaroc* from these shots. It's probably what they used for the charter."

"It just seems like a newer charter plane would have been made from metal, like you said," she said.

"Maybe they ran the charter business in the thirties."

Wren was determined to get answers. "I'll find out tomorrow. One way or another."

31

A DARK AND CLOUDY MOOD

Olivia

No one felt much like attending an award ceremony, as none of the missing fliers had been located. But Mr. Dole had planned a lavish event and he would be handing out the checks, so being there was required. Livy wore a sleeveless red dress she'd bought at a secondhand shop in San Francisco to match *Malolo*, and went through the motions of trying to look presentable, but her eyes were red rimmed and her skin patchy. She mainly hoped to gather more information on the missing planes.

A crowd of finely dressed civilians and men in uniform conversed in small groups, under a sun that threatened to melt your skin off. Coconut trees lightly rustled, and Livy kept to their shade. The hotel was even more grand in real life, all pink with Moorish arches and fancy chandeliers. She grabbed a cold drink with a pineapple wedge from a roaming waiter and went in search of Lieutenant Varney. She found him talking to Mr. Hunt. Livy stopped a few feet away and watched the waves roll in. Men on surfboards glided across their crests like birds in flight. She and the other fliers would have been out there enjoying the waves with them had all gone according to plan.

The conversation between Varney and Hunt grew heated, and Livy heard Hunt say, "You need to do more," before marching away.

Livy stepped over. "Excuse me, Lieutenant, any word?"

He nodded. "I'm about to address the group, so I think you'll have your answers. Please excuse me."

A weary-looking Mr. Dole stood under an arch, shoulders drooping. "Aloha," he said to the crowd, drawing out the *o*.

A few people answered back with an aloha of their own. The mic squealed, and he fiddled with it for a moment. His wife stood off to the side, a solemn look on her tan face, even as she hid behind oversize sunglass. Reporters lined both sides of the grassy seating area.

"Now, I know we all have heavy hearts, and are sick over the missing crews, so I want to start with Lieutenant Varney sharing what all is going on with the search. After that, we'll be awarding the brave fliers their due. Lieutenant?"

Varney stepped up, cleared his throat and wiped his brow with a handkerchief. "As of 1500 hours, there are over forty navy vessels on the hunt, including aircraft carrier *USS Langley* and her tender, *Aroostook*, and three submarines. We have a mine sweeper, two navy seaplanes, and hundreds of Japanese fishing boats searching every inch of Hawaiian coastline.

"Also, new information from the *SS City of Los Angeles* leads us to believe that *Golden Plover* was spotted along the great-circle route not long after *Malolo* passed overhead, at roughly 0500 Hawai'i time. And the *SS Manulani* reported seeing *Woolaroc* and what appeared to be another plane on a more northward course about halfway across."

Livy's ears perked up, and she remembered wondering if Heath had been nearby out there, and how her skin had prickled at the thought. She'd shared her course with him, so maybe he really had been.

Varney checked a small notepad, then went on, "But Watts believes *Miss Doran* likely went down sooner, on account of half her cylinders were misfiring after her first run. That leaves us to wonder if it was the *Soaring Eagle* that *Manulani* saw. Visibility was poor, as you know, so it's hard to say."

Varney paused, and someone behind Livy mumbled that the plane never should have taken off. Livy looked around at all the pained expressions and drawn faces. The mood was dark and cloudy, yet all around, the birds were chirping, the sun was dappling the water and kids of all shapes and sizes were frolicking in the shore break. A funny thing, how the world kept on spinning even in the face of such tragedy.

One of the reporters called out, "Is it true that equipment was tampered with the night before takeoff? Are you looking into that?"

Varney's ears turned red. "Right now, one hundred percent of our efforts are on finding the crews. Time is of the essence. But if there was any criminal activity, you can bet the Oakland Police are looking into it."

"What about the *Dallas Spirit*, is it true they're going to join in the search and fly to Hawai'i tomorrow?" another asked.

"Affirmative. Erwin and Eichwald plan on flying to Honolulu, and then back to Oakland if we haven't found the missing fliers by then."

"What if they go missing, too?"

Murmurs floated around.

"They have a two-way radio on board. They aren't taking any chances. No one is," Varney said.

Livy almost laughed aloud. A radio was no guarantee of anything.

"Now, I'm going to turn the mic over to Mr. Dole. He can answer any more of your questions."

In a light gray suit and tie, looking all business, Dole took over the ceremony. "Thank you, Lieutenant. Now, for anyone who missed my earlier announcement, let it be known that myself and the other sponsors are putting up a twenty-thousand-dollar reward for each aircraft found."

Livy had missed this news. Finding the missing aviators would be more than reward enough, and she planned to partake in the search for as long as it took, but an extra twenty thousand would go a long way. She was still in the dark as to how much Felix would give her, and he'd alluded to having scores of people to pay back. Why she hadn't pressed to settle this beforehand, she had no idea.

Dole's voice broke several times as he continued, "These folks risked their lives to further the field of aviation, and help establish a commercial air route between the mainland and the Hawaiian Islands. They are brave souls and pioneers, and we will not let them down."

Yeses went around the audience. Dole then went silent for a moment, and Livy thought he was going to have a breakdown. If he did, it was all over, as she was holding herself together with a safety pin and a frayed thread of hope.

He inhaled deeply, then held up a hand. "Now, to our winners, will you please step forward."

Goebel and Davis and Felix, all in white suits, joined Dole at a small table surrounded with wicker chairs. Livy came from the other side and stood next to Felix, warm sun on her shoulders. A pretty, dark-skinned woman in a white dress placed a flower lei around each of their necks.

Dole nodded at her. "We have, standing in our midst, true heroes. Three men and one woman who have achieved one of the greatest feats in the history of aviation. They have shown us how to achieve the impossible, and they have shown us the way of the future. Because of them, Hawai'i is now the talk of the world. Please give a hand to our winners, Art Goebel and Lieutenant Davis."

Applause broke out, along with whistles and hollers, and yet you could feel a vacancy in the atmosphere—there were only four when there should have been seventeen. Dole handed the men a check and shook both of their hands, putting on a smile for photos, then turning his attention to Livy and Felix.

"And to second place. Good flying, Mr. Harding," he said, shaking Felix's hand first, then pecking Livy on the cheek with tight lips.

They stood shoulder to shoulder, beaming out at the crowd, as cameras snapped. In the morning, she and Felix would be in papers all around the country. It took all of her restraint not to say, *Had it not been for me flying much of the way, Mr. Dole, you would be searching for another downed plane and two more missing fliers.*

Felix caught her eye and gave a weak shrug of his shoulders.

After the ceremony, they migrated to a poolside area where a Hawaiian trio of musicians played steel guitar and ukulele. Dole offered to pick up the tab for food and beverages. If only they had liquor, Livy would have drowned her sorrows. Iwa left them at the table and set off to the bar for virgin cocktails and pupus—Hawaiian for appetizers.

When she was out of earshot, Livy said, "Did you tell her about the race?"

"Not yet."

"Are you planning on it?"

"What good would it do? Poor woman is already in a fragile state, with all the money we owe." He blew out through his nose like a horse. Scratched his chin. Looked up at the coconuts, as if he might find the words he was looking for tucked up among them. "Which brings me to a most difficult point."

Her whole body went stiff. "What is it?"

"Iwa did the math, and we will only be able to pay you twenty-five dollars."

She must have misheard. "You mean twenty-five hundred?"

"No. I mean twenty-five."

Livy leaned in. "Felix, I navigated *and* flew us over halfway here while you were in the back either knocked out or in a state. Don't you think I deserve a little more than that?"

"I think you deserve all of it, but the money is spoken for."

She was suddenly furious. "This is unacceptable. I make more than that in a weekend of flying for Mahoney! I gave up weeks of a paycheck that my family relies on, not to mention putting my life on the line to get us here. Have you no decency?"

His eyes grew watery and he looked around. Livy had stopped caring if anyone heard. "Dear girl, you think I don't know that? I'm not like the other chaps, where I had a wealthy sponsor dishing out wads of cash left and right. Iwa pounded the pavement and secured loans that need to be paid back. Had we been first, it would be another story."

She collapsed back in her chair and fanned herself with the menu. Nothing about this trip had gone as expected, so why should anything change now?

"I'll find a way to make it up to you."

Unable to control herself, she slammed her drink on the table and made to stand so she could get as far away from this man as she could. Her mother's words came back to haunt her. *Have you lost your mind? You have no idea who this man is and you want to fly across the Pacific Ocean with him in a flimsy piece of machinery?*

Felix grabbed her arm. "Look, my friend. You're knackered and you're worried for Heath and the others. You need a stiff drink and a good night's sleep, then in the morning, we'll regroup, and I will do *everything* in my power to help you find him. Find them."

She tried to yank her arm away, but his grip was firm. His palm was rough, but something about his touch felt comforting.

"Look at me," he said, gently.

Her eyes went to the nearby grassy lawn. "I wish I had never partaken in this whole sorry affair. I should have known better. We all should have."

Felix let go and leaned back in his chair, crossing his hands behind his head. "So, you're going to throw up your hands and give up? Is that it? I wouldn't have pegged you for such a quitter," he said.

Livy felt her face go red. "If it isn't the pot calling the kettle black. And you know I'm not a quitter."

"Well, don't act like one, Slim."

His use of *Slim* caught her off guard, and it was like a pressure release valve had been flipped. Thoughts of better days with Heath and Mahoney drained away the anger and frustration, leaving only fear.

"I'm so scared," she said.

"I know you are."

"I want so badly to believe he's still alive."

"You better believe he is. It's early yet, and there's an armada out there searching. You two have a lot of unfinished business—Hazeltine knows that. He's not going down without a fight."

Iwa appeared with three tall glasses of pineapple juice, and set them down on the table. "These have a little kick, so be careful," she said with a wink.

When Livy raised the glass to her lips, she was almost knocked out by the foul odor. "What is this?"

"Ti leaf root shine. The Hawaiians call it 'ōkolehao," Iwa said quietly.

Felix took a swig. "Stank and rank, but it does the job."

Three sips later, Livy felt the muscles in her neck unwinding. The twitch beneath her eye finally ceased, and her burning anger at Felix dulled. Felix was nothing if not sincere. It was hard to stay mad at the man.

Felix waved over Goebel and Davis, who joined them for a little lubrication. Lord knew they all could use it. They compared race notes and discussed plans for the next day. No one wanted to sit by idle and wait. By the time Livy finished her first drink, she was seeing double. She excused herself, went up to the room and slept for thirteen hours straight.

When morning came, there was news.

32

PROMISE ME

Olivia

The Royal Hawaiian Hotel offered up a small meeting room as an informal headquarters for the search, and Iwa appointed herself as coordinator. No one argued. The room was already equipped with a telephone, and Dole brought in a two-way HAM radio and a very efficient Japanese woman named Ryoko to assist. Livy beelined it there once she got wind of it, and Iwa greeted her with a flurry of information and a steaming cup of Kona coffee.

"Sightings are flooding in, and we're working to check out every one. At nine o'clock last night, two boys fishing from the beach near Haleiwa saw a glowing red object gliding out of the sky and into the water," Iwa said.

"How far out?" Livy asked.

"A mile or two. We have boats and planes out there now, combing the area. But that's not the only report. A few people on the Big Island called in seeing red lights high on Mauna Loa, which could have been flares."

Livy pictured the massive shield volcano, which by all accounts was covered in jagged lava above the tree line. "Would someone be able to land on that lava?"

"Not likely. But the military is sending three planes to search."

"I want to go, too."

Anything to feel useful. Twiddling her thumbs in a hotel room would drive her mad. Plus, it was a big mountain. Three planes would hardly be enough.

"Wait and see what they come back with," Iwa urged. "Also, off Maui, a couple swears they heard a plane engine approaching the coastline, and then suddenly stop. We have boats and planes searching there, too."

Livy waited and waited. And waited. Every so often, she pulled out the letter again, and read Heath's words. *"I'll be thinking of you the whole way across."* Iwa had turned the blackboard into a giant map of the Hawaiian Islands, which was now covered in *X*'s and arrows and notes. Just before lunch Lieutenant Varney called in that the search outside of Hale'iwa had yielded nothing. Iwa drew a big circle with a line through it over the location. They'd all been so hopeful, it was bitter news to swallow.

Livy had begun sorting and collecting telegrams, brought in by Dole's nephew from Western Union. Some were addressed to the fliers, including those missing. One box was full of congratulatory notes for Goebel and Davis and a few for Felix and Livy, and yet another held fan mail for Millie. Livy read the one from her parents first.

MISS OLIVIA WEST
YOU DID IT SWEETHEART! YOUR FATHER HAD NO
DOUBT IN HIS MIND BUT I DIDN'T SLEEP ONE WINK
UNTIL I HEARD YOUR WHEELS HAD TOUCHED THE
GROUND STOP CHEERS TO BEING THE FIRST WOMAN
TO CROSS THE PACIFIC IN AN AIRPLANE STOP YOU
ALWAYS WERE A DREAMER BUT PROMISE ME NO

```
MORE BIG DREAMS FOR A WHILE SEND WORD WHEN
YOU CAN STOP
LOVE M AND P
```

The words hit her where it counted, and swelled her up with pride. But it was that exclamation point that really mattered. Her mother must have been beside herself to pay extra for it. Livy felt a shift in the field, much as she often did with the weather. Prize money or no prize money, the fact that she had made it to Hawai'i was everything. She could picture Pa out back, downing a tequila shot or two in her honor, and her mom in the kitchen manically baking cinnamon rolls with a smile that couldn't be wiped from her face.

Their daughter, the talk of the country.

Next, she read one from Mahoney, who sent his congratulations, offering her a small raise and wondering when she would return so he could throw a party at the hangar. She felt a warm flush of satisfaction. No one at Dutch Flats had really thought she would get in the race at all, let alone place second in a race where only two planes finished. Mahoney would have to wait for an answer, because Livy had no idea when or if she wanted to go back.

When she had finished reading her telegrams, she leafed through those to Millie. Curiosity got the best of her, and she read a few. There were three marriage proposals, two requests for a lock of her hair, six people asking for a signed photo, and an offer for a role in a film in Hollywood. But the one that made Livy break down in tears was the one from Millie's folks.

```
MILDRED DORAN
WE LOVE YOU DARLING AND WE KNOW THAT YOU
ARE SAFE AND SOUND WHERE EVER YOU ARE STOP
GOD ALMIGHTY IS WATCHING OVER YOU STOP WE
ARE SO PROUD OF YOU BUT MORE THAN ANYTHING
```

WE JUST WANT YOU BACK HERE WITH US STOP DO
SEND WORD THE MINUTE YOU ARRIVE STOP
YOUR LOVING PARENTS

She knew it was irrational, but Livy felt guilty that she was living and breathing in Honolulu, her parents overjoyed, while Millie's family felt much like she did—gutted and desperate to hear the words *We found them. They're safe.*

In the bottom of the bag, she found a few telegrams for Heath. She ran her hand over one, feeling the slight indent of the letters on paper, but couldn't pick it up. Let him read them when he came ashore.

At high noon, Ryoko's mother showed up with tins of aromatic chicken and vegetables, and steaming baskets of rice. Enough to feed a small army. She was a tiny woman with shiny hair and an infectious laugh and she brightened the mood, if only for a half hour or so. Felix showed up just in time to join them for lunch, with the depressing news that the planes over Mauna Loa hadn't found anything.

"Seems like they should still be searching—there's a lot of ground to cover," Livy told him.

"You're right about that, but from what I gather, sending those planes over was a formality. No one believes much that anyone is up there. And if a plane went down in the lava, no one could survive that."

"We'd want to know, one way or another."

"That we would."

Livy took her plate and went to sit on the grass under a broad, shady tree. Holding her breath all day, on top of still being worn to the bone, was taking a toll. Bees buzzed and the sound of the waves lulled her into a reverie. Heath was swimming with her off the cliffs in mid-October, the water ice, but clear as spring water. He'd gone under and disappeared for what seemed like minutes and Livy had started to wonder where he was. She spun around and around, concern creeping into her consciousness. Five seconds later, he erupted out of the water, laughing and wrapping his arms around her. They stayed that way, shivering under a wide blue sky, bodies pressed together for warmth. Then he said something peculiar, words that until this very moment she'd forgotten all about.

"Promise me, if I go down, you'll come looking for me."

The next thing Livy knew, Felix was standing over her snapping his fingers. "You'll want to hear this, my friend. Erwin and Eichwald just took off from Oakland in *Dallas Spirit* and they're broadcasting their flight."

He pulled her up by the hand, and they went in and sat by the clunky radio, with all its knobs and dials and wires.

"Lucky bastards. What I would have given for even an inch of blue sky," Felix mumbled.

Livy stayed glued to the radio, as Eichwald and Erwin broadcast their flight across the airwaves, hour by hour, using Morse code. Davis happened to be an expert in deciphering the dots and dashes in real time.

"'Engine purring along just fine… Over *SS Manoa*, dipped a wing and got a blast of steam in response… Just flew over a rumrunner. Could use a drink about now… Love you, Ma.'"

Then, at two twenty-two, a call came in over the telephone. Ryoko answered and began scribbling furiously. She waved Livy over and Livy ran to her side.

"Yes… And they're sure?… The colors match… Any sign of the crew?" Ryoko said into the receiver.

Ryoko had written in large letters on a notepad, *"MAUI, PLANE,"* and tapped it with her pencil. Livy felt light-headed. *Which plane?*

When she hung up, Ryoko said, "That was the sheriff on Maui. He says they believe they've found *Miss Doran* in Honolua Bay!"

Iwa did a little dance and hugged Livy. "Fingers and toes crossed and prayers being sent."

"Any sign of survivors?" Livy asked Ryoko, cautiously optimistic.

"Not yet, but this was just called in. He's on his way there now."

If they'd made it this far, chances were good that maybe they'd just run out of fuel like Smith and Bronte.

"If you're going to crash-land in the water, Honolua is the prime spot for it. There's a long white crescent beach that would be easy to crawl up on," Iwa said, injecting a splash of hope into all of them. "Oh, let it be them!"

A Mr. Lum from the newspaper had been camping out for the past couple hours, and he relayed the message to the *Advertiser*, which then ostensibly led to a special midafternoon radio broadcast announcing that the crew of *Miss Doran* had been plucked out of Maui waters by a local fisherman.

Not long afterward, Varney called again. "Sorry to break the news, but it turns out what they thought was a plane is really a sampan—a fishing boat. *Miss Doran* is still officially missing."

The mood dropped like a lead fishing weight.

Before dark, Goebel and Davis showed up after another sweep around the islands, and were eager to tune into the radio and hear of their compatriots' progress. A silver flask mysteriously appeared on the table, and Ryoko brought them a round of passion fruit juice mixed with guava pulp. Goebel did the honors, pouring a dash of 'ōkolehao in everyone's glasses. The room felt immune from the laws of the outside world.

"Godspeed to our boys in the *Dallas Spirit*," he said, raising his glass. "And to Auggy and Millie and Vilas, to Jack Hunt, and to good old Hazeltine. We're pulling for you, mates."

"Hear! Hear!"

"May they live and breathe..."

Misery loved company, and Livy felt better having the other Dole Birds around. No one else could even fathom what they'd just gone through. They were bonded by extreme circumstance, of having barely survived a Pacific crossing far more dangerous than anyone had expected. Even with ships stationed all the way across, three planes had vanished into thick air.

"You know what gets me? That tampering. No one is talking about that. What if something went wrong because someone messed with these planes?" Goebel said.

"But we were all warned, and rechecked our planes," Livy said.

"You never know. Some obscure bolt comes loose midflight, and down you go."

"That's murder," Felix said.

"Exactly."

Felix scratched his head. "By that logic, the guilty party would have to be one of us four."

"Not necessarily."

"What if the compass was just faulty?" Felix asked.

"What if it wasn't?"

Goebel held up his hands. "We may never know."

A new sequence came through the radio, and Davis translated.

"Darkness is coming. No sign of any downed Dole Birds. Won't be able to see anything until first light. Will resume then. Will keep transmitting through night."

Livy felt a little light-headed, and set aside her drink. These men were in for a long and dark night. She was tempted to stay up and listen to them the whole way across. Her Morse code wasn't as swift as Davis's, but she could get by.

"All is okay, Erwin just used the loo."

"At least he's maintaining a sense of humor in a very unhumorous situation," Felix said.

In between messages, they recounted the hairiest moments of their trips.

Davis shook his head, recalling. "I'll say. When our engine started sputtering in the darkest hour of night, I thought we were toast. I ran through the most probable culprits—blown piston, bad spark plug, some kind of faulty valve and listened closely. I quit what I was doing and moved toward the front of the plane, trying to hear what the devil it was. To me it sounded like the valves were failing, so I pulled out the life raft, loaded her up and got ready for a swim."

Goebel laughed. "Meanwhile, I had no idea any of this was happening."

"What did it turn out to be?" Livy asked.

"Spare ring for the earth inductor compass. It fell out of my pocket and lodged itself under the floorboards. When I saw what it was, I whipped that thing all the way to the moon. You want to talk scared, I nearly wet myself."

Felix shot Livy a sheepish look. "You wouldn't have been the only one."

"All of that aside, those never-ending clouds took a toll on my psyche, like Chinese water torture," Davis said.

Livy concurred. "A navigator's nightmare."

"What was your favorite part?" Felix asked them all.

"That's easy. Landing," Goebel said.

Davis thought for a moment then said, "When I finally saw Diamond Head, and knew where we were, I started dropping all those unused smoke bombs. Felt like the Fourth of July and Christmas all wrapped up in one. And then that army guy held up one finger... Well, that was sweet. How about you?"

"I'm with Goebel. Touching down," Felix said.

They all looked to Livy.

Piloting the airplane more than halfway across, was what she wished she could say.

Instead, she said, "That moment when I first saw Mauna Kea." Iwa had coached her on how to pronounce it. "I will never forget the beauty of that mountain peak as long as I live—"

Their conversation was interrupted by a loud burst of static and a rapid fire of dots and dashes. Background noise made it harder to hear, but Livy already knew. *Dallas Spirit* had run into a storm.

"Getting bumpy."

Cold air blew up her spine. Beneath those two words was an undercurrent of alarm, Livy could sense it. Then, a few minutes later:

"SOS tailspin."

No one said a word. They'd all been there.

"Close call but we leveled out. Scary as hell. Some wild bumps up here. Please tell—"

Nothing more came through.

"Shit!" Goebel said, jumping up and pacing the room. Then:

"Tailspin."

Davis began tapping madly on the lever, while also yelling, "Cut the throttle! Pull back hard on the stick! Full rudder!" Same as what Felix had done during their ordeal. Livy said a prayer, and willed them out of it. When they hadn't heard back after a few minutes, she ran to the phone and called Lieutenant Varney, who no doubt had heard of the transmission.

"Every ship in the ocean is heading to the coordinates," he told her. "Go get some rest, Miss West, we're gonna find 'em."

33

EVERY CANDLE

Wren

Wren bounced down the road down to the 'Upolu Airport, marveling at how close Haleakalā looked. Every crack in the mountain and gradation from green to brown was visible. When she arrived, she was disappointed to find that 'Upolu Point was more of a long strip of asphalt running alongside a jagged, windswept stretch of coastline than an actual airport. The ocean out front was deep blue and wild, a rough crossing to Maui. Other than a private two seater and two old Royal Hawaiian Cessnas, there was nothing to be seen. Wren spotted a man unloading coolers from the plane into a rusted truck.

"Excuse me, do you work here?"

"No one works here, except maybe that flock of birds," he said, nodding to a bunch of cattle egrets in the tall grass behind the parking area.

"Isn't there a manager or someone here?" she asked.

"Used to be. What do you need?"

"Information. Maybe you can help me?"

The man looked around fifty or so, probably too young to know anything, but it was worth a shot.

"One, I'm looking for an airplane mechanic, and two, I want to find someone who knows about the Dole Derby in 1927," she said, half yelling in the blustery winds.

"All the mechanics I know are on O'ahu," he said, then lifted up his sunglasses and gave her a once-over, as if seeing her for the first time. "What do you need an airplane mechanic for?"

"Long story."

"If I had more time, I'd want to hear it, but I'm on a tight schedule. As for the Dole Derby, no idea. Sorry, kid. The twenties are long before my time. I came in the sixties from Florida and never looked back. Go to the Waimea Airport, you'll have more luck there."

Forty minutes later, Wren stood shivering in the small terminal in Kamuela as she waited for the girl at the counter to locate the one man who might know something. He didn't, and it turned out planes were serviced in Honolulu, or mechanics were flown in from Honolulu.

"Try Kona," he said.

In no mood to drive another hour on a probable wild-goose chase, Wren thanked him and drove back to Kohala with nothing to show for half a day of wasted time and burned-up gas.

She stopped in and picked up more beeswax, and on the way home, thought about all those bee boxes and honey back at the barn. She'd even found an old bee suit in the shed. Half-disintegrated, but it gave her an idea. If she could produce her own beeswax, that would help cut costs even more. Plus, the property practically hummed with bees collecting nectar from mac nut flowers, eucalyptus, 'ōhi'a, guava, strawberry guava, Christmas berry and koa trees.

When she got back, she selected an old beam, cut it to three feet, drilled holes, stained it and set it aside. For Pono, at the ranch, she liked the one he'd seen in the mezzanine. Only, instead of blown glass, she cut just the bottom off of a handful of tall mason jars, wet sanded the bottoms and began to fasten gold lightbulbs inside.

As she worked, she imagined the look on Pono's face when she gave it to him, and it brought a smile to her heart. Joe had never been remotely as enthusiastic about her lights. It seemed that he liked the idea of having an artsy woman on his arm, as though she were some kind of rare animal to show off at business dinners. But when it came to actually wanting the lights in his house, he would never pull the trigger. *I love them, but they don't match the furniture.* Now, she could do whatever she wanted, and it felt more wonderful than she'd expected— spiders and all.

The next morning, when Wren arrived at Malama, she was hoping that at least one of the residents would remember the Dole Derby. It was in their era. Last week, she had been so focused on learning the ropes and getting to know the residents, that there had been little time for small talk. Nor did she want to come across as conducting some kind of inquiry. Let it be natural. Someone would know something.

The morning shift came with a different set of challenges than the afternoon shift. Helping brush teeth, wash up, primp— for those who still did—get dressed for breakfast. Some needed all the help, others just needed an extra hand or a gentle reminder. Like Mrs. Inaba, who consistently put her articles of clothing on the wrong body parts. She had come out of her room with her skirt over her shoulders and was moseying out to breakfast when Wren intercepted her, and steered her back into her room to change.

The whole house smelled like fried rice and Portuguese sausage, the delightful smell of a home-cooked meal. Wren, on the other hand, had eaten a hardboiled egg and four guavas for breakfast. Her clothes were beginning to feel a little loose, and

she reminded herself to take any extra scraps home for breakfast tomorrow. Myra had offered, and she was more than willing to oblige.

As with bathing and dressing, several of the residents needed
help eating. Along with Wren, there was Myra and her husband,
Ferdinand, on shift. Myra took Mrs. Obake and Mr. Santos
who needed spoon feeding, Ferdinand helped wipe chins and
cut up toast and fruit into smaller bits, and Wren made sure
Mr. Larsgaard didn't try to keep standing up.

"As long as you play cribbage with me before you leave,"
he grumbled.

"I would love to."

Molly Anderson had to be prodded to eat, always saying she
was waiting for her husband.

"He's going to be late, he's with the horses, but he said to go
ahead and eat without him," Wren said, as instructed.

Molly looked up at her with milky brown eyes. "You sure?"

"Positive."

The others at the table all nodded in agreement. Everyone
at the home was in on it. Wren felt guilty for lying, but Myra
assured her once again that it was the only way to go. Better
than having to break the news over and over that her husband
was no longer alive. There was no need to put her through
that. There were only two couples at Malama, the Kaheles—
who had been married for seventy-four years, and Mr. Hewitt
and Mrs. Akina. At first Wren had thought the lovebirds were
married, because they held hands all day long, until she found
out they'd met at the home last year. Seeing them together,
and the way they looked at each other, was like a warm blast
of tenderness on an icy day.

Then there was Mrs. Wagner, the woman who spent her
time outside with the chickens and the birds. This morning,
she sat alone at the table by the window, gazing out into some
unknown world only she was privy to. All residents came with

a short life history form, but Mrs. Wagner's only said, *"From Kona. Widowed. Early-stage dementia."*

Wren went up to check on her. "Have you seen the mockingbird this morning?"

At first the woman showed no signs of hearing, but then she slowly turned her head to Wren, and took her in. One of her eyes drooped a little, but the other was clear and blue.

"Mockingbird? You're mistaken."

Dodge had pointed one out at the ranch.

"I had no idea, either, but my sources tell me they live on this island, more on the dry side usually. But this one was out front singing to me when I arrived. Seems like a friendly little thing. Did you have mockingbirds where you used to live, Mrs. Wagner?" Wren said, hoping to keep the conversation going.

"Once. Not now."

"Are you from Kona originally?"

Mrs. Wagner looked out the window again, and Wren could tell her mind was somewhere else. "No, not originally. My favorites were the albatross. Wide-winged, soaring beauties. Have you seen one?" she asked Wren.

"Once, when I was younger. My mother took me to Ka'ena Point, and there were two swooping around us. Majestic creatures, too bad they don't nest on the Big Island."

The woman sipped her coffee, hand shaking, then said, *"Mōlī."*

"Excuse me?"

"The Hawaiian name."

Wren had never heard that before. "Ah, I'm so happy to know that. I took Hawaiian in school, but my recollection is pretty sad."

"Memory fades, dear."

"Did you study birds? Or Hawaiian?" Wren asked.

"Neither." The woman turned back and tilted her head sideways. "Say, have we met before? You look familiar but I can't place you."

Wren had to stop herself from saying, *Yes, the other day out back*. The rule here was to always go along with the resident or redirect.

"I'm new here. My name is Wren."

A flash of recognition showed in Mrs. Wagner's eyes. "The bird girl from the yard, yes that's right."

Behind her, Wren heard a loud clinking sound. She turned to see Mr. Larsgaard tapping his spoon against his coffee mug. "Waitress! Another round, please."

"Please excuse me for a moment, Mrs. Wagner," Wren said, then went to refill his coffee.

The rest of the day—and the rest of the week—went much of the same. Getting to know the ins and outs of the residents, and helping them with their ADLs—Activities of Daily Living. The big events of the day were breakfast, lunch and dinner. In the between hours, Wren played cribbage with Mr. Larsgaard, herded Mrs. Inaba back into her room every time she came out wearing something inappropriate and talked story with the Kaheles. As it turned out, everyone who had been in Hawai'i in the twenties had at least a vague notion of the Dole Derby, but no one remembered any more details than Wren had already gathered from the newspaper article.

"I recall it being a fiasco."

"Didn't only two planes make it?"

"Oh, that was a big deal back then. Real tragedy though, wasn't it?"

On several occasions, Wren slipped out back to see if Mrs. Wagner wanted company. Each time, it was almost like starting over.

"Have we met?"

"My name is Wren."

"Oh, yes, lovely name."

Aside from short-term memory trouble, the woman seemed remarkably lucid, and would ask things like, "Do you know of the sooty tern? The Hawaiians call them *ewa'ewa*. Good little fisherman they are."

"I don't know that I've ever seen one. Do they nest around here somewhere?" Wren asked, always happy to learn more about Hawaiian birds.

"I don't think so."

"Where do they live?"

"I saw them on Moloka'i. A long time ago."

And that would be that. Mrs. Wagner would then retreat back into her mind and venture off to a place Wren couldn't follow. Old people were like icebergs, she realized. All you saw was the tip, but beneath the surface there was this long and full life lived. Wren found herself wanting to dive down and see what was under there. Especially with Mrs. Wagner.

Wren rose early and took a cold shower in the outdoor contraption she'd created on Friday, adding a splitter to the hose bib and running a hose up to a shower head and bolting it to the wall. Chester had given her everything she needed. It wasn't pretty and it was cold as Alaska, but it worked. Getting hot water was a high priority that might never happen, so she figured she better get used to it.

Pono rambled in at half past eight, and her stomach filled with moth wings at the thought of seeing him again. It had been five days since he'd last been there, and she told herself this weird elation was purely from being lonely, but the truth was, she missed him. When he climbed out of the truck wearing a flannel shirt and a cowboy hat, it was all she could do not to run up and wrap herself around him in a big hello.

"You swam already?" he asked.

She shook her head. "I built a shower and christened it this morning."

"No wonder your lips are blue."

Pono came closer, then stopped, so Wren held her arms out wide. He stepped in at the same time she tippy-toed up. His arms curled around her, dense and wiry, and she pecked him on a smoothly shaven cheek. For a split second, she was lost in the smell of detergent and Old Spice. The whole thing took less than two seconds.

He'd brought coffee again, still-warm banana bread from his mom and a bag of pipi kaula for Pa'a. It was drizzling, so they sat inside and Wren put out a plate of banana, lilikoi and strawberry guava she'd foraged yesterday afternoon.

"Any more progress with Pa'a?"

"I have her bed right up against mine now. And she comes in earlier—while I'm still reading, and sometimes leaves after I wake up. She has this hilarious but very loud snore that makes me want to throw a pillow at her. But of course I would never, she's so wary. I wonder what happened to her?"

"Probably better you don't know," he said.

She looked over at the two dogs, lounging just inside the barn door opening. Pa'a had an uncanny ability for showing up the minute Pono and Scout arrived. Either she had really good ears or she was hiding out closer than Wren thought.

"What about the job? How's that going?" Pono asked.

"It's hard, but I love it. And the hours are perfect, so I still have time to work around here."

"You know what they say about all work, no play," he said, squeezing a lilikoi into his mouth and getting juice all over his chin.

"What do they say?"

"That it makes you dull. But I guess you don't need to worry about that."

Wren buzzed from the compliment. "None of this here feels

like work. It's just what needs to be done. It feels really different in that way."

"No man back on O'ahu who will resent you being gone so long?"

The question caught her off guard, and when she looked at him, he looked away.

"No man on O'ahu. No man anywhere, and I'm happy that way."

She probably came off as defensive, but it was the truth. Being alone and having the freedom to do whatever she wanted felt liberating. The more distance she got from Joe, the more she was coming to see that she'd been living someone else's life—his house, his friends, dreams. She was about to send the question back his way, but the words stuck in her throat.

Let him tell you when he's ready.

"Fair enough," he said.

Wren then told him how she'd struck out on finding any more details about the race, and on locating an airplane mechanic.

Pono didn't seem bothered. "I guess we're on our own for now."

Somehow, that fact didn't bother Wren at all.

At lunchtime, they took their materials list and went into town. They loaded up at the hardware store, picked up sandwiches and a box of homemade taro mochi being sold on the side of the road out of the back of an El Camino.

When they drove past the Bond Memorial Public Library, Wren said, "Stop!"

Pono slammed on the brakes, holding his hand out to prevent her from slamming into the dash. When it was obvious they weren't going to hit anything, he said, "What the hell?"

"Sorry, it's just that every time I've tried to go to the library, it's been closed or has a note on the door saying Out to Lunch, or Back in Thirty Minutes. Can we just pop in and speak to the librarian?" she said.

Pono waited in the truck with Scout. Inside the New England–style red-roofed house, Wren found a thin, short-haired woman in a yellow muʻumuʻu and a sweater returning books to the shelves. In a whisper, Wren told her what she needed.

"The *Star Bulletin* articles go back to 1912, but you'd need to go to Oʻahu to the main branch for the microfilm. That or UH," the woman said.

Yet another dead end.

"Welcome to the Big Island," Pono said when she got back in the car and told him.

January seemed intent on showing off every weather pattern in her playbook, and come late afternoon, the drizzle turned into a steady downpour, coupled with gusty trade winds. The big eucalyptus out back dipped and swayed, branches scratching the metal roof—an eerie, animal screech. Both dogs had moved inside and Paʻa glanced up nervously each time it happened.

Pono noticed and said, "You're safe with us, girl."

Despite the damage to *Malolo*'s canvas fuselage, the fact that the plane had been sequestered away for God knew how long was to its advantage. Pono had found a book at the Waimea library on restoration of antique planes that proved invaluable, but the advice went counter to what they had already began. Namely, start in the back of the plane and work your way forward piece by piece. That way, you cut your teeth on the less critical parts, not the engine and the prop. Pono had come armed with brown sandwich bags and a black Sharpie, to store and label all fasteners they removed in the process.

They adjusted their strategy, and moved to the tail of the

plane, which seemed like it was already in great shape to Wren. But what did she know?

Pono crouched down, running his hand over the hard piece of wood coming off the bottom of the plane. "This tail skid is obsolete, it's made for dirt runways. If we are to fly this thing, we'll need to replace it with a wheel," he said.

We.

"You seem to know a lot about old airplanes suddenly."

He nodded toward the restoration book. "That book you're holding? I read it cover to cover this week."

"Impressive. So when you say *we* fly it, what exactly do you mean by that?"

"Just what I said."

"So will you be flying it or will I?" she asked, half teasing.

Pono stood up, dusted his hands off and moved away from the plane, taking in her lines as he would a beautiful woman. He didn't answer for a while, and she could tell he was toying with her.

"I guess that remains to be seen. But something tells me it's going to be you, Captain Summers."

She laughed. "You're hilarious."

"What?"

"I guarantee you will be the one flying this bird. She might be my airplane, but you're the one in love. You have been from the moment you saw her," she said.

"Maybe. Maybe not."

Scout, sensing he was missing out, came bounding over. Wren scratched his ears and he rolled over so she could pet his belly. It had fast become his MO with her. A burst of wind rattled the windows, finding its way in through cracks and crevices and sending Pa'a scurrying underneath the airplane.

"Wicked weather, we should probably head out," Pono said.

Wren had been hoping he'd stay for a drink after they'd finished. She had even bought tequila and limes for margaritas.

"Sure," she said, disappointed.

They stood, framed by the barn door opening, making small talk about weather and dogs as the wind kicked around them. Pono didn't seem to want to leave. Then, the spitting rain broke for a moment and he whistled for Scout and made a dash for the truck.

"See you at lunch tomorrow, I have morning plans," he called.

Wren waved and watched the truck roll out, then slid the doors closed and lit the new chandelier, and every candle and lantern she owned. With a few strikes of the match, the industrial workspace became an intimate setting, a romantic party for one. Precisely the reason she loved working with light. It was all about setting the mood and the mood now was glowing and serene.

She prepared dinner for Pa'a, adding fresh pipi kaula to the kibble. If nothing else, the dog was gaining weight by the day, which made Wren happy. She tapped the spoon against the bowl and set it down on the floor alongside the table. Pa'a crawled out from under the plane and ate, but when the eucalyptus branch dragged across the roof again, she bounded up the stairs and slid under the bed.

Long week, long day. The bottle of tequila called Wren's name, so she cut and juiced limes, salted a glass, added a teaspoon of honey and mixed herself a stiff margarita. The stainless shaker had been a gift from Joe, but she loved it anyway. As she sipped her cocktail, she tried to remember what exactly it was that caused her to fall in love with him. Any clear answer eluded her, as if he'd been wiped from her mind. Even more remarkable was how in such a short time here, his emotional pull had dramatically evaporated.

A loud crashing sound outside brought her out of her tequila-induced trance. Wren grabbed the flashlight and went to investigate. Around the corner, a two-foot-wide branch had torn off the eucalyptus and taken out part of an avocado tree, leaves and smaller branches strewn everywhere. As she was assessing the damage, the whole forest lit up, confusing her for a moment, until she realized there were headlights behind her. The headlights flashed, then went dark.

34

FINDING WINGS

Olivia

Livy woke tangled in the sheets, sweaty and poorly rested from a night of fractured dreams and fitful sleep. The thought of standing around in that room all day waiting for news of the missing fliers made her physically ill. She sat up and looked out at the blue water.

Her swimsuit had worked its way to the bottom of her trunk, and she dug it out and stepped into it, sliding on a sundress halfheartedly and heading for the beach. The Spanish tile was cool on her bare feet, the grass dewy and the sand deep and powdery. It still felt surreal that she was on a tiny island in the Pacific. She stood at the water's edge for a moment, with Diamond Head to her left, and Waikiki and Honolulu to her right, reflexively scanning the skies. Canoes were pulled up on the beach, racks full of surfboards, and doves cooed in the coconut trees behind her. The scene was straight out of a postcard, depressing as hell.

When she dove in, the warmth of the water surprised her. Cool but not cold. Her body adjusted immediately, and she swam out to where tiny waves broke over shallower water. The buoyancy was remarkable, and she floated for a while, letting the ocean leach out all the pain of the past few days, temporarily numbing her frayed nerves. Making it here had been everything she ever wanted, and yet now, she felt broken.

A couple of Hawaiian men were teaching two white women—what they called *haole* here—to surf. But the waves were so small and infrequent, the four of them ended up just paddling around, laughing and standing up on the boards. Oblivious to the fact that somewhere in this same body of water, were seven lost souls—eight if you counted Lulu, the Great Dane puppy.

After her swim, which revived her some, Livy returned to search headquarters ready for some good news. All hopes of that were smashed when she saw the faces in the room. According to Varney, there were four ships in the vicinity of where *Dallas Spirit* had gone down, but none had found any trace of the missing airplane. Flights over Mauna Loa had also yielded nothing. The pilots had all come back shaking their heads.

"Talk about a wild-goose chase," one had said.

At lunchtime, Livy persuaded Felix to take her out to Rodgers Field to find an airplane, but all planes were already up in the air, save for an old Jenny under repair. The army and navy deemed the search active until all hope was lost, and the good people of Hawai'i were taking it seriously. For that she was grateful. But she needed to be a part of it, to know in her heart, that she was doing everything she could.

Promise me, if I go down, you'll come looking for me.

"I have to get to the Big Island. What about an army or navy plane?" she asked Felix.

"Not likely, my friend."

A flash of an idea struck her. "What about *Malolo*? She's still at Wheeler just sitting in the hangar."

"Malolo is being refitted, you know that. They're taking out the extra fuel tanks," he said.

"Do you know if work has begun?"

He opened her car door, squinting into the sun. "Not for certain."

Livy sensed reluctance, and when he sat down in the driver's seat and closed the door, she turned to him. "Tell me something, will you?"

He rolled down the window, letting a warm gust blow in. "Shoot."

"If Iwa was lost out there, what would you do?"

"You've got me there. Let's go see about that plane."

Without another word, they were speeding along toward Wheeler and her only chance of getting airborne that day. Felix careened around turns as if they were being chased by the mob, and Livy had to brace herself on the dash. When they arrived at the gate, the guard, who looked about fourteen, was hesitant to let them through.

"For pete's sake, our airplane is in there," Felix said.

"I still need authorization, sir."

They waited off to the side for fifteen minutes. Livy's blouse melted onto her back, and she finally had to climb out and stand in the shade. When the guard came back, he waved them through, then stopped them again.

"What is it now?" Livy asked.

He leaned in and produced a newspaper with a big photo of Livy and Felix standing in front of *Malolo* up to their ears in lei. "My boss wants your autograph, Mr. Harding. Would you mind signing?"

Not a word or a glance to Livy. She bit her tongue, trying not to be bothered, but failing miserably. It was sure to get a whole lot worse before it got better, and unless people knew the truth, her name would quickly fade into the dusty basements of libraries.

At the hangar, *Malolo* sat untouched.

"She looks pretty doesn't she?" Felix said.

No work had been done, but someone had washed her down and her red paint shone. Seeing her again made Livy happy, like seeing an old friend. The place was empty save for an old mechanic who helped them fill up with gas and offered to guide them out.

"Just say the word and I'll spin the prop," he told Felix.

Felix nodded at Livy. "She's flying, not me."

The man shrugged. "Nothing surprises me anymore. Mind the crosswinds on the takeoff, the trades are gaining speed."

"Roger that. And thank you," she said.

He saluted. "Hope you find what you're looking for."

When they hit the Big Island, they flew up the wide saddle between Mauna Kea and Mauna Loa and Hualālai. The summits were all clear, so they had that going for them, but the mechanic had been right—the brisk trades had made for a rough ride over. And now, the saddle was like a wind funnel tossing them around vigorously.

"These mountains are so big, they create their own weather patterns," Felix yelled. "Be prepared for anything. Rain, fog, snow, ash."

"Ash?"

"When Kīlauea erupts."

Livy had never seen an active volcano, and visiting one had been on her list of things to do in Hawai'i when she first started planning for the trip. Now, she was getting that wish. Based on the report out of Hilo, lights had been seen high on the eastern flank of the mountain on the night of the seventeenth. Their plan was to fly a grid from the top down once they reached the general area, and if they found nothing, spend the night at Volcano House and resume the following day.

"We can stay here all week if you want. I'll let you decide," Felix had said.

She suspected he was trying to make amends, and appreciated his efforts. Before they'd left, he had given her a crash course in Hawaiian volcanoes, and Livy was surprised to learn that Mauna Loa was seventy-five miles long and sixty-four miles wide. That meant the mountain was as long as the whole island was wide, making their job of finding anyone all the harder.

"The summit rises 13,681 feet above sea level, but if you count from the ocean floor, she's a whopping thirty thousand or so. Taller than Everest and more massive than any other active volcano in the world. A real beauty, she is."

"How do you know all of this?" Livy asked, impressed.

"Iwa's father is a surveyor. He used to drag his girls to the far corners of the islands on mules, and she retained every detail. Brightest woman around, that one."

"Maybe she ought to come with me instead," Livy said.

"Iwa taught me everything she knows. You're in good hands, my friend."

They flew along the northwest flank of Mauna Loa, a patchwork of black, gray and dark brown lava flows dipping down through moss green forests. Moku'āweoweo rose five thousand feet above them to the right, and Halema'uma'u spread out below them to the left. Felix had made her repeat the tongue twisting names of the summit calderas of Mauna Loa and Kīlauea before takeoff.

"I won't remember these," Livy had protested.

"You need to know your landmarks, otherwise, you're no good to the search."

It was midafternoon, with hours of daylight stretching out ahead, and enough fuel to take them beyond sunset. As they made their way around the mountain, the winds eased and a sea of clouds moved in over the lowlands. They both had binoculars, but Livy was more intent on navigating to the coordinates they'd been given.

"Here we are!" Felix finally yelled.

Livy brought them lower, a hundred feet above the treetops. At this elevation, trees were stunted from the lack of oxygen, and there was more lava than forest. She could see why the army pilots had had their doubts. They flew southwest for twenty minutes, then looped around and came back a little lower down the mountain, then did it again, and again. Trees grew larger and more varied, with older-growth forests and high, lime-green canopies. Other than a couple of hawks floating on wind currents, they saw no sign of life.

Livy wanted to stay optimistic, but with each pass they made, the crack in her heart widened. A few times, they'd seen broken branches or fallen trees, and but the damage must have been from storms. It was agonizing and frustrating, but better than being in that room back at the Royal.

Two hours in, as twilight neared, they approached a dense blanket of clouds. "What should we do?" Livy called back.

They were at fifty-four hundred feet and the airfield they'd be landing on was at about four thousand.

"Continue on. We should drop below it soon, but I'm afraid we won't be able to keep searching tonight."

When they broke through the clouds only a couple hundred feet below, it was like entering another realm. Overcast and moody and downright depressing. The whole of Kīlauea caldera was visible in the distance. Livy took them directly toward the black expanse, which looked more like the moon than anything on earth.

"The runway is northeast of the crater, beyond that high point. And I should warn you—it's short," Felix said.

On the far edge of the caldera, spirals of smoke rose from the edge of the cliffs, dancing in the wind.

"Is that some kind of eruption?" she asked, not sure if it would even be safe to land.

"Steam vents. Not a concern."

Livy wanted to see more, but there would be time for that tomorrow. Right now she was worn-out and needed to get on the ground before complete darkness fell. Below them, she noticed a short strip of cleared land-off to the left, not far from the road. It looked almost as long as it was wide. A death strip, really.

"Don't tell me that's it," she said.

"That's it."

"Damn you, Harding."

Felix guided her to the approach, where they were buffeted by thermals. On one end was a forest, on the other, a rough-looking lava field cut through with a huge crevice. She had half a mind to fly to Hilo and land there, but that would burn up fuel. She wanted to save every drop they had, even the vapors, for the search. It took three harrowing attempts before the wheels touched down, but they made it, once again.

At Volcano House, Livy and Felix checked in and made a few calls to O'ahu, where there was still no news. Now, they sat in wooden rockers in front of a roaring stone fireplace sipping weak hot cocoa topped in whipped cream. The air was cold enough outside that she'd been able to see her breath. The large Victorian-style hotel with a round turret and shuttered windows sat on the edge of the massive caldera, and was packed with visitors from far and wide. A boisterous group of soldiers sat in the lounge singing "Ain't Misbehavin'" and "In the Jailhouse Now."

"There's a military camp across the way. They come here to recreate," Felix told her, eyeing the men as though he wanted to join in.

"Heath wanted to come here to do the same," Livy said.

"Did he, now?"

Up until now, she'd kept his letter to herself.

She nodded. "He gave me a note before we left, but I didn't read it until after we landed. He wanted to give us another chance. I knew it even before we left, but I wouldn't give him the satisfaction. He'd burned me so badly, you know? And now he's gone and I'll never be able to tell him yes."

His eyes began to water. "Aww, shucks. I'm sorry, Livy."

Her own eyes teared up and she stared into the fire. "It still feels surreal, you know? It'd been so long since I'd seen Heath and I had convinced myself I was over him, but the minute I saw him in that speakeasy, it felt like no time had passed."

"That's love for you. It has a way of warping time that makes no logical sense. Two people who are meant to be together will always find a way in the end. Trust that," he said.

"Well, I'm here, but he's not, and it really stinks," she said, holding back a sob.

He stood up and held out his arm. "Come on, you need to sleep. Tomorrow's another day."

35

EUCALYPTUS

Wren

Wren swung her light around, illuminating a big dark truck. Her whole body went slack with relief.

"Pono? What are you doing back?" she called, hurrying back to the shelter of the barn.

He and Scout met her inside, both wet and muddy.

"There's a downed tree about two-thirds of the way out. It was slow going with the weather. You don't happen to have a chain saw, do you?" he said.

"No, but even if I did, I wouldn't send you back into this tempest. Did you see the carnage out back?"

She went and grabbed two towels, one for Pono, one for Scout. He dried off Scout first, roughing him up and wiping down each paw.

"The winds have swung around from the west, so this isn't the way the trees naturally bend. In these winds, eucalyptus turn deadly," he said.

"I'll remember that."

He seemed jacked up on adrenaline, and his eyes swept across the room, reflecting the flickering light. "I really should get home."

"With these deadly trees? Look, I can make you up a bed down here and you can leave at first light. By then I'm sure things will have calmed. And you can take my hand saw, but it'll take forever to cut through a big tree."

That seemed to satisfy him, and he whistled for Scout to come down from upstairs, where he had been clomping around, no doubt trying to lure Pa'a out of hiding. While Wren mixed a bowl of food up for the dog, Pono took off his wet flannel shirt and hung it on the back of the chair.

"Sorry to impose on you like this," he said, hovering near the table awkwardly.

Wren placed her hands on his shoulders and pushed him into the chair. "Sit. Relax. Shit happens. And when it does, I make margaritas. Do you want one?"

"Heck yeah, that sounds good."

"And I have human food, too. Nachos with avocado, guacamole, and topped with more avocado. I wasn't expecting company."

The property contained enough avocado to feed an army, and it also happened to be one of her favorite foods.

"I'm easy."

He didn't seem easy, in fact he seemed preoccupied and wound tight as a wing wire, but Wren was determined to loosen him up. Extra splash of tequila. Check.

When Pono took his first sip, he closed his eyes. "Damn, someone knows how to make a mean margarita," he said, with a line of salt clinging to his mustache.

"I've had practice," she said, tapping her glass to his.

"Cheers…to old airplanes and new horizons," he said.

She met his gaze and smiled. "I'm all about new horizons."

He took a few more large sips, while Wren refreshed hers, just a splash. And another spoonful of honey.

"Hang on a second, did I just see you put the hundred-year-old honey in your drink?" he said.

"Yes, why?"

"Oh, just because I don't want to have to take you to the hospital."

She grinned. "If it was bad, we would both have to go. You just drank it in your margarita."

He grabbed for his neck. "Oh, hell!"

Wren just shook her head. "You won't win any Academy Awards, that's for sure. And the honey is good, I tried it the other day. Just a tiny bit. I'm still alive."

It was true. The crystalized honey had softened up when she put it over her camping stove, and it was woody and warm.

"It's actually pretty cool when you think about it. This honey was bottled by someone in your family before the war, and little did they know that someday you'd be sitting here drinking it," he said.

Wren smiled at the thought.

Pono picked up the deck of cards sitting in front of him on the table and nodded at the cribbage board. "You play?"

"Yeah, but I suck. I've been playing myself at night so I can figure out how to beat Mr. Larsgaard—one of the residents at Malama. You'd think so much of it was luck, but I have yet to win a game."

"Luck has nothing to do with cribbage. Well, mostly."

"You play?" she asked, surprised.

He shrugged. "Just a little."

"Be honest."

Pono shuffled the cards with one hand. "I grew up on a ranch in Kohala with a bunch of old *paniolo* for nursemaids. Of course I know how to play cribbage," he said with that sly smile of his.

"Will you play with me?"

"Nah. Not a good idea," he said, crossing his legs and leaning back in the chair.

"What do you mean?"

"Because you won't win with me, either, and I don't want to break your heart."

Wren laughed out loud. "Now you have to play with me. I won't let you leave until you do."

He raised his eyebrows. "Is that so?"

A hot whoosh poured through her body.

"It is so. Very so."

She assembled the nachos, heating up a can of black beans while putting Pono to work chopping and mashing avocado. At least he'd come out of his funk quickly and accepted his fate. A good sign in a man. By the time they started playing cribbage, Wren had the perfect tequila buzz going, and so apparently did Pono. He cut the low card, so he dealt first.

After a string of bad hands, Pono fell behind eleven points. Wren started to get a little cocky, until he passed her and never looked back. Half his points were made pegging, and she began to see that that was where the real skill came in. Pono played with such determination it was endearing and maddening at the same time. When he reached the finish, Wren had squeaked past the skunk line by four points. They played again. And again. Each time, Pono showed no mercy even though Wren fed him more margaritas in hopes of lessening his edge over her. But her plan was flawed, because her edge blurred, too.

Sometime during the third game, two of the candles blew out from the wind and one of the lanterns ran out of oil. Wren hadn't even noticed. Now, the room felt more shadowy, everything bathed in orange light.

"One more?" he asked.

She threw a wadded-up paper towel at him. "No way. I'm done getting my ass kicked."

He ducked. "I'll admit, you put up a good fight."

Not even close, but it was nice of him to say.

"My heart might not be quite broken, but it hurts," she said.

They looked at each other, but neither spoke. The atmosphere shifted around them, and Wren's pulse picked up speed. Pono reached over and squeezed her forearm in mock consolation. He let his hand stay there, heavy and warm, in no hurry to pull away. Wren sat still as a stone. When he finally let go, his palm ran slowly across her skin—wrist, hand, fingers—leaving sparks in its wake. His touch was firm and sensual, causing a light sensation in her head. Wren closed her eyes for a moment to try to come back to earth. When she opened them, Pono was standing in front of her with his hand out.

There was nothing else to do but take his hand. He pulled her up close, gaze never wavering from hers. He placed his hands on both sides of her face, featherlight. Then he kissed her. So softly, she wondered if she'd imagined it. A fast brush of the lips, a hot exchange of breath.

Wren pulled herself into the hardness of his abdomen, his hip. He responded by kissing her more urgently, and sliding his hands from her face down her shoulders, running along her sides and waist and settling in the small of her back. He tasted like lime and salt.

When the kiss ended, Pono spoke into her hair, "This is not what I expected."

"Same."

"Do you want to stop?"

She wrapped a finger around a lock of his hair. "Please, no."

Another candle went out, and he kissed her again, harder. They backed toward the steps, unable to keep their hands off of each other. Wren led him up to the mezzanine, where they almost tripped over the dogs before falling onto the futon in a tangle of intoxicated limbs. Wren laughed, heart more full than it had been in a long, long time. Possibly ever. Pono leaned up on one arm and ran the side of his hand along her cheekbone. Every time he touched her, her skin hummed with an electric current.

"The minute I saw you, I knew I was in trouble," he said.

"You weren't even that nice to me."

"That was me trying to play it cool."

Wren propped herself up on one arm, facing him. "I don't believe you. You were genuinely irritated with me. I inconvenienced you and you let me know it."

"No. I was irritated with the fact that you were so gorgeous."

She laughed, not sure what to believe. It must be the tequila. Then there was a loud commotion at the bottom of the bed, and then a snout pressed into her armpit. She squealed.

Pono jumped up, trying to steer the dog off the bed. "Get down, you big monkey."

Instead of listening, Scout rolled over and stretched out alongside Wren, tail thumping hard against her.

"I think someone is jealous," she said.

"Someone has his own girl on the floor."

Pono half wrestled, half dragged Scout off the bed, then returned. He didn't say anything, but kissed her forehead, nose, chin and neck. Small, honeycreeper kisses. Then spreading out to her collarbones. His hand traced a slow line of heat between her breasts, around her nipples, to just below her waist, one finger slipping beneath her panties. No farther. Then his mouth found hers again, and they spent what felt like the next ten hours kissing. No one had ever kissed her like this and her entire body was aflame.

When the last candle burned out, and the barn went dark, Pono rolled onto his back and found her hand. They lay shoulder to shoulder, her hair spread out like seaweed, lips chafed. The roof rattled in the wind, but the eucalyptus had ceased its scraping.

"Sounds like the worst has passed," she said.

"Let's hope."

"You have to be somewhere tomorrow morning?"

Waking up with him would either be blissful or terribly awkward she wasn't sure which.

"Yeah."

As soon as the word came out, his grip slackened and he tensed up, his whole being curling away from her. Instinctually, Wren took her hand away. The silence between them grew until it was almost unbearable. He no longer wanted to be there, she could feel it in her bones.

"I'm really tired. Would you mind if we go to sleep?" he finally said.

Wren felt a welling up of dread. This *had* been a mistake. A bad one.

"Good idea, I'm tired, too."

Pono leaned in and gave her a lukewarm kiss, then rolled over, his back to her. Wren lay there for a while wondering about the drastic change in moods. She could tell he was awake, but eventually his breathing deepened and he began to twitch. Quiet as a mongoose, she slid out of bed and went downstairs to brush her teeth and wash her face. In the mirror, her lips were red and her cheeks flushed—the face of a woman who had just one of the most unexpectedly romantic nights of her life. So why did she feel so awful?

Pono was gone when Wren woke up just before dawn. No goodbye kiss. No note. No sign that he had ever been there, other than crumpled sheets and an indent on her heart. Wren had no idea how he and Scout had disappeared so stealthily. Probably something to do with the throbbing behind her left temple, the cotton in her mouth and the breath of fire. Her sleep had been deep and dream filled. In one, she'd been flying above crashing seas, looking for a place to land in the cliffs and fold up her weary wings.

Now, birds chirped their morning songs, greeting the day cheerfully. The sun peeked through scattered clouds, but Wren rolled over and buried her face in the pillow.

36

SEARCHING FOR LOVE

Olivia

Livy went for a walk early in the morning, along the rim of Kīlauea Caldera. One misstep and you were in a steaming crack or off the edge of a cliff. The sun was rising at her back, casting long shadows of 'ōhi'a trees. She walked fast to keep warm, and it felt good to move her body and breathe in the brisk mountain air. Every so often she caught a whiff of sulphur, lest she forget where she was—on an active volcano, alive and ready to birth new earth at any moment. About fifteen minutes out, she came upon an overlook where she could take in the whole of Kīlauea, and its smaller crater Halema'uma'u. In the distance, she could make out white birds with long tails riding the updrafts.

To her right, Mauna Loa lit up in the slanted sun, looking formidable and barren, beautiful down to every piece of hardened molten lava. It made her feel small, her life fleeting. Livy pulled out her binoculars and surveyed the areas they had flown over, hoping something might stand out from a different vantage point. Ribbons of black lava and islands of green. Rugged and unforgiving country, to be sure. But they were here, and she was determined to give it one more shot.

Back at Volcano House, they ate a hearty breakfast of scrambled eggs, 'ōhelo berry pancakes and steaming hot coffee. The staff recognized them and refused to let them pay. The cook packed them a lunch, and in return Livy and Felix posed for a photograph in front of the hotel.

"Will you fly today?" she asked Felix. "I'd like to be the spotter."

He smiled. "Fresh eyes are always a good idea."

They decided on a different tactic today, based on the assumption that the location of the light that had been seen was a rough guess at best. Livy wanted to fly over the zones just beyond where they'd flown yesterday, and she wanted to fly lower. It would mean covering less ground, but they might see things otherwise missed.

Felix had secured more fuel from the military camp while Livy had been out walking, so they were restocked with enough to last them half a day before they had to head back to O'ahu. On the takeoff, Felix went full throttle from the get-go, and Livy swore one of their wheels nicked a treetop on the way out. As they made their way up the mountain, she kept an eye on a dirt road that must have been part of a ranch. They followed that up a way, over a cabin and fenced-in grasslands, cattle and horses—low enough that Livy could see clouds of flies swarming around the animals—then more forest. Livy had never seen a place so unable to make up its mind. Lava. Forest. More lava.

"Where does this road lead?" she asked.

"No idea."

"Follow it, will you?"

"Looks way south of where we want to be."

"Humor me."

The road went up and up, veered south across a pasture and disappeared.

"Dammit to hell," he said, sounding as frustrated as Livy felt.

They swung back around and continued up the mountain. Every so often a clearing would open up, and she would scarcely breathe until they passed over it. Every time there was nothing. They were now way to the south of where they'd been yesterday, and Livy kept checking her watch.

"I hate to do this, but we need to call it quits," Felix said.

"Not yet."

"We have to, my friend."

Desperation clawed at Livy. She *had* to keep looking. Could not give up. Time had just about run out, when suddenly another road appeared out of the trees. Narrow, and overgrown, but definitely a road.

"Over there!" she yelled.

Felix banked. The road continued in and out of brush, and they followed it just above the trees, south, away from Kīlauea. A couple miles on, there was a big disturbance in the road, where the whole grassy surface had been skinned off. Trees on both sides were broken. Goose bumps trailed over her skin and Livy's whole body went cold.

Something violent had happened here, something unnatural. There, just beyond, tilted on its side and almost completely covered by foliage, lay an airplane. Or at least part of one. Yellow-gold with white trim.

37

MEMORIES LIKE TREE ROOTS

Wren

Wren had never looked forward to going to work as much as she did on the Tuesday after making out with Pono. The last two days had been spent not wanting to think about him, while listening for the sound of his engine. All. Day. Long. He never showed at lunchtime the next day like he said he would. She'd also relived their night together seven hundred times in her mind, body burning in places he'd touched her. There would be no time today for those kinds of thoughts, thank goodness.

Everyone greeted her with warm smiles, at least those who remembered her did. Molly Anderson gave her a suspicious look, but the rest seemed genuinely thrilled to see her. Lunch was already *pau*, and people were scattered around doing their usual. TV, cards, reading, talking story. The only person missing was Mr. Larsgaard, who usually held court at the card table at this time of day.

"Where's Mr. Larsgaard?" Wren asked Myra, who seemed to never stop working.

"He fell this morning and Ferdinand took him to hospital. Poor guy was in a lot of pain."

Wren's throat tightened, and she wasn't sure she could speak, surprised at the depth of her concern. He'd grown on her like all the others. They'd become like a whole collection of grandparents she never had. Plus, she had been looking forward to a game with him, hoping that Pono's skills had rubbed off on her.

Her eyes misted up. "Did he break anything?"

"I hope not, but at his age, there's a good chance."

Wren flew through her tasks in the house, ready to get outside and say hello to Mrs. Wagner. She wasn't sure why, but she felt like they were kindred spirits. Light trade winds had blown the clouds away, and the woman sat where she always sat. But today she'd dressed in riding pants and a thick jacket better suited for Waimea weather.

"You're looking sporty today, my friend," Wren said as she approached.

Mrs. Wagner swung her head around, squinting into the sun. "Felix? Is that you?"

"No, Mrs. Wagner, it's Wren."

A look of disappointment. "Come over here where I can see you, dear. And call me Livy, please."

Wren moved to the other side of the bench, and held up a bag of bird seed. "I brought you a present."

The woman took in her face for a few moments, her lined face so pretty still. "Ah, yes, the bird girl. What a delight to see you again."

She seemed clearer today.

"Was Felix your husband?" Wren asked, the name tugging at her subconscious mind.

Mrs. Wagner laughed. "Oh, heavens no. Felix was a dear friend, and he called everyone that—*my friend*." She sat for a moment, as though remembering, then said, "We flew together."

Wren thought she'd misheard. "You what?"

"We flew."

"Was he a pilot?"

"We both were," she said, remembrance lifting off of her in waves.

Wren looked at Livy's outfit more carefully. There were pins on the jacket, and the pants came to her knee where they were met by tall socks. Truth began to dawn. Mrs. Wagner wasn't in riding pants at all.

"Mrs. Wagner—Livy—this is incredible!"

"Yes," she said, wistfully.

"How old were you when you learned to fly?"

"Younger than you are now, I'm sure."

Wren did the math in her head. "Were you in Hawai'i when they held the Dole Derby?" As the words came out of her mouth, she remembered where she'd seen the name Felix. The old newspaper article. "Wait, was your friend Felix, *the* Felix? The pilot in the race?"

"Felix was in the race." Livy laced her fingers together and set them lightly in her lap. "And so was I."

The wind lay down, the birds stopped chirping and a cloud slid across the face of the sun. It felt to Wren as though the earth stopped spinning.

Olivia West.

"You were his navigator. I saw the photograph in the paper," Wren said.

Livy's eyes began to water. "In 1927. The race of a lifetime. I remember it as though it were yesterday. The plane, the clouds, that naked blue ocean."

Wren was still floored. She'd been searching all over town while the one person who knew more than anyone had been hanging out with the chickens and sparrows at Malama Care Home.

"I would love to hear all about it sometime. And about Felix. What happened to him?"

Livy frowned, reaching up to sweep a wisp of hair from her eyes. "The Germans got him, I think. Or was it the Japanese?"

She paused in concentration, lips tucked in on themselves. "My mind has these holes in it, you see. I do know he went off to war and never came back, like so many of our boys."

Wren touched her crepe-paper hand. "I'm so sorry."

"Felix died doing what he loved. He was going to go out in the air, one way or another. It was his wife I felt for. The two were inseparable as peanut butter and jelly. If I recall correctly, she went looking for him after the war, somewhere in Europe, and fell ill. You ask me, she died of a broken heart."

"You knew her, then?"

Livy nodded. "Iwa. She and I became fast friends."

Chicken skin spread out along Wren's arms. *Iwa.* Her great-aunt, oldest of the Kahawai girls. She couldn't believe she was sitting here with someone who knew her.

Behind them, the back door slammed against the wall, and Myra called out. "Wren, I need you in here, please!"

"Give me two minutes," Wren said.

Myra huffed, but went back inside. Wren's mind was a jumble of questions, and she wanted to stay out here all afternoon with Livy—all night if she had to—and gather answers. But they had time, and the woman seemed frail. She didn't want to press her by opening a can of worms that might stir up painful emotions, and then leave her alone with her thoughts.

She turned to Livy. "I would love to talk to you more about this, and hear your story. I have questions, too, that you might be able to answer. Can we talk later today or tomorrow?"

"I'm not going anywhere," Livy said. "At least I don't plan on it."

On impulse, Wren reached out and gave her a quick hug. Underneath all that material, Livy's shoulders were bony, arms thin as stalks of ginger.

"You better not. We have lots to discuss."

Wren was slammed all afternoon, and Livy was eating when it was time to go, so their talk would have to wait until tomorrow.

★ ★ ★

When Wren got back to the barn, she retrieved the wooden box with the photos, and the newspaper article from the dilapidated shed and spread them all out on the table. A twenty-something Livy smiled back at her. Same eyes, different lifetime. It was hard to imagine this vivacious young creature as the old woman at Malama, but the more Wren stared at the photo, the more the two women became one and the same. It was all in the eyes.

She leaned back and thought about this new piece of the puzzle. Felix had gone to war sometime in the early forties and never returned. If the planes had been untouched since then, no wonder they were in such good shape. And poor Iwa, she must have been devastated. Wren felt a strong ache in the center of her chest.

Worlds were colliding, and she wished she could tell Pono, but Pono was MIA. He knew she worked this week, and after their night together, you would hope he had the decency to man up and at least come by to explain his weird behavior. But that heavy feeling remained, the knowing that something was off, and she couldn't quite shake it. Wren grabbed a beer from the melted ice in the cooler, blew out all but one candle and went outside to count stars and look for satellites.

Not ten minutes later, Wren heard a twig break. A small rustle off in the bushes.

"Pa'a, is that you? It better be."

That feeling she was being watched surfaced again.

"Come sit with me, will you?"

There was no more movement for some time, and then Wren heard the sound of paws on hard ground. A dog-shaped shadow approached, eyes glowing in the candlelight. Instead of stopping ten feet away, like she always did, Pa'a kept on coming and sat just beyond arm's reach.

"Well, hello to you, too."

At least someone wanted to be with her.

The next day at Malama, as soon as Wren was able, she stole out back to talk to Livy again. Everyone else was settled and she figured she could disappear for a half hour or so. Mr. Larsgaard had returned from the hospital, hip intact, but he'd been sedated and was in no state to try to amble around on his own.

The winds had shifted out of the north, cooling down the air and brightening the sky. Coming down the hill, Maui had been as clear as she'd ever seen it. The beauty on this island continued to catch her off guard, every single day. Livy sat where she always did, bundled in a sweater and holding a ceramic mug. The bag of birdseed lay on the bench next to her, half-empty.

"Perfect day, isn't it?" Wren said.

Livy sipped, then said, "Reminds me of home."

"And where would that be?"

"San Diego, where my parents live."

Live, not *lived*.

Livy glanced up at Wren, and Wren was expecting her to say, *Have we met?* but instead she said, "I've been waiting for you to come, dear."

Funny how the mind worked, some memories slipping through the cracks, others firmly planted like ancient trees whose roots had taken hold. Wren knew it was mainly the new that slipped through, which was why she was so pleasantly surprised that Livy remembered her now. Their talk yesterday must have opened some neural pathway that bridged the old with the new.

She sat and took Livy's hand. "Yesterday you told me you were a pilot in the Dole Derby, and about Felix, do you remember?"

"Oh, yes."

"What if I told you that my great-aunt was Felix's wife? Not only that, but I've recently inherited an old hangar with your plane, *Malolo,* in it," Wren said.

Livy's eyes went wide. "No!"

"It's true."

Through watery blue eyes, Livy looked more closely at Wren. "Maybe the nose. And that pretty brown hair of yours. Iwa was a real looker, that one. And *Malolo!* My word, I've never loved another plane the way I loved her, quirks and all. When you spend twenty-seven hours in a small plane like that, you become either close friends or bitter enemies."

"It seems inconceivable that a plane that small could even fly that long. Felix must have been a remarkable pilot, but how did he stay awake?"

A long silence stretched out between them, and Wren was about to prod Livy, when she said, "Felix wasn't flying that night. I was."

"You both flew during the race?"

"I flew *most* of the race. Felix was an excellent pilot, but he had a problem with water."

"He ran out of water?"

"No, he was terrified by water. Open ocean. He made light of it until we were well on our way, and then he went and fell apart on me. Had I not been a pilot myself, you and I wouldn't be sitting here having this conversation."

Wren was stunned. "How much of the race did you fly?"

"Twenty hours, give or take."

"In a twenty-seven-hour race? How come there was no mention in the papers of this? I mean, do people know?"

Livy had seemed like just a minor character, an afterthought, if you went by the newspaper story.

"Oh, Felix got all the glory, he did. But there was the prize money to consider, and we worried we'd have been disqualified if the race committee found out I'd flown most of the way.

They were stodgy and particular and the pilots had to pass muster. Us navigators did, too."

"I'm so impressed. What an honor it is to be sitting here with *the* Olivia West!"

Two rosy spots appeared on Livy's cheeks. "It was a dream I went after tooth and nail. Girls weren't supposed be able to fly airplanes, but some of us proved them wrong. Not just me, there were others."

The two chickens, feathers ruffling in the breeze, came over and started pecking around Wren's feet. She threw down more birdseed.

"Flying is one thing, but crossing the Pacific? I, for one, would never have had the guts. Just flying over here from O'ahu was terrifying for me. Not because of the flight, but because I was leaving everything behind and coming to live in what sometimes feels like the end of the world."

"Sometimes the smallest things can be the scariest."

"It sure feels that way," Wren said. "Livy, there's another plane in the barn with *Malolo*. Do you think it might have been in the race, too?"

Livy peered out into the blue sky and Wren could tell she was trying hard to focus. "What does the other airplane look like?"

"It looks old, too. A little bigger than *Malolo* and the whole thing is made from wood not canvas. Same engine, it appears. It's a beautiful plane. Red now, but the paint is chipping and it looks like there's white beneath it. Sound familiar?"

A muscle twitched beneath Livy's eye. "Tell me, dear, what exactly do you know of the Dole Derby?"

"Just what I read in the newspaper article. Who won. That only two of you made it, and several planes were lost at sea. I know that a large search ensued."

A butterfly flew past, almost fluttering into Livy.

"There's so much more to tell. But first, I want to see those planes," Livy said.

"I could arrange that. Will they let me take you out of here?"

"They ought to. If not, we'll go anyway."

Wren wanted to keep her talking. "Can you tell me any more about Iwa?"

Livy took a while to fish around in her memory. "Iwa was a real go-getter. If it weren't for her, Felix would have never gotten that plane. She went fundraising all over creation. I had never met a woman so tough but sweet, and smart as a crow. They had this rare affection for each other, and neither wanted kids because I think they had enough in each other. The sweetness of it rubbed off on everyone around them. Since you're a relation, I will tell you this much." Her voice trailed off, and she glanced around as though checking for eavesdroppers. "Iwa confided in me that one of her sisters couldn't conceive, so she'd given her a child."

Hānai. The act of sharing your children—the reasons many. And since Portia had no children, that only left Lihau.

"That would mean that Iwa is my grandmother?" she said, more to herself than to Livy.

"I suppose it would. Happened all the time in those days, spreading around the children so there was enough for everyone. No one thought twice about it."

Wren felt shaken, her sense of identity shifting once more.

"What about you, Livy? Did you have kids?" Wren asked.

Livy closed her eyes. Her lids were almost translucent, and patterned with spider-thin blue veins that brought to mind the skin of a newborn bird. "I'm tired, dear. Let's save that for another day, shall we? Would you please help me inside before the rain comes?"

There were no clouds in the sky. "We don't need to worry about it raining today."

"I'm not worried. But the rain *is* coming. Can't you taste it?"

Any other day, Wren might have agreed, but the skies were so darn beautiful. And the only thing she could taste was the third cup of coffee she'd just poured down her throat. She walked her, arm in arm, up the steps. Livy was slow and shaky, and her feet shuffled over the grass, but she held on to Wren with an iron grip.

Saturday. Wren would get her out of here to see the planes, even if she had to fabricate a story or steal her away.

38

KIDNAPPING OLD PEOPLE

Wren

The rains did come. Livy had been right about that. It felt like the wettest winter on record, and all the trees in the forest seemed to be growing taller by the hour. The road to the barn had grown so slick that Wren had to cut her speed by half. Her tires were coated in thick mud that kicked up long trails of brown when she turned onto the main road. But without the rain, this whole stretch of coastline wouldn't be so lush, and have so many shades of green you could fill a whole book with them. From lime to huluhulu moss to lizard to shallow-water green.

On both Thursday and Friday, Ferdinand was out sick, so Wren and Myra did double time. Wren stayed late Thursday and came early on Friday. She checked in on Livy whenever she had a chance, but she only had a few moments to spare.

"Are you still planning on kidnapping me one of these days? I sure hope so because I have things to tell you. I wasn't going to, but I've decided I must," Livy said.

Wren wished she could scoop her up and take her to the barn right then, but that was impossible. "Tomorrow," she promised.

Livy clasped her hands together like an eager child. "Is it a long drive?"

"Not too long."

That evening, after eating two burnt grilled cheese sandwiches for dinner, Wren took a lantern upstairs and opened the file cabinet with the box inside, just as she'd done the last two nights. She laid each article out on the bed, still amazed that these items had belonged to her grandfather—if Livy had been right about Iwa giving Lihau her child. The photo of Felix and Iwa fascinated her the most, and she searched for any sign of herself in their faces.

When Wren had had enough, she delicately placed each item in the box and put it back in the file cabinet for safekeeping. She'd set the lantern on the counter and in the bright light, she noticed the top of a small piece of paper slid between the shelf and the side of the drawer. Her heart kicked up a notch as she pulled it out and saw young Livy staring out at her, unsmiling, a sad look in her eyes.

"*Navigator Searches for Lost Lover*" was the headline. Wren sped through the short article, and when she finished, her heart was in her throat. Maybe this was what Livy wanted to tell her about. Her reluctance to talk about it now made sense. What a life this small, bird-loving woman had lived—and Wren didn't even know the half of it. Tomorrow couldn't come soon enough.

When Wren picked up Livy, Livy was wearing her knickers and jacket again, rosy cheeked and ready for adventure. Myra had packed a picnic basket for her, and Wren set that in the back of the truck.

"I snuck an extra cup of coffee this morning, to help pep me up," she said, as they drove off from Malama.

When they reached the gate to Ho'omalumalu, Livy said, "This whole slice of paradise belongs to you?"

"It does now. It's still hard to believe. There's not much out here beside trees and sky, but the place is growing on me with every passing day."

"Inheriting something like this is no small deal. You know, one day, out of the blue, I got a letter from Felix asking if I wanted to come and join his operation. Said he had built his own runway and was going to make the best little airline in Hawai'i. I was seriously considering it, but then the war broke out and everything changed."

"He wasn't too old to enlist?"

"Oh, he probably was, but that didn't stop him. For all I know, he was the oldest pilot in the navy." She laughed. "But he often said that after our crossing, nothing could scare him."

"I'm surprised it wasn't the other way around."

Livy nodded as she gazed out the window. "He marched to his own tune, that one. And wouldn't you know it, sixty years later, I'm finally on my way. That's one thing about life—it will keep surprising you until the cows come home."

When they drove up to the barn, Wren felt a burst of pride. She had cleared and trimmed the front area, and now, with all the rains, grass had filled in, smooth as a putting green. The barn could use a new paint job, but it at least looked cared-for. The Adirondack chairs sitting in a pool of sunlight added charm and a homey feeling.

"Leave it to Felix and Iwa to create something like this," Livy said.

"Wait until you see inside."

Wren helped her out and Livy turned her face skyward. "Ah, if only you could bottle this mountain air. Reminds me of our place at Volcano."

Our. Wren hadn't asked about her husband, the man who gave her the last name Wagner. It had never felt like the right time.

She opened the lock. "Are you ready?"

"Absolutely."

Wren slid the door open, and they went inside, arms hooked together. Both planes stood bathed in soft light. Wren felt Livy falter as they neared the planes, and she held her up.

"Oh, my," Livy said, eyes lasered on *Malolo*.

"A friend and I have been working on restoring her. He's a mechanic, and he got a book on vintage airplane restoration. Obviously, it's a major undertaking, but I think she deserves it, don't you?"

Wren left out the part about the mechanic's disappearing act. She would deal with that later, and could always find another mechanic if she had to.

Livy looked to the other plane, and Wren swore her face tightened, but then she reached out and set her hand on *Malolo*'s side near the cockpit. "I never thought I'd see you again, my friend. We're just two old girls from another time, aren't we?"

Wren stood by with a lump in her throat as Livy slowly made her way around the plane, inspecting every inch of surface, as only a pilot could. The plane held her up, as it had so many years ago.

"They don't make 'em like this anymore. Sure they might be bigger and faster and shinier, but no plane ever built has had so much gumption and personality as this little bird," Livy said.

"Did you ever fly her again after the race?"

There was a long pause. "Once."

"What was the occasion?"

Livy's gaze swept around the room, finally settling at the table. "Shall we sit, dear? This might take a while."

Wren helped Livy get situated, then fished around in the cooler for two cans of Hawaiian Sun Passion Orange. The minute she closed the cooler lid, she heard the familiar clicking of Pa'a's nails on concrete. The dog trotted toward them and sat about six feet away from Livy.

"Well, who do we have here?" Livy said, brightening.

"This is Pa'a, she's the real owner of the place."

Livy held out a shaky hand. "Hello, Pa'a, you're a beauty, aren't you?"

Pa'a's tail swept across the floor.

"She lived here before I did," Wren offered. "She allowed me in, but I'm still gaining her trust."

"Trust takes time. For some longer than others," Livy said, then turned to the dog. "You have nothing to fear from me."

Pa'a looked at Wren, as if for approval. "Go on," Wren said.

In slow motion, the dog stood and slinked over to Livy, sniffing her hand and giving it a small lick.

"You're a good girl, aren't you?" Livy said sweetly.

Pa'a then positioned her side against the chair and let Livy run her hand along her neck and back, fingers buried in the short fur.

"She's never let me touch her," Wren whispered.

"Animals have their own rules and their own reasons for doing things. You may not see it, but this dog is bonded to you, plain as day."

Wren thought about the flash flood, and how Pa'a watched her from the bushes, how she always came home at night. She hoped Livy was right. After a minute or so of back rubs, Pa'a lay down at Livy's feet and let out a blissful groan.

Livy turned her focus back to Wren. "So where were we?"

"You said you'd only flown in *Malolo* one other time."

"Right. Why don't I start from the beginning?" She took a long inhale. "When I was sixteen, I went up in the air for the first time with a dashing young pilot named Heath Hazeltine..."

The sun traveled through the sky as Wren sat rapt, listening to Livy tell her life story. They took juice breaks, food breaks, bathroom breaks and dog-petting breaks—Pa'a stayed the whole time, and Wren had to steer Livy back on track a few times. Her words took on a cinematic quality, as though Wren were sitting in the barn watching an old movie play out before her eyes.

A few times, Wren tried to jump ahead, hungry to know the ending, but each time, Livy firmly said, "Patience, my dear."

39

STATE OF THE PLANE

Olivia, 1927

Felix turned the plane around at lightning speed to do another pass over the downed plane.

"We need to land this thing!" Livy screamed.

"There's nowhere to land!"

She looked around, seeing nothing but forest, and coming to the same conclusion, but blinded by a burning need to be on the ground. "We have to, Felix. We *have* to!"

"Hang on."

He raced beyond the crash site, a couple minutes or so, and they both saw it at once. A stretch of road with nothing but pasture on both sides. No trees.

"There!"

Felix for all his shortcomings during the race, made a near perfect landing on a very imperfect landing strip. *Malolo* did her part, too, holding together and coming to a stop before a fence post ten feet on. Livy was already out of the plane, running toward the crash with a canteen of water and a heavy feeling in her heart. If Heath was alive, chances were, he would have been out there waving.

"Wait up!" Felix called from behind.

Livy only picked up her pace, lungs burning in the thin air. Her hair flowed out behind her and the landscape blurred. Getting to the plane on foot felt like one of those dreams where you were trying to run but your legs wouldn't cooperate and you were bogged down where you were, in quicksand. It took years.

When she hit the grove of trees she began yelling, "Heath! Heath!"

Up ahead, she saw the outline of the plane, a quiet ghost in the shadows. Stillness and birdsong mixed together, creating an eerie backdrop to the loud banging of her heart in her ears.

Livy slowed and Felix was suddenly next to her. "Hazeltine!" he yelled.

Up close, the state of the plane looked even worse than from above. Windshield crashed in, wheels flattened up on both sides of the plane, gaping hole in the fuselage where the wing had torn off. For a moment, the world spun around her and the corners of her vision darkened. Livy braced herself on Felix's arm.

"Maybe you should wait here. I'll have a look."

Livy was torn. She wanted to be the first to reach him, but wasn't sure she could take seeing his broken body. It was a terrible thought, but at least there was no smell, and no flies or vultures or any outward signs of death. Making up her mind for her, her legs gave out and she crumpled to the earth. She sat cross-legged as she watched Felix steel himself, then hoist himself up to the cockpit.

He disappeared into it and before Livy could blink, called out. "There's no one in here!"

"Are you sure?"

"No question."

Relief as big as the mountain they were on flowed through her. But if he wasn't in the plane, where was he? Livy stood up and spun around.

"Could he have been thrown out on impact?" she asked.

Felix then reappeared, waving a logbook. "I think we have our answer here."

He came to her and showed her a message written in familiar but shaky handwriting in the logbook.

Crash landing August 17 at 1920 hours, broken arm and leg, probable concussion, waiting two and a half days for rescue. Going for help.
HH

Livy read the message and watched a teardrop land, dampening the ink. Heath had survived, and there was a chance he was alive. She wanted to kiss the earth and hug the sky and swirl around with joy, but they weren't in the clear yet.

"I'm going to find him. You take the plane back down and alert anyone and everyone," she said.

"You can't go alone."

"I can and I will. But if he has a broken leg, we'll need help getting him down. Get a ranch truck, or any kind of truck up here just as soon as you can," she said.

"You got it. I'll drop the sandwiches for you. Good luck, my friend," Felix said, as he took off back toward *Malolo*.

Livy set out at a slow jog, wanting to sprint, while knowing she needed to maintain a pace she could keep up. The road ran flat around the mountain a way, and she was already out of breath when it turned downslope. Her lungs were pleased with the reprieve, but her legs began to burn and she wondered how much farther she could go without resting. She kept on, and an hour later there was still no sign of Heath. No breadcrumbs or marshmallows or notes. The sun burned hot. A little way on, she noticed a hawk circling above.

A new round of bargaining with God started up, and Livy promised she was willing to give up just about everything in order to see Heath alive again, and to tell him yes, he could have another chance. Then, up ahead under a copse of tall and willowy trees, she thought she saw movement. Her pace quickened, but it was hard to tell in the shadows what exactly she was seeing.

"Heath?" she called.

A silhouette of a figure.

A man.

"Heath!"

She broke into an all-out sprint and closed the distance as fast as her two legs would carry her. He was leaning on two walking sticks, crutches holding up his entire being. You could have sensed his weariness from an ocean away.

He turned around, half his face red and swollen, a gash in his forehead. One of his eyes was sealed shut. "Olivia, that you?"

She stumbled toward him, "Oh, my God, you're alive!"

"My God is right. It really is you," he said weakly.

When she got to him, she was almost afraid to touch him, but he threw down the sticks and held out his arms. She gingerly stepped in, and could feel him leaning into her, leaning *on* her. His skin was warm to the touch, almost feverish, and his hair was matted to the wound on his forehead.

He spoke into her hair. "Where did you come from?"

"Felix and I, we landed up the road. He went back for help when we read your note."

"I thought I heard a plane, but my senses have been playing tricks on me, so I was sure I imagined it."

"We've been searching for days."

He pulled away from her and looked into her eyes with his one good one. "God, you're beautiful. When I knew I was going down, I just kept thinking I'd never see you again. And then some part of me said, 'To hell with that, you aren't gonna die, you have too much to live for.'"

Heath blinked and swayed, seemingly bowled over by the memory.

Livy tightened her grip. "Let's get you down and resting. I have water and food."

She helped him down onto a soft patch of grass so he could lean up against a tree trunk, noticing for the first time that his entire left forearm was purple, with an unnatural bump protruding above his wrist. His leg was covered by his no-longer-white pants, but the way he babied it, and grimaced as he sat, Livy knew it was bad. He had cut the sole off his shoe and wrapped it with strips of material onto his swollen foot. Heath leaned back, legs splayed out, a dazed look in his eye.

He caught Livy sizing up his injuries. "I had to cut my boot off. Nearly died in the process, but the break, I think it's only the fibula."

She held her canteen to his lips. "Drink."

He closed his good eye and drank. "I ran out of water last night, and knew if I didn't get going today, I never would. Can you imagine surviving that crash only to die on the stinkin' mountain?"

Now that Livy had him here with her, she didn't want to think about it.

"Speaking of, where the hell are we?" he asked.

"Mauna Loa. The Big Island," she said.

He nodded. "I thought as much, but it was nearing dark when I came in. I was too far north and when I realized my error, I overcompensated. And when I saw this beauty in the distance, I was sure it was those damn fake islands again, but here I am. And here you are. 'Right joyous am I to behold your face.'"

Livy smiled. Heath would be parroting Shakespeare until the day he died, and she loved him all the more for it.

"I wasn't going to stop looking. *Ever,*" she said.

She may not have been able to save Orlando, but this time around, her persistence had paid off. It almost felt as though he were there, watching from behind the trees, cheering. Or maybe he had been beside her all along. A guiding star.

Heath grinned, then winced and touched a crack at the side of his mouth. "I know I don't deserve it, but I sure am happy to hear those words."

"You would have done the same for me."

"You're right about that," he said, not taking his one good eye off of her.

Sad thoughts moved in. "But I'm not the only one looking. Every fishing boat in Hawai'i and half the US Navy are out there searching, and not just for you, Heath."

"Aww, hell. Who else is out there?"

Livy leaned up on the tree next to him, breaking off bits of the tuna sandwich, and handing them to him as she filled him in on the last few days. Every detail. When she finished, they were both in tears. But being in his presence helped soften the sharp edges of the pain. That was the thing about sadness, when shared, it became softer and that much easier to take.

He swatted at a fly buzzing around his forehead. "You did it, Liv. You beat the odds. I'm so proud of you. I can be heart-broken and proud at the same time, can't I?"

"No one's ever written a rulebook on feelings, as far as I know," she said.

He picked up her hand and held on like he was never going to let go, leaning his head back and closing his eyes. The trees rained down small yellow balls of pollen around them. Heath was asleep less than a minute later. Livy let him rest, keeping a close eye on his breathing. And then she noticed something next to him. *A long, striped feather.* A sign if there ever were one.

They waited and waited, and even though she knew he couldn't hear her, she told him all the things she'd been want-ing to say since reading his letter.

"You know that second chance you asked about? Well, the answer is yes. And I know I was harsh on the mainland, but you hurt me more than you will ever know. I can see now that you did what you had to do, what you thought was the right thing at the time. But it cut me to the bone. Over the years, I picked myself up again, so when I saw you in that speakeasy, I did everything in my power to protect myself. Even withholding help when you asked for it. That was petty and dangerous."

When she finished, Heath opened one eye and, in a hoarse voice, said, "I love you, Olivia West. To Hawai'i and back. Truth is, I've never stopped. Not for one minute."

"Promise me something."

"Anything," he said.

She leaned closer, an inch or two away. "I need to know that you won't up and leave again."

His brown eyes bore into her. "Never, I swear it. You'll have to shoot me if you want to get rid of me," he said.

Life sure had a mixed-up way of bringing two people together. But maybe that had been the point all along. A kind of divine timing that you had to just trust in. Because now more than ever, Livy knew in the deep recesses of her heart that sitting here next to this beat-up man was where she was meant to end up in the end.

"I love you, too," she said at long last.

Even in his battered state, Heath was an instant celebrity at Volcano House. Word spread that the downed pilot was staying at the hotel, and curious guests, staff and reporters came knocking at all hours of the day. His room quickly filled with vases of anthuriums, hydrangeas and orchids, and he answered countless questions about his ordeal. Felix had flown back to Honolulu, but Livy refused to leave Heath's side. They had been given adjacent rooms but she was spending most of her time in his.

Lying in bed was not one of Heath's strong suits, and he turned out to be a terrible patient—disobedient and antsy. After what he'd been through, Livy was happy to let him be ornery all he wanted. They read the paper first thing every morning, sipping coffee and hoping for good news. But time stretched on, and no one else had been found. Mourning together made it a hair easier.

Four days in, when the dizziness from the gash in his head had diminished, Heath asked her to take him outside.

"I want a clear view of where I went down so I can know how lucky I really am," he said, sitting on the side of his bed and reaching for the crutch.

They had been buried in thick clouds for the last few days, but this morning had dawned with an unbroken sky, the blue sharp against the black lava.

Livy made no move to help him. "It would be a lot easier to go in the wheelchair, you know that, don't you?"

"I need to get my blood pumping again. Bedrest is for the birds."

Livy teased, "Are you saying there's something wrong with birds?"

He grinned. "God, I've missed you and that bird-loving mind of yours. There's not a woman in the world who can even come close to you."

"Does that mean you'll go in the wheelchair?"

He laughed. "Whatever you say, doc."

She wheeled him into the lobby, where they were greeted by manager James Gandy and volcanologist Thomas Jaggar, who were tinkering with some kind of metal contraption. Both men had told Heath that his chances of walking away from that crash had been a negative number. Between the old lava flows covering much of the mountain, the harsh elements and the remote location, everyone agreed someone must have been watching out for him.

"Someone named Olivia West," he'd told them.

Once outside, facing out toward Halemaʻumaʻu and Mauna

Loa, Heath grew quiet. He gazed up at the mountain, eventually shaking his head.

"Those men were right. By all accounts, I shouldn't be here," he said.

A cool wind blew up the tree-lined cliff, ruffling up his hair. Purple still spread out beneath his eye and the lid was still swollen. He looked as though he'd been in a barroom brawl, but to Livy, he had never looked more handsome. She couldn't help but smile.

He looked at her and cocked his head. "What are you smiling about?"

"Oh, everything."

Over the next week, Heath mended quickly. Each day, he gained strength and they took longer strolls, Livy pushing him in the wheelchair and Heath beginning to ramble more on the crutches. They listened to honeycreepers chirping and twittering, and they ate hot, fresh cornbread slathered in 'ōhelo berry jam. The doctor had set his bones well, and when he came to check on Heath one afternoon, he gave him the go-ahead to make the journey back to Honolulu.

"To tell the truth, I was kind of hoping he would order me to stay another month here," Heath said, after the doctor left.

She had been thinking the same thing. "We'll just have to come back."

His eyes lit up. "That we will."

Two nights later, at sunset, they bundled up in borrowed coats and hats, and went to the crater rim to watch the sun go down behind Mauna Loa for the last time. As much as she would have loved to stay here indefinitely, she also wanted to see her parents. She couldn't wait to see the look on her father's face when she handed him a check big enough for a new boat and then some.

Steam from the vents lifted from the edge like vapory spirits. Heath had been uncharacteristically quiet throughout the day, and Livy began to wonder if everything was all right. There were still threads of insecurity wound around her heart—how could there not be?—but she kept reminding herself that this time would be different, and that faith was what you hung on to when there was no other option. It was the only way forward.

At the bottom of the sun-kissed mountain, Heath bent down from his wheelchair awkwardly as though trying to pick something up from the ground. He scooted forward and fidgeted, then groaned.

"What are you doing?" Livy asked.

"Oh, forget it." He grabbed onto her arm and stood so he was facing her. "I know I'm supposed to be kneeling for this," he said, voice cracking.

Every cell in her body jumped to attention.

He took both her hands and looked into her eyes. "And I know I should have done this years ago, but I'm asking you now. Will you marry me, Olivia West?"

It was unquestionably the most perfect sentence she had ever heard, and she needed no time to think.

"Yes. Yes, I will, Heath Hazeltine."

He let go of her hand, pulled out a ring from his pocket and slid it on her finger. Small, delicate and square cut, the diamond caught the sun and dazzled in the last light.

"Where did you find this?" she asked, searching his eyes.

"In San Francisco."

She thought back to their encounters, and of how she had given him the cold shoulder, but he'd kept coming back for more. "You knew then?"

"I hoped."

It felt as though the world just locked in place. He kissed her in the most tender way, dusting her lips, with one hand on her low back, pulling her in close. With tears in his eyes, and with Mauna Loa and Kīlauea as witness. A tropic bird soared past in the distance and Livy knew she was finally home.

40

MORE TO THE STORY

Wren & Olivia
1987

When Livy wrapped up her story, Wren went and got a box
of tissues, kept a few for herself and handed the box to Livy.
Even Pa'a had let out a few whines as Livy impressively spun
out her memories, the older the clearer. And Wren was afraid
to ask—because they all knew Livy was not Livy Hazeltine,
but Livy Wagner—but she had to know.

"So what happened next?"

"Felix came back with a Hawaiian man and his son in a ranch
truck. Strong, strapping men with kind hearts. Felix apparently
commandeered them on the side of the road. We got him down,
the doctor set his bones and mended the gash in his head, and
we stayed at Volcano House for two weeks while he mended,
and those people waited on him hand and foot. They became
like family. Felix flew *Malolo* back to Wheeler, but there was
no way I was leaving Heath's side."

"Who got the money for finding him?" The reward money
was a tiny note in the story of the missing fliers—but Wren

had to know, after hearing how little Felix had given her for getting them both across the Pacific.

"Felix let me keep every cent. It worked itself out in the end, like it always does, if you let it. I was able to help my pa buy a far grander boat than the *Lady Bee*, and eventually the old Pa came back."

Wren was glad to hear Felix had redeemed himself. She wanted to like her grandfather, but she hadn't been so sure after hearing Livy's account of the race.

"What happened with you and Heath after Volcano?" she asked.

Livy smiled, and her eyes misted up again. "I gave him that second chance he asked for and we tied the knot at the edge of Halema'uma'u Crater a year later. This time, we came by steamer, mind you. Felix and Iwa, my parents, the hotel staff and a couple of tropic birds were our only guests." She closed her eyes, as if remembering. "Have you been to the volcano?"

"Not yet."

"You must. It's magic."

An image came to Wren of a young Livy in a white dress and a maile lei, volcanic steam rising around her.

"So, where does the name Wagner come from, if you don't mind my asking?"

Livy sighed. "We moved from San Diego to Kona after retiring, but my Heath died a year or so after we got here—his heart gave out on him." She paused, looking distressed and confused. "Or maybe it was ten years? Anyway, it was too soon, and I was so lonely. Our neighbor, Tom Wagner, befriended me, and one thing led to another. Heath would have approved, he only wanted me to be happy."

"What an incredible life you've lived. But, Livy, the world needs to know what you accomplished—that you piloted that plane most of the way to Hawai'i. You're a legend and no one even knows it."

Livy waved her hand as if was no big deal. "Let Felix have the glory. I was luckier than most. So many people lost their lives. I was just happy to make it out with mine, and even more blessed to find Heath. I owe my life to that race, strange as it sounds."

"What do you mean?"

"I almost let Heath slip through my fingers. Oh, I thought I was so tough, and I didn't need anyone. I let flying take over my life at the expense of everything else. Things were safer that way, I suppose. No chance of getting burned. But twenty-seven hours over the Pacific Ocean will shake some sense into just about anyone."

"Yes, but you should still be given your due and set the record straight. You're a real American treasure."

Livy glanced back at *Malolo*, then the other plane. She got that strange, tense look again. "Fine by me if you tell someone, if anyone really cares anymore. But you talk about setting the record straight, there's more to this story, and it's not pretty."

Livy's voice had grown hoarse, and Wren worried about pushing her. "Do you want to take a break? Get some fresh air?"

"Nope. I've been quiet too long, it's time to fess up what I know," Livy said, her lined face set with determination.

Wren opened another can of juice for each of them, then leaned in to hear the rest as a couple of myna birds squawked on the roof.

"It was never reported, but a few things happened before the race that made everyone nervous."

She told Wren about the men who came in the night, and Vilas's missing magnets and how when three planes didn't show up in Honolulu, everyone was questioning if there had been foul play. But there'd been no evidence of any wrongdoing, and they had no leg to stand on.

"Oh, sure, we reported it to the authorities after the race was over, but what could they do? They brushed it under the rug as if it never happened. Everyone was more worried about the search for the missing planes. But, unbeknownst to me and to everyone else, one of the missing planes had already been found. The day after the race, Felix had come across Jack Hunt and his plane, *Soaring Eagle*, in a sugarcane field on Maui. The plane was mostly hidden with coconut fronds Jack had dragged to the site. The only reason he noticed it was because he'd been flying lower than the coconut trees, and he knew what to look for."

Livy took a sip of juice and looked toward the mystery plane.

"Don't tell me this plane is the *Soaring Eagle*," Wren said.

Livy nodded. "According to Felix, Jack was sure his father was the one responsible for the tampering and wanted no part in it. He knew any accusations he made would fall on deaf ears, so he decided to pull a fast one on his old man and disappear. When Felix landed and started poking around the plane, which was in perfect condition, mind you, Jack came out of the sugarcane and confessed. Felix wanted the reward money— he'd come out of the race empty-handed after paying back his debts—but Jack wanted to start a new life, out of the shadow of his father, and he would never be able to do that if his father knew he was alive. Jack offered Felix the plane in exchange for his silence."

"So Mr. Hunt was never charged with anything?"

"The world was a different place back then, dear. Justice was a much looser concept, and in this case, Mr. Hunt lost a son out of it. I suppose the authorities thought that was enough. Felix told me the story years later, when he asked if I wanted to come fly for his new charter. He said he'd painted the plane and made a few modifications, and that no one would be the wiser."

"But why would Hunt sabotage the planes in the first place? It's not like he needed the money, did he?" Wren said.

"No, but he'd invested in the airplane company that built the Vega plane. If *Soaring Eagle* won, they'd have had orders spilling in from all over the country, the world even."

"It's criminal."

"A real calamity. The irony is that Mr. Hunt contracted cancer—the man was a walking smokestack—and died not long before Felix told me his secret."

A sad case of poetic justice.

"Did they ever find the last plane? *Miss Doran?*" Wren asked, still trying to process this news.

Livy clasped her hands together, knuckles red and knotted. "Oh, there were plenty of rumors and possible sightings, plane parts washing ashore, and searches as far away as Johnston Island. Messages in bottles started washing up in California and Hawai'i, all signed by Millie. One estimated they were eight hundred miles off O'ahu and said their engine had died, send help."

"But none were real?" Wren said.

"All hoaxes, if the handwriting experts were right. I suppose it's meant to remain a mystery."

Wren shook her head in shock. "I can't believe I found you. That you remember it all."

"When I close my eyes, I'm right back in that little airplane, soaring above the Pacific, and I can still see the site of Heath's crash, the way those trees were capped right off by his wing. Some things stay with you forever, in a place deeper than memory."

Wren wasn't even aware that she'd picked up Livy's hand. Afternoon sun swept into the barn, lighting up both planes, the song of a plover in flight echoed overhead and, at long last, the story had been told. Passed from one generation to the next, as all great stories should be.

41

THANK GOODNESS FOR BOB SIMMS

Wren

West winds bent the trees backward as Wren walked through the dying afternoon. Night would come soon, but she hardly noticed. All she knew was that her body needed to move and she wanted the company of the forest. Livy's story had shaken her to the core. This land, this barn, these airplanes, this woman, they were all intricately connected, and she felt like a spider sitting at the center of a giant web.

The gears in her mind began turning, and she pondered who she might tell, and how she could get the word out about this incredible woman. She also felt an urgent need to share everything with Pono. He'd been there since day one with her, caringly restoring the plane, and was as invested as she was. Only now, it felt as though he'd up and abandoned the whole thing. Abandoned her. But why? Something had spooked him that night, that seemed the only reasonable explanation. The question now was what was she going to do about it?

She passed the old airstrip and walked the length of the macadamia orchard. She followed pig trails and watched the bottom of the sky fade to orange. Birds flitted through the branches, singing and chirping and tweeting their greetings to one another. Only when she reached an impassable stream did she turn around. When she did, Pa'a stood a little way up the trail, sniffing her scent in the grass. Wren held out a hand. Pa'a took a step, and then sat.

Wren dropped down to a cross-legged position in the middle of the trail. "Okay that's it. I'm not leaving until you let me touch you. You follow me around like a ghost, you saved my life, you practically sleep with me and yet you won't let me get close. I don't get it."

Pa'a's ears twitched. She whined and went down on her elbows, scooting forward in a crawl until her nose almost touched Wren's hand. Wren let her sniff for a moment, then reached a finger out to rub the dog's jaw. Pa'a leaned into Wren's hand with all her weight, and then rolled over onto her back with her forelegs curled up, small tufts of fur poking out between her paws. Wren rubbed the small white patch on Pa'a's chest, and then her smooth pink belly.

"You really made me earn this, didn't you?"

Pa'a rolled around, scratching her back in the grass as she soaked in the love. It was like the floodgates of trust had opened, and Wren wasn't sure who had saved who.

"Now you're stuck with me, sweet thing," Wren said, a huge smile forming on her face.

The love of a dog was more valuable and more steadfast than just about anything else she could think of. Maybe God had been listening to her silent prayers after all.

Flames lit up the trees around the firepit. Wren and Pa'a sat outside watching the sparks float up and disappear into the night. She had made up her mind. Tomorrow, she'd go find Pono at the ranch and bring him his stupid light, which ironically had turned out to be her best one yet. If he was weird, so be it. But she needed to do this. If there was one thing she'd learned from hearing Livy's life story, it was to go after what you wanted as though your life depended on it. Because it did—any life worth living.

When she went to get the hose to dampen the fire, she heard the distant sound of an engine. It was a little late, but every now and then she passed a truck on the road, going to the land below hers. *Her land.* She loved how the words sounded, and could hardly believe how close she'd come to selling it sight unseen. Just because she'd been wallowing in self-pity and worried about the price of an airline ticket. Thank goodness for Bob Simms and his broken-down truck.

Pa'a sat up, ears tuned in. It was ten o'clock on a Saturday night at the edge of the world. Pa'a's tail began to wag, slowly at first, then building to a frenzied sweeping.

"Who is it?" Wren said to the dog.

There was really only one person it could be. She turned the hose off and stood by the side of the barn, unsure how to feel. Pa'a ran up as soon as Pono got out, spun in a circle, then started tearing around in giant figure eights and letting out a series of high-pitched whimpers. Scout tried to catch her but was no match.

Pono stuffed his hands in his pockets and stepped toward the fire. Wren stayed where she was.

"Wren, I need to talk to you," he said.

"At ten o'clock at night? It must be important."

She couldn't keep the edge out of her voice. Even though she'd tried to fight it, she still felt scorned. Abandoned even. But maybe that was her father wound talking. In her world, men left and did not come back.

"Come over here, will you?" he said, voice strained. "Please?"

Wren met him by the firepit. The smell of burning kiawe wood sweetened the air around them.

"I owe you an explanation of where I've been and why I left last weekend without saying goodbye," he said.

"Yes, you do."

"I know I should have told you before, but it never seemed to be a good time. I lost my wife a little over two years ago, and last Sunday was her birthday. I had plans to go to Mauna Kea that morning, as I've done the last two years, to where we scattered her ashes."

He paused, and for a moment, Wren wasn't sure he could go on. Her heart ached for him. "I'm so sorry," she said.

He nodded. "But what I hadn't planned on was what happened between you and me. I haven't been with a woman since Pili died, and for a while I figured I'd just be alone the rest of my life. I was so pissed off, you know? So fucking devastated. But time dulled things a little, and then you showed up. Getting involved was the last thing on my mind. I was here for the truck and the planes, but it didn't take long to realize that wasn't all I was here for."

Wren reached for his hand. "You don't have to explain yourself, Pono."

He squeezed hers tight, then pulled her in and held her against his chest. Wren felt his heartbeat, strong against her own. The smell of leather and grass. Then he pushed away, so he could see her face.

"No, but I want to. I should have left a note, or come sooner, but I felt like a jerk and then I didn't want to lead you on, because what if I wasn't sure? What if wasn't ready?"

"Is anyone ever sure? Or ever a hundred percent ready? I know I'm not," Wren said.

"It's been a rough week of soul-searching, but I'll tell you what I do know."

Wren looked down, afraid he was going to tell her it was too soon, he'd made a mistake.

"Look at me," he said, tilting her chin up gently with his hand. Their eyes met.

"I know that when I'm with you, I'm happy and when I'm

not with you, I wish I was with you. All week long, I wait for when I get to drive over here and see your face. We could be working on the planes, or sitting in the chairs outside watching the flies on pig shit, it doesn't matter. I never thought I would feel that again, but I do. And that's enough for me," he said.

"I've been waiting all week to see you, too. I have so much to tell you—" she said, unable to contain her excitement about her discoveries and the idea she had to bring Olivia's story to the world. "But that can wait."

This time, Wren took his face in her hands and kissed him. The kind of long, slow kiss reserved for beautiful beginnings, for two hearts ready to get back up and try again. Who knew what would happen—life was always a gamble—but this was a very good start.

42

ALOFT

Wren & Olivia
July, 1988

Winds: ENE
Conditions: VFR
No airmets in effect

Pono drove, with Livy in the front seat and Wren and Pa'a in the back. Skies were clear, and Maui looked close enough to swim to. Livy thought that they were going to the airport for the maiden voyage of a rebuilt *Malolo*, but Wren had another secret up her sleeve.

Ever since that first day, when Wren had brought Livy to the barn, they'd been bringing her back and involving her in the restoration. Her short-term memory was tenuous, but those old ones remained rock-solid, etched into her brain like deep canyons. She and Pono had hit it off splendidly, and he loved nothing more than to butter her up with hydrangeas and purple agapanthus from the garden, or freshly squeezed orange juice and mango bread from his mother. The dogs loved her, too, and she them. She was one of those souls who drew people and animals in like moths to a bonfire. There was just something special about her. She also knew airplanes like nobody's business, and turned out to be more of a help than Wren had expected. She had an opinion about everything, wood, paint, canvas, even engine parts. And her opinions usually turned out to be spot-on. Pono found a retired airplane mechanic living in Kona who was more than eager to hop on the project, especially when he heard what plane it was. Who wouldn't have?

When they drew near to the airport, Livy said, "You know, I flew over this stretch of coast all those years ago, when I was searching. I remember bucking around like a bull rider, and then they went and built a runway on it."

"Windiest part of Hawai'i," Pono said. "Or at least one of them."

Cars lined the road, and the parking lot was full.

"What are all these cars doing here?" Livy asked.

Wren shrugged. "Beats me."

Pono helped Livy out, offering a tanned arm. She was dressed in an old flight suit, and for a moment, Wren didn't see an old woman, but a young one, vibrant and colorful, brimming with life and ready for anything the world might throw her way. Ahead, on the narrow strip of asphalt, *Malolo* waited.

When Livy saw the plane, her hand went to her chest and she gasped, "Would you look at that."

Malolo was draped in a long flower lei, just like the one she'd worn all those years ago at Bay Farm Island, and her red paint glinted in the sun. Wren had never been more proud of anything in her life, and she felt herself beaming as they approached a sprawling crowd of people. A man in a white suit waved them over. Camera shutters began to snap, and a woman with a giant KITV news camera followed them as they made their way toward the one-room building.

The man in the suit stepped forward and placed a lei around Livy's neck, and she graciously bowed.

"Mrs. Wagner, I'm Leland Dole, James Dole's grandson. We want to honor you today, and your pioneering contribution to aviation. I understand this is coming sixty years too late, but you have a real champion in Miss Summers and she was determined to see this through," he said.

Livy looked to be in shock, but quickly regained her composure and gave him a big smile. "Better late than never, is what I always say."

The man next to Dole stepped forward. "It's a privilege to be in your presence, ma'am. I'm Jed Washington, president of the National Aviation Association."

Livy shook his hand. "An honor to be in yours, too, sir."

They were ushered to an area where five rows of chairs had been set up, with a mic up front. Livy, Wren, Pono and Pa'a sat front and center, while others filed in behind in them, some military, some civilian. By the way they were dressed, Wren guessed most were pilots. There were also a few folks from Malama Care Home—Ferdinand had brought Mr. Larsgaard, the Kaheles, Mr. Hewitt and Mrs. Akina, and two of the nurse assistants. They had been sworn to secrecy, and Wren had worried some might forget, but they'd kept their word. Livy was too busy looking at the airplane parked out front to notice them. Reporters stood by, too, snapping away. Pono was holding tight to Wren's hand. She loved that about him—how he always seemed to be touching her. A hand on the small of her back, a foot under the table, arms loosely entwined in the bed.

Livy leaned into Wren. "Don't tell me this fuss is all for me."

"You'll see, my friend," Wren said.

Leland tapped the mic. "Ladies and gentlemen, welcome to 'Upolu Airport. I am proud to be here today as we recognize a special woman who has flown under the radar, so to speak, since the days of my grandfather, James Dole, and his infamous Dole Derby. Many of you came from the mainland or from outer islands and I'm betting that when you made your reservations, you didn't bat an eye about flying over here. Book a ticket, show up at the airport and boom, here you are. We have pioneers like Mrs. Wagner to thank for the ease with which we travel around this globe. Hawai'i today, Paris tomorrow. She opened our eyes to a world where the sky is no longer the limit.

"Sixty years ago, Olivia West was engaged as a navigator for Felix Harding in a race across the Pacific. When Harding fell ill, she took over the controls, flying all but seven hours of the harrowing twenty-seven-hour flight from San Diego to Honolulu. This woman not only saved herself and Mr. Harding, but she had the tenacity to go back up in the same plane you see before you, days after the race, to locate and rescue Mr. Heath Hazeltine on the slopes of Mauna Loa."

The wind stole Dole's hat, carrying it up in a swirling eddy. Wren noticed whitecaps picking up in the channel and began to worry the winds would be too strong to go up. A moment later, she caught sight of two dark shapes in the sky, floating in from the east. She nudged Livy, and Livy gave her hand a tight squeeze.

'Iwa birds.

"Thus, I am pleased to introduce Jed Washington, president of the National Aviation Association, who has an important announcement to share with you all."

Dole stepped to the side, and Jed joined him at the mic with a wooden plaque in hand.

He looked directly at Livy. "Mrs. Wagner, on behalf of the association, I would like to share this Pilots as Pioneers award with you."

A big round of applause erupted.

Livy's lip quivered, and she shook her head. "I don't believe this."

Washington held up his hand, "Mrs. Olivia West Hazeltine Wagner, you will be joining the likes of Charles Lindbergh and William Boeing as the newest inductee in the National Aviation Hall of Fame. Your skill and courage and passion are most admirable and you are a true hero in the world of aviation."

More cheers and whistles, and everyone who had been sitting stood. Livy glanced around, soaking it all in, cheeks wet from tears. Then she looked up to where the *'iwa* birds were riding the currents, weightless and majestic, old friends from a time long ago. Wren walked with her to the mic and Livy clung to her arm, whether to keep herself steady or for moral support, Wren couldn't be sure.

It took Livy a moment to compose herself, then in a strong, steady voice, she said, "This right here, this makes my life complete. I think my dear friend Amelia Earhart said it best, 'Everyone has oceans to fly, if they have the heart to do it. Is it reckless? Maybe. But what do dreams know of boundaries?'"

After the ceremony, *Malolo* waited. Soon, she would be headed to the National Air and Space Museum, joining *Spirit of St. Louis*, but not before a final spin in the Hawaiian skies.

Working on the planes and spending time with Livy had given Wren a new appreciation for the invisible pull of the sky. She could almost imagine herself in Livy's shoes back in 1927. *Would she have had the heart to do it?* Maybe. But her flight suit was a little different. Jeans, a white shirt, a flight jacket and aviator glasses. Thanks, Tom Cruise. She and Livy walked out across the asphalt, holding hands. The crowd had quieted. The pilot, Danny Loui, was waiting by the plane.

"Take me with you," Livy said.

Wren had debated sending Livy up on the maiden voyage, but worried about getting her in and out. In the end, they'd decided against it.

"You'll be with us in spirit," Wren said.

"I don't want to be with you in spirit, I want to be with you in that airplane, *okole* in the seat." She got a mischievous look in her eye. "Tell you what, I'll settle for copilot."

Livy might not be as limber as she once was, but she still knew what she wanted. After the past year of blood and sweat, Wren wanted to go up in that plane more than anything. But Livy deserved a ride in *Malolo* more than she did.

Pono was off to the side, talking to someone. She caught his eye and waved him over.

"Livy's going up with Danny," she said.

He looked at Livy. "You sure?"

"Sure as rain."

Myra would probably kill her when this was over, but Wren didn't care. When you were Livy's age, you got to make the rules. Maybe this was reckless, but what did they have to lose? They helped Livy up the steps, and Pono and Danny lifted her into her seat as though she were made of fine china.

Wren handed her the aviators. "Here, take these."

Livy slipped them on and gave her a thumbs-up. Once again, she saw the young Livy, thick hair, sun-kissed skin, brimming with confidence and ready for adventure. She looked more at home in the plane than she did at Malama. The look of pure joy on her face would stay with Wren for a lifetime. Danny waved them away, and she and Pono went up to hand prop the plane. She let him do the honors, and the little plane buzzed to life.

Pono took her hand and they watched Danny and Livy roll down to the south side of the strip, spin around, gun the engine, then accelerate up the runway. The winds had held, and before she knew it, *Malolo*'s wheels left the ground and they were off. Pono held an arm around Wren, and they admired the lines of the airplane. Danny flew low toward Hāwī, following the coast. The plane grew smaller and smaller until she disappeared over the hill. The original plan had been to swing out toward Maui, do a big loop and come in.

"Where the hell are they going?" Pono said.

Wren felt like a nervous mother, waiting and wondering. She thought of Livy back at Bay Farm Island, watching those planes fly off, only to return trailing canvas or billowing black smoke. What a heavy thing that must have been.

Thirty-seven minutes later, they heard the drone of the engine and saw the red speck grow larger until it approached for a landing. Everything looked intact, and the whole field of people started cheering. When Livy came out of that plane, aviators still on, she waved to the crowd as though she'd just crossed the Pacific.

Pono smiled. "That right there is one classy lady."

Wren laughed. "Classy and classic."

The kind of woman who knew how to close the gap between the dream and the thing, and would never keep the world waiting.

Later, when the crowd had begun to disperse, and Wren and Pono and Livy were headed toward the car, Wren thought she heard someone call her name. She turned to see a man hurrying to catch up with them.

"Excuse me, Miss Summers...Wren," he said.

The man was tall with a thick head of brown hair, graying at the temples. He was wearing dark glasses but pulled them up onto his head and smiled. Their eyes locked, and a funny feeling came over her. She knew this man, would recognize him anywhere, even though the last time she'd seen him, she'd been a young child.

Wren stopped. "Kainoa?"

Dad.

Tears pooled in the corners of his eyes. "I didn't think you'd recognize me."

His face had been etched into her mind from studying the photographs in that box in the garage day and night for years. His eyes were still too far apart, his nose wide and flat, but she saw herself there.

He approached her tentatively, as though coming up on a

wild animal. "Look, I know I'm the last person you expected to see here, but I read about *Malolo* and Olivia West in the paper and when I saw your name, I knew I had to come. If you want me to leave, I will, but I want you to know I'll be staying in Waimea for a couple weeks if you want to talk."

An ocean of pain flowed between them, Wren could feel the current threatening to sweep her away. Pono and Livy appeared on both sides of her, and Pa'a sat at her heel. Both took a hand, filling her up with courage.

Finally, her mouth formed the words, "No, I'm glad you came."

She had no idea what came next, but she was beginning to see that life had a way of unfolding in the most unexpected ways. In her case, it had been a muddy and ravine-filled back road to this moment, but hey, she would lean into it and see where it led. Because the people and places, the beauty and the heartbreak, they were all part of the scenery—all part of one imperfect and splendid journey.

★ ★ ★ ★ ★

AUTHOR'S NOTE

I first learned of the Dole Air Race, or the Dole Derby as it was also known, when I was reading through an old book about Hawai'i called *The Saga of the Sandwich Islands*. Right away, I knew this was a story I wanted to tell because it was fascinating and tragic and not well known despite being a major milestone in aviation history. I spent some time dreaming up my plot and characters and how to best meld them in with as much of the race's history as possible. We debated changing the name of the race in my novel, but since so much of the story is rooted in real events and people, we decided to keep it as is.

Though the Dole Air Race in 1927 really happened, my character Olivia West is a figment of my imagination. In real life, Mildred Doran was the only woman in the race, a passenger in the plane *Miss Doran*, which was named after her. At first I thought about telling her story—she was an interesting and ultimately tragic figure—but I couldn't stop thinking about what it would have been like to be a female pilot in that race. There were many fearless female aviators in the 1920s, but none officially entered in the race. I can't say for sure, but I like to believe that at least a few would have wanted to take part had they had the opportunity. But back then, women pilots were not highly regarded by the establishment. Thus Olivia West was born—to represent all the women who were pushing the limits of their time but not celebrated or even recognized.

In real life, only two planes made it to Wheeler Field. In first place was *Woolaroc*, flown by Arthur Goebel and navigated by William Davis, and second place was *Aloha,* flown by Martin Jensen and navigated by Paul Schluter. In my novel, *Malolo* and Felix are inspired by and replace *Aloha* and pilot Martin Jensen, and Olivia replaces Paul Schluter as navigator. I also created Heath and his plane, *Golden Plover*, out of thin air. *Soaring Eagle* is the fictional and highly dramatized replacement for the real-life *Golden Eagle*. The conspiracy around *Soaring Eagle* and its fictional pilot, Hunt, is entirely fictional.

The other planes and pilots mentioned in the story were based on real planes and people, and I stuck to race details as closely as possible in telling their story.

The other airplanes, pilots and navigators in the race were as follows:

Oklahoma, piloted by Bennett Griffin, navigated by Al Henley, turned back.

El Encanto, flown by Norman Goddard, Kenneth Hawkins, crashed on takeoff, and the crew was not hurt.

Pabco Pacific Flyer, flown by Livingston Irving, crashed on takeoff, and the pilot wasn't hurt.

Golden Eagle, flown by Jack Frost, navigated by Gordon Scott, left California and never made it to Hawai'i. The plane was owned by George Hearst, son of William Randolph Hearst.

Miss Doran, flown by Auggy Pedlar, navigated by Vilas Knope, with passenger Mildred Doran, turned back once, then took off again later and never made it to Hawai'i.

Dallas Spirit, flown by William Erwin, navigated by Alvin Eichwaldt, turned back, but later set off for Hawai'i in the search, only to crash into the Pacific Ocean and disappear.

According to my sources, compasses really had been tampered with before the race, and men did visit in the night, though from what I gather, no one ever found out who was responsible. It made me wonder—did all of the planes that went missing really just crash or run out of fuel? Or is it possible they were casualties of foul play? That question was the inspiration behind the fictional Hunt's sabotage.

Several people on the Big Island reported seeing flashing lights high up on Mauna Loa on the night the other planes landed. It seemed impossible to me that someone could have survived up there in that harsh terrain of lava fields and dryland forest, but then I read about Major Harold Clark and Sergeant Robert Gray who crash-landed on Mauna Kea in 1918 and walked out of the forest two days later. Their unlikely story inspired Heath's crash landing on Mauna Loa.

While I was writing this novel, I had been spending time in a care home with my mother, so I had plenty of inspiration to draw on for Wren's experiences at Malama. Sadly, my dear mom passed away in September of 2022, while I was still finishing my first draft. She never got to read it, though I know she would have loved it and shared it with everyone in her nursing home. She was my biggest fan and backed me a hundred and ten percent in everything I did.

This is my first published novel not set during WWII, and it was fascinating to research the history of flight and all of those early pioneers who had more courage per square inch than I have in my entire body. I found Charles Lindbergh's *The Spirit of St. Louis* to be immensely helpful, as well as the book *Race to Hawaii* by Jason Ryan. I highly recommend both books to anyone interested in learning more about early transoceanic flight.

ACKNOWLEDGMENTS

As always, I am so grateful to my supcragent, Elaine Spencer, who is also a great editor in her own right, and my new editor, April Osborn, for taking a chance on me and nurturing this story and bringing these next books of mine to life. Also, for the whole team at MIRA for believing in me and helping me create beautiful books and share these Hawai'i stories with the world. The fact that I get to keep writing novels is a dream come true, and I don't take a second of it for granted.

Also, sending love to Bill Hochman, my expert reader, who for health reasons was not able to help with this book. Instead, pilot and friend Dana Asis provided some much-needed guidance on aviation. And always thanks to Todd who puts up with me through it all—my messy morning hair, peanut butter spoons left around the house and my fretting over every (perceived) publishing emergency that arises, to my ever-supportive group of friends who listen to story idea after story idea and keep acting interested, to my late parents, Doug and Diane, who, among other things, filled me with this great love for Hawai'i, and to you, my wonderful readers. Thank you for being on this wild and beautiful journey with me.

DISCUSSION QUESTIONS

(contains spoilers)

1. What had you heard of the Dole Air Race, or other famous air races, before reading this novel?

2. Could you identify with Livy and her love for flying? Have you ever wanted to do something so badly but the odds were stacked against you?

3. Have you ever thought about the early pioneers of flight and how far we've come in our ability to travel the globe? Have you done anything pioneering?

4. Were you rooting for Livy and Heath to get back together? Why or why not?

5. It sometimes feels like people of past generations were huge risk-takers. Do you think that as we humans progress, we have become less courageous? If so, why?

6. Wren ends up moving into the remote barn in Hāwī alone with a stray dog. Do you think you would have done the same thing had you been in her shoes?

7. Did you know that Mrs. Wagner was Livy all along?

8. Did you have a preference for one storyline over the other?

9. If you could transport yourself to the Hawai'i of either storyline, would you rather be in 1927 or 1987? Why?